CRIMES
AGAINST
MY
BROTHER

for Tony Best wishes Dis

CRIMES
AGAINST
MY
BROTHER

[signature]

DAVID
ADAMS
RICHARDS

2015.

DOUBLEDAY CANADA

Doubleday Canada and colophon are registered trademarks of Random House of Canada Limited

LIBRARY AND ARCHIVES CANADA CATALOGUING IN PUBLICATION

Richards, David Adams, 1950-
Crimes against my brother / David Adams Richards.
Issued also in electronic format.
978-0-385-67116-3
eBook ISBN 978-0-385-67117-0
I. Title.
PS8585.I17C75 2013   C813'.54   C2012-906599-4

Cover image: © Bruno Ehrs/Corbis
Book design: Andrew Roberts
Printed and bound in the USA

Published in Canada by Doubleday Canada,
a division of Random House of Canada Limited,
a Penguin Random House Company

www.randomhouse.ca

10 9 8 7 6 5 4 3 2 1

FOR PEGGY,
WHO LOVED ENOUGH TO STAND BY ME THROUGH DARKNESS

FOR MY CHILDREN,
WHOSE LOVE BROUGHT ME TO LIGHT

FOR PHILIP AND WALTER LEE

AUTHOR'S NOTE

I should note that Sydney Henderson, one of the main characters in *Mercy among the Children*, plays a minor role in this book. For this novel takes place at the same time, and in the same world, as *Mercy* and deals with three people who knew Henderson, and of his pact with God. This is what propels them to make a pact with one another. Those who know my world will recognize certain other characters as well—ones who have minor roles in various parts of the text.

This place is fictional, of course—it always has been. The characters too are fictional. If this novel says anything to the reader, it is what I have managed to learn over many years of being a rather solitary figure in Canadian letters: take heart and know that no betrayal is so self-infatuated, self-serving or brutal it cannot, in the end, be overcome.

In great hearts the cruelty of life gives birth to good.

—Vasily Grossman, *Life and Fate*

CONTENTS

PART ONE

IAN PRESTON HAD SOME GOOD TIMES WITH HIS TWO COUSINS, Evan Young and Harold Dew.

There were two or three things that united them, as if they were tethered together in the hold of a ship.

One, each boy grew to manhood on the Bonny Joyce–Clare's Longing stretch of the river.

Two, all three knew Joyce Fitzroy and Lonnie Sullivan, all of them had to work for Sullivan and all had a chance at getting Joyce Fitzroy's inheritance. But the one who didn't seek it got it. That fact is a strange anomaly in the heavens, one that might make us believe or disbelieve. That is, no matter how things happen, some will say yes, there is a God, and others will say no, this proves no God exists. As for God himself—he has already made up his mind.

I was their cousin too, or at least that is what was said. But I made myself away when young—my mother had that middle-class strain of belief, for the most part full of genteel hypocrisy, that her boy should be better than other boys—and I did not speak of our family relationship with old drunk Joyce Fitzroy, who was an uncle and rumoured to have money; or the local junk wheeler-dealer Lonnie Sullivan, who impoverished so many with his schemes. I escaped that world, and said I would never go back. But these boys, Ian Preston, Evan Young and Harold Dew, each of them every bit as smart as I, grew up in that world and never really escaped it. I remember them in grade two when I was in grade seven, or so says a photo that was taken and laid away; and then in grade seven, when I was in grade twelve, and they were standing together in the snow outside the small shack that was Evan Young's home; and finally as I got older and was doing my thesis on adolescent angst and trying to get accepted to a college in New York, and taking the train to Yale and seeing myself as a winner, I would remember them and how they grew up without a chance— and how they were supposedly less than me. And I believed this until I saw the other world—that is, the world of the university, which held within its fallow bones its own fecal corruption. And then, after that—after my doctorate and post-doctorate, and after the swimmingly grand success of tenure, and after walking the streets of Madrid in autumn and seeing my work published in small academic journals—I longed again for their world. Yes, longed even, at times, for the pain and blood and remorse of that world. I remembered Sydney Henderson too, and how Ian and Evan and Harold turned against his quest for God—how they ridiculed it; that is, ridiculed how a man as hard and rough in youth as Sydney Henderson could turn to God. Sydney was a joke to them, so they made a joke of it all—just as many others did. But seeing how those boys had so little, I could understand why they would mock him. As you may know, this Sydney Henderson became the study of one book and at least seven theses showing how he longed for God in such a lonely place in spite of the odds.

So I want to tell the story of these three, and how they bashed God in the head and refused to believe, and valued one another above all. People initially thought they professed these things as a jest—a practical joke on the world—but by and by it came to be no joke at all.

I spoke to my students often—all of whom had written their inestimable essays, their left-leaning theories on the dispossessed, their brilliant studies of our disenfranchised, every piece so polished you would think it publishable in *The Globe and Mail*—about these three. Yet I realized that not one of my students had ever slept in a room with rats walking across the floor like Ian Preston had. Not one of them, at fourteen, had stood up against men coming in at night drunk to fuck his mother, like Evan Young. Not one had carried a water bucket up a gangplank, or tossed wood all day until dark, like Harold Dew. Not one had cut his own wood for the winter, trapped beaver against a black brook, killed an animal with a stick. Or gone at twelve years of age to work for

Lonnie Sullivan. That is, even as I taught these students, these pleasant, affable, upwardly mobile young men and women, I wondered what could their inestimable essays ever say beyond what I myself had known in my blood by the time I was ten years old? And why did my mother and father want this for me—this world where I had become something of a figure of merit? To fuss and preen over me when I came home?

And I began to think that since I knew all three, I could relate something of their story that my students might not have caught.

Harold Dew was the biggest. He would go bald at twenty-eight years of age. He would become a hypochondriac and worry all his life about colds or some odd disease taking him off. He would be known from Neguac to Boistown as "Big Harold Dew." He would be as well known on the river as anyone here, and at times just meeting him would make your day.

Ian Preston was the smallest. His hair was ginger and his face fine—or refined, as if in the pale backwoods some grand nobleman had stopped 143 years before and put down roots near a stream, and built himself a shack. And there in that shack, near some hidden brook, Ian Preston would someday be born. And when he was, the first rocket ships would be blasting away from the earth while his weak mother would be alone, on a rusted cot, in a soundless room.

Still, though I say this, touching Ian was like touching a piece of steel.

Evan Young was the toughest and kindest. He in some ways was the most enigmatic, the most secretive—perhaps too the smartest.

But all of them were smart—that was the problem. My students would never understand how each one of the three—Harold, Evan and Ian, standing in the snow against an old dark shack, waiting to have a bolt of the moonshine that Joyce Fitzroy ran off—how all of them were smarter, more resilient and more joyful than they.

———

The three of them, Harold, Evan and Ian, went to work when they were kids for Lonnie Sullivan, who hired boys to work the woods for him, for he could pay them less, and impinge upon their freedoms more and more as the years went on and they accrued more debt. It was an honourable idea: that workers themselves would accrue debt, not for God's sake the man they were working for. In fact, Ian was told that when his grandfather retired from Benson's store after forty-seven years of work, the old man had exactly $11.95.

So the boys worked for Sullivan. He would pay them ten dollars— easy enough for boys to live on at the start of a week. But before half the week was over they would want or need more money, and Sullivan would say, "I can give it to you—but you will have to work this long."

And he would hold out his hands as if it was a joke and say, "You have to work as long as my dick before I can pay you more." The conditions were always to his benefit. And their working environment at the time was harsher than most. In fact, I knew two dozen boys who worked this way for people much like Sullivan from one side of the river to the other, children who were thrust into the world with few options and little hope of finding ones.

Over those years Lonnie Sullivan had a host of women. He impregnated more than a few—usually widows or old spinsters, many older than he was. I know this now for it was researched in depth by one of my students, Ann Marie Delong, and she came up with many things—old baptisms and confirmations—that told a tale. The tale of long ago. That is, it was part of his nature to start out helping those he would eventually inflict with pain; that is, his great broad back and happy-go-lucky wave would seem like a blessing—for a tiny while.

From what I see, it started years ago, when he got the local contract to plow snow. He was a man of thirty-eight or thirty-nine then, unattached, big, brawling and loud.

Sullivan would use his snowplow to help certain women out. That is, he wouldn't charge them a cent. He'd clear those roadways and drives with his old plow, the smell of diesel in the air and the pipe stack billowing out against the cold. He would park his tractor with the plow up, and let it idle as he went up the stairs of country houses; and he'd stay for an hour or two, sometimes leaving close to midnight. There were at least three women in their forties, widows with school-age children, making do on pensions, whom he impregnated and then left to fend for themselves in the boggy lands below us. They would end up terrified of him in some way—understanding too late that he meant nothing with his endearments. In so many ways, this was talked about and laughed at. And those women were left by themselves, alone in a house off some dark winter turn along the road.

Still, Sullivan's main interest was in repossessing things from people who owed him for loans he gave at a horrible rate. This was a broad business and took him from one side of the river to the other, winter and summer, and indentured many. There was a story that he had knocked up Mrs. Brideau and left her husband to take care of the child. And this child was Anncttc Brideau. Most of us came to realize that this story was false, simple gossip, and as harsh as gossip can be in a small town—a story that made the rounds because the husband was a weak man who Sullivan often bullied. But Sullivan did have a certain power over this girl, just as he did over most others he knew for most of his life.

I met Annette when I was young, around the same time I first noticed these three boys whose story I am telling. I did not know what role she would play in their lives, or how their lives would play out in my life—or how I would come to view them at first as unsavoury backwoods examples of Bonny Joyce, and then come to recognize in all of them, after a time, my own history's brutal and tender blood, hidden as it may be under my suit and tie.

Annette was an only child and from the age of fourteen a strutting beauty—and she could not help this. She could no more help commanding attention than a meteor bursting out of the dark air, or a metaphor so beautiful you put it in a song. Lonnie Sullivan had many youngsters hanging about him, but she was his favourite, and she designed to be his favourite from the first—just as she designed to be everyone's favourite as much as she could. Nothing exemplifies rural life more than those who with longing and hope want, in one fashion or another, to escape it.

No matter how he spoke about helping others, Sullivan committed offences against these people, almost clandestine, almost whimsical and almost unnoticed—a dollar here, a quart of oil there, a mistake in numbers that lessened your pay or a bill you paid back in agony and destitution that was not counted in your favour. Sullivan would sniff and shrug when you tried to plead your case. Or look hurt when you happened to catch him in a lie. But this was true: it could happen in any life, urban or rural. And Sullivan from the first moment he spoke to someone—as he stood in his office with a cigar in his mouth—never really hid his intention. We must, in some way, give him that.

I discovered this next part of the story almost by accident—and have no reason to disbelieve or discount it. It starts out one early spring long ago, with a thousand board feet of lumber that Sullivan told Ceril Palmer he could have to redo the back of his house. But when it came time for Ceril to take it, Sullivan demanded the price be deducted from his pay. A pay that had been withheld since April 15.

"I have had enough of your lies," Palmer said.

"I have never told a lie," he answered, and went in and closed the office door with a quick snap of the lock.

The quick snap of the lock allowed some to think Sullivan was frightened. It was a careless assumption.

Over the next month or so certain of those men came together and plotted their revenge like you would an assassination. Where to do it, who would be involved and how to get it done consumed many people for a long time. Sullivan had six men who worked for him full-time, and at least four of them were included in this conspiracy.

In mid-May a Barryville man attacked him, punching him off his milk box at a horse haul at the community centre. Wearing a white shirt and tie, and heavy old suit jacket and frayed suit pants as part of his obligation as president of the Bonny Joyce Community Centre, Sullivan stood and fought back with two quick punches to the ribs and a left hook, delivered so fast and hard that he left his opponent prone on the ground. And the two others waiting to attack, seeing their biggest ally stunned, left off and moved away. In fact, they snuck away in the confusion of the crowd and loitered together behind the tents.

This was always remembered by us as a strange and pivotal moment in Lonnie Sullivan's life.

There was a sickening pause as the man lay there, beaten, his blood on the dirt, unconscious, like a sleeping child, with Lonnie Sullivan standing above him in triumph. But *how* in triumph—in what way was it a triumph? It was the triumph of a great man burdened by sudden betrayal, and looking from side to side to see who he might or might not implicate, and wondering about those who now stood together behind the dinner tent. The look in his eyes, and on his brooding, callous face, was almost depraved, and everyone spoke of it later.

Few ever bothered Big Lonnie again. Yet he was hurt by this incident, deep in his soul. He smoked his cigars in the dark by his work shed. He accepted no offers of copper or tin roofing, but whiled away his time playing crazy eights with a boy who came by. And it was then, while talking to this boy, Harold Dew, that he decided he would hire boys instead of men. That he would reorganize his little empire, and it would be "done right this time."

And a week later he sent Harold Dew to find out who had set up this attack on him.

"You come back with that information and I will be in your debt—and it is a debt I will carry," he said. He said this most solemnly, and with great feeling.

So Harold left the shed. I saw him as he walked away, seemingly almost stunned by a certain obligation, incurious and detached as he looked at me and passed by, nodding only at the last moment in recognition that I had come home from my college courses. He disappeared down the road, a youth conditioned already to be who he was and nothing else, already blunt, brutal and brave.

Harold went back to see his mentor in the rain three days later, as drizzle was falling off the porch roof. He had one name to offer—a name he had heard while playing horseshoes, and that he'd carried with him until he found out the other names.

Hank Robb. Hank Robb and two others had set up this attack.

"Ahhh," was all Lonnie Sullivan said, "ahhh"—as if spellbound, as if he had known it even before he sent the boy to find out. As if he believed he had done so much good, and so much injury had come to him because of it.

But for some long time—some many excruciating days and weeks— Lonnie Sullivan seemed to do nothing. Hank Robb and the other men came and went from work, and the endless days tagged onto one another, filling the void with agitation and worry, until Sullivan had settled not only on who might have done it but on how he might gain retribution. And so when he had blackballed the men from any opportunity for a job or other employment—from the piles to the wharf, from Neguac to Doaktown—he called them to come see him. The first he called into the office on October 27; the second, on the twenty-eighth. Then he waited a day, to let the last one suffer and not know.

On October 30 he called Hank Robb into the shed, into the back room, where he looked over the receipts he kept in the drawer and threw Robb's severance at him: eighty-nine dollars. The other two fared better than Hank Robb: both had jobs offered to them within a month, and nothing Lonnie said about them stuck. But with Hank Robb it was different. He was considered a disgrace to begin with. I know, for he was my uncle; and in that way, I am connected. Robb went into a grave depression, and three times he brought his daughters with him to the shed and asked for his job back, using the daughters as leverage without a voice, their presence more conspicuous than their little bodies could imagine.

"Ahhh. If I got up from this here seat at this here moment, on this here afternoon with this here cigar in my mouth—you would run hind yer daughters and let them be beat for you," Lonnie said the third time Hank came begging him.

"I wouldn't," Hank said. But he was trembling and alone. He was scared and sad and defeated.

And from what I have heard, as soon as Lonnie stood up, Hank ran and hid behind his daughters; and what is more, little Sara Robb tried to protect him.

Hank Robb's torment was exacerbated by the deliberate taunts of others, some of whom had said they would stand with him if he took up the cause. And when he left the cold shed at night, holding his daughters by the hand, his former compatriots not only ignored him but enjoyed doing so. With the dwindling of the money, with the absence of work and with the idea, constant and unremitting, of his own shame, he began his drinking again, after seven years away from the bottle.

Before Christmas that year, Hank Robb drove his car off the Portage Bridge with his family still inside. The incident didn't make many papers. My mother phoned me when I was in Boston, and asked me to please, whatever I did, stay away from the funeral.

One child, Ethel Robb, lived because of the courage of her sister Sara, who, shattering her left leg with the effort, kept Ethel's head above water in the submerged car. Joyce Fitzroy happened by, and was able to rescue them both. Hank Robb was dead on impact.

"Why I came this way—why I walked down toward the river—for the life of God I do not know," Joyce Fitzroy was heard saying later, wrapped in a blanket and drinking a cup of tea.

After that, Sara went from one doctor's office to the other, in her one print dress, to try to repair her shortened leg, but it could not be done. She went to Dr. Mackenzie many times in the days just before Mackenzie retired. But except for the doctor taking off her sock, and tickling her foot on the bottom until she giggled, nothing more was done.

Then these visits to the doctor's stopped and a kind of whimsical tragedy set into her lively little face and features. Soon she rarely went out at all—or only at night. For she was teased about her leg and how she walked—never by the majority, yet we all know the world is not made up of the majority and never has been.

Neither Harold, Evan nor Ian teased her.

But others did, and would.

———

I will skip ahead now by a few years.

Annette Brideau was Sara Robb's friend, and liked to tell people that she was. It showed her to be kind and thoughtful, and she liked this too—that is, she liked that with Sara tagging along, limping behind her, she would be thought of as kind and thoughtful. And indeed, she could be both kind and thoughtful when she wanted to be, or had to be.

Annette Brideau was the same age as those three boys, and she was also beautiful. At fifteen she scraped together what she could to dress like twenty. Her heritage came from the very earth and trees around her, from where she was born. The trouble was, and it was not entirely her fault, she was often enticed to do mischief, and to be mischievous against her better nature, or in contest with someone else, to prove that she, Annette Brideau, did not have to follow rules. Then she would go to church and pretend to pray and look at the statues and declare she would do better.

Many times her mother took a belt to her. Many times people could hear her screeching as she was whacked. Then the house would go silent and the beaten child would remain inside, upstairs in her small room, where the roof angled over the porch. Many times I have heard that her mother, pious and respectable, was jealous of Annette's beauty and of how so many youngsters loved her.

But her willful nature would overcome her, and Annette would find herself once again doing something she should not. And this led to a pivotal moment in our story. It happened in a small room at the convent on a spring day when she was in grade eleven. Annette was caught cheating on exams. (I sometimes wonder, did it matter that it happened at this moment in her life—that she was not caught cheating on her English exam the day before, or her mathematics exam the day after? Is there any answer to these things?)

She had cheated at school many times since grade eight, and many times her marks showed how competent her cheating was. She had the answers to questions about the Carthaginians written on some pieces of paper and was busy saying the rosary as she wrote, praying seriously while peeking into her sleeve. Mother Saint Silvia realized Annette had never prayed so ferociously before; she made her stand in front of the others, between two rows of old black grade-school desks, and searched her roughly, patting her breasts and hips while the child squirmed and others watched.

"Give—me those—notes, Annette! You behave! Those notes—where are they? I will—take—a ruler to your—fingers!"

Finally the small pathetic crib notes fell to the floor, and Annette was pushed to the door.

"Leave," Sister Silvia shrieked. "Down the hall to Mother Saint Beatrice—NOW!"

"Go to hell," Annette called back, "go to hell—all of you," as she ran, the two books in her arms falling as she herself fell against the corridor wall.

"Go to Mother Saint Beatrice!"

But Annette did not go. She ran down the long hallway, down the back stairs and onto the side lane. There, her face filled with hot and furious tears, she took the apple from her lunch bag and threw it at the door.

She did not want to go home; she wanted to run—away.

She crossed the street at exactly ten in the morning and stood with her thumb out, hitching a ride. And in fact, this ride changed her life. But of course, like so much else, this would not be known for some years to come.

Hitchhiking back downriver she was given a drive by Lonnie Sullivan himself, who had just come from getting his hair cut at Nick's.

Annette began to tell him about Sister Silvia, and how awful she was. And then she played with the dial of his truck radio. And then she took a cigarette when he offered her one. And then she took a drink of wine. And then Lonnie said, "Never mind nuns—nuns are worthless creatures most of the time. I have a job for you."

"I will have to ask my mom and dad."

"Well, you can if you want—but in fact you don't have to ask no one. I will tell them, so you won't have to. I'll pay you good and treat you right—and that will be the end of the convent and Sister Silvia. Let your parents say what they want—I think you should do what I say."

So Annette Brideau took a job at Lonnie Sullivan's, filing certain papers in his big cabinet, answering the phone, cleaning up at the end of each week, both the bathroom and the office, and being at his beck and call to make him a sandwich or find him a drink of pop. She learned to type a letter or two, and to put his to-do lists in order. And he seemed to be appreciative and like her a good deal.

She would go home at night, and for the first time she was allowed out after nine o'clock. That is when she began to wear makeup and perfume. That is when the Annette we all know began to emerge. By this time, those three boys were often at the work shed as well, and for the most part she ignored them. That is, she seemed much older than they. But all of them looked at her and spoke to one another about her—for they could not help it. Of the three, Evan seemed far less interested in her than the other two. But the other two could not, for the life of them, take their eyes off her when she walked. And for the life of her, she could not help but notice this as well.

One day Lonnie asked Annette, as they played their third game of checkers, to watch those three boys and pick who she thought would succeed. Would it be Ian Preston, Evan Young or Harold Dew? Whoever she picked, he said, he would be kinder to and help more. That is, whoever she picked he would pick too, to be his favourite around the shop. "Can you pick the one who will succeed?"

"It is Harold," she said. "He is the one who I would put money on."

"If you had any money, Annette," Lonnie said, biting away at his cigar.

"Yes, if I had any money, it would be him I put me money on!" she said wistfully and with a kind of adolescent regret as she moved a checker, which Lonnie quickly jumped. "But I never have any money—and Daddy doesn't even give me an allowance like the other kids."

Lonnie laughed, looked at his cigar philosophically and shrugged. "You might be right about Harold—you might be indeed right!" Then he stretched and said he did not wish to play anymore.

Lonnie was a philosopher. He spoke endlessly about the plight of others—determined not only to look wise, with his cigar, and seem wise with his cigar smoke, but in fact to *be* wise, with and without the cigar.

————

At that time, the three boys worked in very dangerous places for measly wages, and did so with the exuberance of youth. Sometimes they worked up on Good Friday Mountain in the blinding and terrifying snow. They earned about twenty-eight dollars a week working after school and on holidays from the last of November until December 23, cutting and hauling Christmas trees and piling them on Lonnie's two trucks to sell in the lots in town. Then, during the Christmas holidays, they would stand in the lot from seven in the morning until eleven at night, selling trees at two dollars a foot.

But there was a pivotal moment on the ridge near Good Friday summit. They got caught up in the terrible ice storm of 1974 and stayed together in a small shelter they had constructed. This storm happened late in the winter of that year, in March, when many people were known to have died from the cold.

Lonnie had sent the boys up to the ridge—and people later said it was on purpose, knowing they might die, and to see if they would or wouldn't. But that wasn't the case. Lonnie simply had an abundance of ignorance about what he put his workers through. He may have been selfish and vain, but he wanted no one dead.

He went home and ate dinner, and simply didn't think about where his boys were.

They were stuck for three days, and no one went to find them because Lonnie did not report that they were missing, and their families, thinking they were sleeping safe in Lonnie's bunkhouse, made no inquiry.

They almost froze and had almost nothing to eat—for they were supposed to have returned at noon two days before.

It was then and there that they became blood brothers. They challenged one another to be heroic and loyal. Then they each cut a finger with Evan's buck knife and drew out a spot of blood, that bright sheen of life, and mixed it together. They spoke of Sydney Henderson, who had made a pact with God not to injure, and how others on the flats below, like Mat Pit and the Sheppard boys, tormented him now because this pact made him weak, and they wondered how long he would carry on, and if he would snap out of it and go back to being himself. That is, they thought Sydney's pact was a desperate sham, just as everyone on the road and along Arron Brook did. Oh, they would never be so careless as to make a pact with a Catholic God they did not know or believe in—and all of them were tough enough not to be bothered by the likes of Mat Pit. Ian, the smallest, was as tough as nails, and an ordinary boy would never want to try him. He had slept in the cold, been alone at nights, walked for miles to earn a dollar—and was known to have thrown a man down an embankment who once made fun of his torn jacket. Ian joined the others in becoming a blood brother that night and mocking Henderson as well.

But it was strange, and I might say even otherworldly, how this Sydney Henderson bothered them, not only that night but for years to come. And this Henderson, I would come to find out, bothered many—at the university and even within the church. So these boys were no different when it came to Henderson than most others in society. Henderson would bother them for the rest of his life, for they would see in him a virtue they would by times try to match and by times undermine. In a certain way, this became their quest.

The darkness pulsed around them, and they saw a vein of fool's gold that ran in the rocks nearby; and sometimes in the midst of the snowfall thunder rolled and lightning bolted down. And once, when lightning bolted, Harold stood up, his face contorted in wonder, and yelled out, "Kill me now if you will, or forever leave me be."

He waited, hanging on his own words, his body slightly weaving; if it wove too much, he would tumble two hundred feet into the Arron Brook below. But he not only seemed unworried, he seemed not even aware of the great danger he was in. And he only laughed when the others told him to come back in. They said, with youthful eagerness, "Please watch yourself, boy."

Harold said he would never fall. And he added, "I challenge God of the weak liar Sydney Henderson, and say it is impossible to kill me without a gun!"

The idea of those who don't believe in God (or say they don't) is always to challenge God to prove himself. And this was in fact the mantra of those three that night, as the dark sky produced thunder and lightning in great swirls of angry snow. "God will never bother me— there is not one thing he will do to me. If he couldn't make me fall, then he won't make no one else fall either." And Harold spit his certainty over the side of the cliff.

The other two laughed, not at his statement so much as at his antics. Then they each made a cut and mixed their blood, and the mixed blood dropped into the snow.

And so the blood brothers' bond came to be without God, and they all of them swore to that as well. They all spit, at the moment of the bond, in the direction of the church.

Let Syd do as he would; they would do as they did, and they would see who triumphed in the end. The challenge seemed worst for Syd: people used to fear him, but now he was mocked and scorned. He had become little and littler in the eyes of the community. Yet not one of the boys thought, in that moment, that their youthful celebration against Syd was in the least convenient. (This is what I much later told my cousin Sara Robb, and my students, those sometime young firebrands at Saint Michael's University, who longed for truth in a perfect world, a world so perfect it would make us shudder.)

"We won't be mean to him, or impolite—but we will see. Let's just see how this will play out from here on in," Evan said.

The boys looked at one another with carefree exuberance, knowing it was so cold that they might die in that moment. They were thrilled by this thought of their brotherhood. The idea of their pact without God not only enthused but enthralled them. It allowed them the freedom to do what they must—or in time, perhaps, to do what they wanted. They had seen little enough piety in the priest's weary look to ever think anything could come of religion that wasn't false and contrived. God: what a way to live; better to die.

So they agreed, although they might face death right here, this terrible night, or they might come out of it—whatever happened, life or death, pitiless or free, they would rely upon one another and no one else.

The night became cold and then colder still, and the small half-cliff they sat on became their universe. The vein of fool's gold captivated them, shining against the blackness of the cliff with inordinate force, sometimes wrapped in a resplendent gauze of snow. They whiled away the hours, listening to the storm, sharing remnants of stale bread and hamburger almost burned black, and speaking of two things: women they wanted to bed and riches they felt they would someday have. Both Harold and Ian spoke of Annette, but Evan did not; he spoke only of Molly Thorn.

The snow swirled in the great sky above them, covering up all the paths along the great hills. It was as white as the purest soul, and as scattering as gossip.

Yet to those boys stranded halfway up Good Friday Mountain, the meaning of riches was less than what you might imagine. They huddled into one another in the storm. They stared at one another's boots and hands in the thick darkness and felt the sting of cold and the taste of metal. But they spoke of a future as bright and alive as that of anyone who, at that very moment, was preparing to attend Harvard or Yale in the fall. They thought that if they worked hard, maybe they could earn twenty thousand dollars a year. All of them decided that twenty thousand dollars a year would be the most anyone could want—and to ever want more would be greed. And they agreed they would share all of these riches if they got them. Twenty thousand dollars to these boys was like a million to others. And they had seen one another's loneliness and poverty through the years.

It was a great thought, and in that moment Shakespeare was right: love did feed on itself.

Evan Young said he would someday have the Jameson sawmill, the mill the Jameson family had owned in the 1920s and '30s. He would refit it and dedicate his life to making it work. Not only would he bring industry back to Bonny Joyce but a sense of community as well.

Ian Preston said he didn't know what he wanted to do. Perhaps he would work in town because he was good at fixing appliances and was a fine electrician. Yes, he often thought he would move upriver and work there. This was a town of six thousand people then, a town that was very large compared with what Ian had known.

Harold Dew said he would inherit some money and open up a pawnshop. He had seen the pawnshop Lonnie Sullivan had opened in the late 1960s and he was intrigued by that kind of enterprise. That is, people live according to their own level, and perhaps, even if he made a million, Harold would still need to have the pawnshop to satisfy himself. For in the pawnshop he saw the whole town, and the people in it, and the rise and fall of fortunes, and those who he felt he could know and help. They would all come to him someday, as they did to Lonnie now. And those long, warm, summer days in town with the pawnshop door open, and a breeze blowing the curtains slightly or a fan ticking in the corner, was for Harold the emblem not of success but of peace—something he had never had. He remembered Lonnie's pawnshop just like that—the items all catalogued, and people coming in with little trinkets or wares to trade—and his feeling was one of calm and fulfillment.

"But do not worry yourselves, I will share it with you all—I will make sure nothing I have will be mine alone," he said.

"And I will too," Ian said.

"And so will I," said Evan.

In mixing their blood that night on the hill in the storm the three truly felt they were united in a way that nothing could pull asunder, and that the boy Sydney Henderson who had made a pact with a Catholic God was nothing more than someone who challenged them to do better and to prove themselves. In a circuitous way, then, all of them by this challenge were trying to prove themselves to Sydney's God by disproving that He was ever needed at all.

Then the three of them spoke of the church, and how they had been forced to go to it when small. How the priests were like old women, how the sacraments were false. They now hated the idea of charity and nuns and the church—they were smarter and understood more. And because the priests wore collars and the nuns wore widow peaks, these boys could say that the hypocrisy and untruths of the nuns and priests was greater than that of others. But they ignored this fact: by committing to be blood brothers, they were exercising the same hope as a priest with a collar or a nun with a cap, and the road was a long one yet.

"Sydney's a fool," Evan said, spitting over the side of the drop. "I never thought I would say that about that man—but there, I did say it about him."

And the others complied. And to a boy they nodded in disdain. Then, though they were supposed to take turns keeping one another awake, they fell asleep, all of them. And if the wind had continued, they would all have died—but for some reason, the wind changed within an hour after sleep came, and by morning the temperature had risen substantially, and all of them woke up in the sun to the smell of melting ice and the first sweet tinge of spring.

Harold looked over the cliff the next morning—and realized how close he had been to it, and smiled. "No, I didn't fall."

———

The three went along this road of mocking for well over a year, and made so many jokes about religion that people called them the "devil's advocates"—which they all enjoyed immensely. And some said they

were "the wickedest three in Northumberland," which they also liked
to hear. They loved to hear this because of two things: it made them
seem and feel like renegades—and the world never had enough of
those; and it made them believe that all others about them were pious
and meek, and not so witty or brilliant or daring as themselves. So they
walked past many others in the night with a satirical sniff.

Some people, in fact, thought they would burn the church—old women
especially, who went to the Catholic Women's League, and worried much
about it. It did not help that Harold told a young woman that he would
put firecrackers in the holy water.

"Boo!" Harold would yell to various old ladies, and they would look
at him with great trepidation and alarm. The other two, of course, did
not do this, but as Harold said, he "booed" for all three. And all three
would laugh in hilarity. Yet once or twice, in a state of euphoria brought
on by widening vocal swipes against the pious and the meek, a draft
would sweep across their eyes and make them blink.

"Nothing will come between us now!" Harold said one spring night
when there were warm pebbles under the ice and the smell of old barn
straw in the wind. He took out his last three cigarettes and shared them
about. God, that was such a night, with golden stars and warm trees in
the moonlit forest.

No one touched them during this time—neither Mat Pit nor the
Sheppard brothers, who they sometimes saw along the road, nor any of
the Delaney men—for everyone knew: go against one, and you had one
hell of a time on your hands.

But the boys remained fascinated with Sydney Henderson on the one
hand, who took any job he could find from anyone, and Lonnie Sullivan
on the other, who gave and took jobs like fate took lives. (Though, in
truth, Lonnie Sullivan was the least exceptional of men, and much like
thirty others on our river.)

Sydney had to find work, and would take almost any job that was
offered. People said he was brilliant, but he certainly did not seem so. And
he would at times find himself at Lonnie Sullivan's looking for a day or

two employment. And so it came to pass that Sydney did work with the three boys at Spine's Grey Landing in early April the next year, when the ice broke and roared and piled ten-men high in the woods. The four of them had to cut ten cord of wood for Lonnie's furnace for next year. Lonnie demanded it be done and laid out this early because he could; and he wanted the boys to have to do it, and then to have to do more for him.

It took the boys a good while to get it done, for the saws kept breaking—the old Husqvarna was fifteen years old, the great Massey Ferguson had a bad spark. All the while, determined to do his work, Sydney kept their spirits up with jokes and songs—songs of a Miramichi and a world now gone, of men of the bogs and woods now gone, of traces and sleds and poles now gone. And not only did the others realize that his jokes were hilarious, but they heard that his voice was pristine. And they knew as well that he had been shot as a youngster—and had once, and probably still was, able to fight like a wild animal. They had called him one when he was thirteen, and in fact, all of them had once been terrified of him. But now so many others said so many lesser things about him, they joined those others in saying the same.

On the night of April 9, they finished. They brought the wood out, and in the great field behind Sullivan's it stretched back and away, and they said to themselves: Lonnie must be happy with us now. None of them had escaped a cut or bruise, and all of them, in spite of what they said, and how they said it, admired Sydney Henderson in that moment. But it irked the three that Sydney might think that he was their friend when he wasn't, and they made that clear by ignoring him as soon as they were done with the work. And so he stood alone. For they were bonded by blood; not he.

Nor would they ever forget that Lonnie, in a foul mood, buttressed by rum and a loss at bingo—as well as the turning of a horse's ankle that made short work of the ceremony of payment—gave them less than he had promised and confused the payment with their past obligation, which they were sure they had previously worked off, and then paid Sydney less than the others by seventeen dollars, when he had children and what everyone said was a beautiful but simple-minded wife to feed.

Yet all three boys—and this happens everywhere when man deals with man—committed the sin of omission, and did not defend the one who should have been defended, and said nothing more. And Sydney walked home alone in the bitter dark with puddles freezing over and snow falling close on Good Friday in 1975.

I remember I saw Sydney Henderson around that time. It was at a wedding—I do not know when exactly, but sometime in the summer that same year.

My mother insisted I go to this wedding—put in an appearance and tell everyone I was a Rhodes Scholar, as if they would be impressed. I loved her, but I realized I was an oddity; and in fact, I always would be.

Still, I went to the wedding because my mother asked me to. And I saw at this wedding—as at all weddings—the kind of finery that shows us to be rural people. The kind of people who will always, no matter what tux they wear, have broad backs and uncomplicated smiles; no matter what dresses, have the feel and look of the earth; and no matter how proudly they walk, exult in the strains of fiddle music only a half-step away.

I told my students later on that this was the first time I remember seeing Sydney Henderson. I had heard so many stories about him I stared at him too long, until he noticed me and smiled.

He was standing off to the side of the large yard where cars were parked. He had long had the reputation of being an oddity, something of a soothsayer—and I remember he was speaking to Annette Brideau. I did not recognize her at first—it took me a while to place her, to remember who she was, because she had become a young woman now. She was in fact one of those few people who would always stand out. Still, I remember that she was looking frightened or concerned, as a person will who is suddenly told some unexpected bad news.

I later learned she had been teasing Sydney, asking him to tell her a secret she had about herself—for this is what Henderson was supposedly able to do. And Annette loved to have her fortune told. All her life she wanted to hear agreeable things about herself. Especially, I found out, if she was told she was both pretty and wise, and that all nice things would happen. So she smiled tenderly and readied herself to be pleased.

At first Sydney did not answer her; he did not want to. He seemed to want to ignore her, without giving away the reason. But she continued to press him to tell her something about her future.

"Tell me now—what is it you know, Syd, what big secret do you know? I know you are keeping it all from me—something you know!"

She grabbed his arm and then took his hand in hers; she waved to passersby and winked at them, as if all were engaged in her tender conspiracy. So finally he bent toward her and whispered something. She was smiling as he bent and she winked at a friend. But bit by bit she turned white, and then backed away.

"That is not true! You are being mean—that's what everyone says about you—you are mean and stupid! Why would you say this to me?"

"No—you are right—I had no right to say it," he said, suddenly very upset with himself. "I am likely very wrong. Why, you ask Elly. She often says I am wrong."

Annette was now scared and stammered, "Well, your wife is as dumb as you, and you have an albino daughter as far as I know, and you can't even afford milk for your children as far as I know—and you write stupid poems as far as I know." She gave a lilting, defiant laugh.

Then she ran across the lot, and sat on an old wicker chair and stared out at the bay, now and then swatting at a horsefly circling her. Henderson turned away and started to walk toward the lane, the dust of it over his shoes and pants. He seemed rattled that he had upset this young woman. Then he started walking back toward Annette as if he wanted to apologize. But he stopped and looked in the direction of Verna Bickle and her son, Wally, as if he was very startled by them too. At that time it was a standard joke that wherever Verna was, her son, Wally, was too. Whatever Verna gossiped about, Wally would as well. And just as some people could be called professional Catholics, Verna was a professional Baptist.

Now Wally stood beside his mommy and the other grown-up guests, a rotund little boy with a red bow tie, and spoke about someday being in the student police. There was nothing about him that struck me as unusual—except that Henderson looked at him intensely, almost sorrowfully, but only for a split second, then looked over at Annette again quickly, seeming troubled.

Then he looked at me and said, somewhat joyfully and almost as if we had known each other for years and years, "I am going down the highway to hay. You are going back to university. That is a great and good thing to do. But you will come home someday, and help solve something important for us—perhaps!"

"What did you say to Annette? She seems very upset."

"I told her that what she is led to believe about her firstborn might someday destroy her second—and I should not have said so, it was foolish of me. But I have had that feeling now for some while, each time I see her."

And that was that: the only time Henderson ever spoke to me. But no one ever believed Henderson, or really cared what he said. And it was only recently I remembered this incident, when I started to compile notes about the three boys to write this book.

I remember as well how Lonnie came down the lane that day, driving his white Eldorado, wearing a gold chain around his heavy neck, and picked young Annette Brideau up. She slammed the car door and glanced at me with imperious and startling beauty. Then Lonnie roared up the lane past Sydney, covering the man's old suit in pebbles and dust.

"She is one of his many little urchins," someone said as we watched them drive away. That is, so much that people believe is hidden, is not.

By now, as we know, Lonnie had amassed a large car, a few trucks, a pocket full of cigars, bottles of old navy rum—and horses he raced, whenever they weren't down, in Charlottetown. And the three boys were certainly charmed by that. And he seemed to have Annette Brideau as his mascot in his car on those long summer afternoons when he would drive down to the beach and call the boys over to him.

"You want to make some money?" he would say. Boys would clamour around his car like a swarm of petulant bees—half of them just to look at Annette, who in the swell of heat and early blossom was a rural and earthen and ethereal presence all at once. But it was also the smell of his car, the look of the big cigars sitting in the pocket of his white shirt, the way he drawled his response and took out a wad of money to pay for something small, that impressed them. He would send the kids scrambling to the corner store for a chocolate bar, pulling from his pockets a wad of twenty- and fifty-dollar bills.

But this secret was well known: Lonnie Sullivan did not have all the money in Bonny Joyce, as he said he had. Joyce Fitzroy too had a good deal hidden—at least as much as Big Lonnie. And so Lonnie would lie awake at night wondering how to convince Joyce to share it with him. Lonnie was obsessed with always having and obtaining more. He also believed that Fitzroy did not respect him, and this irritated him terribly. And from that first moment when he saw Annette hiking home, these impulses in him would in some way destroy her. That is, whoever he drew to him he must, by his nature, twist to his purpose. At first, as always, he was thinking only that he would be her mentor. Still, being her mentor, he felt she must think like he thought, and act the way he told her to. And after a year or so he began to include her in his long-term plans without ever thinking he would harm her. But there was never a person Lonnie knew who, at some point, he did not hurt. If there was a man who kept secrets on his friends in order to turn on them when he was given the chance, that man was Lonnie Sullivan.

One of the boys who gathered around the car on those lost summer afternoons—so long ago that transistors were still in fashion and no one would have known what a computer was—listening to the corrupt ramblings of Sullivan, was Ian Preston himself, who could not take his eyes off Annette. So with timidity and love he asked her out. Annette did not know whether or not she should go. So, as always, she went to Lonnie and asked him what to do.

"Oh, he's a little twit," Lonnie said, while he busied himself polishing and spitting on a boot. "But still, it's very interesting—very interesting that he would get up the nerve. So go and have a good time. He has saved his money—so you may as well enjoy it." He looked up and smiled, and then spit on the boot again.

Then he added, in a sardonic voice, "All the boys are after you. Harold is too—don't you kid yourself. You watch that they both don't come to blows over you."

At sixteen years old, this both shocked and thrilled her.

"But I want you to take heed."

"What?" she asked.

"Don't pick the wrong boy. You have to think of yourself in all of this." And Lonnie wagged his finger and looked sternly at her. "Don't think of anyone else—time is on your side now, but someday it will no longer be. So if I give you advice like a father, you should take the advice I give. You come back and tell me everything."

So Annette telephoned Ian and said yes, she would go out.

She went to a movie with him that first night, and after that whenever he had the money, and soon she took a milkshake from him at Bobbi's Dairy Stop. Perhaps she did not know just how much this cost Ian out of earnings he himself was trying to save. And he did not understand at that time how little of what he said could impress her.

Still, on a summer evening so long ago—the trees waving, as if with the kind of passion that makes one think they not only are alive but vying for attention; on one of those summer evenings so long ago, when the sky was warm and black—there was a moment when Ian tried clumsily to sneak a kiss. He put his arm around her so abruptly that she almost fell forward, and then he tried to draw her to him. Annette looked at him in sudden—for it seemed to just happen in the moment— superiority, and turned her head away.

"No, you can't," she said. "Uncle Lonnie wouldn't want me to!"

Ian was a little shocked at what he had attempted, and angered that she had refused. He went home, hands in his pockets, and looking up on the crossroads he saw Joyce Fitzroy, drunk as arse, dancing with an axe.

I will someday get out of here for good—I will be better than I am today, Ian thought. In seven years people will know who I am! And he thought: Someday I will kiss her—and at her cottage too!

————

I think Joyce Fitzroy's money obsessed all who knew about it. For there it was in his house, hidden somewhere among the rafters, and nothing was being done with it. And he, Joyce Fitzroy, was a drunken half-illiterate man, never farther than fifty miles away from Bonny Joyce in his life. His photo, taken when he was twenty and on a river drive, looked fierce: he up on the little sou'west, working for Jameson. His picture at thirty-five, he with a heavy black beard, sitting in a lumber camp, showed a man resilient, a man who on his own could terrify a half-dozen other men. But now he was old and alone; everyone he had ever loved was gone. And the worst of it was, he had money. At least twice, people had tried to rob him—derelict men into drugs in our town. It was rumoured that Lonnie Sullivan had set these attempted robberies up—but nothing was ever proven against him. However, Lonnie had set his mind on this money years before, when he drove a snowplow in the winter—and though he had become wealthy since, he had not lost interest in it. Fiztroy knew this, but he also knew those sad women Lonnie had visited when he ran his plow, and from that moment on never spoke to him. This enmity between them was silent, and therefore deep and bitter.

So now our story turns slowly toward this money.

One day in 1975, shortly after that wedding I attended, Annette awoke and went to see Joyce Fitzroy because Lonnie Sullivan had asked her to. "Find out what he needs," Sullivan told her the night before, "and come back and let me know. I want to help him. So many people have abused that poor old man, Annette—and you know it for a fact!"

Lonnie often said "you know it for a fact" to those who did not know it for a fact. He looked at her strangely, seriously, as if trying to impart some message without saying exactly what it was.

She arrived at the old shack that Fitzroy lived in, and sat on a chair in the centre of the room. The walls had been peeled down to nothing, the stovepipe was black and corroded, and the windows were so thick with grime it was hard to see through them.

She asked Joyce if she could make him tea. He said no. She asked him if he wanted something to eat. Again he said he did not. She sighed and nodded and tried to tell a joke, although she could never seem to tell them right. She fumbled with her hands, then filed her fingernails for something to do. She watched as the flies alighted on the oilcloth table and got caught in a flycatcher hanging from the middle of the ceiling. Finally, after the old man started to fall asleep, she ran back and reported all this to Lonnie.

"Did you find out where the money was? Did you get near it at all?"

"No."

"You didn't?"

"No."

"I thought that's what I sent you there for." Lonnie glared at her, as if she was suddenly the worst person on earth. He raised his hand to strike her. She fell back terrified, and he put his arm down. He smiled slightly and whispered, "I guess I can't trust you—I thought I could." And sweat broke out on his face.

They were alone in the office and Annette felt confused and frightened. For the first time, she saw a different Lonnie Sullivan from the one she knew: he had never told her what he'd wanted, and yet was furious she did not deliver what he had not asked for. She stumbled backward and tried to smile.

He lit a cigar and puffed away on it, then went outside and sat alone. He refused to speak to her the rest of the day and finally she sat at the checkboard, tears running down her cheeks.

"I'm sorry," she kept saying, "I'm sorry, Uncle Lonnie—I am!"

Finally he came in, and stood over her as she wiped tears away with her hands.

"Next time I ask you to do something—you will do it," he told her. "That old man is going to burn his house down some night by accident—I want to take that money and make sure it's safe for him. He has nobody but me—and you know that for a fact."

There was a list of who knew and who did not know about Fitzroy's money. This list was made up after the fact, when things became serious.

Lonnie knew Fitzroy had money.

Annette knew it too.

Harold knew about it, and most everyone assumed Ian knew of it as well—for him not to have known would be peculiar. Still, it is my contention that Ian was ignorant of it. That is, I remembered him from long ago, and I told my students later on that, yes, this idea of who knew about the money was instrumental to understanding all other things concerning these blood brothers.

Of course Evan knew about the money because he was the boy who tried to take care of Joyce Fitzroy when he went on his three- or four-day drunks; he was the one who tried his hardest to get the old man to take his pills. And one time, Joyce had shown the money to Evan, nodding in the prepossessing way only a drunk can.

Joyce told Evan he had no use for the money and was going to give it all away.

"You think I care for money? Do you want it? Here, take it—now is your chance, you won't get a better one! Take it now! Or never ask me for it no more!" Joyce smiled at him, his beard grey stubble and his face deep red, a Copenhagen snuffbox in his pocket.

Evan told Joyce not to be so foolish and helped him put the money away. The thought of the offer was both repugnant and enthralling to him. He went home and thought on it. He sat on the chair in his bedroom, already broad shouldered, committed, and grimly focused on doing something special with his life. Should he have taken the money, or no? This was a question to plague him for years to come. But no, he could not take it from a drunk and remain a man.

During this time, Ian Preston's mother was dying in a room alone at the hospital downriver. Ian had not been close to her in the last few years. He had tried to be someone else and had developed a kind of officious and regimental attitude. He was snobbish toward her, just as people had been to her most of her life. Often she waited, in that last year of her life, on the couch in her small living room, hoping that he would visit while the clock ticked away the afternoon. She would sometimes get up and busy herself, but always come back, look at the clock and think: Well, there is still time for him to visit.

And now, of course, as with so much in life, it was too late.

Ian went to the hospital to be with her. He sat in the chair and listened to her breathe and watched the monitor; the instruments set up to keep her living were seemingly too advanced for such a small heartbreaking life, and the beeping of machines contrasted with such a frail body.

She was being given liquid and nothing else now. Ian would look at the orange juice in the cup, the small straw, and feel embittered and depressed. He wanted to take her suffering away but could not. He even hoped that this transference of suffering might happen if he closed his eyes and thought hard enough. But it did not.

Then a priest was in the room, looking at his notes to see who it was he was visiting, and accommodating Ian with a false smile. Ian walked over to the window and looked down at the parking lot while the priest went to the bed, made the sign of the cross on his mother's forehead, blessed himself and prayed.

The priest then came over to Ian; all of a sudden he was at his neck, whispering. He said that if Ian prayed, he might be able to alleviate some of his trouble. And the feeling of the man's breath on Ian's neck infuriated him. He turned to look at the man—this was the same priest who had hit him some years before and made a remark about his family. It was a final insult that he was here simpering like a weed, asking him to pray. No, no, of course—the man would never dare to hit him now. He would be too cowardly to do it now; Ian was not a child of twelve now.

"You will find it less difficult if you pray," Father LeBlanc said.

"Lies," Ian whispered. "Do not speak to me again!"

"What?"

"Where were you when we were trying to buy food—except drinking booze with old Jim Chapman, and sniggering at people on the Bonny Joyce?" The worst of it was, this was true. But what was truer was that this feeling of outrage and this outburst came because Ian wanted to exaggerate and perform. And when he said all this, his mother was lying on the white bed, the sheets whiter than any she had had the pleasure of lying on before, with dark rapid shadows playing across her face. The bed was tilted forward so she could breathe better, and her eyes opened suddenly as if she had recognized Ian's voice, and she tried to shake her head, to tell him to stop. But even in looking at her and seeing her distress over what he was saying, he couldn't stop.

"Just a Hail Mary," the priest said kindly.

Ian raised his fist, ready to strike the man, thought better of it and left the room.

He sat alone for the longest time that evening, tears running down his cheeks. Half were for his mother, his guilt over abandoning her, his belief that he was better than she; and half were out of anger with the priest, who had gone away now.

Later in the evening, Evan came to sit with him. Neither of them knew where Harold was. Evan was silent about one thing—what Harold had asked him two days before: would it be right to steal Ian's girl? That is, he was as plagued by Annette's beauty as Ian himself. And Evan had decided he must stay out of it. But he knew this was the reason Harold did not come to the hospital.

"Never you mind, he must be busy," Ian said. "He wouldn't *not* come unless he was in some bind."

The next evening, after Ian's mother had died, both Harold and Evan went to Ian's house, and they stuck by his side until the funeral was over. Harold and Evan did not know what to do or say, but they were there. Ian looked at the small living room, the TV that almost never worked, the knickknacks his mother had collected at fairs and picnics, and he picked up a chair and calmly threw it though the front window.

When he woke the next morning, the window had been repaired by Harold Dew, who had walked to Clare's Longing to get a new one.

During the funeral, Harold was preoccupied with one thing: how could he betray Ian and not have it looked upon as betrayal? Ian had asked Annette to stand in line with him at the funeral parlour, and Annette did so because she felt it made her someone special. This was all well and fine for Annette until she actually saw the body of the little woman, cold and utterly artificial, and yet with a look of grave warning and anger that seemed to be directed at Annette herself. Afterwards she could not go into the parlour again.

Harold stood outside the funeral parlour in the strong wind, hoping to talk to Annette, now and then picking up the twigs that had fallen from trees and tossing them high into the air. He was thinking of one thing: how would his life be without her? And: If Ian thought enough of Annette to ask her to stand with him in line at his mother's funeral, what was he, Harold, to do? How could he change this in his favour without hurting his blood brother?

Only if she was not Ian's girl would he feel justified in doing this. But as we know, there are ways to convince yourself that the direction you want to go in is the direction you must take.

Is she his girl or what? Harold asked himself, walking alone that night toward Clare's Longing. No, he had been told by Lonnie yesterday afternoon, Annette was no one's girl. Harold had said nothing. Still, if she was no one's girl, that certainly meant she was not Ian's.

But there was something else he thought about on the way to Clare's Longing. Harold believed his mother, Goldie Dew, was in

Fitzroy's will and would someday claim the old man's money. For Goldie had come into their house one day most excited, and said that Fitzroy had exclaimed, "You may as well have it—I don't want it. I will give it all to you after I go—just use enough of it to pay for my funeral, and the rest is yours."

This had been said when Harold was only fourteen, but he had remembered it ever since. And now, the more he thought of it, the more he was certain that this money would someday be his.

But Joyce Fitzroy had said this to a dozen others when he was drunk—others who visited his little clapboard structure off the beaten road. Fitzroy liked saying it, and in fact, there was a bit of a taunt in it—even more of a taunt than one might first imagine. He knew very well why certain people visited him. And he always liked them to assume he didn't know. Then, after they left, he would spit his snuff into the hot stove and look with disdain at their departing snow-draped figures.

So Harold had begun to brag about his mother's place in Fitzroy's will. He'd done it in front of Lonnie one afternoon, just before the funeral, saying that someday he would be as rich as Lonnie Sullivan.

Lonnie had nodded and said, "You might be richer, for sure." But he was definitely bothered by this.

The day after Mrs. Preston's funeral, Lonnie spoke to Annette about it. "What are you doing with that pipsqueak Ian? Harold is the one who will get the money—it would be a shame to see you spend your life in some shack."

"I don't care about that," she said.

"It's not up to me—but if you don't, you are stupid. That's hundreds of thousands."

Annette was flustered and said nothing, and looked ashamed.

It was true that Joyce Fitzroy's money was thought to be in the hundreds of thousands of dollars. And Lonnie added more to the sum the more he spoke about it. During this time it obsessed him so much he was only sleeping three or four hours a night.

"I want you to find out everything, and tell me what you find out. I don't want any mistakes—like last time," he said. And when she looked at him apologetically, he shrugged.

A week after the funeral, Annette heard Harold talking about money at the horse haul in Lower Newcastle. He was not talking about Joyce Fitzroy's money, but about twenty dollars he had won playing horseshoes that day. Still, she tried to get closer to see what it was he was speaking about, so that Lonnie would be pleased. She went around by the back of the large tent and came up behind him to listen. He spoke loudly and brazenly. And suddenly, turning his head, he saw she was there—only ten feet from him!

That was the day, well recorded here, when Mr. Laws's Belgians got hyped on rum and tea and were crazy in the eyes. The handlers had a hard time bringing the team back to the pole to hook the heavy load, and most of the women and more than half of the men stood well back. As Annette herself said, she was scared "of them awful horses." She did not say this to bring attention to herself—but it did bring attention.

"What are ya scared off? Stick with me, for I'm scared of nothing." Harold laughed, walking over to stand close to her.

The horses' great hooves pranced in the dirt, their eyes looked strange and startled, and their massive backs rippled as they were forced into place; and all the men around them looked ordinary—even, somehow, fragile. Annette again said she was frightened of those awful horses, and so Harold put his arm about her, and she stood where she was, Harold with his large arm hugging her.

Ian saw this. He and Sydney Henderson were the only two brave enough to hook. Hooking a team of horses to a giant slab of wood, when the team is trained to bolt as soon as the clamp is set, is as dangerous a job as one can have. By hooking, both boys were risking injury or death to win fifteen dollars.

Harold knows she is my girl, Ian thought, looking over at Annette's wilful and beautiful and taunting face. But he was so upset he almost did not get out of the way of the sled when the horses lunged. Afterwards, he went to the tent and sat in his place, waiting for Annette to come have dinner with him. He held the money he'd won in his hand, hoping to pay for her dinner. But she did not come. He could not eat, and when he left the tent, one of the horses had gone down with a heart attack and was lying on its side in the dirt, a half-metre away from the tonnes of wood it had been forced to haul—the tonnes of wood Ian had hooked on.

Ian looked up at the sky and cursed—but he did not know if he was cursing Harold or God. He walked all the way back to Bonny Joyce, stopping every little while to wait for Annette. The day was empty and the wind had turned cold.

Later, when he went looking for her down at Bobbi's Dairy Bar, he heard from Mat Pit that she had left the horse haul to go swimming with Harold at Arron Falls.

Over the next few weeks, as warm rain began to spit down, Harold ignored Ian, not saying hello when he met him on the long lane by the piles and bypassing him as he walked to Annette Brideau's house.

Ian was struck dumb by this. But Harold, one evening, said to him, "All is fair in love and war."

Then Ian walked to Annette's little cottage with flowers, trying to win her back. But she ran into the house and her father told him to go away. After a few days of Ian staying away, Annette asked Lonnie what to do.

"Do you want to see if he will still follow you about, if you still have some control over him? Then write him a little note," Lonnie said, chuckling at all of it. To him, it was innocent fun—that is, he had these youngsters fighting and upset, and he loved the spectacle. So Annette wrote to Ian, with this line: "Meet me now—I will explain everything to you, but you have to come at once to Fallon's Brook."

Ian ran there, up past Fanny Groat's on the Gum Road, past old Harold Tucker's and the stretch of Arron, and into the great fields beyond. He got to Fallon at supper hour, covered in muck and brine, filled with the scope of Annette's majesty, her imperial beauty, her charm that erased all thoughts except that he would die for her—at once. And yet, she wasn't there. And the day darkened little by little in the stifling afterhours. It became still in the after-supper hours and full of the scent of rain, and then the low clouds tormented the bushes.

He thought there must be some mistake—or perhaps she had hurt herself and was lost. He finally walked down the Gum Road, and around eight o'clock suddenly heard tittering like that of little blond birds at the edge of the highway, near old Jim Chapman's grader. It was Annette—and two other girls—who had come to watch.

"There he is," they were whispering, "there he is."

Then Annette teased Ian when he ran down to see her swimming at the wharf. "I wouldn't go out with you if you were the last man on the river—even if you owned the river, would I? If they said, 'Oh my, that Ian Preston, that pipsqueak won the entire river,' I'd say, 'He is still a pipsqueak to me.'"

She knew she was being cruel but could not help it. It seemed like so much fun for everyone. Lonnie was pleased with her again, and everyone seemed to like her.

Harold did not know about Annette's game playing or tormenting, but who knows if it would have mattered if he had. Lonnie knew, and enjoyed it. So he went on blindly, this Ian Preston, scratching himself against the surface of Annette's soul, unable to understand or wound—and he certainly wanted to wound them all. But how can you wound someone else when you are heartsick?

We know how love tormented the lover—but must also realize how much the torment pleased the beloved. Annette said she did not wish Ian to follow her but was pleased when he did—and more pleased when her friends had to tell him to leave her alone. And so Ian did leave her alone. He went back to the small house on Swill Road and sat on the porch staring out, almost in madness, at the trees. He wandered through them from Badden Brook all the way down to where Little Hackett flowed into Glidden's Pool—and there he hid.

And Ian did think of suicide at that moment—and eventually Annette was told this.

"My God," she said, somewhat thrilled. "I don't want anyone to kill themselves over me."

"Why not?" Lonnie said, and pontificated on life, liberty and love: "It's the way of the world—it's all in how you move your sweet little ass." Two years previously, he would never have been able to talk to her so freely—but two years is a long time. And during those two years Annette was continually told she must get from the world what she could; that people were out to use her, so she must use them. Now, it seemed, she had everyone on a string, and it was a beautiful string. It arced out like her body against the pale evening sunlight, wearing a light summer dress. The string moved, and the young boys danced. And Lonnie sat with his cigar, the tip of it wet with his spit, and listened to the tapping feet against the hardwood floor.

So, for a time, Ian went away from the other two boys, and those two became closer to each other than Ian was to either—for Harold said that Ian's jealousy was not his concern; it was, in fact, only one person's concern: Ian's alone. Besides, Annette did not love Ian and had made that clear—and Harold said that since this was clear, Ian should not harbour a grudge.

"I don't know what's wrong with him," Harold would say to Lonnie Sullivan, in a bragging fashion. "He should soon get over it, shouldn't he? I'd never be caught harbouring no grudge over a woman!"

"You are by far the best lad for her," Lonnie would say. "I always said you was."

And Ian was alone.

This is how it came about that one night Ian got close to the Sheppard brothers, who were going to raid Sydney Henderson's store. By this I do not mean a retail store, I mean Sydney's store of smelt nets in his shed. The brothers wanted to take them and sell them to Lonnie Sullivan, who would sell them again to his friend downriver. Still, when it came to it, something prevented Ian from doing what he'd told the Sheppard boys he would do. He remembered Sydney working with him and Harold and Evan, and sharing his Thermos of tea—and he'd also heard that Sydney's wife, Elly, had been accused of theft. Now, people who knew her said she couldn't have done it—and yet, much was to be gained in gossip and fun by saying she had.

"No," Ian said to the Sheppard brothers that night, "it is not right. Sydney has a wife and a boy and girl over there, and is just making do. His wife probably didn't steal McVicer's money, anyway."

"He's an enemy of ours."

"That means nothing to me. You aren't doing it, and I will stand at his store all night to make sure." Ian did not know why he said that; he did not have anything but contempt for a man who would not protect himself. But still, it is what he did say.

The next day he took his fishing rod and went to upper Hackett to catch trout. He had been alone—that is, without his friends—for five weeks now. He could not speak to Harold, nor did he want to see Evan. So he was alone, and he came to the river's bend—called Toe—in the late afternoon. There were raindrops on the water and he walked down over the shale bank to Lion's Den Pool. He was alone in the midst of all his agony, and yet he soon had two fish. He laid them up on the shore, keeping an eye out for mink that would steal them. He was changing his leader when a man moved downriver toward him, and he realized it was Sydney Henderson—the man who had made a pact with God, an idiot making a pact with the vespers of an idiot.

Ian wasn't planning to speak, but Sydney did—he came over to Ian, and exclaimed, "You are lucky—two nice trout!" He said this even though he had more fish than Ian in his own basket. He watched Ian work his way down through Lion's Den and then come back, and he sat with him a moment.

"So God keeps putting you out, don't he?" Ian said. "Your goddamn Catholic God. Elly herself is now being accused. I'd go after anyone who accused my wife—I would tear them apart."

Sydney laughed. "Elly did nothing and I know that. And those who accused her do too. You will have hardship in your life, as well as me—and even more, I do think . . . though I am not so sure, and don't want to presume."

"Presume what?"

"Oh, I have made a pact with God, or at least people say so. And people say it is an impossible one." Sydney laughed. "Some lads even stole my smelt nets to see if I would attack them." Here he smiled and sniffed, and looked down at the clump of weeds growing up through the rocks. "But you have made a worse pact—a pact that is virtually impossible to keep, really. You have made a pact with men. Yes, I have heard about that too—up on Good Friday in the snow. And I do not know which of us is in the more difficult position, but we will see, we will see. I know this God business is a terrible responsibility—almost impossible, Joseph Conrad said. But this man business—this blood-brother business—it's like making a pact with a shadow of smoke. And your wife someday will be accused of thievery too."

"By who?"

Sydney did not answer.

"By who?" Ian said, grabbing him, and suddenly realizing how strong the man actually was.

"By you," Sydney said.

Ian watched as Sydney worked the pool and hooked a fish up against the far bank where Ian wasn't able to cast and then asked Ian if he wanted it.

"No."

"But you were in this pool first, so I do not mind."

"No—of course, not at all. Go on down."

Yet Sydney released the fish anyway. He said, "It is most awful to be betrayed, and it is just as bad to be accused of betraying friends when you did not. Life is hard enough without that."

Ian would remember this conversation years later, when Sydney Henderson died. And he would think then, how right Sydney was. But none of that mattered in the moment.

Ian went home filled with envy—envy over Harold and Annette, and envy that Evan and Harold were still such friends, while he seemed to be on the outside. In this desolate moment he thought of what Henderson had said. And he felt he had no blood brothers at all.

"Lucky" is what Henderson had called him—but in what way?

———

I knew when I was at Yale about all of these events—in dribs and drabs news came to me, as if by whimsy, and I would suddenly hear that Harold had got into a fight at the station, and Evan was seeing Molly Thorn. But during this time in my life I had dined out so much on being understanding and progressive toward everyone except those I had once known, I simply sniffed when I heard anything to do with my remote and tedious birthplace far to the north, a place many of my new colleagues did not know existed, nor ever care to know. I have come to accept my foolishness, to realize that no one was more intolerant than many of the academics I met during those long-ago days. But back then, I believed I was the one in the know. And that those three boys were not.

So I ignored much of what I heard. Until I read this headline in a paper that my mother sent down to me: GLEN DEW DIES IN FALL FROM BONNY TOWER

There was only one person Harold truly loved—his brother, Glen. And so I must mention this incident briefly, for it cast a shadow over everything else. And we must understand now, and keep it in mind, that not a moment went by that this tragedy didn't take its toll. Was Harold's fight at the police station before or after this event? It was sometime later, I am sure, that he was thrown in jail. Still, what happened to Glen must have been the genesis of the coming storms.

Evan Young got his nickname "Lucky" because he lived, while a younger boy was electrocuted and died, on a transformer tower. The boys had been hired to clean off bird nests from the tower. It was a job

Lonnie Sullivan had been asked to do, and he planned to hire the three sixteen-year-olds, Harold and Ian and Evan, for twenty dollars apiece.

Lonnie waited for the boys all morning. But on that day Ian was not at home, the loss of Annette having made him solitary. Harold would be back only in the afternoon because he had promised to take Annette to town. So Lonnie waited in his car—angered not only that Harold was not forthcoming but that Annette was the reason.

"He likes the money, but he don't like the work," Lonnie said to Evan, who was waiting with him. "And all Annette wants is attention. Well, we will see! We will see. Someday I will pay her back as well. She pretends to, but she does me no favours at all."

Of course this was not true about Harold, and Evan told Lonnie so. And then Harold Dew's brother, Glen—only fourteen years of age—said he would go up instead.

"Harold didn't mean nothing," Glen said. "Don't fire him. Let me go." For Glen worshipped Harold and longed to please him. And everyone knew, as he roamed about the lanes and backfields of Bonny Joyce, that Glen was, as they said, "Not quite right, not all there." And this is why Harold knew his blood brothers would protect the boy, come what may.

Without hesitation, Evan told Glen to stay where he was; there were others they could get to do the job.

"No—there is no others. So you go, Glen." Lonnie spit a bit of cigar out the door of the car.

"I don't want him up there," Evan said. "I can do it by myself to save you money. He's not good on his feet, and it's a long way up." He looked at Lonnie with the eager and urgent gaze of a man wanting to convey a message of importance without speaking—a message about Glen's world of play, his childlike being.

But Lonnie smiled in a fatherly way as Glen said, "Oh, I don't mind."

Evan took his time getting ready, looking at his old watch and hoping Harold would return—but ten minutes came to twenty, and Lonnie became more and more impatient with him. So he could hesitate no longer.

"I can go up alone," Evan said again. And wind blew down from across that tower in a duct of hot and scalding air.

"No," Lonnie said, moving his cigar from one corner of his mouth to the other. "If you don't want poor Glen to earn a spot of money, you are a poor friend."

Glen looked from one to the other. Lonnie, I am sure, enjoyed himself with all of this, never thinking of anything but how the moment reflected his enormous power over money, poverty and love.

"You stick near me," Evan said at last.

"Okay. Stick near you, sure," Glen answered, already seeming to tremble, half in excitement and half in dread.

Evan and Glen climbed up the tower. When they reached ninety feet, they stood out on a small, triangular metal catwalk, without a rail, and carefully picked off the large bird nests that had accumulated for four years but were now a deterrent to workers coming in the next few days to sandblast and paint. The two boys looked like clothespins against a dreary summer sky. The scalding air still swirled out of the harsh blue sky.

It was just after noon when Harold came rushing to the job site, knowing he was late and knowing he might lose out on pay. Seeing him run up the hill that long-ago afternoon, so frightened of displeasing his harsh and ignorant boss, one sees the tyranny over youth of small-minded men.

"Who went up there instead of me?" Harold asked Lonnie, bending over to catch his breath.

"Glen," Lonnie said.

"He shouldn't be up there," Harold said suddenly, wildly, glaring first at Lonnie and then at the tower. "He's not right in the head—the whole Bonny Joyce knows!" He said "the whole Bonny Joyce knows" as a sacred plea. Everyone knew—surely no one, then, would allow this; who then would allow this?

"I know—but it was Evan who insisted. It's always money with fuckin' Evan. You know that!" Lonnie said. The hand in which he held his cigar trembled slightly—for he now realized what he had done. And his body shook a tiny bit. And he wouldn't look Harold's way. He struck a match again, relit his cigar and looked up. "It's a bad spot for that youngster to be in," Lonnie said, with sympathy. "But what are we to do with the likes of Evan Young? Don't think he is not in everything only for himself."

Harold was now beside himself with panic and worry—no, it was worse than panic, worse by far than worry; it was premonition. And this premonition gave him a dull heaviness as the hot gusts of wind blew. He walked toward the tower, over the stubble of burned and desperate ground.

Glen was frozen in fear at ninety feet. That is, he had not known he would have to climb so high on a ladder, and now he did not know how to get back down. He looked around like a lonely bird, his small neck craning here and there in gloom and desperation. And the reason he did this was that he could not for the life of him attempt to lift a leg over the top of that ladder. He felt he would lose his balance. Nor was there anything to hang on to. So he froze, and tried not to look down.

"Hold on here. I'll be just a second, then I'll take you back down," Evan Young told him.

Young decided to climb up the thin ladder the rest of the way by himself, and he did so hand over hand, like you would do on a ship, picking up the innocuous raven nests from every cross-section of pipe and tossing them out of the way, while Glen looked at him, watching those nests falling down, out of a bluer sky than he had ever seen before.

Onto the highest perch Evan Young climbed, straddling two beams, and even Glen Dew was far beneath him. He managed to reach the osprey hatch and reel it over the side, so it fell like a shadow against the sun. Then Young let out a whoop, and laughed for the sheer delight of being so high in the air. But beneath him on the tier things were not well.

"Harold, come and get me!" Glen called, and Harold shouted that he was going to climb.

Young yelled out, "Harold, there's no room for the three of us up here. I will bring him down, and he can have my twenty dollars for being brave."

So Harold stood where he was, looking up one moment, looking away the next.

"I want someone to get me down," Glen yelled. His state—which was often the case—was one of perplexity, and his hands began to flail about like those of a boy of three or four, and he decided it was time to walk down by himself.

"Don't move," Harold yelled up at him. "Don't move your arms!"

By this time Lonnie had moved back to stand beside his car, with the door open. He had only sent Glen up as a joke, something he could relate later to someone, to prove his power over children. And now it stunned him: his own useless folly.

"I'm coming down to you now," Young said. "And you can have my twenty for all yer help!"

But before he reached the catwalk, Evan saw a ball of fire, orange in the bright sun.

Glen Dew had grabbed a heavy wire above him. In a second, electricity shot through him and caused his hair to flame orange and smoulder. He was sent flying from the tower. The flash caused Harold to look up as the boy fell from the sky. "Like Icarus," the paper said later.

The heat caused Evan to fall the last fifteen feet to the catwalk and lie there, strangely hearing the ticking of crickets, while Harold Dew's brother fell, both sneakers burning with blackened thick smoke, the eyes melted from his head.

When Evan came down, he was poled back by a jarring straight right from Harold. It put him to his knees as he staggered, but he did not retaliate. Lonnie backed his car up into the gravel ditch and drove away. He threw his cigar onto the side of the road.

And even into the dead of winter, when their houses were settled under great wisps of snow, people talked about poor little Glen Dew and his melted eyes, and how Evan forced him onto the tower when he didn't want to go. All for twenty dollars' pay.

PART TWO

Evan's girlfriend, Molly Thorn, told him to forgive himself and forget the threats and treatment he now endured at the hands of Harold. But Evan told her that Harold would always want to pay him back.

"He's still your friend," she would say. "You cut for blood with him and Ian. Why don't you come to church?"

At first he did not respond, but when she asked the third time, he yelled, "Church! Leave me alone about fucking church! What happened didn't have anything to do with sin, and why should I go confess?"

"I am only saying it might make you feel better!"

"Priests jerking off little altar boys and then handing you the Host!"

Molly worked at church picnics and sang in the choir, while Harold's girl, Annette, wore her Catholicism as a virtue, without worrying one way or the other if she was being particularly virtuous. Catholicism to Annette was a way of the world—and if someone else had another way, so be it. Practising writing her name—"Mrs. Harold Dew"—was her great celebratory occasion in front of other young women.

"When we have the money, we will go far away from here and never come back," Annette would tell Harold when he became depressed over Glen and many other things. For she did not want to spend her life there—not in Bonny Joyce or Clare's Longing. At moments, when she thought about this—that is, how her life would go—there was a vague, faraway and dreamy look on her countenance, a look that not everyone understood. It was especially noticeable when you walked toward her on some late-spring evenings when she seemed unaware that it was cold and that the rawness had penetrated her skin. And of course, it was clear that she had to leave behind her house and her servile father, with his obsequious daily journey to his job in the Department of Motor Vehicles, his training manuals for teenaged drivers, and the one big dinner he treated his peaked, selfish wife to once a year. If she did not leave all that, if she could not—if she relented and stayed—she was doomed. I knew this when I saw her once, dancing at the Byron Creek sock hop with five boys surrounding her, all vying to be her partner, while she remained steadfast, solitary and alone. She wanted the right boy—the right boy to be her partner—and Lonnie Sullivan had promised her he would help her find him.

But after the debacle on the tower, Lonnie secretly decided to destroy them all—including Annette. And the gullible child in her did not understand this. She did not know that, as I was writing my master's thesis on disenfranchised youth, Lonnie would begin to ask her to do things for him—and little by little, because of this, she would turn into the Annette that everyone came to know, or worse, to hear about, from one end of the river to the other. She would steal this or that, betray this friend or that, all the while hoping it would make her someone special. Soon that little child within her would disappear, and eventually she would struggle against the odds to get her back.

But there was something else—an open secret among the boys. The secret was this: the third boy—the third blood brother, Ian—felt he would not be happy until he was with Annette Brideau. She was the girl he believed he loved, and he also believed she would someday love him. All it would take was the right moment. He did not know when that time would be, but he did feel he would someday win her for himself.

I have to prove myself, or die trying, he thought. Then she will be mine. And do you want her to be yours?

"I would give a life for it," he said aloud.

So in a way—a very real way—Annette Brideau made Ian resolute and ambitious. He became more and more solitary as he tried to decide what he wished to do with his life. He gave up watching hockey because it cost him two dollars at the rink. He gave up fish and chips on his way home from the field. He gave up everything he possibly could. And in some way he was doing it for Annette, who for the most part did not know he was alive.

Ian knew he would have to have money. That is, if he was to have Annette, money would be part of his allure. And this was Ian's first disobedience to his larger soul. He lessened his opinion of himself in order to charm her.

I am not good enough for her, he would think. I will never be good enough for her—even if I have money. I know that!

No, I will have someone else—and she will be sorry, he would tell himself other times.

Then: Why should I need money? If I need money, she's not worth it.

Then: Yes, I will have her—I would give a life for it, he would say. But when he met Annette, he would look in another direction entirely and pretend to ignore her existence. On occasion she would become pleasant, look his way and wave, in the innocent way young girls do to flirt. But as soon as he acknowledged her in any way, she would turn away.

In this fashion, she and he conned each other. She did so by pretending she didn't want him to be attracted to her. He did so by pretending that Annette would someday tire of all the others in the whole world, even Harold, and seek him alone.

But by this time, Annette also believed she was nothing. That is, in a profound way she believed she could be nothing without Lonnie's validation and blessing.

"Find the right man," Big Lonnie would say. "For Christ's sake! Don't end up with a man who'll be a burden."

"I won't, I promise, Uncle Lonnie," she would say pensively, her eyes brilliantly dark and mysterious.

"Anyways, Harold is okay. But sometime when you are in the mood, and everything like that there, and Harold is not around, maybe you can come with me to PEI or somewhere like that there. I mean, I know families over there in construction who have, like—well, I hate to tell you—"

"Tell me what, Uncle Lonnie?"

"Have, like, seven million dollars!"

"Seven million dollars?"

"Upon me soul ta God. And there is a young lad over there who is I think is interested in you too. I mean he saw you when he was over here looking at that filly that time—remember? I don't know if you remember."

"Do you want me to go?"

"Not yet—not right away. We will see how Harold does with the Fitzroy will. But if that doesn't come off for you—well, don't settle for nothing but the best!"

Annette, when she first went to work for Lonnie, had thought all of this talk of money untrue. But that was well over two years ago. Now it pleased her, in a strange way, to listen to this talk, because it meant Lonnie was interested in her getting a fortune. By now Annette did not make a move without Lonnie, and in this way he had taken over her life.

———

When he was eighteen, Ian decided to do something that no one would have guessed. He determined to leave Bonny Joyce, and leave it forever—leave his friends, and leave everything he had ever known.

So he worked all summer, haying in the big fields in Millerton, to pay off the debt he owed to Lonnie Sullivan. And he did owe $442—an amount compounded by the piddling amount Sullivan paid. No one believed he would be able to work it off. But Ian went to the hay fields in mid-July and worked for nothing more than lunch and supper, supplied by a vending machine at the corner store. In fact, for the last three weeks, he worked for nothing at all, and slept in the woods and ate bread and drank water, and though Lonnie called him out in front of the others, he asked for nothing.

"Don't you need more money?" Lonnie would ask obsequiously, for he did not wish to lose a good worker, and the only way to keep him was to loan him money he would then have to work off.

But Ian said he wanted not a penny. "No" was all he said, and all he seemed able to say. "No." He was working his debt off and would not accrue any more. And the debt dwindled to two hundred dollars and then one hundred and then $38.50, which is what he was paid for a day's labour.

But on the last few days, Lonnie picked a Mandeville boy from Millerton to drive the tractor and told Ian he had enough men to throw the bales.

So Ian sat far back at the edge of one of the huge fields, watching. At night there was a great moon, and it bathed the land, and the last of the bales looked like blond wheat rolled against the sky. Down below, the lights near the river flickered out while the cement plant shone white behind the scattered machines. He looked down the hill at the cement plant, at the waves of soft cement that had drifted over clumps of grass, at the chalk-white building where the office was, with its three windows and its hum from the generator. And looking down at this he thought of himself as a Frankenstein creature that no one would ever love.

He determined he would sit where he was all the last day, and watch the workers work—to prove not his, but Lonnie Sullivan's, disloyalty and madness.

But on that last day the boy from Millerton did not return. He had broken his wrist in a fall at the river, having gone for a swim after work. And so Lonnie, cigar in his mouth, looked about for someone to help— and spied Ian four hundred yards away near the very back of the field, and called him down.

Exhausted, tormented by both hunger and thirst, Ian went to work. He repaid the last of his debt that night.

Annette heard all this from Lonnie, and understood it in the way Lonnie himself described it.

"He is crazy," Annette said. "After all you did for him—it makes me almost cry."

"I do cry," Lonnie said. "You help a man out and he spits in your face. It's a shameful old world we live in, pawnmesoultagod."

Ian had a tiny bit of money. It clung to the pocket of his suit jacket like dirty coins. It had come from his mother, from a small bank account that she had put aside for him before she died. He moved to town and got a room near the bridge, where he could listen to the hulking of trucks in the night buckling the spans as they moved back and forth while a perpetual warning light flashed on and off.

Far away from home he was quiet and obscure, a faceless journeyman neither happy nor sad. Of all the pictures from his past, he took only one with him: a picture of Annette standing beside Lonnie Sullivan's car one summer afternoon. He put this in his room and looked at it as he ate his solitary supper. People assumed she was his girl from Bonny Joyce. But he quietly told them she was not his girl, but his friend's girl. Or perhaps she was no one's girl; he did not know. She was, he said, an uncertain girl because she was uncertain of herself, and he hoped the best for her, and could say no more than that. They looked at him with a kind of strange curiosity, so he said that she was elusive and unhappy and wanted more to her life—but who among us does not? And then he would stroke the picture just once and turn it away, as if to keep her memory pure.

This caused him to be looked at and spoken about in a peculiar way. That is, he was soon mocked behind his back by people who heard of him, and his antics became known at the mill where many worked. And this, I know, played a part in his life as well.

Ian sent Harold and Evan letters and Christmas cards, but they have not survived, nor were they answered. He was lonely, and walked by himself along snowy streets at dusk, wondering what would become of him—not fitting in, not knowing anyone. His two uncles were both town drunks, and sometimes came by to ask for money—and he felt obligated for the first little while. Then in anger he chased both of them downstairs, furious, saying he would kill them if they tried to rob him again. This was the first indication of his violent temper and it brought the police, the two uncles standing sanctimonious behind the officer, as filled with civic duty as mayors, ready as always to tattle.

Ian spent that Christmas by himself, with a small Cornish hen he had scraped together enough money to buy. The mill stank in his lungs, but in desperation he applied to work there so that he might impress

Annette with a big mill job, and a man from middle management—the kind most of us know if we live in small towns, a man who curls and belongs to the Kinsmen, who has ordinary ideas, a man with a fine and open face, happy-go-lucky, with nice wavy hair, and who couldn't seem more pleasant—dismissed Ian outright because no family member of his had ever worked there. The mill glowered in the night air like a giant red sore over the river, and Ian was left to walk the road back to his room and open his door to a small couch and a night table.

He walked back in the February slush for four miles, his feet soaked and his suit pants covered in salt. He counted his money, quarter by nickel on the metal table, a plastic curtain over the window. He looked at the calendar and wondered where he would be in seven or eight years. He would see that man from the mill again, he thought to himself—yes, someday this man would come to him. Someday he would stand in a place Ian owned. And when that man did come to him, when he did, the tables would be turned. This is what he hoped for and prayed for— though he said to himself that he did not believe in prayer. But he thought about how the town, this town, orchestrated itself into a hierarchy of small-minded businessmen and conceited mill officials, all succumbing to the idea that a paycheque in their back pocket and new pants on their arse made the man. And then he was ashamed to have been thinking such unkind thoughts.

He was brighter by far than they were, and he would prove it.

So Ian rented the room in town, and fixed radios for money. No one knew much about him, and that, it seemed, was the way it would always be. He took jobs when he could—mainly lifting and carrying, and working the boats. He did this for a year. At the first of each month he struggled to make the rent. And he promised himself that he would not drink, for drink had destroyed his family for three generations.

Although he was alone, his reputation for being able to fix whatever he put his hand to grew, so after being out of work for some time he finally got a job at a large second-hand appliance store on the square. There people noticed him, and some—more than some; many—called him brilliant, for twenty-year-old radios would find a spark in his hands. But this was nothing to him.

In a way, it was Annette who kept him from drink—for it was she who he kept hoping for. He kept her picture in his room, and his ability to stay sober helped keep his hope of being with her alive. Oh, it was a false hope and stupid, and he felt stupid too, and he thought of how foolish a hope it was. But he was proud of his ability not to drink; so many around him had already succumbed to this very thing that had destroyed their fathers.

"I don't drink," he would say to people who offered him an ounce. "Drink is a whore that doesn't charge you but robs you blind."

His uncles now came back to see him—both speaking about how much they had loved his mother and tried to take care of him. He knew they had robbed her, and many times made fun of him, and he also knew this: that they were filching spies for Lonnie Sullivan, who wanted to know what Ian was up to. Lonnie envied anyone who got away from him, who made it out from under and directed their own life. So Ian put each of the uncles on an allowance of a bottle and a half of wine a week. And he bought them new rubber boots for the winter, so shiny and black you could pick them both out standing at the corner.

And he thought: Yes, I am a blood brother—but neither Harold nor Evan ever take the time to say hello. And in his reverie he would think how both had cheated him, and both had neglected him when he was down. He would not have done so to them. Stung by old memories, he decided he would remain living on his own and make it on his own, with no help from his two former friends. When he was rich enough, they would see who he was. And this he longed for.

Ian's first month on the job, he heard that Harold had bought Annette "the diamond." It was tiny, not much bigger than the smallest stone—but she wore it and showed it off everywhere she went. People told him he would no longer recognize her, that she was someone different now, and different in the way she acted. She was sure of herself now, and sure of her destiny.

"What do you mean?" Ian asked when someone said this one night. He was hardly able to breathe, asking about her again.

"She dresses the part," the man told him.

"What do you mean, 'dresses the part'?" His throat was dry and his voice seemed to come from someone else.

"Well, what Lonnie wants a woman to be, Lonnie gets."

This stunned him. For the first time he understood how much Lonnie controlled her, that she was Lonnie Sullivan's shadow—and how had he not seen this before? It all came back to him, how she'd smiled at him from the car window. The man he was with continued to talk, pleased at the information he was divulging, declaring first this and then that.

"Say nothing more about her to me," Ian said, feeling blood rise to his temples and his eyes flame. The man turned white, shrugged and left. But when he got halfway down the block, he yelled, "She's just a fuckin' downriver twat. 'Lonnie's twat' is what she is called. Ha, you don't know. You're as dumb as Harold Dew. She is with Lonnie in the car every day— she is on the road with him every day—so what do you think they do!"

Ian started toward him, and the man turned and ran again. Ian went back to the store, sat on a stool and stared vacantly out at the river.

Why was this story surfacing now about Annette?

It had begun five months before. Annette had gone to Lonnie wondering, in her innocence, about the boy he had told her about, the boy with the seven million dollars. She thought Lonnie would be pleased with her inquiry. But Lonnie, having just lost on horses, was furious, and said he would not be going back there and for her to stop pestering him. His shirt was covered in sweat, his shirt sleeves rolled up to his elbows, exposing his two tattoos. He counted money and now and again looked up at her. He called her greedy and said the one thing he hated was a gold-digger. (This is what someone had called him in Charlottetown.) Then, still counting money, he calmed himself and told her that he'd thought she was going with Harold anyway. So she should continue with that.

"Harold?"

"Why not—go get engaged to him, why don't you?"

Lonnie had not thought of Fitzroy's money in a long while, and it was because of his falling out at the races in both Truro and Charlottetown, and his conversation with Annette, that he began to think of it again. He needed money, was always trying to determine ways to get it. And he had the idea that he would rob Fitzroy and be done with it. As he sat there that afternoon, this is what he began to think.

What he hated was, in fact, how much this money plagued him. And how much Fitzroy did not like him. Fuck him, I'll just take it, he thought. He don't like me and I don't like him, and that'll be an end to it! And he looked very self-righteous and stern when he thought this.

Robbery was not at all a new thing for Lonnie Sullivan—nor was using Harold Dew to steal. In fact, by now he had enough on Harold to turn him over to the police without implicating himself in the least. That is, Lonnie always had something on his friends. The younger they were when he met them, the more he held on them.

So now he said to Annette, with paternal caution, that she should look for someone closer to home. He asked her if she had seen Harold lately, if they were still dating. She told him they were, now and then. But she was not really in love with Harold. Not really.

Lonnie shrugged.

"Love! Love is nothing. He's a good lad—and smart," Lonnie told her. "And you are going on twenty now—perhaps he will be the best deal for you. Not that you ever need a man, or anyone. I am not saying that any woman needs a man—just saying." And he shrugged.

Soon, in spite of all Annette's plans and Lonnie's promises about men in distant places who had seen her, rich young men he knew; in spite of Lonnie acting as her agent and speaking about what he intended to do for her; in spite of all her wild, unrealistic hopes that Lonnie had fed for five years, she was suddenly engaged to Harold, a man from Clare's Longing. And she became engaged without even knowing she would be, or that she would accept when he asked.

"It can't be," she would say some days.

And yet it was. And she was exactly like twenty other young women she knew, and not one bit more satisfied.

"Things will be different with me—won't they, Uncle Lonnie? I mean, there is still a chance?" she said one gloomy day, sitting on the porch couch, staring out at nothing at all.

"With you—oh, of course! A chance?A woman like you will always have the world by the balls."

Would you kill for her? Ian was haunted by his declaration, and told himself: Look at the girls in town and forget her forever.

Yes, kill for her, Ian thought—my God, what a thing to say. But then, just the memory of Annette running to Harold at the horse haul was enough to enrage him. How *could* she have done that to him? How could she have done that—to *him*?

So after she was engaged, this is what he resolved to do: He took her picture off his mirror and put it in a drawer, determined never to speak of her again. He ate alone at Susie's steak house on the corner, and went to work in a blue-collar shirt and pair of workpants. He read serious magazines and had a subscription to the *The New Yorker*. Of course, there were many jokes about Bonny Joyce and the Clare's Longing stretch that he had to listen to—about the skanks that lived there and how many children could be accredited to any of their husbands. And once others in the city knew where he was from, it got worse.

But people relied upon him, and his one ambition was to work hard and keep his mouth shut. In fact, people went to the store where he worked because of Ian—his expertise in dealing with electricity and plumbing and all things of that nature was natural and profound. Soon customers were asking to deal solely with him. He found himself indispensable. It was at this time he was offered another interview for a job at the mill. He declined in a stiff, formal fashion. He remembered and hated the personnel manager with his wavy hair and small red tie. His bosses at the store knew about this and raised his salary twice. So he knew that someday—somehow—he would save enough to buy the huge appliance store he worked in. He began thinking that someday he would own his own house too.

The store owners were two elderly brothers, who had over the years borne a grudge against each other to the point where they did not speak. Many times Ian would have to act as a go-between, and he became familiar with their finances and knew about the younger brother's desire to sell. This brother muttered to Ian many times during that long first winter, and then into the second, that if he could find a buyer, he would convince his brother to sell.

So Ian began to save toward this eventuality.

———

All through his adolescence and into manhood, Evan Young had his hopes set on buying the old Jameson sawmill, and he had often walked up to the siding to view it, to walk its grounds, to stumble over its buried artifacts used by men dead a generation ago. He had been inside it many times, always in secret—for he wanted no one else to get ideas about it. That is, as old and decrepit as it was, to him it was a treasure. But over the last few months something had come up. Lonnie Sullivan had been to the grounds twice.

For seven years, the estate that paid the taxes upon the mill had offered it for sale. No one had even looked at it. But now Lonnie thought he might buy it and sell it for scrap, and he was in the process of deciding if it was worth it. Evan kept silent when there was any mention of the mill, because he did not want to give his plan away. But Lonnie knew his plan, and just for torment decided one cold spring day to buy it out from under him. For there was always money to be made some way.

So Evan knew if he was to own the mill, he had to buy it now. But where would Evan get the money? He was in worse financial straits than he had been three years before, with no prospects to get out from under. That is, he owed at least nine hundred dollars to Lonnie for loans he was trying to work off. So there was only one possible way. There was only one place to get the money: from Joyce Fitzroy, the person who had once offered him that money years before.

Evan knew that if Harold got Fitzroy's money, Annette and he would have it gone in a year. He had watched them from a distance, and knew this was the truth of it. Whereas he was certain he could both borrow and return this money to Fitzroy, and have the mill turn out finished product, in eighteen months. Then, if Fitzroy wanted to will his money to Harold, he could still do that.

Yet Evan felt he needed someone to go with him if he was to broach the subject with Fitzroy. That is, as strong and as powerful a man as Evan was, he felt he had no ability to position himself as being different than society saw him to be. He was frightened to ask Fitzroy on his own. But he knew someone who seemed to have this trait he needed—that is, a clear vision about his own will. Evan needed someone sure of himself to come with him as support: a man who had thrown away booze at seventeen and said he would never again take a drink.

So two years after Ian had started to work for Craig Electric, Evan Young showed up at the store. He stood inside the door, a huge man in work clothes and heavy boots, and asked Ian if he would like to go hunting.

I suppose neither one knew the other was longing for money to go into business. Yet the one thing both men possessed that trumped everything else was honesty.

Three years ago, as he'd left the mill that did not hire him, Ian had said to the smiling personnel officer, "You will never cut on Bonny Joyce." And soon after that, he had started a group called "Save the Joyce." He wore a suit and tie to the conservation meetings, and spoke to retired coast guard captains, widows, two men who lived together at Grey's Brook, and a former teacher of mathematics, Miss Finn, who was now seventy-nine years of age. These people not only admired Ian Preston but somehow believed he could do whatever he said he could. Evan, in a way, thought this as well.

So Evan met Ian that day with a particular request in mind. To have Ian come with him to Fitzroy and help him argue his case for the loan.

Evan had decided he could sooner or later put twelve men and three women to work at the mill. He would cut out what lumber he needed from the area below where Ian's concern lay, and this, in fact, would help re-growth. He felt this is what Ian could explain to Joyce Fitzroy, who was against cutting on the Bonny Joyce as well.

Evan knew that a single sawmill had never been Ian's or anyone else's concern; the worry was over the huge pulp and paper mills mainly owed by foreigners, mills that would come in and clear-cut a place down to the ground A sawmill, on the other hand, was looked upon as being the most traditional and the most caring way to use a forest.

"I know I asked you late, but was thinking if you could make it, we'd go up to my camp and hunt awhile," Evan said.

"I don't have a rifle anymore."

"I have a shotgun and you can use that. It was Harold's—that little .410."

"How did you get that from him?" Ian asked, because he remembered the shotgun and its beautiful stock and silver barrel. "He wouldn't give it away?"

"He did not give it away—I won it. On one horseshoe toss—my old Chevy car for the shotgun."

But Evan did not complete this story—that is, he did not tell Ian that Annette had prodded Harold all afternoon into doing this, because she wanted a car to ride in and Harold was a great horseshoe player. But he lost on that toss. Annette could never have imagined how much that shotgun meant to Harold Dew.

Ian agreed to go hunting on one condition: he had to be back by Friday morning for business in town. So the two men went to the camp deep in the black woods near the south branch of the Sevogle. The sun shone lonely through the cabin's one window, and the wind rattled it half the afternoon. Ian took four birds that day at dusk and went back to the cabin, took the breasts from them, placed the guts and feathers in a bag, then cut up onions and green peppers, carrots and potatoes, and made a stew.

But it was long after dark when Evan Young arrived back.

Ian went to the front of the cabin with a lantern, and watched his friend carry his nine-point buck into the front of the yard. Evan must have been far away because Ian hadn't even heard the shot.

The night was warm, and smoke drifted out over a space near the lake. They had the buck hoisted and were taking off the hide. Evan did this with a small buck knife, starting at the hind legs and cutting a strip away to the haunches, and then rolling the hide back from the fat. The two men talked in special and spectacular ways, in an idiom that was peculiar to the river. Evan spoke of having to defend his mother, of being alone from the time he was seven, of always wanting something better and not knowing how to attain it. He finished by saying he was about to ask Molly to marry him. He was hoping to be married in a month.

"It's about time," Ian said.

Evan paused, flustered, then looked at Ian with great seriousness. "Well, if I ask you for a favour—would you help me?"

"Of course."

"I mean, I want you as best man, and you could put in a good word for me . . . Would you? It is the biggest favour I'd ever ask you, and I'll help you in return, in any way I can."

"Of course—when?"

"This Monday—come down!" Young said quickly. And then, determined not to give away his reasons, for he wanted nothing, not a word, to get back to Sullivan, he said little else. "Please come down," is all he said. "I will wait for you. And then I will tell you what the favour is."

Over the years that followed, Ian Preston always maintained that he thought the support Evan sought was for Molly's hand in marriage, not for Fitzroy's money. And the fact becomes more and more apparent as time passes that Evan did not tell Ian what this request was—not at all. I have wrestled with this riddle myself, in classes I taught when I came back to the university here—for I vainly used those boys as subjects—until I saw how little the clever people I taught respected the subjects I spoke about. Some young ladies in my class came to their conclusions by saying, "I wouldn't have anything to do with any of them."

Or: "I wouldn't clutter my life up with people like Evan Young, or anyone else from there." Yes, with a grandly schooled middle-class sniff of disapproval—the first of many tyrannies associated with liberty.

Still, my classes did reach this conclusion: that Ian never knew what Evan wanted from him. After all, Ian was to be best man, so it was not inconceivable that Evan would want him to approach Molly about his feelings. He didn't know that Evan was asking for another favour. He thought that Evan, after all these years, and about to be married, had now come to ask for his friend's good word.

So Ian decided he would wear his suit jacket, and his new fashionable pink shirt and his big yellow tie, and speak to Molly about Evan. Perhaps, he thought, he would bring a bottle of Mateus wine down to celebrate, even though he himself did not drink. So he bought a bottle of Mateus. And maybe he would bring some of that new cheese that he liked. So he bought some Gouda cheese as well. And maybe he would tell Evan and Molly how he was saving for the store, pinching every penny.

But nothing like this happened.

Evan Young never got those funds; and neither did the man who most coveted them, and thought of them as his, Harold Dew.

Ian Preston, who I maintain never knew about this money, did, however, acquire it all.

———

Ian Preston worked at the big electrical appliance store for one reason: if you had no connections in town, you were dead at the mill. It was that simple. People here will deny that. But people will deny anything that makes them look weak and selfish. They will parade their paycheques and their cars, their camps on the river, and many will not take the time to think that they never managed to do one independent thing in their lives, that they were both selfish and vain, as were their wives, believing that the cheques would never stop, when in fact the thousands of acres of moulted and thrashed timber was their own death warrant.

So Ian hated the mill. He hated its smell. He hated its smoke. Everything about it irritated him. He could not stand that so many of the men who worked there, not half as bright as he, made much more money by killing the very land they were born to; and he hated that they were men who all their lives had been told what to do by outsiders and how and when to do it, and they did so without question. That they would scrape and bow and cheat in order to be the number-two man on a paper machine.

But here is why he disliked the mill even more: he disliked it because of the man who did not hire him. He could never forget that man's smile and thin wavy hair, the picture of his wife and family on his desk, the pin that said he belonged to the Kinsmen.

What has he ever done to deserve this power over me? Ian would think. And he would dream of a day when he could pay that man back. That is, even his conservation group was formed to pay that man back. And everything he decided about how he would stop the mill was to pay that man back. He secretly knew this about himself. And twice he'd had meetings with the minister of the environment to relay his concerns about the greatest tract of timber in the north, the Bonny Joyce tract; and twice the minister had assured him that no cutting would be done along that stretch. And yet both times Ian was a little disappointed— for he actually wanted a confrontation with that man, and he wanted to tell everyone at the mill to go to hell.

Two months before Evan visited him, Ian had discovered that the family he worked for wanted to sell the store he worked at. Now all his energies were directed toward one point: Ian wanted to buy this store to prove to himself he was better than those men at the mill, to prove he was better than that man who took his application and smiled and never thought of him again.

But now, looking over the notes I have written on these three blood brothers, I will jump ahead just a bit.

The store Ian Preston soon owned refurbished second-hand appliances. It was a very good, sound business. He had many new appliances for sale. But he also received second-hand goods twice a month, and worked to make them ready to sell. He also sold gyprock and plywood, cupboards and cedar and roofing shingles—and therefore he relied upon economic benefits from the mill he hated. This was the quagmire he was in, a quagmire that he did not admit to. And that was the flaw in his "progressive" stance. He believed the only thing he wanted was to save the river basin and the prime wood that stretched back beyond Good Friday Mountain. This is where he pulled the wool over his own eyes. And this was to become his fight with the very town he had adopted and loved.

So what happened to Ian after he and Evan went hunting?

Ian had to be back on the Friday to go to the bank and see about a loan to buy the store. And so, on that Friday, he travelled from one bank to the other. He began in the morning and ended late that afternoon. Yet, as everyone knows, he was refused in each bank.

Here is what every banker saw: This was young Ian Preston from way back on Bonny Joyce Ridge who had worked himself to exhaustion and now wanted to buy a store on his own. What would they look like giving him a loan? The store would go to ruin, and they'd be laughing stocks. Besides, he was asking for far too much money without any collateral.

As Ian sat in the offices with loan officers, all this became apparent to him. It left him desolate. And now he had to go down to Bonny Joyce and witness on Evan's behalf to Molly Thorn. But, as bad as he felt, this is what he was prepared to do. That is, he was prepared for Evan's and Molly's sakes to be as joyous and as celebratory as he could be.

And then, while there in Bonny Joyce, Ian suddenly secured his loan from a man he'd never thought had any money—an old man who was just enough of a relative to say yes to the $125,000 he needed. The man wanted only to be a partner until he died.

This man, Joyce Fitzroy, lived another four years.

People later said Ian had cheated the old man, who had Alzheimer's disease. Everyone said it; it did not matter if it was true or not. And it *was* true that the old man had Alzheimer's—but not when Ian got the loan. Still, he had used an illiterate old man for gain—and if any of that was true, then he was a conniver. And more to the point, a Bonny Joyce conniver, which meant that he'd always been that way—that was the interpretation. It was said that he had got Joyce Fitzroy drunk and had stolen the money—though Ian himself did not drink. That fact was really the mark of Cain—it showed the calculation involved in this conniving.

Soon people became very righteous in speaking against Ian Preston. Someone so crooked shouldn't be allowed to swagger into town with money and set himself up in business, they said. He was in a way like the robber baron they hated, or like Lord Beaverbrook himself—one day broke, and looked upon as having a trade in town; the next buying out people and reinventing himself. So Ian was distrusted after this. Especially when those who knew Joyce Fitzroy—and knew him to be a stubborn man who lived alone in a house with three rooms—saw the old man out in the winter in a frayed sweater, chopping his own wood for the wood stove that was his only source of heat.

Evan and Harold heard the rumours in the town swirling against Ian and believed them all. Evan distrusted Ian ever afterwards, and so too did Harold. Both of them became bitter in ways that were to cause enormous difficulty. Both felt betrayed in equal measure, and both felt more injured because they were Ian's blood brothers.

"I will ruin him one day," Harold boasted. "I will." He said this to Annette as if she too should relish the idea of ruining Ian. But after listening to Harold rant, she would whisper to herself: He is crazy as a bag of hammers. And her knees would begin to shake. Then Harold would begin to break things around the house—once he threw an armchair down the stairs. He said he might cut Annette's ears off; and then he said he was just fooling about cutting her ears off. "I must have been drunk when I said it—don't believe what I say when I'm drunk!"

He's a lunatic, Annette thought. I am going to marry a man who is a raving lunatic. Already a lunatic and he is only young. And he is poor besides. I am going to marry a poor young lunatic. What happens when he gets old? I will be married to an old lunatic. In her little life, she had no one else to turn to. So, scared and defenceless, she went to speak to Lonnie.

Lonnie said nothing for the longest time. But he thought about how his plan—the plan he had to use Annette—had come to nothing. And now he was disappointed in her.

"Well, where then is the money?" Lonnie asked Annette. "Look what you got yourself into. I told you not to—I told you, didn't I? He's a madman. From what I heard, manic depression runs in his family."

"Runs in his family?"

"The whole lot of them, manic-depressives. Might kill someone, that Harold. I told you one hundred times to stay away from him."

"I don't remember," Annette said, leaning forward with her forehead in her hand. "But I am engaged to him, and I will see it through."

"See it through—good for you. But I am often worried about you."

"Worried about me?"

"Well, how will you cope down at Clare's Longing? You think you can cope down there? Living where four generations of fuckin' Dews have lived and died and fought over every morsel of food? That's no way for my favourite girl to live."

"Your favourite girl—?" Annette blushed.

"Well, who else would it be? Who is the prettiest, most—well, has the best . . . well, looks like a princess all the time, but you? Knows how to dress but you? Wearing white gloves to church and never without a necklace. But I want to tell you—this is between you and me—you got a nice body, so use it. What about the man down in Nova Scotia I was telling you about? Now, he owns his own gravel pit and everything. I could introduce you, if you want."

Annette blushed.

Lonnie bit the tip off his cigar and spit it away. He looked at her as he lit it, from under his eyebrows, and smiled as he blew out the match.

But then he said this: "Oh, oh, oh—how you made fun of Ian Preston!"

"I never did!"

"You laughed in his face, didn't you! You said he was a little nit."

"I never in my life did. I always thought he was sweet—it's Harold what tricked me!"

Annette suddenly realized how awful everything looked for her at this moment. "What will I do?" she asked.

"Well, you come to me again—you come to old Uncle Lonnie when things go bad. But when things are good, I'm not good enough for you. I knew what Harold was—many times I didn't want him around here, but I allowed him here because of you. That's a fact. But now I see—I see. Old Uncle Lonnie is nothing when you think you have no more use for him. Well, well, well. I don't like your conniving, Annette—that's a Brideau streak, I feel. No one else on this here river has it. I was honest, and expect others to be too. Anyways, I'm pretty much done with Charlottetown, and you should be too. Thieves and bastards and what-not over there. Someday I'll take you to Truro and introduce you to a real good lad. Now, he's about my age—but he saw you last year over there, and really liked what he saw, I tell you that!"

"What does he do?" Annette asked, without any feeling.

"Owns a mortuary—has a horse or two—bides his time, likes to make pronouncements. Well, you know—big feeling, thinks he is something special, not like you or me."

I want to be a good person, Annette said hopefully but to herself. For where had that little girl gone?

Lonnie was very upset himself by this turn of events with Ian. He had now lost the money he'd thought he could get if Joyce Fitzroy died without settling on a benefactor. He knew ways in which to move into an estate and take over—settling old back taxes was one. He was always prepared for a fight, and had assumed he'd take over Fitzroy's house when he died. He was annoyed that Fitzroy was clever enough to keep his property taxes paid, and that too seemed like an insult.

But now it was beyond him. The money had gone to Ian Preston.

From that moment on, whenever he looked at Evan and Harold he thought of them as grown men. That is, the fact that they had allowed themselves to be betrayed made him disrespect them intensely. So there were many days when he would not call them to do jobs for him—or when they did come over, he would force an argument between them. He treated Harold worse than Evan because Harold felt the worse.

"Oh," Lonnie would chuckle, "how is Annette ever going to get along in Clare's Longing swamp having ten little Dews? That's paying her dues for wanting the money, isn't it."

And Harold, who up until that moment had thought nothing could ever come between him and Annette, began to realize that Annette wanted in some desperate way to rescind their love and escape. Harold begged— literally begged—Lonnie for money, any money, to prove himself to her.

"To prove to her what?" Lonnie said.

"To prove to her—just to prove to her," Harold pleaded.

"I have no money for you, Harold. You shouldn't have bragged so much about what was coming to you. Bragging is a terrible thing—it allows for terrible things in a person's life, and causes enormous difficulty, don't you think? Let her go off and get screwed a couple of times by someone else. She'll see what it's like—one cock is good as another and she'll be back!"

This caused Harold to go into a rage, stand up and look with blearily hateful eyes at his tormenter—but he was no match for Lonnie Sullivan then.

Lonnie chomped his White Owl cigar, and after taking out a crumpled bunch of bills put them in Harold's hand.

"That's the best I can do for you, boy—and I do it 'cause I liked your mom."

———

"Yes, the Ridge," I would say to my sociology class when I came back here to teach in 2001. "The Ridge is hopeless. The girls get pregnant by seventeen on the Ridge, and their lives are set. The boys become drunks and hit their women. On the Ridge this is almost uniform policy."

You see, I never said that the people on the Ridge were less than we were; I just indicated that they did not have the same chance, that they were disenfranchised. Those youngsters I taught always wished to compel those who were not like us to become like us. This attitude, in fact, is what people used against Ian and the others. Of course, it was some years after the events I am relating when I taught my course, but those three boyhood friends figured in the course I taught. And I want to tell you one more thing: I did not believe what I said to my students about the Ridge. I said it to see if I would get an argument. If I did—and at times I did—I would show them a picture of my house, and tell them of the years of my youth I'd spent there.

But often I found there was no argument, even from those who had lived close to the Ridge. Why was this? Because talking about Ian and Evan and Harold gave many of my students an incredible feeling of being concerned without suffering themselves, which is what our society, especially a university-educated one, is after. Concern without suffering allows us to think we are fine men and women, although none of us is required to prove it. We live in a country full of fine men and women who wouldn't hurt a fly—who wouldn't say "Indian" but "First Nations," and who wouldn't know one First Nations person if they met him on the street; who would ban *Huckleberry Finn* but never be able to create one. This is the country of transgressionalists who deplore religion yet have created their own, more sanctimonious than any other you could imagine. The university bred this kind of sanctimony; it was a place where moral positions were so often paid for by inherited money or student loans.

In the world of my students, Ian and Harold and Evan—and Molly, Sara and Annette—did not have a chance. There were actually better off with Lonnie. And when I began to realize this, what I knew of Ian and Harold and Evan—and Molly and Sara, and Annette with all her small hopes and dreams—changed me. I began to argue with my own students, and with other professors like Jonathan Mittens, my one-time high-school friend, in defence of something that I no longer was. And so I became a pariah, just as those three boys were. The university sooner than later wanted rid of me. Professors spoke against me at certain faculty meetings I did not attend. The most vocal was Jonathan Mittens himself.

Once, I took my students up to the Ridge and showed them what was left of the houses there and the great tract of lumbering land Ian had once wanted to save, which was now plowed into the earth and thrust up against a grey-black sky, a sky turbulent in its very silence. And in that silence, as sometimes happens, it began to rain.

"My God, who could ever live here?" one of the girls said, accentuating *here*, the sound with its own sense of middle-class condemnation.

At the turn just before Ian Preston's lifeless, bulldozed homestead, there was an old Pepsi sign tacked against the side of a barn, and in the distance the desperate tower where small mentally disabled Glen Dew had lost his life. Some of the students looked at it all as if excavating a sight for bones. I had tears running down my cheeks.

"Is this where it all happened?" one of the brighter students said, looking over at me pensively. "Then it is true. Human drama, and human greatness, unfolds wherever humans are—and that's a fact." He did not know we were standing beside what was left of my parents' house.

So let us become ghosts and return to those days just after the hunting trip.

Evan Young had hoped Ian would help him ask Joyce Fitzroy for the money, and then he would pay the loan back. But Ian believed Evan wanted his help in asking for his girlfriend's hand in marriage. The hand of Molly Thorn. That quiet child whom Evan loved.

Ian knew he had done nothing wrong. He reacted to the silent accusations of others by being silent, and this was to his own credit, in hindsight—but in hindsight only. Now he was certain both of his blood brothers hated him; and he was even more certain it was not his fault.

Fitzroy had wanted to be a partner in the store until he died. That was all. Sitting by the stove and chewing snuff, his false teeth in his pocket, he still smelled of the woodchips and ice he had worked with for almost sixty years.

He had $125,000 to show for those sixty long years and he had given this over to his youngest sister's grandchild, Ian Preston, a boy he had spoken to only a dozen times before.

And so Ian's great store became, to some, "the stolen store," and remained so until it closed in disgrace some years on. Did it matter if this was untrue? Not one of my students thought it was untrue—yet none of them wanted to investigate it to find out. The stolen store had variant meanings—that is, it was stolen from Harold Dew; or, as most thought, from Joyce Fitzroy; or, as was hinted at times, it was stolen from Lonnie Sullivan, who always sounded hurt when he spoke of it. But the one point that never varied was this: it had been stolen.

So how did this happen? How did a man who was above reproach in his dealings and scrupulously honest, who refused drink and did not condemn others, come to be blamed for something like this?

Ian, who was not only primarily moral but primarily loyal—even if the tendency among those who knew him was to dismiss him—had gone on the Sunday before he was to visit Evan Young to Joyce Fitzroy's house, hoping to buy a small travelling trunk in the old fellow's possession, one that had come over to the river on a ship out of Liverpool in 1840. He had seen it as a boy, and once again when his grandmother died. He had thought to himself, late the night before, while eating supper alone and listening to the transistor radio in his small room, that he would buy it as a wedding present for Evan and Molly.

He had the funds from saving for three years toward the store he would not be able to buy, since he could not secure a loan, and so he decided he would buy the trunk if the old man would part with it, which he believed he might. If he wouldn't, Ian decided he would give Evan and Molly the three or four hundred dollars he was willing to spend on it, to do with what they wished.

He remembered from years gone by that the trunk was in remarkable condition, made of teakwood, with leather straps, spotlessly polished and never damaged in any way. He had been thinking this before he went to see the banks, and thinking more about it after he was refused his loan. How foolish he had been to think that the banks would give him a loan. Now he wanted to part with all ridiculous notions about himself. He was, he thought romantically, tough and brave enough to labour as a common working man.

He said to himself: Since I will never get the store, why be so scrupulous about saving for it? I haven't spent a dime in three years. So I'll buy the chest for Evan and Molly.

This decent thought was to cause his calamity, and the calamity of many around him, even some as yet unborn.

Ian was prepared to offer three hundred dollars for this trunk, and had the money in his pocket. He could not have known that the trunk was worth more than that—in fact much, much more. (At an auction in New York City, I could have easily sold it for twenty-five hundred dollars.)

However, the trunk was long gone. The old man did not remember where it had gone, but knew he had lost or given it away some time before.

"I don't know. It's gone away, boy, wherever," Joyce said. "I might have given it away. I don't much remember—I was probably drunk at the time!"

Joyce sat by the stove chewing snuff, and every few moments he would lift the lid, and spit into it, and after hearing the scald of his spit, he would put the lid back on and then wipe his chin with his hand. They talked of Lonnie Sullivan—always putting boys to work, and how it was a shame at that, for now Rueben Sores was working in the woods for him. And that Lonnie went to Sara Robb's mother to get his tea leaves read.

"Does he still?" Ian asked, proud to be away from all of these things. Proud that he had escaped when his two good friends, his blood brothers, had not. Proud that he would have nothing to do with Sullivan again.

"More now than ever," Joyce said, almost gleefully. "He still thinks he should be rich—that is all he ever wanted! He believes he is the smartest one on the river. You know that! All his conniving and cigar smoking, and looking up land deeds, and trying to find riverfront that is back-taxed. And that young one of Harold's is here half the week— asking to help me out." Here he laughed. "Annette is pretty, though— and don't mind showing herself off!"

Ian said nothing. He felt hot and horrible. Even the mention of Annette caused him to feel a pang. Would he still kill for her? Gladly, he thought, and then cringed at the idea. He was well away from all of it. And now he was so temperate and so stingy that no one would want him, he decided. His whole life had been to scrimp and to save and to be alone. And right now that suited him just fine.

Then Fitzroy sat up straight, with his hands on the knees of his Humphrey pants. He had the peculiar gaze that men in the woods have: determined, far-reaching and silent.

"And what Preston, then, are you?" old Joyce Fitzroy said.

"I'm Ian Preston."

"Well, all them Prestons are brown-skinned."

"Just a bit."

"Black Irish and French."

"As they say."

"Where do that come from?" the old fellow asked.

"What?"

"Black Irish."

"From the Spanish taken in by Ireland—after the sinking of the armada."

"Oh—is that a fact?"

"It's what I heard."

"Then my, oh my—what are you doing, working the wood like me?"

And so Ian Preston, who was actually fairer-skinned than the relatives they spoke about—ginger-coloured, in fact—mentioned that he was an electrician at the large second-hand store in town, and that he was secretly trying to buy it, and that only a few people knew it was up for sale and he did not want to advertise the news himself. But here was the problem: he had been turned down by the banks. Now these bank managers, as much as they had clay feet, had various friends who did not. So he was worried now he would lose the enterprise, for he was looked upon as both an outsider and a loner. There would be someone these bank managers would want to tell or go to. He began to use a profusion of big words because he was angry.

"Can you get the loan someplace else, then, and make yer deal?" the old man asked.

"No—I've been everywhere."

Old Joyce Fitzroy stared at Ian Preston for a moment, as if accusing him. Then he lifted the lid and spit. "I never keep my money in the bank," the old fellow admitted perfunctorily. He didn't trust the banks. He didn't like them. He admitted that since before starting to work for Leo McVicer in 1947—before that, he had been working for Jameson, cutting wood—he had kept his money safe in the house.

"'Cause of the Depression! Banks would steal from anyone." Fitzroy sniffed again in proud unawareness. "They stole from Janie McCleary, who owned the theatre back then—the Dime, as we used to call it. People will sell their soul for money, and it's best to just work the woods."

Ian Preston was silent. He wanted to leave. It was as if he was being kicked in the guts. He had spent half his life in these silent, cramped rooms, with winter outside. And he was the only one of his family left, the last of the Prestons. And no one who knew him had been sure about him. That is, they had not known if he could stand on his own two feet as a man. And a couple of days before, at one of the shops downtown, Annette Brideau had tossed her head as she walked by, as if to mock him. As he thought of this now, it infuriated him (although in fact, she hadn't even seen him).

I will still become rich—and have nothing to do with her, he thought again. But his anger remained.

The old man kept looking at him in sardonic silence, a kind of impetuousness on his old, hard face. He straightened his back, as if to stretch, and then opened his Copenhagen tin and took a bit more snuff. The wind blasted against the house. "Get up boy, now, and make us a cup a tea," he said quickly.

Ian Preston put the kettle on.

It was nothing to the old man to drink tea with a mouthful of snuff. He laid the snuff full in his puffed-out bottom lip. "Yup, them banks—they know nothing, and never did. How big is this here store?"

The old man kept up bursts of subtle but self-important comments as the tea was made, and telling stories about banks.

Finally Preston said, with a laugh, "I'll never get the store, Joyce, so it is best to forget it! I'll bet everything you have in this house that I won't."

"Oh, is that so?" old Fitzroy muttered. "You just made quite a bet! I will show you why young Harold Dew shovelled my driveway and his little vixen charmer Annette brought me a boiled dinner."

Then he went into the back part of the house. The clock ticked and almost fifteen minutes went by before the old man, his heavy pants sagging and his top shirt buttons undone to show his hardened red chest bones, came back in with a heavy tin box with a small lock. He put it on the table beside his great-nephew. He opened it with a small key—jiggling it to get it to open.

In the tin were four faded and yellowed newspaper articles—the first about the moon landing, the second about the assassination of John F. Kennedy, the third about Germany surrendering, the fourth about Canada declaring war on Germany . . . and under this was money, a lot of it, very old money.

"How much is in that there tin? I think it's enough to buy yer store! That is, unless you take this money I will hold you to the bet!"

The old man sat back down and looked startled, even fatigued, by what he had just offered. But the deal was struck. He would be a partner—a silent one—and would have a say in what happened. The money came to just over $125,000.

The deal was finalized in town later the next day: Ian Preston bought a store from John Craig that had been in the Craig family for sixty-nine years. He was to give them the money for 75 per cent of the holding, with the option to buy the whole store outright within five years. He did this, and within seven years would make it more than twice as profitable.

On that Monday, Evan paced outside his house. Ian had told him he would drive down about three in the afternoon. It was a cloudy day, warm, with the scent of snow and mild earth.

Ian was the one who could help him convince the old man; Evan felt going there by himself would be like walking the street naked. But Ian did not come. Finally, feeling he could wait no longer, at about quarter to five Evan went to the old man's house alone, to ask if Joyce might help him buy the old Jameson sawmill on Upper Arron.

Fitzroy listened to him with a quizzical expression and then blurted, "Everyone wants money now. Well, I can't help no one else of yas. I already helped Ian Preston. I asked you before to take the money—and you didn't take it. You didn't—so now you get nothing!"

Joyce said this with sudden glee, as if he had just played a joke on someone.

"Ian! When did he come here?"

Fitzroy saw the crushed look on Young's usually buoyant face and said, "Why, now what's the problem? Did I do something wrong?"

People along Bonny Joyce Ridge believed Ian Preston had indeed done something wrong, that he was so desperate to get something for himself that he had betrayed his friend. They all knew how he had scrimped and gone without—but in their eyes, this simply showed him to be what they'd always thought he was.

Evan married Molly three weeks later. The room where the reception was held was cold. Molly did not know why her husband seemed so bothered, nor that the wedding present he'd wanted to give her was not possible. Molly was already pregnant—so people said Evan married her because he had to. Harold and Annette were invited but stayed away, for Annette had suddenly stopped speaking to everyone, Harold included.

In fact, Harold too had arrived at Fitzroy's the very Monday Evan had—but late, when it was almost eight o'clock. Lonnie had decided to get the old man drunk, make him sign a will, and take the money. He'd convinced Harold and Annette to do this for him. The scheme, as they say, was hare-brained, but Lonnie was desperate. He felt if they got Fitzroy drunk enough, they could convince him to sign. He would use his two friends to help him. If anything went wrong, he would say he'd had nothing to do with it.

When Harold and Annette arrived, it was dark and very windy, with the smell of dried and dead leaves on the walkway. It was three hours after Evan had left. The old man was sitting in a stupor; he was already dead drunk. There was no light on, and the stove was cold. There was a statue of the Madonna on the shelf, a statue that seemed to glow in the dark. Annette, who was frightened of what Harold and Lonnie had got her into, saw the statue and froze.

Harold kept moving into the room.

"Come back, Harold—never mind," Annette said.

Harold and Lonnie had told her what to wear, and her hair was teased, her skirt was short, her blouse half-unbuttoned, and her face was covered in makeup. But she could not look at the statue of the Madonna without closing her eyes.

Music was playing: some long-ago country tune, some Hank Williams song about loss and sorrow and regret. And Annette was the first to see it: that is, the tin on the kitchen table, emptied of whatever had been inside, while old newspapers lay on the floor. She pointed at it. "Look," she whispered. "Is that it? What is that? Shhh, Harold," she said. "Let's go—please!"

At first Harold did not understand. He picked up the tin and looked back at her. He shook the old man and yelled at him, and told him they had brought him over a bottle.

Fitzroy kept waving him away. He was crying and asking who was there.

Harold realized then what had happened. "The money!" he said. "Where is the money?"

Fitzroy could only wave his hand and tell him to go away.

"It must have been Evan," Harold said. "That bastard got the poor old lad drunk." He grabbed the old man's shoulder. "Hey!" he yelled. "Hey— what did you do with my money? What did you do with my money!"

He knocked the tin off the table and watched Annette run out the door. The door banged in the wind.

"'Leave me be!" she said.

A cold mean snow had started to fall.

"Wait—" Harold said. But Annette would not.

No one saw her for the next three weeks. And in fact, she almost escaped. She was packing to leave when Lonnie phoned and told her it had not been his plan to get Fitzroy's money that way. He had never wanted a nice girl like her to act like that.

"What did I tell you when you were sixteen? Come on, now, what did I say?"

"You said I would be rich—"

"Well, do you want to be or not?"

Annette did not answer.

"Well, you and I are going to be."

"Who—who got it?" Annette asked, finally. "Who got that damn money?"

"Ian Preston—can you imagine? The most underhanded of them all. He deceived us all. He deceived me, dear, and he deceived you. We made that wrong choice in picking Harold."

Lonnie would never get over losing that money—and he was determined to make everyone pay. And for some reason, he wanted Ian and Annette to pay more than anyone else.

———

Since this comes into the story now, I will mention it. That is, the discussion of God. People always said I wasn't cut out for academia— and, well, I suppose this is part of the reason.

Some of my students over the years have asked me, do I believe in God? I am not sure, really, one way or the other. I will only say the concept obsesses us all. By this time, none of the three blood brothers believed in God. God was an absurdity, hocus-pocus concocted to disable the weak and control the poor. They believed everyone knew this—especially the priests, who clung to their fallacy out of fear, and justified their malevolent and even sadistic behaviour with penance. And there was good cause to say this was true. At times I too have said that the College of Cardinals is filled with dupes and whores.

And just as Sydney Henderson had made a pact to honour God, the blood brothers made a pact not to. But now all three not only suspected one another of betrayal but hated one another.

Over time, Molly began to realize that Evan might have been abused by a priest when he was young. And if that was the case, she knew his rage was justified. But she could not join him in it. That is, she could join in his rage, but not his lack of belief—and all his anger directed toward her belief made her belief more important.

So Evan was filled with jokes in bad taste, thinking them very witty—and then told her she was skewered by his wit when she did not laugh. That is, Evan did not only want to mock the church; he seemed, like so many modern thinkers, academics and film stars, to want to be in direct competition with it. And he loved to compete against Molly—the last person who ever wanted to compete with him. He never abused her, but little did he know how much he scarred her soul.

"So," he said to her once, "Christ walks into a hotel with three spikes and says to the manager, 'Can you put me up for the night?' "

Molly knew something had happened that had scarred Evan deeply. When, as a boy, he had gone home to tell his old drunk father about the priest, his father had turned and punched him hard in the face—blackened both eyes and broke a tooth. "You don't talk about Fadder like dat," his father said.

Besides, Evan had long ago realized you determined your own life, and if you did not, you were doomed. This is why Evan needed the old

Jameson sawmill. And it is also why Harold, some months after he discovered Fitzroy's empty money tin, was doing jobs for Lonnie Sullivan, and repossessing furniture and cars, and sometimes took things out of people's back sheds that were worth almost nothing because Lonnie sent him to do so. He also had pushed weaker men down when they were trying to protect their houses and their wives and children. He was compelled to repossess and steal because he felt others had stolen from him. He knew that if he did not do it, someone else would, and he would be out of a job. And if Harold began to be called heartless and mean, so what? And he told Evan this, and Evan said, "Do what you have to, I suppose!"

So this was what the blood-brother pact came to in the end—three men injured by one another and inoculating themselves from the consequences of what each had done.

Yet Evan, for the first time, saw how this determination worked when applied without scruples. *He* would never have cheated and betrayed his friend. He could never, ever have done so. He sat in a stupor for many days before his wedding, staring out into the back trees on his small property, overcome by a kind of shame. He couldn't look at anyone and he could not mention Ian's name. He felt so slighted, and yet believed this slight was deserved. He felt conned by his only friend—for by this time he did not consider Harold a friend as much as Ian. Yet Ian had turned on him without a qualm, taken money he must have known Evan needed, and then gone back to town without so much as a goodbye.

But in point of fact, if there was no God, had Ian done wrong? And if he had done wrong—as Evan now believed—how did one demand retribution? For retribution was needed, and yet would not come in a court of law; a court of law would not, and could not, deal with this. This had just been proven to him by a lawyer named J. P. Hogg, who for a while was interested in helping Harold with a lawsuit against both Fitzroy and Ian but realized soon enough that it was fantasy, and so begged off before his reputation was tarnished.

This to Evan proved not the existence of God but the absence of God—or at the very least, the uncaring nature of what we chose to call "God." Even this was not the main issue, however. The main issue was to haunt him for a long while: how to deal with this fracture between him and a man he had once considered closer than a brother. It was a fracture that had happened so instantaneously, and yet seemingly with so much guile. And Evan had another, more secret feeling about this kind of cunning—that is, to take action against it was to admit you had been duped and that you had trusted someone whom you should never have trusted. And Evan could not do this. He simply could not admit this betrayal to himself.

Soon after the wedding, Evan was berating Molly for going to church. He berated her, and all Catholics, in a way that was sanctimonious. But, because it was also comic, he believed the sanctimony was hidden; in fact, Evan liked to think that his observations were not sanctimonious if they were against religion.

"If God really saves," he would start off at dinner when Molly was blessing herself, "why can't Father Tom afford to fix his roof?"

Molly would try to defuse the tension by speaking in a straight-forward way about things happening at the church. "I told Father Tom you might be over to fix it, or look at it, someday soon."

"Me? Don't pick on me! I have used up all my goodwill. I was filled with goodness and will, and goodwill, for a while. It ruined me!"

"I don't know why you are so angry. Is it me—did I make you angry?"

"No, you did not—at all. But someone else did."

Evan believed Ian had committed the greatest sin: betrayal. And he was right to think betrayal was the greatest of sins. The problem was, he was unsure of why he thought this, nor did he ever think that he himself betrayed others. Yet every time he berated Molly, in a way he did so.

"What in Christ has Christ ever done for us!" Evan bellowed once during grace, slamming down his fist so forcefully he frightened Molly and spilled the tea.

She was at that moment seven months' pregnant with a child both of them would adore.

Harold, meanwhile, knew he had nothing to hold Annette. The end came unceremoniously and suddenly. She gave him back the diamond ring. She was shaking when she did so. But when he began to curse, she became spiteful—her dark eyes flared and her lips curled into a small sneer. She would never be beholden to him again.

This left Harold broken, and he blamed one person: Ian Preston.

After this, Harold would arrive at Lonnie's worksite at seven in the morning, sit on the old bench in the shed and wait it out, his leather mittens in his hand, his breath sharp and his eyes anxious. He was a big, brooding man now, with black hair and a swollen face. His shoulders were broad and his chest large, and yet he held his leather mittens like a little boy.

Finally Lonnie, coming into the room, preoccupied with the day's activities, chomping on his cigar, would shake his head, pull a fistful of dollars from his back pocket and hand them, crumpled, to the man and say, "Two weeks' work, and where I want you to go."

Then he would lecture Harold about getting out from under him as Harold eagerly counted the money.

"Do more with yourself than Evan is going to do. You know I had high hopes for you!" Lonnie would say, blowing cigar smoke. "Ian was the only one to have everything figured out. There was no one slyer than a Preston when I was growing up—I could have told you and Evan not to cut for blood with a bastard like him. They are bluebloods from way back, turned to peasants by Canada. But there you have it—all of them are scoundrels."

And the smoke would curl away, like an unobtrusive shackling of the world.

———

By the third year of owning his own store, Ian was making a very good profit, and he had all but forgotten about his great-uncle. And some who were envious of him realized this. That is, they realized that it did not matter if he was truly unkind or unfair to his uncle; the appearance of impropriety was enough to cast doubt on him.

Ian was very strict with himself, parsimonious even, and yet he demanded respect—and people did respect him. But they did not like him. He would not spend a nickel on anything or anyone; never gave to the March of Dimes, never to the Cancer Society; would pass by kids on the street selling apples for hockey and wore the same poppy three years in a row. He was tough too, and kept something in his store that guided him through any dark night of the soul: a baseball bat near the front counter. His parsimony was much spoken about in the houses of the middle class, and his store, now prosperous, became a target among those who heard what was spoken against him. And since he was not protected by connections in the town, he was an easy target. Yet one night, he dealt with the toughs of the town in this way: he grabbed the bat and chased three men out. He was wearing a shirt and tie, and his body and his face trembled with rage. This only increased the talk about him and his reputation, and even more than before his position as an outsider was sealed.

Men from the mill and the mines laughed about him (behind his back) and spoke against him (behind his back). They were all great men crowded together in a union hall and as priggish as schoolmasters or civil servants, without the suits or ties.

So Ian's trip to Evan's camp was retold many times by people in those union halls until the story became that Evan's plea to Ian was unquestionably about the money—that Evan had told Ian about this money and his plan to ask Fitzroy and had begged him to keep it secret. And soon Fitzroy himself believed this story. That is, Fitzroy believed Ian had duped him, that he himself had always planned to give the money to Evan, and that Ian had not only talked him out of loaning it to Evan, he had talked him out of giving it to Harold in his will.

Not only this, but the rumour surfaced that the banks had warned old Joyce not to let Ian visit him because he, Ian, was a thief. And this was said so often that Joyce himself believed it too, and believed that all the banks on the river had been worried about his fortune, worried that Ian would steal it.

"I should have trusted them banks to do right by me, like I knew they would," Fitzroy said. He said all of this because he was a lonely old man and knew he would entertain people if he told this tale.

Hearing of the old man's suspicions, Ian Preston felt guilty, though he had been innocent. He went down in a snowstorm one night to visit his great-uncle, bringing him coffee cake and a box of tea.

But his uncle seemed less than aware of who he was—and almost afraid to make a mistake about who he wasn't.

"Harold," the old man said. "Harold—is that you? Is you back in here?"

"No, it is Ian."

"Who—?"

"Ian."

Harold no longer came. That is, now that the old man truly needed someone, and might need a warm meal, no one came to visit but Molly Thorn.

The storm had crept up to the doors and back shed; it had covered the dark windows; and all of those so content to say Ian had stolen the money were not there to help he who had supposedly been robbed. The old man had not been taking his pills, and pill bottles lay on the table, empty—and people said he did not have insurance and could not afford to refill them. Ian had not known this, and all of it was put onto his shoulders now.

Ian Preston saw the old fellow was ill and made preparations instantly to take him to the Mount. He did not like to spend the money—that was his problem, and always would be—but he went to the Mount and found a room, fussed over every detail, and made a deal based on how long he believed the old man might live.

Yet this act was now viewed with the same suspicion as all his other acts. That is, people said that he was preparing to settle the old man's affairs in the best possible way for himself so he wouldn't have to bother with him again or pay a thing back. At this point, his reputation as a thief was sealed, and would be going forward for years to come. Worse, others suspected him precisely because he did not drink. That is, they believed that parsimonious people like Ian who did not drink could not enjoy themselves and thought only of money.

Just over four months later, Ian's great-uncle died, and the loan was moot. Suddenly Ian had an extra $125,000 in his pocket. In fact, Fitzroy had left him the money unconditionally.

He thought of giving the money to charity—to the local Salvation Army—but now that he was in the midst of buying his own house, he felt he couldn't. He also thought he really should give some of it to Evan, and was kept awake late at night thinking this: He needs it. He is married with a child. I have it. I can loan it—and he will pay me back. But Evan had not spoken to him since the night at the camp. No one spoke to him unless they were in the store asking for something. In fact, he was known to refuse service to people if he discovered they had gone to another store first.

"You should have come here first," he would say. "You better go somewhere else."

"But I thought we were friends."

"Friends? No, I have no friends," Ian would say matter-of-factly.

So now no one would ever know he had not offered Evan the money he'd thought of offering—no one but himself.

And by now it was clear that Evan blamed him in some way that made Ian feel terrible. So he became, in his own way, as resentful of Evan as Evan was of him.

There was one other important rationale for not giving the money to Evan. Giving the money would only allow people to believe they were right, that he was trying to salve his conscience. More than this, he knew Evan would refuse the money outright, and perhaps tell people he had. Besides, he could not think of parting with it. His family had had so little; there had been many days when there'd been nothing at all to eat in the house and he was told to drink water to fill his stomach before he went to bed.

Now that he had money, why should he give it away?

And Evan, the man who had said they were friends, had proven one thing: that he, Ian Preston, would have no one.

Ian tried to elaborate on this train of thought one night but was not able to—he was not able to call to mind what the poet said, that "too long a sacrifice makes a stone of the heart."

So, thinking of what to do with the extra money, he bought an older three-storey house on Pleasant Street—because he had loved those houses when he was a boy and his father used to deliver stove wood to them. He had never forgotten the smell of apples in the yards, the old carts filled with pumpkins from the garden, the soft mellow look of leaves on the trees, the backyards surrounded by well-kept fences. He himself took to rewiring it, brought in breaker switches instead of fuses, got rid of much of the drywall, had the driveway paved, and repainted the exterior then rebuilt the veranda. The first summer there he spent by himself, putting on a new roof, jumping from the staging to the roof with a seventy-five-pound bag of asphalt shingles over each shoulder.

That is, he did the work on the house himself once he discovered how much a contractor was going to charge. He figured that if he'd spent money on the house, he'd saved on the renovation by being able to do the work with his own hands—and being alone and doing work never bothered him. But again people saw him as a miser—and he reinforced that by arguing at the bottle exchange over the bottle count. But why should people be so upset about that? It was an extra six cents, and it was not their six cents—nor would he allow them to have it. If he allowed them to take six cents, it might as well be six dollars. And so, putting the extra six cents in the change pouch of his wallet and zipping it up, he never noticed how many eyes were looking at him. But he heard the words: "That's him—Ian Preston—that's him."

He ignored what he decided he could not change—although he did tell the people at the bottle exchange again that the six cents was his money, not theirs.

One night some months after he had bought his house, Ian was passing by the jail on his way home and heard his name called in a harsh whisper. He almost never bothered with people now—and he never bothered with them because they had hurt him, and they had hurt him because he had trusted. So he was sure that as long as he did not trust, he would not only be happy—he would be safe. It was his main objective, in fact—not to be happy but to be safe. The baseball bat under the counter was insurance for that.

The harsh whisper annoyed him, and he didn't look back. Yet the voice beckoned again, this time with his name. And it was a voice he knew. So he went over to the jail and looked through the mesh over the window, and saw the face of a man staring out at him with a kind of peculiar glee.

Harold was inside—Ian could make out only part of his face. They tried as best they could to shake hands.

Harold had come to town and got into a fight with a policeman. He said he was searching for Annette. He had less than four dollars to his name. "If you see her, don't tell Annette I'm in here," he said. "I'll make it all up to her—I will. Tell her that she has to come back—she promised me. She is hanging around with people that she thinks care for her, but they don't—she just doesn't know. In this life, you know or you don't. She doesn't KNOW—tell her I will make it up to her."

"I will. I will tell her," Ian said. But Ian had also heard this about Annette—that Lonnie Sullivan was taking care of her. And he too had thought: She cannot know what he will demand.

Harold, in all his confusion, knew this too. "Do you think you bear some of this responsibility?" he asked suddenly.

"How?"

"How?" Harold laughed sardonically. "Boy, you are something. You robbed us, you did. Annette and I. You robbed Evan too."

"I didn't know about the money," Ian said. "I promise you—*I never knew about the money until that day!*" He gave Harold his cigarettes and wished him well.

What Ian did not know was why Harold had come to town.

Furious that his life had taken such a harsh and irredeemable turn, Harold had arrived the night before and watched as Ian closed the store and went home. Then he'd waited until it was completely dark and the snowbanks hid him, and he went behind the building. But though he had two rags in his pocket soaked in gas, and though there was no one in the world near him, he couldn't get his old Bic lighter to light in the cold wind. He cursed it, and after a while, seeing some people (he did not recognize that they were Ian's old troubled uncles) coming through the alley, his resilience failed. He begged off and went to the tavern.

There he drank the last of his little fortune down. As fate would have it, at the tavern he tried to light the rags once more. This time the Bic lighter worked, the rags caught fire, and the waiter finally called the police. He was fined and spent twenty-eight days in jail.

Annette was told by Lonnie that Harold was in jail because he went exceedingly berserk and wanted to cut her head off with a pair of grass clippers. "I put a stop to it," Lonnie said. "You do not need no Harold Dew—not now."

"No, I will never need him again," Annette said. "Nor any other man."

PART THREE

WE HAD NOT SEEN ANNETTE IN ALMOST THREE YEARS. She had been involved, with Lonnie, in four scams in two different cities. She was afraid of him, and always felt a certain kind of relief whenever she pleased him.

One day, he said she owed him $5,300 for clothes and jewellery and transportation. And he asked her to help him out in some way, just once more.

"How?"

"I don't know, Annette dear, I don't have all the answers—maybe a trip someday."

She stood off to the side in Lonnie's shed. You could still tell it was Annette—no one could ever deny that. But now, though she was still lovely and seeking love, her eyes had the look that would distinguish her to those who observed closely enough—the look of a predator.

Like all true victims she had been trained for this role since she was a child, since she had run away from the convent school that day. And now she was part of the con that would eventually destroy her.

————

It was later that month that Ian met Sara Robb—that is, the oldest daughter of the man he and his friends had put out of work years ago.

On Thursday nights Ian would go for walks. He owed no one and had no friends.

To meet young women he had joined a dance club, called the Bright Up 'N' Comers; he shined his shoes and wore his best suit.

But because he did not drink, and could never see the day when he would, he was less fun than the other men. And this is how most women viewed him. Nor did he spend money on them or even offer to buy them a drink. So he most often arrived and left by himself.

Then his life changed. He met a woman who couldn't dance and did not go to dances.

He literally bumped into his future, and the tragedy that was to come, three weeks after he gave Harold his packet of smokes at the jail. He turned the corner one Thursday night on lower Pleasant Street, well after ten o'clock, and bumped into a young woman on her way home from the Heritage Foundation. She fell backward as her blue tam came off, and dropped all her brochures. He helped her to her feet and helped her pick the brochures up.

"Oh, I'm okay," she said, gathering the papers back, now covered in snow. When she pulled her tam on, it fell almost over her eyes and pinned her ears down. But as she turned away, he saw that her left leg was injured; she dragged it slightly.

"What happened—did you hurt yourself?"

"Pardon?"

"To your leg—what happened?"

"Oh, I got that years ago—everyone knows." She glanced at him and shrugged. But her eyes shone with a peculiar brightness that told him she knew all the ways this could be used against her and wondered if he would.

Ian, holding one of her brochures, watched her go along the street with streetlights shining down on the pale snow at intermittent spots. He followed her at a distance. She turned from one street to another and entered a small house at the back of a lumberyard.

He did not know what to do after that, but he felt very sorry for her. Eventually he went home and put the brochure on his fridge. "Richie's Wharf must become a historic site!" it read.

He went to the young woman's house the next day and knocked on the heavy door. The house was so low to the ground its windows were only inches above the snow, and a snow angel left from Christmas still clung to one of the faded crinoline curtains.

She lived with her mother and her younger sister, Ethel. Ethel reminded him of a dozen young women in these forlorn places. She was incredibly thin, with milky skin and big scared eyes, and sat near the stove in the damp hallway, bearing witness. Her face was covered in shy, almost invisible freckles.

"I didn't get your name," he said to the young woman he had knocked over.

She stared at him for a second without recognizing who he was, as heavy wind rattled the window and blew snow across the street.

"Oh! Ian. I'm Sara Robb—you must remember me!" Sara had heard most of the rumours about Ian but did not care to believe them.

"I know you—we were in school together back at Bonny Joyce!" Ian said. It seemed a hoax by God—the God he and his friend Evan detested and had decided not to believe in when they were sixteen—that this most beautiful one in the household was, because of an accident, burdened and deformed.

So Ian started going back to that little smoky house, which in so many ways reminded him of his childhood house, every few days after that. After a time he told people about Sara. Perhaps even too soon, and perhaps wanting to be married now that he had moved into his house, he told his staff he loved her. He even bought the family groceries and paid their oil bills.

There was one other eventuality—something else—one more thing. Here is where he ran into two other people: his old boss Lonnie Sullivan, who teased him mercilessly about stealing Fitzroy's money; and Sara's best friend in the world, Annette Brideau. They both would come to the Robb house, sometimes together and sometimes separately, to have tea-leaf readings done. Annette would say little to him, but now and again he would see her glancing his way with her black, beautiful eyes.

—

Sara was very bright and she certainly soon loved "Mr. Ian," as her mother called him. Mrs. Robb seemed frightened to call him anything less. "Sara," she would sing when she picked up the phone, "it's Mr. Ian."

Sara sat out in the sun reading on spring days when the wind blew sulphur smoke across the backyard fences. But for Ian, she would have been off to university that fall—for him, she put her studies aside.

"I am well off," Ian told her one night, "and my wealth will grow."

"But that's for you—what about for me?" Sara smiled.

He told her he loved her, and he did. Ethel was ecstatic, because of Sara's predicament—the fear that, being lame, she wouldn't find a man. And she was the gifted one! Ethel had been terrified that Sara would be marked as deficient because of her heroic act long ago.

But Ian, though he said he was well off to Sara, did not speak of money to anyone else. He was more guarded about money than anyone Sara had ever met, and she soon realized this when she mentioned his money in front of her family.

"I don't talk about money to anyone," he said to her later, and as sternly as he could.

And so she did not mention it again. But her family loved him in spite of his taciturn ways.

An effusive attention was given to Ian that might have seemed calculated if it had not come from such innocent, kindly and simple people. They were kindly in the way they talked about everyone, from their neighbours to Sara's friend Annette, who often borrowed money from them when in fact she was supposed to pay for her tea-leaf readings. This, of course, was the same Annette Brideau Ian had been enamoured by, and who was now a hairdresser at Cut and Curl up near the highway. Annette had allowed her benefactor, Lonnie, to pay for this course some months before.

Now, Annette at Cut and Curl had been hearing about the boy she had so rebuffed in high school. And hearing about his success felt akin to a stab in the back. She had come a long way from those early days. . Lonnie had taught her that she must do something with her beauty—

she must take the world by storm. In fact, he was planning a trip for her to meet a man in Truro, a trip that would help him absolve a seven-thousand-dollar debt he owed. Recently one evening, before setting out to town, Lonnie had again told her that she had picked the wrong man when she picked Harold. But Annette had long ago given up on Harold.

"Picks can change," she said, lighting a cigarette in the dark. To look at her now was to see not the young girl who had hoped to be someone special but a woman provocative, beautiful and susceptible.

"Ian's already taken," Lonnie said to her.

"I don't mean Ian—I am not interested in stealing someone's man."

"Though you could if you wanted—with one look," Lonnie said. He said this in a husky suggestive voice, but she was nonchalant in her agreement.

"Sure—in a New York second."

The air was as cold in the shed as out when he said this; the smell of cigar permeated the grey room. All of which caused a sadness within her, sadness that her life might be no better—and that others she had never thought could do anything were moving ahead. Not that she needed a man to get ahead, or even thought of it in that way. She was too bright for that! Still and all, to think that Sara, who she liked to pity, would have something she herself would not.

Lonnie was commiserating and his cigar smoke seemed to indicate this in the aluminum air, with the sweet smell of ice and falling snow. He wore an old worn jacket, with a battered fur hood. And he had a bundle of money that he hauled out and flipped through before tucking fifty dollars into her blouse.

Her eyes looked at him, steady, without emotion, as he tucked the money down.

"In a second," she said, almost to herself.

A week later Ian was in the small foyer of Sara's house, while Annette was in the awkward position of asking Mrs. Robb to throw down the tea and tell her if she would ever find a man, a man she could trust.

A man who was sensitive, said Annette. She leaned forward in her chair, wiggling her beautiful bum, her legs entwined about the chair legs and her face almost beatific with interest in those squelched and squalid tea leaves that held so much more romance for her than the confessions or masses that Sara still attended.

"I have been broken-hearted many times," she said, smiling at everyone with a kind of summer whimsy (even though it was not summer). "I probably will not be able to find true love, or take much more of bad love!"

"Yes, of course you will," Mrs. Robb said.

"You see, Annette, we all told you so—didn't we tell you so!" Sara exclaimed.

"Well, it's been my fault—I have not been as good a friend to some as I should." And she glanced quickly at Ian and then glanced away.

"Of course you have," Ethel said.

"Well there!" Annette said. "Thank you, Ethel. If I ever get a house, you can come work for me."

Ian stared at her, slightly open-mouthed; here she was in front of him. The woman he would have killed for. The woman who'd had that awful relationship with Harold—who, she said, had broken her heart. My God almighty, Ian thought, she is even more beautiful than before.

In a strange childlike way, Annette believed herself to be the most progressive person in town. For she had read all the magazines that told her she was, and held all the opinions they told her to. But now she exhibited a trait to Ian she did not know she revealed: self-absorbed naïveté, with her sweet vulnerable hope in a tea-leaf reading. He found this in its own way brilliant. For the first time since entering Sara Robb's house, he felt weak with old autumnal desire—of sunlight flashing on a late-October afternoon against the side of a house, or the smell of auburn hair at dusk—for as any rural man knows, it is autumn, not spring, for breeding.

Annette did not want Ian and she did not want to hurt Sara—but she realized Lonnie was right: she saw Ian's infatuation with her, and she smiled and winked.

So she set her sights on Ian. And there was no one she had ever set her sights on that she could not have.

Nor did it matter that Harold still phoned her, in complete despair over his loss and her betrayal. Once, he waited for her behind the building across from Cut and Curl. When she came toward him, he grabbed her by the arm.

But Annette could always assume an expression of grave sorrow— and she assumed it now. "Let go of me—you are hurting!" she said. She did this not because she was mean but because she had been taught to use the weapons she had.

"Someday you will come back—I promise you that," Harold said. And as she walked away, he yelled, "Don't think I don't know what you are up to. I will tell Sara!"

He saw that she stopped for a second, and knew he had not only hurt her feelings he had revealed her to herself.

The one who could see a plan within the fabric of Annette's whimsical beauty was Corky Thorn—Molly Thorn's brother. He was a tiny thin man, ugly and happy—kind to everyone and hoping the best for others, harmless to a great degree. He had been bullied most of his life and made the best of it. He was dating Ethel—and no one thought more of Sara than he, for it was Sara who had saved Ethel's life. This fact made him silent in Annette's presence, and once made him say she was a phony. He had not thought she was at first—but in the last while he had become more and more reticent to speak about her to the Robbs.

"Oh, come on—she is a good friend," Mrs. Robb would scold him, in the way people who do not know the implications (or do not wish to know the implications) of something will often scold those who do. Then she would look hurriedly about, as if distracted.

"Well, just wait awhile and everything will turn out I am sure," Ethel would say.

And Corky would mutter something that Ethel couldn't hear or understand.

"What, what, what?" Ethel would say. "You have to speak louder, Corky."

"Well, did you see them going for walks? Ian will be walking and all of a sudden Annette starts walking faster, so Ian keeps up with her and leaves poor Sara behind with me and you—and I don't like it."

"Oh, Sara doesn't mind that!" Ethel would laugh.

Annette noticed his dislike and countered it by scolding him about his treatment of Ethel and his poor view of women. And she would evoke a time when things were different, and say that now women did not have to be so abiding. That is, she'd decided that anyone who disagreed with her must have a poor view of women, for this is what magazines told her and this is what she believed. It cost her nothing to believe this and made her feel special. And this was the way, since she was a child, she'd found her right to feel.

"I don't have a poor view of women," Corky said.

"You do."

"Don't."

"You do. So someday I will just take Ethel to find someone new if you are going to be so unpleasant and suspicious, Corky," she would say. And then she would smile in a generous way. She enjoyed that she could get the best of him. She saw that everyone was a little frightened of her—and she enjoyed this as well.

Corky was indeed worried that Ethel would find someone else, and was jealous, so he would frown. Everyone would laugh at how witty Annette was, and Corky would grab his jacket and leave, walking though giant puddles with his hands in his pockets.

Someday they'll all be sorry, he would wince. Someday.

Annette worked at Cut and Curl, and there the owner, Diane—or DD, as she was called—often talked in an immature, self-infatuated way.

Diane was married to Clive. She'd got married young and was often confiding in Annette about her problems with him. He was too possessive, and now she felt—since she owned her own place—she must leave him soon.

Clive sold hair products for men and beauty products for women and travelled along the lonely coast with his boxes of radiant-smile hair tonic. He laughed almost idiotically and would gawk at others with dull perplexity—the first time he saw Ian he'd stared at him with such an insolent gaze that Ian simply looked at him and said, "Anything wrong?"

And he'd answered by gawking more and then looking about and laughing, as if sharing a private joke with others. That is, he had heard all about Ian, and since he had now seen him for himself, he believed he was in the know and could say the exact same things everyone else was saying.

But when would Annette get married? This was the question at the Robb house. That is, there was a good deal of false concern, brought on by Mrs. Robb because of Sara having found Ian.

"Oh, men—I've given up on stupid whiny men," Annette would often tell them. "No matter what the tea leaves say. I had my man, and Harold turned out to be such a disappointment. You know he follows me about. He threatens me—off and on."

"Well then, you should get the police!"

"I will—if he does not watch out!"

Then she would smile, take a deep breath and trump a king of diamonds with her ace of hearts and laugh a wonderful provocative laugh. "Youse didn't think I had that ace up my sleeve, did you? Well, there you go now—I did. So now you all have jam on your faces!"

That is what captures you, really—innocent charm. It is the great and glorious cloth of seduction. Ian tried not to be seduced—he forbade himself to allow it. That is, he tried not to look at her.

Ian now had the money he'd once said he needed in order to charm Annette. He really, if he was careful with it, had money enough to last two lifetimes. He had once said he would murder for her. Well, now perhaps he wouldn't.

He did not know that Harold had planned a murder over Annette as well. He had planned to murder Ian.

———

All this time Ian thought he was secure and that his business was private. He did not speak too much about it but kept every cent in his head. He had about two hundred thousand dollars on hand and his house was paid for.

Yet for all his supposed wiles, Ian had no idea how the world really worked. Lonnie, however, knew how the world worked. He knew what Ian's store brought in, knew what his house was worth—knew that he had been planning other investments. And why was Lonnie observing all this? Well, because he could, and because it might be an avenue to get money—he just didn't quite know how yet. But he would know within a short time. One spring day his features would change; he would become buoyant and almost uncontainable—it was that day when he discovered how to make it all work. Lonnie Sullivan may have never heard of Machiavelli—but Machiavelli would certainly have heard of him.

At first, I believe, Ian did not catch on. Perhaps Annette did not either. But over time he realized that each conversation she had was directed at him and him alone.

This was his plight: to remember those long-ago days of warm summer breezes and Annette's multicoloured dresses and the soft lilt of her white breasts in a swimsuit at the shore, and for her now to act completely differently toward him—that is, to be interested in every word he now said. And for him to catch her staring at him whenever he glanced her way.

But I have long maintained there was only one Sara Robb, and this is what poor Corky in all his humility tried to tell Ian. And this is why Corky got into such trouble with Annette, who was furious when anything about her true motives (motives she herself was uncertain about) was discovered.

"If you are going to be rude or unpleasant to me, Corky, I will take Ethel away on a trip and we will find some—well, we will just have fun. You know, I know boys in Nova Scotia who are rich and kind and who would love Ethel as much as I do. You see I have travelled a bit and have a bit more experience with how to handle people like—well, people like you."

And Corky would stare at the wall, his arms folded, his untied boots half off his feet, his cup of tea steaming. Annette would walk by him, the swaying motion of her dress enchanting—enchanting, it seemed, to everyone but him.

"Yes, and you always have Ethel make you tea. If you really cared for her, you would make it yourself, Corky—so don't be so unpleasant."

Corky would mutter and look away and say he did not want the tea at all. Ian would not interject in these squabbles, but somewhere in them, he knew, there was a hidden warning, some caution light he should recognize. But that feeling would pass.

Ian had promised Corky a job, and told him that once he was married to Sara and Corky was married to Ethel, they would live like a family. They would run the business and Corky would become a partner—and they would get into the siding business before anyone else in town.

Ian still really hoped to help both Molly and Evan too. So he planned to help Evan buy the old Jameson mill. And he thought that by hiring Corky, he would demonstrate that he intended only good. He was serious about it, but he did not know that Corky Thorn had placed his entire life into this dream.

This is what Ian often told Corky: Evan could run the mill, but if Ian was going to solve Evan's problem, then Ian should actually own the place. "You will come to work here with me, Corky—just wait! Everything with me and Evan and Harold will be worked out. Harold will come around too—I am sure of it."

And Corky would beam.

There was something else. Ian was no fool. During this time, aluminum siding was starting to replace wood, and he knew that someday he would involve himself in this. In fact, as ugly and as simple as poor Corky looked, he was indispensable to Ian's plan, for he knew how to work both with siding and in a sawmill and he was far brighter than he seemed at first glance.

So Corky was devoted to Ian's idea, was overcome by it, and could only see one danger. "There is only one great gift in a man's life and you have found her. Do not throw her clumsy grace away for the smell of perfume on the inside of a thigh!" is what Corky would have liked to say if he'd had the ability to do so.

But how many hundreds of millions of men have thrown away their gifts? Or, as I have long maintained—and I once mentioned this to Sara, who refused to speak about it—perhaps Annette too had no choice. So one should have mercy.

"The virtue of Mercy is not strained," I said, misquoting Shakespeare and liking the misquote.

"I have wrestled with that and found it true," Sara told me, in her lilting Miramichi accent that seemed to cut the air with love.

As much as Corky was indispensable to Ian's daydreams, Annette became indispensable to Sara's in hers—in her planning the wedding that was to come. Soon every decision Sara made had to be approved by Annette. She liked this or did not like that. This bridesmaid's dress was too plain, that one was too full, this one didn't show the boob, that one had a too-narrow line. The wedding dress should not be radiant white but pearl coloured because of Sara's pale skin. The aisle must not be too, too long so the procession should start closer to the altar (Annette whispered in discretion) because of Sara's limp.

This gave Annette more authority in the young couple's lives than any other person—and no one fussed more about protocol.

"A young priest to marry and old priest to bury," she said when they went to visit the rectory one afternoon, and settled on Father MacIlvoy, who was their age, though Annette disapproved of him.

Sara was clumsy-brilliant—by that I mean she could neither be brilliant without being clumsy nor clumsy without being brilliant. And I wanted my students to understand that characteristic, although if they ever did I am unsure. The great defining forces in our lives are not uniformly good or inglorious—that is, traits that would cripple us are present in all great men and women and are fought against every step of the way.

There were things Sara was not good at: friendships were hard for her to form because too many had inflicted pain. But the prettiest girl in the world seemed to like her, and this made up for much, and so she was completely devoted to her one friend, the prettiest girl in the world.

Nor did she mind that Annette did not see her brilliance. That is, from the first Annette wondered why she kept Sara as her friend. It was a challenge. Especially when Sara went up to Diane's Cut and Curl to have her hair done, thinking Annette should welcome her, even though she was so out of place in that place of beauty. Her pale face was offset by a new hairdo that only showed her to be unaware of the world Annette knew.

Sara's world seemed backward, going the other way—she studied the poetry of someone called T. S. Eliot and the war of some year, 1812. She had tried to speak of T. S. Eliot once at Cut and Curl, of his objection to knowledge without faith, and so much hooting and laughter followed that Annette became embarrassed.

Besides which, Annette was as good and comfortable in her world as any woman. And hers was not a little part of the world but a great part, a large part that those with small eyes and pale skin did not see—and therefore, as Annette knew, could not join.

They played a Ouija board game and Annette asked the board if Sara would find true love.

"I don't need to ask." Sara laughed. "I already know."

The answer came back: yes, she would. And they all laughed harder.

———

Harold had lost everything and he blamed his two friends for it. He thought of killing himself, but though he held the knife to his jugular, in the end he tossed it aside. It was a grey and morbid night when he decided not only to live but to exact revenge on those who did not care if he died. That was it: no one seemed to care if he died.

He wrote Sara a letter, saying he believed Annette was after Ian:

> You had better watch her—she had me steal money for her. That was eighty dollars—imagine what she would do for Ian! And what is more to the point—imagine what Ian would do for her. Take one look at them when they are in any room together and you will see.
>
> Your faithful friend from youth, Big Harold Dew.

But there is blindness in love and friendship is love. And Sara was determined to be as kind a friend as she could. And some part of the reason for this was to prove Harold Dew and his letter wrong.

Cold toward her all day, Annette would lighten and warm when they were alone—when, as far as Annette was concerned, they were out of sight of those whose opinion so counted. These were the best moments for Sara, who waited for the change to come—and often worried that it would not. But then, all of a sudden, Annette would say something or ask a question in such a particularly affectionate manner that Sara's troubled little face would brighten. GOOD! Annette was back—the real Annette, who loved her again.

The young women walked down the back streets together, with mud still on the sidewalk and the pale evening spending itself like love over the great spring trees, and the buildings casting out evening shadows. Sara was concerned that she did not know what was important about being "feminine." And now, for the first time, she had a man and needed to know. (Or at least, this was the idea Sara wanted to promote, in order to make Annette's expertise valuable.) So she asked Annette's advice about what to wear and how to dress—and in some way she did this only because Annette expected to be asked and would have been disappointed if Sara did not. So the advice had to be given, in the same way it had been for generations—not because it was needed but because it was expected. Therefore they spoke only about things Annette assumed Sara did not understand, and Sara pretended for Annette's sake she did not. And finally they came to this: "Are you a virgin?" Annette asked.

"Yes."

"Is he?"

"I'm not sure—I think probably he is."

"People say he is rich. Is he rich?" Annette asked. "Or probably he isn't." Then she lit a cigarette and tossed the match aside.

"I'm not sure," Sara said, waiting for her. "But I think money will be no object for us—at any rate, he made a lot of money in the last three years because of the hospital, the school and nursing home—he supplied them all with their pipes and heating systems, had a contract for the windows in the hospital and still does. And then there was over three hundred appliances he sold—and besides that, he bought and sold two other properties and invested the money in his warehouse. He is smart like that. You know he is also sad—he is sad at times that his mom and dad never got to see him grow up or make all this money."

"Really?" Annette said. And since it was the first time she had ever seemed impressed, Sara bragged about Ian's yearly salary of over a hundred thousand dollars, which would be comparable in any large city to three times that. (In fact, over the next two to three years, because he supplied both the community college with all the gyprock and lumber for its new structure and all the wiring to replace the knob and tube, and did the same with the senior citizen homes, and bought and sold two warehouse properties, Ian would earn close to $150,000 a year. And that is one reason the townspeople simply took him to be a cheat.) The only thing Ian worried about was the two strip malls coming in and offsetting his business, for he had no control over them. And he knew that when those malls came in, he would lose contracts, and perhaps much more. He felt if businesses expanded outward, the centre of the town would die.

There was one more thing the two women talked about. Sara was giving up a scholarship to university to marry—she had applied the very day Ian had met her, and a scholarship had been offered.

"I'd give up a dozen of those," Annette said flippantly. What was this scholarship worth? It was worth some twelve thousand dollars a year. "Ha!" Annette laughed. "And by staying at home you'll have a hundred."

"You've reached the big leagues now," that beauty said, with such unaffected innocence that both she and Sara laughed.

Sara, without telling Ian or anyone else, wrote the university, thanking them but saying she would not be attending. Then, with resolution, she walked to the post office and mailed that part of her life away.

There was another, hidden, part of her life too—a part that you might see if you looked closely and carefully at Ethel's face. She and Ethel—they had grown up as little Injun Town girls, with the pulp yard just down the way. On sunny mornings in the old back porch, near where Ethel once saw a huge black rat, Sara and she used to set out their table and have a tea party, and Sara would read Trixie Belden books. She would read very professionally too, turning the pages with a good deal of form. But one day long ago, in that old lopsided porch where they were having a tea party, something happened. They were both there at 10:32 a.m., and then ten minutes later they were not; they had gone somewhere with someone.

No one but Ethel knew how Sara had protected her sister by saying "No, no, no!" and stamping her foot. And if you'd looked at her face at that moment, the word *no* meant more than refusal—it was a declaration that the act being committed was such a betrayal, and that she, as a child, understood this. The man she was talking to had given them candy and told them he knew where a prince was. And they had run down past the blocks of wood in the pulp yard to see—both little girls.

The man then told Ethel and Sara that if they drank what he gave them, they would see a prince. Sara had nothing to her name but one dress, and neither she nor Ethel had ever seen a prince. So they drank and got happy and then dizzy. And Ethel said she wanted to lie down. And suddenly Sara realized she had put Ethel in a terrible danger, because it seemed neither girl could walk well. She looked up at the man and smiled timidly, and then looked at the ground and pretended to be looking for something special.

She told him they had to go back to their house now, but he told them if they took their dresses off, they would be able to put other splendid dresses on because the prince was coming.

The man told Ethel to come back behind an old cardboard siding, where the new dress was. It had stars and diamonds on it, he said.

"No," Sara said. But the man took them behind the pulpwood, in behind the cardboard. Ethel said she wanted to see the dress, and the man began to take Ethel's dress off. But Sara stepped in between them and tried to tell the man she didn't want the dress, that it didn't matter if she saw the prince. That is all she could remember, stepping between him and Ethel and stamping her foot: "No, no, no."

Sara was a little girl of six then, and now she did not know if she was still a virgin or not—she did not know anymore what it was that had happened. Only that Ethel had stood there watching as Sara said no. She thought Ethel too had forgotten it all. But one day last month, as if she remembered something, her eyes brightening, Ethel had said, "Now, Sara—your really, really prince has come, just like I prayed for you. See!"

———

There was one thing that worried Sara about Annette. And that was Annette's friend, the young man who worked at the stables downriver, Ripp VanderTipp. And the very day she went to show Annette the diamond Ian had given her, Ripp was with her. Annette was troubled and worried when Sara came up to her, and Sara knew she had picked just the wrong time to show the ring.

When Annette saw this diamond, her face turned and her features distorted. She tried to be happy for her friend, but she knew she didn't sound like she was. It was three times the size of the little diamond Harold had once bought her, when she had stayed up late practising how to sign her name Mrs. Harold Dew—with a flourish.

Ripp was there to tell Annette that Lonnie wanted to see her, and so she had better go down.

Annette went downriver, took off her shoes and sat in her little bedroom, where her life seemed very dark, where she could recall not one
pleasant memory—where all her thoughts of being loved and wanted
seemed a lie, and she had no idea what to do. She thought of the odd little
house she lived in—thought too of her mom and dad and how they themselves lived, bickering over nothing. What, then, would happen to her?

She had trusted Lonnie—or had she? Well, she was wilful as well. And
now, she realized, she had been naïve. She did not know if she was pregnant, because her periods had been irregular since she was fourteen. In
fact, Dr. Hennessey had often been concerned about her, worried that
she might develop blood clots, and had her tested at the hospital here
and in Moncton. Yet nothing seemed to come of it except blood pressure tests. Dr. Hennessey told her that in years to come she must have
regular checkups and perhaps someday she would need blood thin-
ners. Why was that? Well, because he was an old man and believed he
could tell things because of how thin the veins in her fingers were.
Strange, she thought, that he'd picked up on this instantly when she
turned thirteen. Twice since then she had developed blood clots in
her legs; and for Annette who loved to dance this was now painful,
and she had to take medication.

What was now happening seemed far more serious, however. And as
yet she had gone to no doctor.

She'd had a pregnancy test, and had handed it to Lonnie yesterday
and then left the shed—not able to look at it herself. And now he had
told Ripp to have her come see him, and he was going to tell her if she
was or was not pregnant. And if she was—because she had done what he
had asked her to do—what would happen then? She thought about her
mother, and what the gossips would say, and what others along Bonny
Joyce would say. About Annette, who thought she was so much better
than everyone else, who was so full of herself! And what about that man
who supposedly had millions and was in love with her? It was a lie she
had wanted to believe, because then she would get back at Harold—and
them all. Yes, get back at them all—for why had nothing spectacular

happened for her? So this rich man was her way to be spectacular. Yet she didn't even know where this supposed millionaire really lived. She would be a laughingstock.

And when she had asked Lonnie about him two days ago, Lonnie got furious and it frightened her. He'd called her down, told her she still owed him $5,300 and that she had ruined herself. So now she was not only worried but sick and ill. She thought of Sara and all her happiness, while she, Annette the wise one, was alone and pregnant.

"What will happen now?" she asked the statue of the Virgin. "Please help me!"

A voice—and she could never say what voice it was; in fact, it must have come from deep inside her—said, "Sara. Go to Sara. She will know what to do. She will help you because she loves you. You must rely on her. She, in fact, loves you more than anyone else."

But Annette's deeper secret and more envious thought was this: if she did go to Sara, Sara would protect and help, which was fine—but then what would happen? There would be no chance with Ian—and this is what she was now secretly hoping for, a chance with Ian. So no, she couldn't go to Sara. And this moment brought it home and she could no longer deny it.

She went to Lonnie Sullivan. As soon as she entered his shed, he looked at her sternly.

"Well, I thought you had more sense," he said. "He didn't use protection and either did you—what kind of girl are you? I had you pegged for someone a lot smarter than that there—I should have nothing to do with you." He sniffed and rubbed his nose and looked at the newspaper, and made pencil marks on a certain page, trying to solve a crossword puzzle. "All you wanted was his money—he caught on."

She sat down on a little stool and started to cry; she had never cried so much in her life.

He read the paper while she did. Then he tossed her a box of Kleenex. "There is an easy way to get out of this mess—go back to Harold and have him marry you. He'd be so happy to have you back he'd never know the difference. "

"No," she said. "Leave me alone—leave me alone—I just want to be left alone."

"Then there is someone else—just maybe?" Lonnie said. He sounded compassionate; he smiled and his eyes shone just a little bit.

"There is no one," she said. She looked up at him, thinking exactly the same thing that he was. Their eyes met and both of them knew it.

Then he said, "But it's too late now. You can't hurt Sara—she has been too kind to you."

"I don't want to hurt Sara," she said, lowering her eyes, as if he had read her thoughts. She began to tremble.

Lonnie thought for a moment, twisting a plastic cigar wrapper in his hand. "Well . . . who's to say? All is fair in love and war! In fact, didn't she steal Ian from you once? As far as I look at it—"

"No, she didn't do that!"

"The way I look at it," Lonnie said quietly, smiling, "as soon as he went to town . . . The way I look at it."

She wanted to believe him more than she'd ever believed anyone in her life. In fact, she had to.

"Oh, I don't know. I don't know. What will I do?" But she glanced at him—yes, she knew whose fault this was. What a fool she had been to travel down that long ugly road to Truro with him—and for what? Why had she believed anything he said?

Lonnie only smiled. "Do you love him?"

She made no answer. She just stared out at the clouds that seemed to rush by the window.

"Then use what a woman has to get him," Lonnie said. "And if it does not work—go back to Harold, have the kid, and I will be there for you."

"Who will find out?"

"Find out? No one in the world—who can you trust if not me?"

She left the table, left the shed, left the yard, shaken and confused.

Lonnie stood at the door watching her go. After a while he waved.

———

At this point there seemed to be nothing for Sara to worry about. Sara certainly loved Ian. Ian thought things were settled. Ethel and Mrs. Robb did as well.

So why did he marry Annette?

Many in town a generation ago say it was because Annette was Annette and simply willed it. It was as if suddenly she decided enough was enough: she would not give up a chance at a man with a small fortune—to her it was that—just because of loyalty to someone so plain who relied upon her so much.

The destructive forces in any friendship always end in betrayal.

It started simply enough. And Annette was in fact sent by Sara to him. That was a stroke of luck. Did Sara know this? Begging Annette to go, did she relinquish some superior hand to an equally superior twist of fate? As the brightest of my students, Terra Matheson, mentioned: just as Ian in his heart of hearts thought he must fail because he felt unworthy of the money, Sara's test to Annette was of a friendship that was impossible.

Still, Sara herself bade her go to Ian. Annette needed this opening; she could not have done it by herself. And this one request by her friend made her determined to see it through.

So Annette went to Ian's store one evening a few months before the wedding, a deceiver sent by the one she needed to deceive, to tell him that Sara was sick and could not come by to see him—they had been out shopping all day for things for the wedding and she was exhausted.

"She said she will call first thing in the morning," Annette said.

Ian thanked her and stood a little apart, near two fridges that were pushed out in front because they were on sale. The place had the smell of wiring and lights, and a feeling of dispossession that always permeates dry electrical places, that always gives the impression of man at odds with himself and his own nature. It was a place where a somewhat gangly, serious and naïve boy was surrounded by things he had "fixed up."

"I am a fixer upper" was how he described himself to her. He wanted to impress her finally. (But he also knew the large store was much more than that—it supplied two-thirds of the river with appliances, wiring, lumber and wallboard, and lumber and lights from his store had built fourteen houses in the upper subdivision in the past two years. That made him one of the most important suppliers on the river and one of the richest—and he had reinvented the store since he had bought it, to make all this possible.)

Annette turned to go and then turned back. "I think it's her period," she said. "It always gets to her!"

Embarrassed, he looked away. His hair was combed back on both sides and twisted at the front and top, like those boys from the 1950s. He put his right hand over his left elbow as if to protect himself from something and smiled clumsily.

Annette did that something: she touched his right arm quickly, squeezed it and then let go. He was staring at the spot on the arm she had touched, when she suddenly said that Sara owed her thirty dollars for a manicure and haircut, and she didn't want to bother her now because she had so much on her mind, but she needed the money herself.

The lights shone like a draft or a funnel behind her, as if she stood directly inside some splendid radiance that allowed her dress to become almost transparent. It was at this moment she realized that he could not take his eyes off her.

"Well," he said, coming to himself, "here." And he immediately put his hand in his pocket and gave her thirty dollars. (He had a lot of money in his hand, but he did not hold it as Lonnie held his.)

"Oh," she said. "Sara said she would pay it."

"Don't worry about it." Then, seeing her peering here and there, he asked her to come in and see his store. He took her from one end to the other—up the stairs to the second and then the third floor. Everything was in order; everything had a price tag and a serial number—it all looked so impressive to her. From the top-floor window she could see all the way to the bridge, and beyond—to small lights twinkling far away in the darkness.

"Is that Bonny Joyce Road—that small speck way off?" she said in a capricious beautiful tone, turning her face toward his.

"No, it's another ten miles down and beyond the islands."

"Ah yes—but this river is where we spent our youth."

"Yes."

"And now our youth is gone—drifted away somewhere. I do not know where—but it has, hasn't it?" she said. "Well, let's go back downstairs," she said, to indicate propriety.

It was a warm night and she lingered. So he locked up (childishly a bit pleased to have keys that hung off his belt) and they walked down the street together, he slightly ahead of her and not knowing what decorum was. He could hear the sound of his shoes on the sidewalk, the smell of darkness in the warm siding. She was Sara's best friend, he told himself, so walking with her was fine—and even more than fine; it was somehow required. That was it: it was a requirement to walk with his fiancée's best friend. There. He felt better saying this and sighed.

"Maybe I should go over to see Sara—is she running a temperature?"

"I think she'll be fine," Annette said. "Besides, she was sleeping when I left."

It did not matter that this sounded false—or, in fact, it mattered in a good way. It surprised Ian how some small part of him wanted it to be a lie, for that indicated something else, something new and special, between them. He knew this was how shallow men thought—and he knew too that at times this is how all men thought when it came to someone else's fiancée or wife.

They watched a nighthawk fly beneath the streetlight near Fransblo's and heard a bicycle up the back lane.

She wore a short strapless summer dress. She had her nails painted pink and had a small ankle bracelet. She was, to him, spellbinding.

He noticed now how she had done Sara's hair and nails to be exactly like hers, and how this suddenly defined the two women. More importantly, she wore the same perfume that he remembered her wearing that day she'd tossed her head and turned away from him.

She was, in fact, a small-town girl trying to look chic, and in a way this was flattering to him, flattering and poignant—it made her seem exposed in a melancholy way, teetering on the brink of an elliptical desire that could never be fulfilled, like those young country girls he remembered standing in white high heels in the lime-coloured dust of evening. He remembered so many women like that now—and all were remembered in a sudden affecting way—their dreams so elusive, and in the end unfulfilled. In some way he wanted to take all the burden of pain away.

He drove a Mustang and smoked cigarettes—all this was, in a way, self-deceiving. That is, he thought that in order to be perceived in a new way, he had to look like a new man, whether he was or not. Now, suddenly—and it gave him almost a fright—Annette looked at him with a glance that said she understood all of this. It was a glance that could make men go weak with autumnal desire. And men did and would. And Annette knew this in a second.

Caught in that moment, she said, "Do you know what I need the money for?"

"Not at all."

"Well, the money isn't to buy dope—I'm not a dope fiend," she explained. That is, she knew quite well his reputation for being old-fashioned—and of course, in most ways she was too. She loved old songs that spoke of broken hearts and women who had been deceived.

He laughed uncomfortably and turned to wait for her.

She pulled up her skirt very slowly now, to beyond her thighs. "Legs waxed." She winked. "I need to get them done as soon as I can—hopefully tomorrow."

She dropped her skirt quickly, and blushed.

He stared at her legs and then turned his head.

"My legs look bad?"

"No" was all he managed to say. Anyone else doing this would have been more than obvious. Annette doing it was lively, and somehow wonderfully and innocently expected. That was her terrible potency—like a small pinprick from an exotic flower that caused a poisonous heartache. He lit another cigarette with his Zippo clicking in his hand, that self-aggrandizing motion on a dark street that is always a moratorium on class. But he could not be blamed—he had struggled so hard to be one of the bright young men in town.

Her face was full and mischievous, and had a kind of remarkable maritime beauty, beauty hereditary and complemented by her accent, which was a mixture of French and Irish lilt. Ian thought of her as "new" in the way she moved and attracted him. Not new in the way the university kids were, with all their baffling and self-conscious concerns so bogus to him—but new because she was of a tradition that would never change. When he had known her before, she had acted nothing like this with him. She had really tormented him, like a cat might with a mouse. Now everything seemed to be done only for him. She took his cigarette, held it and took a dismissive drag, and handed it back to him as they walked. When he put it in his mouth, he was overcome by the idea that their mouths had met.

That is, she made him feel exactly as she wanted him to.

He was now worried she might change her mind again about him. And without knowing it, he was as infatuated as he had always been.

But she became coy and said nothing for a while. Then, as they turned along the lane toward his car, she told him he should improve his looks for Sara's sake.

"What should I do to look better?"

"I would cut that big snip of hair right there," she said, touching the twist he had at the front. "And maybe pin your ears back a tad."

Then she started talking again, quicker than before. She had nothing but kind things to say about Sara Robb. "And her leg—her leg. If I had a leg like she had a leg, I would jump pell-mell off a bridge," she said. This did not sound demeaning but kind.

But there was something else, almost immediately. He had noticed it when he'd first seen her while visiting Sara's house. It was her insistence— in how she spoke to him, looked at him and then glanced at Sara and back at him—that said: I can have you anytime I want, married or not. Get married and I will still have you. I remember the day I made you walk all the way to Hackett Brook—yes, you remember that day too! You couldn't take your eyes off me back then, just like now. So she was telling him now, and once and for all, she could have him. And more than that, she was insisting it was only fair if he succumbed. And more to the point, he knew—and she knew he knew—that he would, sooner or later.

But what was most profound was the self-deceit. Both knew and said nothing.

He went to flick his cigarette into the darkness and she said, "No, here," and took it once more and had a final drag before she crushed it with her foot. They had almost come to his car and his mind was racing. That is, he was confused about what to do next.

But bending down to pick up a piece of coloured glass to look at, bauble in her hand, she stopped walking and said, almost as if she was out of breath, "You scared me when you were a boy—back then."

"I scared you how?"

She shrugged, looked at the glass and began to walk once more. "Well, I would have loved to have gone out with you, but you were so wild. Oh, you were so damn wild. Sara will probably tame you back down so women like me won't be scared of you."

Of course he knew she was saying this to please him, and it wasn't true—Harold and Evan were far more wild than he. He had always been innocent without being stupid—but even this was flattering.

"God—you don't remember me, but I remember you," she said. That is, she completely reversed reality and made it sound utterly true. And Ian found it wonderful, like a soft reassuring moment in youth when one becomes suddenly glad and in love with life.

"Oh, you remember me with Harold—but you don't remember me when I was so alone at night, sometimes waiting in my house for some-one to come and see me."

That is, Annette's insistence was collaborative, for sin is always col-laborative. It was as if she was willing him to agree with her plans, and he was too weak not to—just as she had done in high school with others.

Was it, then, a sin? For nothing had been done yet. But betrayal is always a sin—at its worst, it is in Dante's furthermost reach of hell. This is what my students and I spoke about, discussed and argued about, many days in a small dark classroom in a cold red building at the top of the hill.

So to accomplish this sleight of hand, Ian pretended he did not remember her very well. He also pretended that this conversation was not out of the ordinary because Annette was Sara's friend. She then mentioned other men, men he had heard of, who were part of the great collection of men who hung around the new bars in town, and who laughed and rollicked about other people's failed dreams and marriages, as if tragedy itself was nothing.

She mentioned these men to see if he approved and then redirected her talk to something else. In this way she was placing him.

He had heard of these other men, Ripp and Tab and Dickie—but only on occasion, and they seemed distant and remote from anyone he or Sara could know or ever want to know. One of them, Ripp, often bullied people where he lifted weights, and someone said even the police were frightened of him—and he liked it when he heard that people were frightened of him. He wore white T-shirts showing his arms with their tattoos. He had an absolute conviction that it was wonderful to make others fear him. Ian, in fact, disliked him intensely.

Seeing his reaction, Annette simply laughed. It was her laugh that really placed him, that told him she already knew more about the world than he ever would.

"Well, don't pretend, love—you are as wild as they. That's what makes you so attractive to all the girls! Oh God, is that your car?" She wisped her hand along the top of the black hood and then took it away quickly. A certain flirtation began that was, in fact, the point where there could be no turning back. Ian was struck by how much she wanted him to realize this—and how much he desired her now, just as he had when he was fifteen. It was much more than desire. It was the idea that she was the one thing he'd longed for and needed since he was that boy from Bonny Joyce Ridge who'd vowed to be a success. But it even went beyond all of that—he knew at this moment that she had settled on nothing less than his complete betrayal of his fiancée; or at least, he had a strong indication that this was what must happen. And both of them in their minds were planning this in intricate ways, without speaking or considering the consequences, while at the same time pretending that this was not at all what they were thinking of.

Suddenly he was angry. For how could she come back to him now, just when it was too late? Why hadn't she said any of this before? And this made him upset with Sara. But by this time, none of it mattered. Really, by this time it wouldn't have mattered if she was saying and doing everything just to spite Sara. In fact, he at one point felt she was, and still it did not matter; so, in fact, from the moment he and Annette began to walk together he was spiting Sara too, and he knew it. Nothing mattered except that now he had a chance with Annette; and he could not say he didn't know what he actually knew and did not see what he actually saw: that is, her previous complete dismissal of him had been replaced by a subtle but lavish desire for who he now was.

Still clutching the flat green bit of bottled glass, she unexpectedly squeezed his hand. Both of their palms were cut by this. She squeezed his hand hard once more and then let it go.

"Oh my," she said, "blood!"

She turned and walked away in the night, with her head down as if deep in thought, in remorse for love. She looked back once, stopped abruptly, looked at him, then turned and ran. It was as if she had just said:

Try to forget me.

———

Ian did try to forget her completely. He tried to forget that he had touched the same cigarette she had, that his blood had mixed with hers.

He went a week or so not seeing or speaking to her. He trembled every time he thought of how awful he was. And this was because of Sara's innocent desire to please him and how annoyed he was with her.

Yet in that week there were moments of the sublime, where he felt he had become exactly what he had set out to become, and for some reason he believed it was he who'd achieved this on his own. He visited the old Jameson sawmill twice—imagining himself the new entrepreneur who would take Evan's dream and fashion it for him. He would buy the mill and give it to Evan as soon as he could. But then, at his most sublime moment, the thought of what had happened would darken his mood. For now he knew he could have Annette, but having her would end all his dreams. In a strange way, he thought he must decide between success and her, and it was his success that allowed this. How strange all of this was to him now.

She wants me now, he thought. Well, no matter, I couldn't care less.

But then, impulsively, he tried to find her. This was on a day when he helped Sara set up chairs for a Heritage Foundation meeting. He had expected Annette to be there and she wasn't. So he went to Cut and Curl pretending to be looking for Sara, knowing Sara was at the meeting. But Annette was gone for the day with Lonnie. DD wasn't sure where. He was tormented by this and depressed. Why was he depressed? Because she had left without telling him that she was leaving, even though, as he said to himself, he couldn't care less.

Something is going on that I do not understand, he thought. What is *really* going on? But that thought was fleeting, and soon forgotten.

Then, a few days later, he heard that she was back. He heard this one rainy afternoon when he was home, looking at saws he could buy for the mill—he had made inquiries into the land below Bonny Joyce that Evan wanted and felt that in two more years he would have all his ducks in order. He was thinking that he and Evan would be back on track then; and he was thinking—and this was a distinct possibility—that they would make a million dollars together.

Out of the blue, Ethel came over to see him, and he blurted out his plan: "Tell Corky to get ready—we are going to do what I told him. We are going to make a sound offer on the mill in the next six months. He will have to break the news to Evan, though. I am just going to stay in the background until I can patch things up a bit. I think in two years everything will be good." And he smiled and shook his head at his own ruefulness.

Ethel laughed and clapped her hands like a child and sat on his knee—for to Ian she *was* a child. She kissed him on the cheek and said, "Sara is some happy today to have her bridesmaid back."

He picked up a magazine and looked at it. "Oh, she's home, is she?" he said, too flippantly. At that moment he believed he had no desire to see her again.

Later he went over to see Sara, hugged her and kissed her as if he had not seen her in months. And when Annette came over that night, he didn't look her way at all. He left by the crooked back gate in a rainstorm.

———

Sara and Annette were planning the engagement party, and Annette came over every day to the little house on the side street, bringing ideas, decorations and balloons for the "buck and doe," as it was called. That is, the men and women would join in one party. They were doing this because it was Sara's party—she was paying and would not allow Ian to. So things were done according to her budget.

The desk was to be used as a dining-room table, with the living room serving as the dining room. Those who came to help spoke of what they had been through and how their lives were similar. All of this made them feel a kind of reductive gaiety, a pleasant truth about the circumstances in which all of them had grown up, and a sense of fierce loyalty toward each other. Most of the men had never cut for blood—but they would cut you in a second if you hurt one of their friends.

Annette was there each afternoon. So finally Ian had to speak with her. And eventually he had to move a table, with her picking up one end and he the other. But something strange happened: she either ignored him or looked at him with furious cold eyes. This fury in her, this queenliness she exhibited, was strangely ordinary and, just between the two of them in the sour little house, somewhat pathetic. Yet she, not Sara, became the one he went to see on those days, the one he couldn't wait to close the store for. Now that she did not bother with him, he thought he might have been mistaken about her intention and wanted to win her attention back.

Annette was the maid of honour. And each day she spoke of how spoiled she would make Sara and how smart Sara looked. And this in itself bothered Ian, because it seemed untrue, somehow superficial and even disrespectful. So he tried to be more kind to Sara than usual.

The idea of him having to be kind to Sara showed already how complicit he had become—and how little it took for him to be complicit. So he was wounded by his own betrayal even before the betrayal happened. And now he longed for Annette to come to the house and was agitated if she did not. He went looking for her three or four times. Once he even took a chance and went to see Ripp to ask him if he had seen her.

"Oh—haven't you?" Ripp VanderTipp smiled in the affectionate, gloating way egotistical men often have.

Ian went back to his house and locked the door as if locking out his own desire. But then, in a moment of anger, he looked at himself in a side mirror, saw the lonely boy from Bonny Joyce everyone had laughed at, and decided he wouldn't speak to Annette again.

"No, she had her chance. I am not playing games with her anymore!"

That night when he left Sara, he went to the lanes beyond the wharf. Looking back, he could see his grey store in the distance. If he did not have this store, would Annette have ever become close to him? No, he knew she would not. She once mentioned that she had never thought he would be capable of "untold riches." So she had told him no lie. Yet still he felt pleased that he had suddenly won her affection.

He could not separate himself from the store, could not separate himself from the man he now was—and that was *because* of the store. So he was very different than he had been before. He had different plans because of this store. He was going to help Evan, Harold and Corky because of this store. He had in fact managed to save three-hundred-thousand dollars because of this store.

So to say he was the same man was wrong. So to say she wasn't right to see him as a different person was also wrong. This is how he thought: he owned a house, drove a sports car—so he *had* changed. So last week when Annette had made fun of Corky, he had allowed this because he wanted her to presume that he was above worrying about Corky Thorn; he had allowed it even though it hurt him when she said things like that and despite the fact that so many of his plans involved Corky Thorn. And so, without even wanting to, he had changed to please her. But he knew that if he kept changing to please her, she would not consider changing to please him.

More importantly, the idea of how he could live his life—of the help he could give Corky and Evan and Harold—would have to change forever if he was with her. And there was one final factor to consider: he would do Annette a disservice if he married her. Why? Because as much as he wanted her, now in the deepest part of his being he knew he did not love her and that she did not love him. So if anything happened between them, he was culpable, not she. So, knowing this, knowing they would destroy each other—knowing now that she was wilful, spoiled and vain, all as he had to do was say "no."

How did Annette know where he was that night? People long after said it was Lonnie Sullivan who'd kept an eye on him and told her where to find him. Lonnie knew this about human nature: that they who pretend friendship often want most to destroy the luck you have and take it for themselves. He knew that the two men he could get to tattle on Ian were his own uncles. It was a Wednesday night—and Lonnie had discovered where Ian had gone: to a place overlooking the great river, to be alone.

At this particular moment, Ian's life spread out before him in an unerring way: the sawmill, the lumber, the expansion to a new warehouse, the idea of constructing houses; all of this was possible with Corky and Evan—and possible too with Harold, for Ian had not forgotten him. And as he stood looking out over the river at this moment—a quarter past eight on a white spring evening—he was secure. And Sara was, in fact, that beacon that made him secure. That is, without her he had no idea what might or might not happen.

Ian was standing at the opposite end of the field just beyond the last lane, down near Sky Town, staring at the great river where the evening swept over the black water and lights were coming on in the distance. He was smoking a cigarette and looking out into the darkness as the great ship the *Liverpool Star* came into the channel and was now dropping anchor.

Suddenly she stood beside him, both of them looking at the same great ancient river and the great blackened ship with its deck lights looking like a separate city. Suddenly Annette was there, and he knew it without glancing her way. They stood for a while in silence. Then she asked, quickly, almost broken-heartedly, "Are you looking at the same river I am?"

"Yes," he said.

"I know," she said, "I know you are!"

Both of them were again silent. She stood close to him so that the back of her left hand touched the back of his right, and he trembled slightly. Neither of them moved.

"Let me see your mark," she said. She held up the hand cut by the coloured glass and he held up his. She placed her scar against his, so that they fit almost perfectly. Then she said, "I have to go."

He almost turned and went in the other direction, toward Injun Town and Sara, but he did not. He caught up to her and told her to slow down. She seemed terribly upset and he didn't want that—and the feeling that would become the signature of his life came over him now: a heavy feeling of remorse and guilt.

"Where are you going?" he asked. He saw that she was crying.

"Down to my cottage," she said.

It was an old clapboard shed separated from the other cottages by a wild beach fringed by wood, and it rested out on a point of the bog. It was a cottage, however, and she had used it as such in the summers since she'd been a girl. In fact, back then she would not let him near it.

Now she told him she had to take some fuses and open the place—that she had been waiting to do this for a week and had to go now.

Ian told her it was too late and there might still be snow on the camp lane. "Why don't you go tomorrow?" he asked.

"Because I'm morning and afternoon at Cut and Curl."

They walked together back across the field with the wind blowing, toward the old hotel and post office looking, like so many other places, vanquished and deserted in the once-proud town.

At the edge of the field, Annette took off her shoes and walked barefoot over to her car.

"Well, I guess I'm on my way," she said. She turned away from him impatiently, angrily. Her eyes were sharp and black as coal.

She said, "You love tormenting me so I can't think straight. Do you want me to have to say I want you? That's what you want. Stop following me and go away, why don't you? Go back to her!"

Stung by this, he heard himself saying, "No—push over and I will drive."

He would, as the years came and went—flew by, actually, from this moment—never know why he'd said this impulsive thing.

She herself, in her white skirt and blouse, was in fact trembling— thinking strangely how this would be a disaster. And she knew her temper and her self-will would cause this disaster.

Yet both of them were unable to say no.

And somehow Ian knew already, for a fleeting half-second, that once this betrayal happened, his life would be over. That is, he knew he should never think that what was forbidden was somehow not forbidden. Both of them, in their own ways, realized this.

She was betraying Sara Robb as much as he was. The idea was that not only was this clandestine but, by its very nature, it lessened Sara's humanity, and made them both feel devious. They did not— and would never—say this. It was to them not important to say it, because they would bring furious voice to what they wanted to hide, and what they must end up doing. Those questions could and would all come later, after it was over. Then, as much as they wanted to, they would neither be able to love each other the way they needed, nor escape the attachment that they had formed.

My point is that what Ian and Annette did was not considered much of a betrayal by some of my students—not until I pointed out the minutiae of how it had happened and chronologically set it up in the way I have just described, and so allowed them to temper their feelings about sexual freedom with what liberty actually is and what it allows. Still, in doing this, some thought I was ponderously old-fashioned. A "square daddy-o," as one person said to me. And in those old rooms at Saint Michael's University, where a certain brand of radicalism disguises many kinds of youthful self-delusion, I was seen as an outsider. Well, yes—as I have always been.

Annette's car was small, the seats sunken. She did not push all the way over, so they sat very near to each other. And that perfume, Evening Surprise, that Ian so delighted in, lingered—not because of the perfume but because of who wore it.

They drove off along the dark highway toward the little pedestrian cottage by the small inlet beyond Bartibog. He remembered her father putting the run to him when he'd come to see her one afternoon with a few wildflowers in his hand, the flowers dropping and falling as he walked. He had been fourteen then. He'd loved her then and had watched her walk past him in her two-piece bathing suit. Now he was driving her down to this elusive place—which was simply an old clapboard camp that had been moved to the edge of the water by her family years ago. Nothing at all special about it—homely and vacant it had sat—except that it belonged to her.

The roadway to the place itself was filled with ruts and puddles, and so they parked halfway down and journeyed on foot the rest of the way. She walked ahead of him—enticing him by not looking back. The waves, warm and cluttered, could be heard on the shore.

The cottage lay bleak against an old bog that was still fissured with slivers of ice. It existed in a kind of squalor, imitative of what other cottages were, and in defiance of others' whims and fancy.

It was called "Earned My Leisure."

Out beyond the point was a small island and the lights of the far shore. The cottage was surrounded by the sound of those insolent waves and the continual noise of washed-up derelict boards. They stood a moment—both pretending to each other that they were doing something ordinary and innocent. The wind blew and they saw the scrape of an old bird nest in a dying tree.

She fumbled about in the dark, beside the broken steps. The wind caught and lifted her skirt, and she seemed too preoccupied to notice. Finally she apologized, told him she couldn't find the key to the door and asked him to help her through a window.

He found a stick to wedge under, opened it finally and helped lift her through. She put her legs up over his shoulders.

It was the first time he had ever really touched her.

Once in the cottage she ran to open the door, the running itself more proof of something covert. She was out of breath, and taking his hand asked him to help her up the loft ladder, where the fuse box was. They went up the loft together, she before him. He placed the fuses in, but when he went to push the handle, she said, "Please—don't turn it on yet. I have to ask you something. I know—but I want you to under-stand—that I like Sara and I think we have to realize what it is—"

This made him brave and important. He pushed her back against the wall and lifted her short skirt up over her panties.

"No," she said. "Lie down here."

"What if I am pregnant—what will we do?" she said later, almost instantly, as if it had been the question she was asking even at the river, when they stared out at the *Liverpool Star*—or even before then, when she'd looked up at him over the tea leaves at Sara Robb's; a question not only in response to the fact that they were lying on the old mattress in the upstairs loft.

"I—I am not sure—if—"

"No, you came inside," she whispered. "You know you did, as soon as I moved my hips!"

It sounded like a scold, a small moral scold, something to hold against him and sober him up, and they were silent.

But then she added, "I have been with almost no men myself, so do not think I have—please."

And in that she was being truthful. But he could not look at her. A feeling of shame came over both of them, and into the entire room, as they sat up to put on their clothes.

"How do you know you are naked?" God asked Adam and Eve. Strangely, both thought of this old lesson as they dressed.

Ian sat in his house after this night, shaken by what he had done. Perhaps, he decided, it would all blow over, be a fling and nothing more. He felt a dislike for Annette now—and he tried to take stock of himself. Yet he knew he should not feel dislike for her but for himself. Still, in some small way—in the way they had closed the cottage up and silently and quickly walked back to the car without looking at each other—both of them seemed terrified. The only thing he was good at was fixing appliances, and he should stick to that, he told himself, because he knew there were two more stores coming, Venieux's and Foggarty's, and those stores would have clients too. That is, just as he had been certain of his life while staring out at the *Liverpool Star*, now everything seemed disjointed and clouded.

The next day, he could not go to work. And late in the afternoon his old-fashioned doorbell turned. It was Sara in her new summer dress, the sun in her eyes, smiling at nothing, filled with joy. That night when he went along Pleasant Street he saw Corky at the lights by the bank, and turned up the street before he reached him. He knew Corky had seen him, and this knowledge filled him with dread.

———

A few nights later, they had the engagement party. Sara's mother had saved her money and gone to Moncton with Ethel two days before, and had bought Ian a set of expensive screwdrivers. The delight on her face, and on Ethel's, when they gave him this present magnified his treachery.

Diane was seated beside Annette and had her own hair brushed back from her forehead, mimicking Annette, making her own eyes small and severe. She smiled at Sara and said, "Oh my God, you look so sweet, sweet enough to eat!"

By now the rumours had started. Ian knew this. But they were still only rumours, and some of the men looked at him now as being luckier than they were. This should not complicate matters—in future years, Ian thought, it would simply be known that he'd had an affair, a little fling, and life would go on.

But soon Diane and her husband, Clive, were saying that Annette and Ian were deeply in love. For Diane, deep love, true love, had to do with scandal and opposition and ruin. It had since she was a girl, not only in the magazines that exploited this but in the human forums, where it took great shape, like small little ghostly forms of erotica at any given time. You cheated and you were cheated on—that was Romance. That is what love was for Diane, and that is what it was for many other people in those long-ago days. Oh yes, there was also a feeling of remorse that clung to it all—that would show up now and again, among the old weeds at the sides of brown houses, but overall, the feeling of scandal and ruin that might attend someone who was never a part of the scandal themselves was an exciting one. And as things would have it, this was the feeling of many of my students, who said I was making far too much of a piece of tail, a roll in the hay—and one or two questioned my own life of lapsed morals.

The fact, however, remained: Sara was left alone during most of her own engagement party, and came to the realization that the town knew something about her that she herself was unaware of. She thought it was about her leg, and that she had been made fun of—for to have an affliction seemed always to alarm others in a strange way. There was a moment when all her guests were dancing, the music was loud, and she realized she did not want to get up on the floor—even when Corky begged her to. It was not her own concern that embarrassed her; it was the concern of others.

So the next day when she saw Ian, she stood up straight and said, "Look—I think it's improving. What do you think?" And she began to walk toward him—trying to walk as straight and natural as possible. But suddenly she faltered, her step slowed, and she smiled timidly.

Suddenly Corky did not want to speak to Ian. And Sara did not know why.

Over the next few weeks the rumours became heavier—rumours stating that Ian was really in love with Annette Brideau, that he had used Sara to get reacquainted with his old flame, and in doing so, he was despised. That is, the reverse of what had actually happened now settled in people's thoughts. And yet to call him innocent in any of this was preposterous. And he knew this. He also knew he sometimes felt toward Annette something akin to rage. And she must have felt the same toward him. So if this was betrayal, I told my students, this is how it felt.

Annette telephoned Ian every evening after work. Sometimes he no more than got inside the door and the phone would ring; at other times the phone would be ringing when he got to the front steps.

"What are we going to do?" Annette would ask. "You haven't told her?"

"No, of course not. I don't know. Why didn't you come to me last year?"

But Annette told him that last year he wouldn't have looked at her.

"That's a complete lie," he said. But it was a lie he was willing and able to believe because he wanted to remain as he was to her. The secret, clandestine nature of their liaison—known by everyone—seemed to him unique, and beguiled him into thinking it was more than real, that true love was always hidden and covert, like in the movies he had never seen.

Suddenly Ripp VanderTipp came to see him, and gave him a fresh salmon. "For you," Ripp said.

Then one afternoon Lonnie phoned him, asked him how he was and if he needed any of the copper tubing he had taken from the old reservoir.

Of course Ian did not need the old copper tubing, but was startled that Lonnie too was suddenly his friend. That is, Lonnie looked upon him now as an equal.

"You did well. You did so well. I always knew you would," Lonnie affirmed. "Watch those other two—they is jealous of you now. You knows who I mean—Harold and Evan! They talk behind your back all the time. Say the worse terrible things about you—and I take up for you—say you stole what you got. I say it looks good on them is what I say. You just did right to fool them."

"But I didn't fool anyone," Ian said.

"Oh, I know that—but the two of them had it comin'!" Then Lonnie paused and said, "The only one who ever really and truly stood up for you down this end of the river is Annette Brideau—she was always a tiger if anyone said anything against her Ian!"

The next night that Ian went to visit Sara (bringing over the salmon that Ripp had left him), her mother asked to read his tea leaves. And Ian blushed and said he did not feel comfortable with this. He had, in fact, gone there to see if the relationship with Sara could be saved, to admit what had happened, and hoped to resolve it. He wanted to talk to Sara alone, but he couldn't seem to find a way. His courage failed him and he looked guiltily around the room.

"No, I don't want my fortune read," he answered.

"Why? I want to know how many children you and Sara will have."

"Never mind it now," he said. "It's bad luck, I think!"

Sara said nothing. However, she knew; she had known for two weeks. She simply smiled at him and said, "Some other time, then."

Sara's mother was bitter, however. After he left, she grumbled at Sara, as if, after all this time, Sara had done something to displease him and destroy the relationship.

"Well, there you go—there you go! Such a fine man too," she kept saying, fidgeting and coughing. "It's your leg, and that's the end of it!"

Of course, Sara's mother wanted the marriage because it would free her daughter, and in some mysterious way it would free her as well. So she gave in to her weakness to be like others and say what others did. And what others were now saying was that "one look at Annette and Sara was a memory!"

The rumours Sara heard could not be substantiated, and no one told her much, but the actions of those around her did.

Ethel became silent, her expression perplexed—as if the warning Corky had given, and that she had not heeded, had come true, and this seemed to have stunned her into silence. For little ugly Corky Thorn, who everyone teased, was the oracle people should have heeded. And she remembered him that one day, walking off through the puddles in the rain.

After this, Annette stopped showing up at the Robb house. After this, she was not seen. And it was, as is usual in these cases, Sara herself who felt she must have done something wrong: she must have insulted her friend, and if she could make it up by taking the blame, things would return to that happy state they had once been in. Yes, it was because of the bridesmaid's dress, and how Annette didn't like it; they'd had countless discussions about it—that must be it. She phoned Annette twice and asked her to visit. And Annette said she would visit, and then did not show up. So Sara phoned again and said, "Annette, I know it's troublesome having a friend like me—not many would put up with me."

"Don't be so damn foolish," Annette said.

Ethel too spoke about the silly bridesmaid's dress. For she and Sara had to make it all about that in order for things to remain how they had been, and for Sara to remain in love with the man she loved and have that man respect and love her.

So then, on a rainy afternoon, Sara walked up to Cut and Curl and stepped into the smoky cloying room. Annette had a woman's hand soaking in creme, and looked up startled and unforgiving. Suddenly Sara had done her a grave injury—that was the import of the look. Sara trembled. She was not used to having her only friend hate her.

The warm wind blew as she went back outside. She thought, after a while, of the hundreds of dollars she had given Annette for the brides-maid's dress. Worse than anything else, she felt like a fool. As she walked down the street, Ethel ran out to meet her, and suddenly saw Sara's face, devastated. She had been weeping since she'd left the beauty par-lour—and all Annette and Diane had done the week before to make her pretty, to make her more like them, had been sapped away.

Ethel was not good at fixing things. And she did not know what to do.

She walked up to Ian's large house but didn't go to the door. She simply stood outside looking at it, then turned and rushed back home.

Then she phoned Molly Thorn—now married to Evan Young—and asked her to come to Sara's aid. She was trying her best to help, but this in itself seemed a defeat. Molly and Ethel decided to try to make Sara into a brand new person. But this was a futile hope, and the attempt only made Annette furious with Molly and Molly's brother, Corky, who was Ethel's boyfriend, and Evan Young himself.

"Love is love and you can't change it," Diane said romantically.

"Shut up, DD—please, for God's sake, just shut up," Annette said.

Molly told her husband she had a premonition.

"What kind?"

"This is going to destroy us all in some terrible way."

"Don't be so goddamn silly," Evan said. "Go pray to the Virgin Mary and all your troubles will be over. I remember when Ethel was a little girl, she found an icicle shaped like the Virgin Mary and tried to save it—but lo and behold it melted in the sun—maybe you could look and find another one."

But Molly was sure that betrayal was a cannibal and ferociously devoured anyone and anything it could. That it would, as a cannibal, turn someday on Annette herself—and yes, very likely on foolish Ian Preston as well.

Soon even Ethel left off trying, and Sara was alone. That is, totally alone. No one wanted to speak to her. And when she went into her house, her mother busied herself in the kitchen, and Ethel ran upstairs and hid. Worse, she thought back to that horrible day, which she could barely remember, when she and Ethel were talked into going down to the chip yard—the chips looking like gold in the sunlight—to see the prince. Could it be that people had heard about it—could it be that? Could it be that Ian was worried about . . . ?

The weather turned cold and rainy, and the small garden was saturated, and the round snowball flowers shook in the wind. Sara decided to do things for herself and showed up at Ian's work in the pouring rain a week or so before the wedding date, her face less filled with pain or anger than sorrow. He had not returned her calls for the past three nights, and yet everything to do with the wedding was proceeding. So she had to know. And she was shaking, her legs trembling. She reflected on how ordinary he was, how small his ambition really was, and how fine she knew her own mind was—and this made what was happening all the more poignant.

"I love you," she said. She blushed, strangely feeling that what she had just said was inappropriate. He smiled slightly and then his face went blank. That was because he realized this was her last desperate gambit to save their relationship—and that, in fact, it had come to this.

"It's all right if you like Annette," Sara said, speaking rapidly. "I like her too—and if you fell a little in love with her, that's okay as well. She makes everyone love her, everyone give her money, has everyone do everything for her—that's the way it is. But I think we have to protect her too—it's our responsibility to protect and love her so she doesn't do something terrible. You know, just between us, I think she's been involved in things—you know she doesn't want to be and is scared, but something is troubling her. I don't want to say this," Sara said, and as people who are rarely spiteful do, she now sounded dreadful when she spoke, "but you know, more than once she stole money from me. I didn't want to tell you—and I think it was because she owed Lonnie Sullivan. She told me once she owed him $5,300 and everything. So, we know how he is. And once she took a deposit from the Motor Vehicle Branch where her dad worked—Harold Dew took the blame and then she left Harold as soon as you got the money. For you see," and here she looked around and whispered, "she asked me how much you made—she did!" She nodded to affirm the veracity of her statement just as someone left the store.

"Stop gossiping now. All those stories are nonsense! You don't think I know?" Ian said. "Fifty-three hundred dollars—what nonsense. Lonnie is her friend—and I guess he is my friend too. I never thought I'd hear a girl like you talk like that. For God's sake—go away if you are going to talk like that in front of my customers. I have a business to run."

And as he said this, Sara knew she would never marry him, that she could not; that whatever it was between them was destroyed; that he was who he was, and she was who she was. And that he had made a desperate mistake, and she had not.

He looked away from her and then he said something he never forgave himself for: "Don't worry, I'll still give Corky the job he wants even if I don't marry you! So Molly and Evan should be happy. We'll get them in business too, so Evan won't be going around talking about me behind my back just like you are doing behind Annette's. Hell, I thought I had friends, but I guess real friends are hard to come by. It's best to remain unaffiliated."

Sara looked startled, and then she turned and walked away, dragging her left leg as she did, like a little girl.

The next night Corky came to the store. He said he couldn't take the job with the siding, that he could not help repair the relationship between Ian and Evan that they had spoken about because he'd decided he might go out west to work. He apologized.

Ian nodded and didn't answer. He felt ashamed.

Corky went toward the door and opened it. Standing outside, under the awning, he said, "I wouldn't have minded working here, though. I could have helped you real good! You and Evan would have been best buds again. If you don't watch it—well, you have to expand or lose. That's what I was hoping to help you with."

"Well, why don't you still?" Ian said, smiling weakly.

"You know she gave up her scholarship," Corky answered, tears in his eyes. "Now, I don't know what a scholarship is—but I know that is what she gave up!"

Ian had not known. That is, he had not known about the scholarship at all.

———

After this, Annette stopped calling him. So he telephoned her. She said she had heard the wedding was called off. He said he did not know one way or the other.

"Is it me?" she asked. "People better not think that!"

She asked him to write a letter to her, explaining that he was the instigator of their relationship and affair, that it was he who had wanted to leave Sara, and that she, Annette, had tried to prevent it, that she was the one who had arranged the engagement party.

So he was struck dumb.

Then Lonnie Sullivan telephoned him, saying he worried about Annette's overall health—that she might kill herself. She might jump from a bridge; that's what he was most fearful of. "Do you know she was ill as a little girl? I got her to Moncton when she was thirteen. Probably saved her life, knowing me. So there you go. Something with her blood in her fingers or something. Now she falls in love— but thinks you only took what you wanted and don't love her. She is really desperate. I'm afraid of what might happen. That bridge looks awful enticing when you are depressed. You couldn't act like that, could you, Ian?"

"Act like what?"

"You know, hurt that little girl," Lonnie said. "I look upon her as my own!"

Now Ian was plagued by the residual effects of his duplicity—and he was burdened by phone calls telling him his unfaithfulness had created a victim not only of Sara but of Annette. So now he was pressured toward something—some masterful untruth, some golden lie like the veins of fool's gold he'd seen that night up on Good Friday Mountain.

That evening he decided to do what Annette wanted. He wrote the letter. Now more than ever he was plagued with the idea that Annette and he had been destined to meet again, and that meeting Sara had only allowed this destiny.

He was still torn about what he should do when Lonnie came to his house and stood inside the foyer. His face pensive and somehow sad, he looked at an old painting on the wall that Ian had bought in support of the Heritage Foundation. He could only stay for a minute. It was raining; his hat was spotted with grease, his white shirt open, a cigar in his pocket. He was out of breath too and had to wait a moment before he spoke. He looked at Ian with great sorrow, and within the bones of this sorrow was a kind of historical dislike for Ian and his family.

Ian looked beyond him, into the yard, and saw Ripp VanderTipp sitting in his truck. And as Ian was looking at that person he detested, Lonnie told him that Annette was pregnant. Lonnie and VanderTipp were at his house because it was a terrible thing, and she needed all of them now more than ever. They had come as a reckoning. Ripp was especially upset, Lonnie said.

"That poor little girl got herself in some fix. If you just go off marrying someone else, what will become of her? That's what Ripp is so worried about—a man has to do the honourable thing. That's all Ripp talked about on the way up here."

Lonnie stood there for another ten minutes speaking, but Ian did not hear what he said. Then Lonnie gave him a note from Annette.

She asked to meet Ian downriver and so he went. She was in DD's car at the end of the old road that led to her cottage. When she saw him, she flicked the lights. He ran up to her and saw she was crying; desperation and self-pity had overwhelmed her. At this moment he knew he must—had to—choose her or Sara.

The next day he went to see Annette at work, with a dozen roses. As he entered, a few of her friends were tittering. Annette, not knowing he was there, was imitating how Sara walked across the beauty shop floor.

———

Suddenly and quietly, Ian and Annette married.

Molly went to Sara's to let her know that this was about to take place—to prepare her. Molly tried to say something positive, and to be spiteful toward Annette—but she had no more real ability to do so than Sara.

"We are all in trouble," Molly said. "I do not know why—but life now is upside down, and will remain so for years. My husband is a changed man, and Harold is changed too. What has become of them?"

Corky Thorn paced the room, and finally, seeing the expensive set of screwdrivers that Mrs. Robb and Ethel had saved for and picked out for Ian Preston, broke down and cried.

But there was one reason for this marriage happening, beyond all other reasons: Ian's self-will demanding that he do it, and telling him if he did not do it, he would lose out on the person he had loved since high school—and that it was inevitable, because he had loved her in high school. And since he had been waiting for her to love him, he could not let this pass him by. He had been spurred on when she rejected him, and this became the spur that proved his worth to her—and Sara was but the route that determined how she, Annette, who he truly loved, would come into his life again.

In fact, feeling guilty, this is what he tried to explain to his old friends Corky and Molly, and he became stern with them as he did so—even self-righteous, telling them they had better understand that Annette was not at fault.

Annette tried to smile for photos and make her wedding day the best of all days. She wore white with blue sequins and Diane was her maid of honour. And because the wedding was so rushed and there was no time to consider anyone else, Lonnie Sullivan was Ian's best man.

Before the marriage, Sara wrote Ian a letter where she returned the diamond ring (though he had never asked her to). He had bought Annette her own—she had picked it out with Diane.

Sara wrote: *My dear, dear Ian (my love). Ethel and I were sitting out in the back yesterday talking of all the good times and how much fun it all has been.*

Sara left town because of the very scandal, and delight in scandal, her wound had created. People could not help looking at her and showing this mirth even in their true sympathy, especially with Annette pregnant and showing.

Nor did Sara want such sympathy. For a long time she could not stand to see people who knew what had happened. That is, she was now plagued by this as never before. Whereas before, even when rebuffed in high school, she had always thought: Someday, someone will come along. And she had believed what her mother had told her in a reading when she was fifteen: "Someday you will meet someone who will love you for who you are!"

At the time Sara, of course, had said this did not matter to her, and nothing like marriage interested her at all. "Unlike Jane Austen," and she had laughed, "I don't think marriageability is the most important thing in the world to women!"

Now it seemed that both the tea leaves and what she had said were proven false.

Ian learned one day, when he asked after her months later, just before Annette was due, that she had borrowed some money and had gone to university.

"University?" he said, mystified that she had taken this step. It was a world neither he nor Annette would ever know. He now realized he was married to a woman who had no use for anything like that, and though she read a dozen books a month, each of these romance books were ones that told her she was right, she was acceptable, she was the one person entitled to love.

The rumour that had started earlier was even worse after he married: the unquenchable rumour that the child was not his. He went to Lonnie to talk to him about this, as a confidant, as his friend and his best man. "What do you think, Lonnie—who would spread such talk?"

Lonnie said only the cheapest of people would bother saying that, and shrugged, and looked away. Ripp VanderTipp was there that day, looking at Ian with incurious self-serving eyes.

Ian stared back at him and Ripp smiled, the gentle aloof smile of a thug.

There were other rumours as well. Ian heard these rumours—he could not help but hear.

Once, coming home late from work, seeing the house once again empty and his supper cold, Ian lifted a quarter out of his pocket and in a heavy moment, leaning against the iron rail, he said, "If it comes up tails, she has been unfaithful."

Their only son was born that December, well over twenty years ago now.

On that same night, Evan Young was trying desperately to save the life of his only boy.

PART FOUR

FROM THE TIME HE WAS ELEVEN YEARS OF AGE, EVAN "Lucky" Young had the kind of fortune that would seem to be everything to others and nothing to him. He swam the river when he was twelve; climbed out on the high tower at fifteen to clean up bird nests. He took dares to prove people's faith in him. He believed he must do this to have honour, and so he was honour-bound to do so. He joined the cadets, and he was knowledgeable and tough.

He thought of Ian as a brother, and protected him like one. He also got along with Harold, and considered him a brother as well. He believed to have honour he must not believe in God—for no honour-bound person would fall back on God. And he realized when he came up against many people who believed in God or the Divine that he shocked them, not only by his great strength and his great dares but his willingness to die without the security of what they themselves believed in, while they were not willing to die at all. He played the bagpipes in a sorrow-filled way at night among the dark shanties of Bonny Joyce. He had a feared reputation in a fight, and on more than one occasion thought of joining the military. He hitchhiked to town to see a recruiting officer, yet he did not join. Two days after this, Joyce Fitzroy asked him to take his money, and he did not do that either.

This, to Evan, proved his greatness of feeling and temperament. He had amassed a good deal of knowledge about heroes, from Marshal Zhukov to Churchill, and realized a terrible truth: that he was, or could be, as great as any of them. He was a brilliant marksman, and in a fight he never cowered but became resolute.

Certainly he had a command and a presence about him that other men recognized and other people followed. So he knew he could prove himself to be as great as other men he had read about, men on a battlefield or stranded in a desert. And he knew he was as great as the Jameson brothers, Will and Owen—both legends here. And in each moment of imagining this, he saw his little brother, Ian, with him. Because he saw in Ian a spirit not unlike his own.

Molly was, of course, perceptive enough to understand what may have occurred far back in his childhood, and why he now hated the church, but Evan would not admit that anything had happened—he only wished to denigrate that which he found both odious and absurd.

"There is, and never has been, a thing in Catholicism worth saving," he said.

This was his view before he and Molly were married, and became much more pronounced than she ever thought it would be afterwards. On the day of the marriage he did not speak to the priest except to say his vows, and to her shame refused communion at his own wedding—the only one in the church to do so.

The truth was, she was far more tolerant of his denial than he ever was of her acceptance.

Men who are fortunate enough to have size and charisma at their fingertips are often unaware that they possess anything special, and waste what they have before they realize it can be wasted. They see the world through a gaze that is blessed, and from a point where others look at them in awe, and they see nothing strange about this. But each one of these men and women find, sooner or later, a wall in their soul they cannot climb.

The fact is, Evan proved to be limited—and he was limited in a fatal way, which he did not know for some time. That is, all his life Evan would try to escape Lonnie Sullivan, just like those others who worked for Lonnie, but he could not seem to do so. And he believed after a while that it was the oath of loyalty to his blood brothers that caused this. For what had happened to his blood brothers? Where were they now?

Somewhere along the line Evan's reputation stopped growing, and he became less than people thought he might; his bagpipes put away and his kilt soiled against the rain. And this decline started when he believed Ian Preston cheated him.

The one thing Evan "Lucky" Young wanted was the Will Jameson land—that land that had once belonged to the Jamesons in the 1940s.

Yet, as we know, when Young went that late Monday afternoon to ask old man Fitzroy for the money for the land, the money had already been given away.

"Who did you give it to, then?" Lucky asked.

"Yer buddy Ian Preston—you know him, he just was here yesterday. I didn't know what to do—he pressured me—he came in and pressed me down for it," the old man said. He said this because he suddenly felt both guilty and cheated, and didn't want to be blamed for being a sucker.

Initially Young did not blame Preston so much as himself. He felt his friend would not cheat him.

But then he heard that Ian had deliberately gone to get the money, and had taken it home in a large bag and sat with it, staring at it open-mouthed. He heard Ian had phoned the banks and told them of his triumph, and gloated about it. That Ian had done this to him was so contrary to what they had spoken about when they had been stranded on the mountain that long-ago night, it was impossible for Evan to reconcile one act with the other. Soon after, he could not stand to hear Ian's name— in fact, just as he cringed or guffawed when he heard God's name or the name of a saint, now he had the exact same feeling about Ian.

What was very strange was an event that happened soon after this.

Remembering how Sydney Henderson had worked with them on the log cut, Evan took some of the deer chop from his recent hunt with Ian down to Henderson's house. He did this because he wanted to see the man and how he lived; now more than ever, he could not believe any man would live in such a deliberate state of denial. Yet when he saw that it was true, he couldn't help but be even angrier.

"Syd, I will never hurt my wife like you hurt yours—living here in the worst place on the river and trying to bring up kids while everyone takes advantage—no one will hurt my wife or kids, and no one will take advantage of me. It's a poor man who has to trust in God as much as you! There is no fun in your life—you have been repressed by that which you now cling to." Evan looked determined as he said this, and stared straight at the man, hoping for a bad reaction.

Why he was so furious at this man, Sydney Henderson, who had done him no wrong, he did not know—nor could he be rational about it. He even wanted Sydney, who had given up all violence, to take a swing at him, just to prove that he could provoke him. But he could not get him to. So he said again, "The church has repressed you, and made your children slaves to dickless priests!"

"My only caution is that blood brothers are not to be relied upon," Sydney said. "And," he continued, "high seriousness is always out of fashion until fashion changes, and I have as much fun as you. Still, if you can advance a theory that is greater than that advanced by Christ, I will believe what you have just said. If not, you should be wary. You might make promises to yourself about your own wife and child that you cannot keep."

"You know nothing about it—nothing about us. Go back to your stupid church!" Evan yelled. And he felt desperate and went home and brooded in the back shed. He thought of Sydney's children listening to his outburst—the young boy, Lyle, looking at him in silence and consternation—and he felt terribly ashamed

And that moment was the beginning of his ill-luck. Because he could no longer think of the majesty of his friend but saw only what others saw: his small-mindedness and tight-fistedness. If he wants money that bad, let him swallow it, Evan thought.

Evan travelled the river to find a bank that would help him, and he sat in their offices, from Doaktown to Neguac. But as with Ian, no bank would offer money to him. Here he sat in his workboots. Here he sat in his blue shirt. Here he sat with his ragged tie askew, and here he sat in work pants pressed to look new.

He married Molly Thorn without his dream of a lumberyard or contracts, or any other thing he'd promised himself he would have when he proposed. The one thing he had counted on had not come to pass. He had spent half his life dreaming about something that was not going to happen—and he was exactly like Harold in that regard, yet he felt he had been far more honourable than Harold to all concerned. Evan and Molly married, and he was obligated to work hard and to earn little, and there was no money for the land. He'd had no money for a diamond either.

They lived in the small house that was surrounded by its share of spruce and birch trees. In winter the snow lit on the back shed, and sunlight struck the panes of glass. He spent the summer fishing and trying to save money—desperate never to work for Sullivan again. But coming unto a year after Ian had bought his store, Evan's fortunes had sunk to nothing.

And so Evan had to go back and wait in the office, near the huge red box of tools that Sullivan kept, as Sullivan had his lunch of tea and tomato sandwiches. Sullivan said nothing to him as he ate, and downed his food with hot tea, and looked at the racing form from Charlottetown.

Mr. Sullivan said work was slow and didn't give him back his job. He looked at Evan as if Evan had done a great wrong, and this great wrong was simple: he was now no longer the boy he had been, no longer Lucky. And Sullivan looked as if Evan had personally injured him, and sighed whenever he saw him coming.

———

Evan tried to insulate his place, and made sure his wife was taken care of as best he could. But the winter was hard. Each piece of insulation he put in by hand between the beams of his little house ripped at his heart. Worse, people who didn't know of their falling-out spoke to Evan about how well Ian Preston was now doing. He went into the woods so as not to hear about his former friend and how successful he was. And in the woods, to be away from Ian's fortune, he began again to take up trapping. But there was another dimension to this agony. Molly was happy— content with so little; having him and the boy, Jamie, was all she wanted in the world—and this simple happiness plagued him, because it seemed to him a betrayal. Why didn't she feel like he did? And so he took to being angered with her so she would feel like he did. Sometimes, knowing she was only trying to be kind, she would try to tease him out of his bad mood. Once he came close to striking her he was so upset. Another time he threw a beer against the wall and left the house.

"How could Ian have done this!"

Yes, I will kill him, he thought one night. And that seemed to settle it.

One day he said this: "I will get the money back—I promise you that."

"What money?" she asked.

"Money—DON'T YOU UNDERSTAND! The money that your God seems to delight in keeping from me."

"Why are you talking so silly?"

"We will see how silly. No one will cheat me—not Ian and not you."

"How did I cheat you?"

"You cheated me too!" he yelled, exasperated. And this was overheard, and people became aware that they were an unhappy man and wife.

But he was determined to get back every cent that he felt Ian had taken from him. He began to work himself to exhaustion, doing what- ever he could for Sullivan, whenever Sullivan did decide to call on him. Then, to make ends meet, over the next two years he trapped beaver and marten along the left bank of Arron all the way to upper Little Hackett Brook, and used Leg Hold and Conibear.

There, he spent his days off alone, trying to get enough pelts to do him. A good marten pelt would bring him two hundred dollars, a mink one-hundred and twenty, beaver, though more abundant, much less. He kept imagining how much money he would make if he could just find the right method—that someday he would be rich and Ian would be poor—and that is what he wanted most of all. That is, not just for him to be rich, but for Ian to be poor.

So he went trapping and guiding, and even prospecting, up on Good Friday.

Trapping was dangerous work, for Evan was in deep wood alone in winter and without a vehicle. He carried his traps on his back and sometimes broke ice against the brooks to lay them down in a pattern near the water's edge. He worked as his great body was meant to, and that was all there was to it.

Still, if anything happened Molly would have no way to find him, and her nerves were bad. They became worse as the days bled away. She did not know why Evan was so consumed with money, or why he hated Ian, who now had it. Often she lay in bed alone and Evan would sleep on the cot in the kitchen—and sometimes, exhausted, he would sleep on the floor.

Every Sunday she went to church. To her, taking the Host—that piece of bread that Evan and millions laughed at, and millions upon millions never heard of—was the most significant event in her day. To Evan it was more than just a silly superstition; it was deeply offensive and hypocritical. Did she not know how he felt? Yes, she must know—so then, it was an offence against him that she perpetrated. He showed her an article that a nun who had left the convent had written, who talked about the greed, hypocrisy and sexual frustration of the women there—and how finally she and a priest had an affair.

"What do you think of that?"

"We all know sex is not a bad thing," Molly replied. "Nor can everyone keep the vow of chastity. Yet if there are those who wish to and fail, it doesn't mean their wish was absurd or the church wrong in asking it. It is asked freely and accepted freely—and not everyone can do so. It seems everyone nowadays talks about sex not being a big thing—and a private matter, until someone else falters and they hoot and laugh as if they are schoolboys seeing their first titty."

But her answer, given while she looked at him straightforwardly, only frustrated Evan enough that he threw the article across the room.

Sometimes he would naïvely bait her: "Is there gold in heaven? I mean, not everywhere—but in the streets?"

He disliked it when she spoke of the Virgin or saints. To him, the Virgin could not have remained a virgin. This is what he told her.

"How could she remain a virgin?"

"Because she did."

"How?"

"Because of God."

"In what way?"

"In a way God decided."

"Well, that's a pretty neat trick."

"It was no trick."

"I wish I could discover his method."

"His method is as beyond you as heaven is to earth," Molly said, hopefully, because she had been taught to say this. And she smiled at her own cleverness. "Mr. Fitzroy always prayed to the Virgin Mary," she reminded him.

"Ya, look what good it did—he gave his money to a cheat who stole from us!"

"We can't be sure—"

"I can be sure. I can be sure. Maybe the Virgin told him to give his money to a cheat—so, my my, sweetie-pie, your Virgin is a robber. Going out and about robbing people. That's what she is—a bandit!"

"No—but I am sure she told Fitzroy to go in the right direction when he found and saved Sara and Ethel that day."

"And how do you know?"

"Because that is who Sara was praying to at the time!"

Again he told her the story of Ethel—the little one who believed she had found the Virgin Mary in an icicle and tried to take it home, and it melted in her hands. He laughed loudly at this. But what he did not say was how he himself had taken the icicle and had tried to keep it intact for the child because she seemed in such wonder. And afterwards Ethel had said, "Never mind—I got to see her for a moment—and that's what she wanted and allowed."

He did not tell Molly that.

If anything, it pleased him to hate—it was a superb way to be intellectually, and even morally, superior to his wife, without committing to anything, and it gave him an aura of instant mockery, which he knew troubled her terribly. But in order to have this state of instantaneous mockery, he had to in some way live with it, and prove its rightness to her and to himself.

Once he crossed a lake in a thaw—just to prove to her that man was his own animal and there was no other animal than man! Goddamn— where had his life got to if he could not do what he had set out to do? This is what he insisted to himself as he crossed toward Darling Shore on the far side of the inlet.

"Someday you will cross and be frightened—I am sure of it," she said to him when he bragged to her about it.

And he answered, "I will go out for two days along the north branch and I will be back for supper on Wednesday—you can pray or not, it will not matter a good goddamn!"

"I will pray for you," Molly said.

"Why?"

"I have to, now that you've mentioned it."

"Do as you do," he said, "and I will do as I do! I need to do it, not that you seem to care—but I need to do it. If even one of my traps is sprung, we lose one hundred dollars we can't afford."

"I wish I could help more." Molly looked up. "But I do get twenty-five a week cleaning the altar."

"You should join that cult. That Sydney Henderson lad—he believes in all of that, and look where it got him now. Rumour says he murdered a kid on the bridge that collapsed out there—that will never be said about me."

"But I do not think Sydney would do that," she said.

"Well, what does it matter? He probably didn't, but most think he did—and why shouldn't they? He never was right in the head."

"But what if people said that about you—about your child?"

"I guarantee they never will!"

Molly kept telling him she wanted to move away—he might even try finding work at the warehouse in Moncton where her uncle worked. She wanted him to forget about Ian and the money, forget about how humiliated he was. And she herself wanted to forget about how Annette had married Ian.

"Life is no different than it should be," Evan told her. "I'd bet one million dollars that Corky would have been a drunk no matter what."

"Why?"

"Because you are driving me to being one. But Corky is weak and I'm not."

She came home with the job offer from Moncton, worth thirty thousand dollars a year. It wasn't bad, she said, and if she worked too, they would be fine. They could, after some time, buy a house and settle there. "Please?" she asked. "Think it over!"

Evan thought they were better off staying where they were. He would not be able to take Moncton. And he made fun of the Moncton boys who came up here in the summer to fly-fish, and of how poorly they cast a line. Did she want him to look like that?

So this is the way things stood with Evan a few years after Ian got Joyce Fitzroy's money. He could not have the name Ian mentioned in his house—and once he threw a man up against a camp wall because the man had asked him if Ian was doing well.

————

So the idea of being blood brothers had unravelled, it seemed, without Ian or Harold or Evan doing anything to unravel it. Not an ill intent had been formed to make ill intent blossom. Not a hard feeling existed before hard feelings swept them all—and none of them believed in anything but themselves.

With Harold Dew it was much worse than for the others. He still had to go to work each day for Lonnie Sullivan, who had many things on him and his family over the years. So his tie to Sullivan was even more binding than it was for the others, and he would wake in the cold at 6:20 in the morning and make his way, getting a drive to Grey's Turn with Jimmy Chapman's grader operator Sam Patch, and walk to the work pit of Lonnie Sullivan, who would sit in the office pondering over what to have him do. Mostly he acted as a repossesser of engines, and at times cars, which Lonnie took from people who could never pay what they owed him.

When Harold became depressed, Lonnie would commiserate. "They both did you wrong . . ."

"I know they both did me wrong. Of course they did—from the time I was in grade school!" Harold would shout. "You don't have to tell me!"

"Well, then, get even," Lonnie said, "rob the store and get even. I'd love to have some of that money back here." Then he would wink as if he was joking.

And this would scorch him—and sometimes, sitting in Lonnie Sullivan's office, tears would run down his cheeks.

So one day a few months after this, as he was sitting outside on an old half-burned couch listening to the snow and sleet fall on the porch roof above him, he too thought of Syd Henderson, who still clung after all this time to a God who could not care and did not know. Then he thought of how in their youth he and Evan and Ian had cut their fingers and proclaimed their state of honour against everything Syd believed, so as not to become like him. And then he thought: What had happened? What had happened in their own lives? He looked around him, and saw how little he had, and remembered everything: he and his blood brothers had planned nothing, but still Glen was dead; Annette was gone; and where was he compared with Syd at this moment? In fact, the truth was that Sydney was being looked upon as more and more heroic, and many now said he may not have been guilty of a thing, even though people had accused him of terrible things his whole life.

Whereas all of them—Ian, Harold and Evan—had wronged each other, and were certainly guilty.

Harold decided that he would wait, and strike Ian at another time. Then he thought of the other man who had betrayed him—his other blood brother, Evan, the one who had allowed Glen on the tower. He would do something to get even—just one more thing.

So it was at this time that someone began lifting Evan's traps. For some time Evan couldn't find out who was doing so. Then he realized it must be Harold Dew. Evan said this was childish, even for Harold, and fretted about what to do.

"All this has happened because Ian got some stupid money!" Molly said when Evan told her of his suspicions. "Harold was never like that before!"

"Oh, Harold would have acted this way anyway, wouldn't he?"

"No, your friendship kept him in check. But now things are terrible, and I am sure it's all because of Ian's trip to see Joyce Fitzroy."

"Yes, but you don't believe Ian is a cheat, do you? You're too Catholic and pure."

"I think he did cheat, but not over the money. I think he didn't even know about the money. I think he cheated Sara—and that came because of the money."

"Shut up," Evan said. "Shut up, shut up. He cheated us all—he wouldn't even have got off Good Friday Mountain if it weren't for me. I mean that and he knows it. He knows it—HE KNOWS IT!"

Still, the lifting of the traps continued into the next month, in the belligerent unthinking way cruelty has of showing one up, and Evan knew that this act of Harold's was about Glen. And though Harold believed him at fault, Evan knew he was innocent. He had done nothing but try to help (though he could not imagine or think this about Ian's actions toward him). Yet in all of this, he saw the peculiar limitations of revenge itself. That is, revenge was a false and vainglorious moral template that people fed on. And in his mind, here is how it worked: Evan could be angry at Ian—and rightfully so. But because of what had happened to Glen, he could not be angry with Harold—even though he, Evan, had tried to keep Glen alive. So Harold, seared by betrayal, needed revenge more than the other two. Evan too believed he needed revenge in a grand way—but against Ian.

Molly did not see this clearly; she only knew as Corky did, that nothing was now like it was supposed to be. Corky visited her and Evan often—upset that Ian had married Annette Brideau; upset that some people were saying it was a great coup, a victory. How in God's name, even if you did not believe in God, could that be a victory? Yet millions of people in the most diverse circumstances believe that cheating a friend is a victory.

Evan tried to forget about Harold's theft, and even moved both his mink and otter traps and put them high up toward Buckler Stream, though it took an extra half-day's walk.

On a particular morning twenty years ago, when it was snowing grey on the spruce, and the roads and paths were blurred, and the sky looked like late afternoon, Evan saw even from a distance that two of his traps had been sprung, close to Boiling Brook, near upper Hackett. He had moved them thirteen miles for nothing. This, I think, is what infuriated him.

That is, he had his mink and marten traps close to the water, and had laid them along a line over twenty yards, beside poplar shafts, and had lost the martens in them.

At first he thought it just might have been a coyote that had followed his line, until he saw in what direction the thief went.

He crossed the brook as ice broke around him, and moved into the trees above Little Hackett. It was strange how every part of the woods carried its own scent, its own history—even a bog of a hundred feet had an inestimable life. The bog here was dried by snow, and frozen and soundless.

He climbed the great hills to the south of Good Friday Mountain, and looked down at the small country road that stretches back from Arron Falls. And he could see distant houses, ramshackle dwellings in the middle of nowhere. The place was called Clare's Longing.

Evan decided it was better to get out of the woods and go down to the road and wait for the thief, who would probably appear within the next hour.

It was a small matter, one might say—but small matters are not unimportant, and in a year those two pelts would be part of a lovely fur hat. After a time, almost five years from the day Evan was watching this very road, that hat would find its way to Frenchies second-hand clothing store just up the highway from Ian's store. And that too would have a drastic consequence.

Evan waited, solitary and alone, more alone now than he ever had been, to get his two small black pelts back. He looked at his dark hands with the big wide thumbs and dragged on his smoke in silence, knowing he and Harold might come to blows and Harold was a tough man. But Evan was a tough man as well.

However, he saw no one come along that blank stretch of black icy road, and eventually he went home. He went home and sat for supper of homemade macaroni and cheese. And he rolled himself a cigarette and put the child on his knee. He knew Harold had seen him first and gone in another direction. Part of him said: Let this go—it is Harold and you used to be his friend, and he is desperate. But part of him would not or could not allow this. Being betrayed by a former friend before, he chose not to be betrayed again, no matter what Harold thought he had done.

After supper he went out and tried to fix the radiator in his car, the lantern hanging over the hood in accordance with a particular kind of destitution. There was a smell of raw metallic evening, a kind of tininess in the hollow frozen air around him now.

But the theft of the pelts bothered him. He could not let it go.

Perhaps he might have let it go in earlier days, before his luck went bad and before Ian had cheated him. But he knew that this would never have happened had his luck not deserted him.

He breathed in his cigarette's languid smoke then exhaled, watching it dissipate in the cold frost air. Putting the antifreeze on the kitchen counter with his tools, he told Molly he had to go out. He decided he would walk to Clare's Longing and take his pelts back—that is, if they were where he thought they would be: in Harold Dew's shed. And this is where he was *sure* they would be.

But that night of all nights, Molly herself had to go out. She couldn't take the child because she would not get out of planning the church's Christmas pageant until late, and then she'd go to her great-aunt's to sleep. So she told Evan he would have to be at home. She told him she had mentioned this to him many times over the last two weeks, but he had not heard. Before he could argue with her, the priest's grey comfortable Pontiac drove up to the door, and she waved to him and ran to catch the drive.

He always comes at the wrong time, and whatever time he comes is wrong. Evan thought. Goddamn old woman—what a way to spend a man's existence. Who knows what he does with them altar boys too!

He rolled himself a cigarette and had a beer. He stared across the small dining room, where a biography of General Montgomery sat. He had loved the military and he should have joined it—now his life was in tatters, and the love Molly and he had for each other had been stretched to the breaking point. He was afraid she would leave him, but he could not stop tormenting her because he himself was so tormented, and once he had pushed her down when she insisted he go to the church picnic. He'd told her he wouldn't go to any goddamn picnic, and was furious when he saw his clothes lying ready across the bed.

"There." She had smiled. "All your best clothes!"

"Goddamn it, I won't go," he'd said and pushed her down.

He had told her it was an accident—but they both knew it was not.

The pelts would be gone if he did not get them. Besides, the child was asleep and he would be back long before dawn. And if Molly must pray, why didn't she pray for the pelts?

He waited, and wondered what to do, and then decided that wondering had made him hesitate too long. That is, he wondered what had become of him. Had this marriage racket made him so soft that he could not go for a walk at night? He stared at the biography across the room of the man who had defeated Rommel at El Alamein. He, Evan, was not as great as Zhukov or even Rommel—but by God, he was much greater than a lot of people said.

He made sure the boy, Jamie, was sleeping. He would be gone only a few hours. He made sure the boy had his favourite blanket near, and closed the door silently. Then he set out for Clare's Longing in the cold, carrying an old muskrat pelt as a joke. He would take his pelts and give Harold the muskrat, so he would know who had changed them up but not be able to prove it.

He got to Harold Dew's past midnight, and waited for the light to go out at the top of the house. Then he went to the small low barn, crawling on his belly across the snow, still lit warmly by the moon. The barn itself was dark and cramped but had the wondrous scent of lost years embedded in its flat rough board.

He went in among the stalls that still retained the last feeble scent of horse, though Harold had never owned any, and found the three pelts he was looking for. He gasped at how pristine they actually were. He took his buck knife, the one he had cut the blood-brother bond with, and gently removed the pelts from the drying tacks. Taking them and nothing else, not the beaver that he knew was not from his Conibear, and after placing the muskrat on the wall nail, he made it out, with the moon high. And holding the fine glossy pelts in his hand said, as if to the moon, "No one takes advantage of Evan Young."

Who was he talking to as he strode back to the road and made his way along, between the ragged spruce and iced-over streams? To what deity that he no longer believed in was he exulting?

Evan got home sometime before dawn, re-tacked the pelts to his own broad boards and fell asleep with his boots still on.

The next morning Jamie was sick, and Evan was cradling him when Molly got home. She gave the child aspirin, and that seemed to take his fever away, so Evan went down the road and sold the pelts to the buyer, Mr. Doyle. But by the time he got back home the child was worse, and Molly was bathing him in tepid water to bring down the fever. Only, that did not help, and sometime near supper convulsions started and the boy threw up blood.

"Call the priest," Molly said, "to come to our aid."

But Evan said no, they would take the child to the hospital. "We don't need him," he said brashly. "It is nothing to worry about—just a little fever."

"But the priest could drive us. Please!"

"No!" Evan ran to the two nearest neighbours to find a car, but no one was home. He phoned Lonnie's office, but Lonnie was closed down for the holiday. And so on a dark Christmas Eve, he and his wife bundled the child up and took him in a pack on Evan's back to the hospital. Halfway there, they flagged down a half-tonne truck and got in.

As soon as they got to the hospital, a nurse grabbed the child and disappeared.

Evan and Molly sat alone in the corner waiting room on stiff auditorium chairs with snow melting off their heavy boots, while Christmas music played from somewhere down the hall and an artificial Christmas tree glowed, cardboard boxes wrapped in Christmas paper acting as presents underneath. Evan stared at them, somehow ashamed of having nothing. They heard "Ave Maria" playing faintly, and it filled him with a sudden unexplainable dread. The child was hooked up to all the machines that monitored the beat of life, as that song played in the corridor.

After a while the doctor, abrupt, in a white coat open to show his grey flannel pants and a shiny belt, came and sat beside them. "Poison," he said, showing them a swab. The swab itself he jutted toward them like an indictment. The air in the room was stale and enclosed, and yet now had the distinct but subtle scent of peppermint.

"Poison," the doctor said again, allowing himself a quick scratch of his left cheek with his right hand, and then becoming very still for a second as he stared at them.

It had taken some time for the doctors to realize the boy was sick from drinking antifreeze. The doctor asked where the child could have got it, and Evan realized it must have been the antifreeze he had left on the kitchen counter when he had gone to take back his pelts. He reasoned that the child must have woken up, seen the container and, thinking it was Kool-Aid, drunk from it while sitting at the table waiting for his dad. Then, after an hour or so, he must have crawled back to his bed.

"Oh" was all Molly managed, in the most plaintive way she could. "You were out of the house, Evan." She did not ask this; she stated it, as an affirmative.

The doctors decided to transfer the boy to Moncton, and Evan and Molly got into the ambulance. It was storming heavily and a plow was sent in front of them to open the road. The driver of both the plow and the ambulance were heroic in attempting this, in the worst blizzard of the year, as Evan and his wife sat beside the child in their heavy winter clothes, making their pilgrimage in stunned and muted silence, the child bundled on the gurney and still wearing his best white shirt. Their progress was reported on the local radio, and people sat mesmerized listening to it. Molly knelt and asked God for help, tears in her eyes. But before they could reach Moncton, the child died.

Money came in to help them pay for the child's funeral, and Evan was ashamed when he received it from people as poor as he. His wife did nothing but stare out the window at the barren little yard, holding the baby's blanket. He set out to kill Harold—with his bare hands if need be. He took the beautiful silver-barrelled .410 he had won from Harold himself. But when he got to Harold's house, Harold was gone; he would not be seen here for months.

But even so, nothing would take Evan's own guilt away.

He felt Molly's pain for months. He couldn't leave her side. He begged her to eat. Two junked automobiles lay in his yard, soundless and cannibalized, the new radiator he had bought for the Chev nestled in the snow. So finally, getting himself together, he put it in. Then he tried to find a flywheel for his old car and travelled the roads to buy a used water pump.

Sullivan allowed him to go back to work. He would sit in his office, shake his head and speak about how troublesome Harold had become. "Yer right to suspect him—I suspect him too," Lonnie would say in an astonished tone of voice.

As spring came, they moved to cut bush along the Tabusintac. Evan lived in an old squatter's cabin behind Legaceville, alone. At night he thought of one thing: revenge against Harold Dew. He would plan it. They would have to be alone—but someday they would be. He might let it go for a year or so—but someday he wouldn't. This is all he thought about when he was by himself, and all he planned for three months.

He was away from home, and asked people to sit with Molly, and women took turns doing this for days and nights. They would gather and play auction or cribbage. But there were rumours too, started at the tavern and other places where men whiled away time and charity. The child had not been his, the rumour stated, and he had set the anti-freeze out to get even with Molly when he found this out and she was out of the house. Molly was nothing but a Bonny Joyce twat, some who had never even met her said, so what do you expect? She had been screwing a man she had met at the church picnic, these people said, and they knew this man well.

But if Evan wasn't the child's father, they said, whose would the child have been, then? Harold Dew's people said. That is why Evan wanted to kill Harold. That is why he'd set out that very night to do his dirty work—and, they said, after all Harold had done for him! Then they said it was a pattern—yes, it was: Glen and others too.

The young social worker, Melissa Sapp, hearing about all of this, and being as committed as most social workers are—young, entirely earnest and forthright, and almost soulless in her devotion—reported all of this to the authorities immediately.

Soon Evan and Molly came under great suspicion of the police and the Crown.

One night out of the blue, three months after the child had died, Molly said, as if to herself, "The priest could have driven us to the hospital—and Jamie would still be alive."

Her form was in shadow, only one side of her face visible, and she did not look Evan's way when she spoke, her hands folded on her lap.

Not a day went by that he didn't think of the little child and how he couldn't afford to pay for the funeral. If only he had taken the time, like he usually did, to put the antifreeze in the box behind the pit props, out of sight and locked away.

The woman from Social Services almost drove Molly to distraction with her questions about how she'd treated the child. But behind her eyes was not concern for the boy so much as surreptitious self-anointment, a kind of distinctive arrogance found in people who believe that in the future people like Evan and Molly will be eradicated by some form of education or advancement.

Melissa Sapp, along with young Constable Michaels, soon decided to take the baby's blanket away, along with many other of the boy's things, to check and see if a timeline could be established that might engulf the parents in homicide. Also around this same time, a bright young man named Wally Bickle from the collection agency was phoning Molly three times a week about a two-hundred-dollar debt. She would listen to him bemoan the fact her debt was overdue. He'd once thought of her, he said, as a friend, but now he believed she was a woman who thought she could steal.

"Hey, Molly—now you've had five months. You can't steal, you know."

"No, sir."

"And what did you blow the money on?"

There was a long silence. It was as if the phone itself went dead.

"Come on, tell me!"

"I bought things—things for Jamie."

"Now, who is Jamie—a boyfriend?"

"Jamie is my son."

"Oh, come on, dear. I bet you don't even have a son—do you?"

"I have Jamie."

"Do you now!"

"No."

"You see how I can get the truth out of people? Now, you better pay up, fair is fair."

"I am going to get the money."

"Well, you had better not forget."

Evan did not know of this loan that Molly had taken out last Christmas—had never known she was being phoned by a Household Finance collection officer.

"I spent the money on Jamie," Molly would say so softly on the phone to Wally Bickle that he could hardly hear her, and it was as if her breath was more constant and louder than her voice.

And how had the animals suffered in those traps? Molly asked this of Evan one night after he returned home. "Is that why the child died, because we got money in such a cruel way? Is that why God is paying us back—paying us back for killing animals in a trap?"

"No, that is not why," Evan said. But he couldn't convince her and she peevishly turned away from him. Then she did something he really worried about. She refused to go to church.

"You have to go," he told her.

"Why?"

"Because it isn't like you not to!"

She turned to him, smiled unnaturally and said, "Oh, I don't need church either. No one needs church—church is a lie, just like everything else. And you don't really know what I am like."

"Sure I do."

"Men don't know what women are like or can be like. You don't think I like other men. I like other men a lot. So, why are you special? I could go out and get gangbanged tonight—at any tavern on the river!"

"Most women who look as fine as you, could anytime at all." He smiled.

But he tried not to look at her, for her sake, for the talk humiliated him. She wore a pretty white blouse—one of two she owned—and a pair of pure white sneakers on her feet with little pink socks that she had gone to town to buy. She had come home excited about her trip, and then turned again to depression.

"You don't think I like other men and that you are the only one. There was a man I met at the church picnic you wouldn't go to—and I liked him. We played horseshoes together—did you know that? He was kind, and when I go to church, I see him too."

Evan was angry at her for saying all this. For why was she saying it now that people were saying that he killed the child because the child was not his? An hour later he smashed his fist into the wall. And that too had a consequence. It broke his hand.

Then Molly said she wanted to go to a movie—even though they had to walk most of the way in the rain. She kept asking him what a movie was like. And he realized that she had never been to one, and that he, who didn't care for movies, had never taken her to one. She was dressed in her white blouse and new sneakers and her new pink socks, and they made it to the movie just in time.

Next morning he woke and she was not beside him in the bed. He got up and searched for her here and there. By afternoon he became worried. He called on the priest, who hadn't seen her either. They went all along the road, and into people's houses to ask. No one had seen her at all.

At ten that night, just as he was going to telephone the police, the door opened and she came in. She was dressed in her second-hand blue suit and had her suitcase with her. "Hi," she said.

She sat down at the kitchen table but did not look his way. That in itself was heartrending. But he was too confused to react to anything. For there was a man with her. The man who'd brought her home was named Leonard; he was the man she had played horseshoes with at the picnic. He was a bus driver for S.M.T. He told Evan he had found her in the bus terminal in Fredericton. She had said she was going to New York. He'd told her she should go home, that Evan would be out of his mind with worry and she didn't have enough money for the ticket.

Evan did not know what to do or say. He offered Leonard money for bringing her home.

"Don't be ridiculous—she is my friend," Leonard said.

Molly sat at the table, not looking at either of them.

For a few days after that—perhaps a week or so—she seemed fine. Evan asked her once about Leonard, but she wouldn't talk about him. She kept phoning Social Services to get their child's blanket back.

"This is Molly," she would say, and she would be put on hold. At night she would look at Evan and say, "I think tomorrow they are going to give me Jamie's blanket back."

Then, one afternoon, Hanna Stone came for a visit and breastfed her own child in the small parlour wearing a look of startling motherhood.

Molly stopped speaking. She took her life on May 25.

"I will never treat my wife as you treat yours," Evan remembered telling Sydney Henderson all those miserable days ago.

———

Evan was investigated until late September that year by the police and by the social worker.

All sorts of people were interviewed—even his old math teacher from high school. Yes, they all said, he must have done something; there was no reason *not* to suppose a man from Bonny Joyce couldn't, in a moment of anger, decide to kill.

So Evan decided to leave his torment, just as Sara Robb had done.

He went north to work. People said he was crazy, and the other men complained about him and how dangerous he was—how he was prone to arguing, how he was dangerous to himself and others. He was called into the head office twice, and was told the company had him under watch. Still he worked as he always had and listened to no one else. For instance, anyone who did not wish to work above six metres could simply say he would not. But Young worked far above ten metres every day. Yet another man's mistake almost proved fatal for him.

No one was supposed to leave tools lying anywhere. But someone left a huge industrial wrench on the staging where Young was working. When he accidentally stepped on the wrench, it slipped out from under him and he fell almost thirty feet. He hit the ground on his right side.

He was unconscious for almost two weeks and in hospital for six.

When he regained his senses, a surgical pad on his head and a bandage collecting a spongy ooze from his right ear, he started his fight for compensation. He began his fight when he was still wearing a hospital johnny and walking about with an IV pole. But he hadn't been belted the day he fell, and in the end the courts went against him, and he spent his few savings on the lawyer's fee. And when the company found out he had previously broken his hand and had hidden the fact, they were ruthless in protecting themselves from litigation. He should never have been climbing a scaffold with that hand—even though climbing the scaffold had nothing to do with his fall.

For eighteen months Evan Young refused to give up, and tried to get a union disposition against the company and the Workers' Compensation Board. This finally failed. In desperation, he took the beautiful shotgun he had loaned Ian to hunt birds that fateful day and decided to go to the Workers' Compensation Board and hold a hostage until he got a hearing.

And what happened?

He got to town at the same moment that Ethel Robb was hauling a sleigh with Ian's little boy in front of the doors of the WCB building and was kneeling to wipe his nose. Remembering how he'd talked to Molly of the Virgin Mary melting away in Ethel's hand when she was a child, Evan became ashamed, and turned and walked away with the shotgun well hidden.

He remembered too how he had won this gun in a toss of a horseshoe against Harold Dew. All of this played on his mind as he walked away.

Harold had bet the shotgun for the Chevrolet. Evan had won the toss by less than a centimetre. The shoe he threw had caught his fingers and that slowed its trajectory, and then it seemed to pivot and stand on end for a second before falling in the direction of the spike. It could have just as easily fallen the other way, or if it hadn't caught the tips of his fingers, it might well have gone past the spike. He would have lost his car to Harold, and he would have had no radiator to fix, and his child would still be alive.

So it was winning the shotgun that had caused so much pain—caused everything. And he had been about to use that shotgun in a crime. And what would that prove to those who suspected him?

He sold the shotgun the next week for a hundred dollars to Hanna

Stone's husband. And he looked at their boy, Terry—the one Hanna had ruthlessly breastfed the day before Molly's death.

Evan went back to trapping along Arron Brook and living in his small shed. He still had the coverlet that had belonged to his child, which had been returned sometime after Molly's death. Some nights he would sit in a spell, holding the coverlet, looking out at the snow as it came down over the black trees or as the wind whipped down from the hills.

'Why?" was the question he continued to ask in those years. And the only answer was "Because."

Evan applied for a job to operate the plow in town and had an interview, but because of his known temperament and his eighteen-month-long dispute with the WCB, he was turned down.

So then, close to Christmas, five years after his child's death, he made his way in a gale toward town to do some work for a wholesaler moving boxes. Six dollars an hour was not much, but to Evan at this moment, it was all the world.

It was snowing. The small garages were covered with snow and ice; icicles hung from the old buildings around the square. The Christmas lights shone from the tree in the park, and the holly and candles glowed down from poles along the streets.

Just after noon, Evan passed the large house of Ian Preston.

When he got to Victory Warehouse, there was only one forlorn light shining from a mesh window, and the garage doors were blocked in snow. The office itself was closed because of the storm, and a note said it would not open until the morning.

He had come to town for nothing at all. Furious, he turned toward Ian's store with the idea of robbing it and going away. This had been in his mind since Molly had died. He had been offered a job on the ice roads up north by a Casey man he had worked with—all he needed was twenty thousand dollars to buy into a rig and start his life anew. How did he know there was money in Ian's store? Because everyone said that nine-tenths of the money Ian had, he kept in a safe in the office of the store—a safe that could be carried away in a storm on a strong man's back. Like old Joyce Fitzroy before him, Ian distrusted banks.

———

Harold Dew spent these same five years overwhelmed in one way or the other by the fact that because he'd lost this inheritance, his girl had left him.

Annette would not return his calls, although he'd tried many times to see her after he came back to town—a fact that Ian did not know. He knew she did not love Ian but was content to spend his money. No, he did not think she'd planned all this; he believed it had just happened. How could she love a pipsqueak like that?

Some nights he passed Ian's store with one thought in mind: to burn it to the ground.

"Burn the fucker out. He had it all figured," Lonnie would say to him.

Then, one February night, it all came out. Harold and Lonnie had been drinking most of the day, burning old cedar shingles as the snow came down and blurred the lane. Lonnie went out and got one bottle and then another. Harold brought over a salmon and poached it on the stove, and they drank and ate. All day Lonnie had been giving away tidbits of information, first about this widow and then about that— first about this married woman and then about that. How he drove the snowplow, how he kept information on people—how widows were frightened of him. How he disowned one of his own children. He told Harold many terrible things. First about this mill worker and then about that miner. And the one thing Lonnie believed was this: he was better than them all.

Then he told Harold that he had set up the marriage between Annette and Ian from the start, and that Ian knew nothing about any-thing. He said he would destroy Ian, because he wanted to. And he smiled in the self-infatuated, calculated way he had. It didn't matter why he wanted to, he said; he'd simply decided he would do it. Then his thoughts returned to Annette.

"But how could she get him? That was the big thing," he began. "How could she get him away from that little Robb cunt? Well, she came to me, asked my advice—I set the thing up." He laughed. "Go ask her if you don't believe me. She had a pregnancy test and gave it to me— she was scared to death she was knocked up by a guy in Truro. I looked at it, kept it and told her to get married. Now, was she knocked up or was she not? I could tell her now, but I won't—she handed the test to me to look at. She was real scared, and I simply said, 'You better get married—it's Ian or no one.' And that was that!" Then he laughed again. "She actually thought that the man in Truro would marry her. She went back to Truro to see him—but nothing came of that."

"She was pregnant and the child is mine," Harold said. He muttered this as he looked at his large hands.

Lonnie gave a start. He looked at his young friend, saw utter delusion, and shrugged. "Think what you will," he said. "But I tell you this—she had only a few weeks to snare Ian, only a few weeks. Or she was going to go back to you. And so I planned it all very meticulously. So someday she will have to pay me. And she will pay me twenty thousand and that will be it. I need the twenty thousand pretty damn soon—so she had better realize it. If she thinks she can get off scot-free, she should go ask some of them widows I had. Then she'd know. Once I get my teeth in, I keep them in—and who can blame me? Life has done me no favours."

But Harold was no longer listening. He was in a daze. "I want to see the pregnancy test!" he said.

"I can't get it for you right now—but I will," Lonnie said.

"But where is it?" Harold asked.

"Can't say. I am looking for a good payment—I can buy up three places here for back taxes and sell them to the government. You know why the government is buying? Because a new pulp mill is coming to cut."

But Harold was no longer listening. His heart had turned sick. He looked only at his hands, and mumbled incoherently to himself.

The one secret Lonnie should have kept his entire life he couldn't keep. In fact, he woke the next morning in a stupor, wondering if he had actually said it. But Harold was long gone, the stove cold.

"I hope I didn't go too far," he said. "Oh, he'll get over it—he'll realize the child isn't his. He'd be a fool to think the child his, wouldn't he?"

But Lonnie was wrong about Harold getting over it. It was such a whimsical deception that Harold was crushed by it. And the boy . . . The insane question was planted in Harold's lost mind: what if the boy was his?

It was as the poet said in a brief moment of clarity: too long a sacrifice makes a stone of the heart. Harold asked to see the pregnancy test three more times. But Lonnie told him he couldn't show it to him. Finally he told Harold that the man who'd knocked Annette up was now dead—and that was that, and not to bother him about it, and not to come around if he was going to talk about it.

Then Lonnie did not see him for months.

Harold knew (though he pretended he didn't) that he would rob Lonnie Sullivan to find the pregnancy test and get his own child back. He began phoning Annette when he knew Ian was at work, and talking about old times. And from time to time he would ask how her son, Liam, was.

———

Ian and Annette went to Jamaica for their honeymoon because she had heard so-and-so had done so. Then Annette came home and got sick. She cried a lot over nothing. People were frightened she would lose the child. Ian himself was plagued by the idea that she would lose it and blamed himself. What would the marriage be without the child?

Days would go by and she would not speak. When she did speak, she said he had tricked her.

He would stand at the door of their bedroom, in the dark, looking at her lying there with a facecloth over her beautiful forehead. Now and again he would whisper, "Is there anything I can do?"

They went to other doctors in other cities.

Her face was pale and her blond hair fell about her white cheeks. She began to take advice from a foreign woman about natural healing and went to classes. One snowy afternoon her fortune teller told her that many things would happen to her that were strange and wonderful and that she was extraordinarily gifted. And had she ever thought of writing a novel? That is, everything she wanted to hear from that woman she heard. And everything she heard was about herself, and everything about herself was extraordinary.

Ian found himself arguing over nothing with customers. Then, after a while, the few friends he had in town seemed to drift away—like Little Corky Thorn, and the man Ian played chess with, from the furniture store.

Still his pride told him he did not need friends, and if they left him because of Annette, so be it! That was the price he would pay.

People saw him driving around in Ripp VanderTipp's truck. Lonnie was often at the door. Then Ripp and others came to the house. In fact, Ian wanted them there to cheer her. But she was still ill. They all worried—Lonnie even more than the others—that she would lose the child. It seemed to Ian that she wanted to. Once, she was put on an intravenous drip and DD came to the hospital.

Time passed, and the child was born. Annette was in labour for hours and hours. Ian was told to leave the delivery room, and sat alone in the waiting room with his hat in his right hand. It was storming, and he heard that someone had come into the hospital with a poisoned child.

"If Annette dies," her mother said peevishly, "if Annette dies—you'll be sorry."

He was shaken, and went to a window and stared out at two attendants loading a child into an ambulance. "God, please let them live," he said.

The next morning he heard that the child was Evan's little boy. He looked at his own infant and thought: What kind of a friend was he to own a large house when that little boy had lived his entire life in two rooms?

A few months later, he and Annette hired Ethel. A few months after that, Annette wrecked the Mustang. She rarely came home. And then the money began to disappear.

———

"I would have been much better off without the money—I would have been much better off if Evan had got it. He would have been better off as well, and perhaps Molly would still be here with us," Ian told Lonnie one night—for he spoke to no one else now, and trusted no one else. Lonnie had told him that the man Ian used to play chess with had said terrible things about Annette.

"I don't know about you—but, well, I wouldn't trust him," Lonnie said about Ian's only friend a year and a half after Ian was married.

"But I have done nothing to him," Ian said. "And now I have no friends."

"Never mind—things will turn out," Lonnie said. "Don't you worry about no one else but yerself! And what do you mean you have no friends? Ha!"

When I related all this to my class, my brightest student, Terra Matheson, did say, "Who the Gods wish to destroy they first make mad." And she may have been right.

PART FIVE

ONE DAY, IAN WAS TAKING A FRIDGE DOWN THE BACK STAIRS by himself. Suddenly, thinking of Sara—as if she was right before him again at that moment—and thinking too of how she had walked way from the store, dragging her leg, he fell sideways against a rack of standard parts, lost his balance and tumbled downstairs, with the fridge crashing into him. But he knew in his most secret heart that some part of him had wanted to fall—for why had he done such a reckless thing?

He lay in pain and blood for over an hour before he was found, coming in and out of consciousness. The rumour started that he had been pushed by friends of old Joyce Fitzroy—and yes, he must have deserved it.

But as my student Terra Matheson would write about small-town betrayal and gossip, nothing ever really *had* to be true. And so Ian woke up in the hospital, the same as Evan had, and at almost the same time. His operation was performed in Halifax on a snowy evening in March. He was surrounded by his new friends: Dickie and Ripp and DD and Annette.

Everyone said the operation was a success. The doctor said he would have only mild to medium pain from now on but prescribed him a heavy painkiller, Dilaudid. He came home and went to sleep, certain everything would be fine. Yet he woke in the middle of the night with the same tinge in his back and a sudden feeling of terrible foreboding. So what the doctor had said turned out not to be true—within three weeks the pain was twice what it had been, and the doctors felt that another operation at this point would not solve things. If he didn't take twice as many pills as prescribed he would find himself in agony.

It was at this time, when Liam was about two years old, that Clive and Diane were going through their divorce. The divorce was very public, and everyone was gossiping.

Annette would wait for Ian to come home and would try to fill him in on the sordid, terrible details—details of abuse and misconduct he knew but kept to himself.

"Whose side are you on," she demanded one day, "if you are not on DD's?"

"Clive is a bastard, but DD is a fraud who will betray anyone," he said.

"Well, I knew you didn't like my friends—you think you are way too good for them," she said. "*DD a fraud who will betray*—shows how much you know about women. Shows how much. DD will never betray me!"

One night, walking home from work after an argument with a customer, Ian suddenly thought: What if I had not walked back to her car that night? What if I had not walked along that wood road to her cottage? Yet that was a foolish thought—he had done what he had done and no one sympathized with him now.

———

Phone calls started to come to Ian when Liam was four years old—phone calls where people would ask for Annette and then hang up. And even though he did not pay attention to them, he could not put them out of his mind. That is, Annette had made dozens of enemies in the town, and this was the result. It was the result of her arguments at the store—with one woman named Julia, and another named Bernice, and a third named Sherrie, whose husband Ripp VanderTipp and his friends had beaten up. These were things that Ian could not imagine or comprehend a wife of his being involved in, things that seemed to be happening now every month or two. Ian paid fifteen hundred dollars to Sherrie's husband, who came to him with his arm in a sling, saying Annette herself was involved in the assault and he would contact the police.

The phone calls came late at night, always when Annette was out and Ian was getting ready for bed.

Do you know what Annette is doing now?

He would hear laughter and tittering before the line went dead. What infuriated him was how innocent he was, and how mocking the laughter seemed.

Annette must have been aware of these calls because she began to question him about them. She sometimes came home late and would sit by the phone in the upstairs hallway.

He questioned her—just once.

"They are just jealous of me," she told him about certain people she'd had run-ins with. "And don't dare you believe what Sherrie Tatter says about me."

But he had never mentioned Sherrie Tatter to her.

He said nothing. No, he did not believe those phone calls. Yet now, whenever he answered the phone, he felt sick. Annette wanted to change their number, have it unlisted. He would not do that.

Still, the most damning phone call came one day to the store itself. It was a woman, her voice taunting.

"How's Annette?" she asked. Before he could say anything, she continued, "How did she make out in jail in Bathurst?"

"Pardon?"

"Oh, that's right, you don't know—but you don't mind Dickie?"

"What?"

"Dropping in to see her? Well, they fixed that little Bathurst thing. Now they say they are going into the tanning-bed business together once they get the money from you. Besides," the voice added sweetly, "Liam doesn't look much like you, does he?" Then the phone went dead.

Ian was suddenly filled with a sick feeling in his stomach; then rage overpowered him, and he walked to the front of his store, and in front of two customers flung the cash register down. It fell into the same arc of light where Annette had stood that night, years ago. He remembered her touching his arm—the touch that became the betrayal. He felt trapped in some monstrous treachery. He went home and stared at his wife as if he didn't know who she was. His heart was pounding. No, he did not know her at all—so why in God's name would he think that he did. The child was not his. It couldn't be.

Now he saw himself as others saw him, and hated what he saw; and he remembered the surprised and angry look on the faces of certain men when they saw Annette and him together—a look that said they didn't even know she was married.

The tanning beds—no, he had heard nothing about them. Yet one day the next week, Annette was waiting for him when he came home. It was in the late afternoon, and the sound of traffic had died. She wore a green dress with a small necklace that had belonged to his mother—one of the few things he'd given her that did belong to his family. She asked how his day was, if his back was hurting—had he taken his medication? She told him what Patsy Mittens was ordering for her upstairs office, and how she wished she could have an upstairs office too. She said she wanted to be a businesswoman.

"Yes, yes," he said.

Then she tried to tell a joke—but for the life of her she could not tell it. He said nothing.

Then, just as he was going to leave the room, she asked him for money: eight thousand dollars for second-hand tanning beds. She asked for it in an offhanded way, just as she had asked for things before. He stared at her a long moment as she began to explain all the benefits of opening a salon now.

For a long time he said nothing. He tried to think, and he tried to speak. Finally he refused. It was the first time, in fact, he had ever refused her anything—and he was as surprised as she was. He looked guilty. "No," he said. "I mean, I cannot—"

"But it's the new thing—tanning beds!" she said. "It keeps us girls nice and brown for the summer. Dickie will be a partner—he knows the man who wants to rent the building."

"Tell Dickie to go to hell!" Ian said. "He and Ripp have already gone through my money as if it was water."

She looked at him, confused. "Ripp and Dickie—they never went through any money! When?"

He did not look at her now. She stood there for a long time, waiting for him to look at her, but he could not. Going out of the living room, she slammed the big French doors.

They did not speak for days. In fact, he stayed at the store late, trying to decide what he should do.

But suddenly Lonnie came to see him. This happened three or four times in a row. They would go out beyond the garden to talk as Lonnie smoked a cigar.

"You know that little girl has no one but you, Ian—she relies on you now. You knocked her up some good, and she was alone. She is worried you are up to your old tricks." He clutched Ian's arm.

"What old tricks?"

"Maybe you found someone. You stay down at the store—she worries."

"That's nonsense."

Lonnie only shrugged. He would look at Ian in perturbed silence, then flicking the ash of his cigar, he would say, "She is not eating right, she is not taking care of herself—Ripp told me yesterday. I was your best man. I feel bad."

"I know," Ian would say, "but there is something I want to ask you. I mean, a question I have."

"Ask whatever you want," Lonnie said with a big generous smile.

But Ian hesitated, then said maybe some other time. He thought about how Ripp had taken money by moving into the cottage, using the phone and electric heat and sending Ian the bill.

"I sometimes feel like a sucker," he confided, like a strong man who does not want to admit weakness.

Lonnie looked at him. "What?"

"You know—something makes me think I am a sucker."

"A sucker! With the big store and most beautiful girl? A sucker—you!" Lonnie said he could not believe his ears. "No," Lonnie said, "you made everyone else the sucker!"

If Annette could have said "I do not love you" then, perhaps afterwards everything would have been fine.

From the very night Lonnie had acted as Ian's best man, and put his arm about Ian in solidarity, the white carnation already faded on his sports jacket and his inside jacket pocket torn because he had placed there too many racing forms, he believed he had a proprietary right over this couple. They were his because he had brought them together. Not that he wanted anything. Initially he thought he did not. They were a treasure, those two—best people in the world.

But then after a few months he felt Annette did owe him something; so he took a few hundred dollars here and there.

But then, some years after they were married, something terrible happened to Lonnie Sullivan out of the blue, as changes in life often do.

Someone reported that Lonnie had not filed his tax returns.

People—a small man and a woman who looked at him as if he was nothing—came into his office, and sifted through his private papers in a way that infuriated him, seeing his racing forms, his bets, the pictures of naked women he kept in the third drawer. He could have broken the man's skull with one hand. But he had to be obsequious and say he wanted to help. The two of them looked at him as if he was nothing—and Lonnie could not stand that.

There was an audit and he had to pay fifteen thousand dollars in fines, along with the fifty-three hundred he owed. A lien was put on his house until he did so. Though the total was just over twenty thousand dollars and would not break him, he was furious—and determined to get vengeance. He paid it all off with funds he was going to use for something else. Something he was privately hoping for.

Then he sat alone, took no calls, said nothing for weeks.

When he did speak, he told people he had forgotten all about the fine. It was his own fault, he said, laughing, and he should have been more careful. This is what he told everyone: "They are only doing their job—it's a hard job they have too. I know that!"

Still, what he told Rueben Sores in private was this: He wanted all of his money back. Someone had told on him, and he wanted to know who. So the same machinations as he had used during the time of Hank Robb were the ones he used now. He sent young Rueben Sores to discover who might have spoken to the tax department.

Both Lonnie and Rueben knew it had to be someone who worked either with someone or near someone in the tax department in town. Maybe someone in the same building. And there was only one person who knew Sullivan, who, young Rueben Sores felt, could have done this. This was a person Lonnie had helped many times in his life. "Not only helped him, but his daughter," Rueben said bluntly.

This person worked in the Motor Vehicle Branch right beside Canada Revenue: Annette's father—a short, chubby, balding man named Symion.

Lonnie gave Rueben his thanks and shrugged. "Nah—I don't care." He chuckled. "Serves me right."

But he would not rest until he got the fifteen thousand back; and more than that, the fifty-three hundred as well. It did not matter that Annette's father came to him, and smiled timidly, and said there was a lot of talk about what he had said to a certain person, but none of it was true. He was terrified as he spoke, and trembled. Lonnie could see his shirt sleeves shaking.

Lonnie said, "Oh my God, I never in my whole life listen to that nonsense," and stared down at Symion with bright happy eyes.

That he said this did not matter at all.

Soon it became obvious to Annette that she couldn't escape Lonnie— and the reason was that her mother and her father, both silly gossips, might find out what she had done in Truro, and how she had been so foolish as to think she could trap a millionaire. Lonnie, furious with her parents, with Symion's timid smile, wanted to tell them what their daughter had done. He wanted to post it in the paper, just for spite. So she had to beg him—actually beg him on her knees—not to.

He had a few people make phone calls to Ian. Then he waited and waited.

Annette was terrified. Her friends too would discover it all: Ian, of course; but it was Sara knowing she feared the most. She could not allow that Sara would ever know. The idea that Lonnie would tell Sara was all she thought about. So the sooner it was done, the better—she knew she must rob Ian's store.

In fact, this is what Annette had hoped the tanning salon would allow her to do: she had planned in her own simple way to make her own money and to get the pregnancy test back. Ian did not know what his stubbornness had caused. That is, he did not know that she wanted to help him and earn her own money in order to free them both.

Many nights during those two months when Ian and Annette did not speak, Annette would sit in Lonnie's car on one of the derelict side roads of Bonny Joyce, smoking one cigarette after the other, staring out at the bleak trees. Sometimes hunters would pass by, and she would duck down in the seat so as not to be seen. But of course she was seen many times by many people.

If everything Lonnie did was calculated, nothing he did was designed. That is, he'd had no idea when he'd picked her up hitchhiking long ago that this would be the result—and yet now it seemed as if all of it had been planned.

She would stare out the side window of his car saying nothing as he spoke to her about these horrid things. She hated him more than anyone in the world.

"I told you—I told you not to go to Truro. I begged you, and told you what people might think of you. Did I or not?" he would ask.

But Annette would not answer. She was only waiting to hear how much money he wanted.

"Fifteen thousand," Lonnie told her a few weeks later. "I need it—I wouldn't ask if I didn't. And the way it will work is you will probably get it all back. Ian won't even miss it. I am asking for a favour, really."

"And the test will be destroyed? So Ian will not be put to shame?"

"Absolutely!" And Lonnie blessed himself.

So Annette began to plan the robbery of her own husband's store for Christmastime. That was when the store would be locked and closed. Annette also planned to leave Ian before then. She felt that to be magnanimous and fair, she had to.

She decided on two occasions to go to the police and admit what she was planning. But for some reason, she could not. She was weak, and in her weakness she had to go along with the plan—and there was at least one point every day where she thought: Yes, it is getting closer. And she would feel as desperate as a person might who is about to be executed.

———

This was the state of things that day in December when Evan Young passed Ian's large white three-storey house. It was the only time he had ever passed the house. Annette's friends were over, and he could hear Annette laughing almost crazily beyond the decorative lights inside.

As Young walked, he thought: What if Joyce Fitzroy's money had come to him—what then might he have been? His child would still be alive! His wife, whom he loved, would still be with him! And all of this death and sadness had happened and would continue to happen because he had broken no law, he had taken no money, he had betrayed no promise. Nor had his wife, nor had his son. But in reality he was angry because the treasure his wife had built up for him was gone. And what was that treasure? Well, it was a smile, two dresses and a new pair of sneakers she had bought on her last trip to town.

Alongside all of these thoughts was something else. It is what he had learned by accident just the week before, when he had gone unto a side road up near Bonny Joyce to check a coyote snare, and saw a surveyor taking a long-distance scope from a brown bag and looking at him, Evan, as if he was a local yokel.

"Oh," the man said when Evan asked him, "all this will be gone in a few years if my company has their way. Oh, you didn't know? Well, I'd line up for a job if I were you."

That is, as with every other mill in any depressed country, owner-ship was always changing hands. Here our large pulp mill at the fork of two great tributaries had gone through three ownerships in the last twenty years, and as always, the government was trying to impress new owners by accommodating them.

Now there was to be a fourth owner.

So Helinkiscor, a Finnish-Dutch company, had sent agents from their company to look at the wood, the size of the mill, and to see what the mill would require in upgrades, and to ask the provincial government to vouchsafe their requirements. The one thing this company wanted in the agreement was allowance to cut Bonny Joyce. In fact, this had to be the very first principle in the agreement—and nothing else would suffice. So the government went back on its promise never to cut out this land. That is why the surveyor was there, and that is why Evan had met him that day.

So the very land Evan had wanted for his little sawmill would be given in a deal to this pulp and paper company called Helinkiscor, along with hundreds of thousands of other acres to be plowed under all the way to Good Friday Mountain, with a guarantee that they would keep the region at work for twenty years.

Lonnie Sullivan had bought the site and the ruined Jameson saw-mill, with all the old saws as well, for a little under twenty thousand dollars. And it had sat there for almost three years, without Lonnie doing a thing with it. After Evan had come back from up north he had asked Lonnie four times to sell it to him. Lonnie had said he would want twenty-five thousand for it. Evan said he would work off the payment over three years. He went to sign the contract, but the price Lonnie wanted for the mill and the time it would take had mysteri-ously gone up to thirty-five thousand dollars and four years. Again Evan had said okay.

But just when he went to sign—desperate as he was to do so—
Lonnie said, "Now that is only 50 per cent of the mill, and the price has
to be fifty thousand." He'd looked at Evan with a strange curiosity, and
held the pen in his hand.

Evan could not sign.

"That's too bad," Lonnie said, dropping the pen with a thud. "Maybe
you feel too proud to go into partnership with me, do you?"

The very next day Evan had gone to the sawmill and sat among the
ghosts—the ghosts of great men such as Will and Owen Jameson, the
ghost of Reggie Glidden and of Meagre Fortune, who was Evan Young's
great-uncle. All those men who worked fifty years ago far up on Good
Friday Mountain. Their last run was at the very spot where he and Ian
and Harold had become blood brothers.

He looked down over the small scrub along the flat vacant lots and
wondered why his one dream was eroding before him.

Sydney Henderson once had walked out on broken ice all the way to
the icebreaker, to try to find the boy he had been accused of harming.
That was over six years before. But they said that Evan had harmed his
little boy, made him drink antifreeze. This is what the rumour was, that
men of little conscience could so readily repeat.

"I didn't!" he would scream, but to himself alone. Still the rumours
persisted. Just as they had for Sydney Henderson, who, people now
were coming to believe, had been innocent as well.

So Evan, sitting on a plank beside the padlocked door that now
read PROPERTY OF LONNIE SULLIVAN—TRESPASSERS WILL BE PROSE-
CUTED, decided he too would prove to the God that was no God that
he was every bit as brave as Henderson. He would walk all the way
across the inlet.

He stepped out on the newly formed ice in a blanket of snow, with his
hands in his pockets. Now and then he would stop and stare beneath him,
see in the blue ice his own reflection and feel the ice still soft. He needed
to shift his weight and move right or left—either that or plunge into
twenty-seven feet of water. But he refused to pray to the God that was no

God that had taken his son and killed his wife. Snow wisped over ice, the day darkened and wind cut through his coat. And strangely, his lips had to press together tighter and tighter so as not to pray—and the one constant on his mind except the bubbles of ice under him was the idea that he would not pray. He would never pray! In the last hour of the sun, in the mean space of nowhere, he thought he could hear Molly's voice saying: Poor dear Evan, you torment yourself, and all the angels in heaven know.

He made it to the far side, crossing below the cliff called Bennie's Rock, and moved up into the frozen turbulence toward his little shack, shaking and sick and unable to eat, for what he had done was such folly for an unlucky man. But he had a letter in his pocket from Norman Casey, who had offered him partnership in a truck that ran on the ice roads. He would have to buy into it by the end of December, for they started the runs in January. The letter said: "You will make it all back in a year—and be set in four—if you can come up. Let me know."

So now Evan decided he would get the money and go, or he would end his life. He was driven to this and felt he had no other options in the world.

The very next day he woke and made his way to town. He knew even as he put on his boots that he wasn't really thinking of working in the warehouse but of robbery. He knew this and pretended he did not. He would rob his best friend's store, just as his friend had robbed him of his dream. And in the wild snow he set out to do this.

Onlookers may think this is a story where people are always thinking the same thing—and as I told my students, they would be right, except for the fact that, even now, Evan had taken years to decide to do something he was still, in his heart, against doing.

The damp soaked through his torn boots. The small houses looked shuttered up in the storm, and the bridge was closed.

The lights along the streets in the centre of the town were out. And wires glistened and rubbed against one another in the wind.

———

What was true, then, was what the money caused.

"If only Lonnie Sullivan would leave me be," Annette had confessed to Ian two years before, when he was with her at the hospital and the reason for the cramps in her stomach could not be determined. But he had not caught on to what she was saying. He'd looked puzzled and nodded. Then she had realized that he didn't understand what she'd said, so she had touched his face as if he was a little boy and smiled.

Now, on this winter afternoon, she helped their son, Liam, dress in his blue suit with a red bow tie and new black shoes.

She knelt beside the boy and kissed him quickly. Her mascara sparkled in the light of the upstairs Christmas tree. The carpet was soft, and the window behind her head was adorned, and seemed to illuminate her. She was, Ian realized again, beautiful. And he had been frightened of her beauty. Perhaps, he thought, that was the reason she was unhappy.

"You are like a saint, Mommy," Liam said suddenly. "That's what I will always remember. Isn't she, Daddy—she is a saint?"

"Yes," Ian said, "yes, Liam. Mommy is like a saint."

Annette smiled strangely, a smile that would be affixed for all time in Liam's mind. He would carry that smile with him forever, and one day on a golden windblown stretch of Australian beach, he would remember it like yesterday, and be sad.

Ian had heard by now that Annette and her friends were planning to rob him—and though Ian did not know the particulars, he was certain that sometime today, or at the very latest within the next week, she would attempt to remove funds from his store. His uncles had come to tell him this, wanting a thousand dollars apiece for the information— but they had settled on a hundred between them.

"I don't believe it," he'd said. But in fact, the very way she and he had acted toward Sara, that very betrayal, was to be re-enacted with him.

His uncles had told him he had one friend in town who'd informed them it would happen the day of his party, when the store was closed. Ian knew no other details. (My student Terra Matheson found out later that this friend most likely was Harold Dew, who had discovered what was happening from Ripp himself.) So Ian had had two weeks to do something to stop her, to pick up the telephone and inform the police.

But he had not. At first he did not think the story was true. Then he began to suspect it might be but was not sure. Now he was certain that she would leave at some point if the robbery was going to take place. And he felt she would leave with Ripp and Dickie. However, he still did not phone the police.

If Ripp comes first, I will know, he thought that morning. He was nervous, and shook so badly he could not shave. Even as he dressed, he was in a state of numbness. Worse, the pain in his back increased as the day went on, so by four in the afternoon he could barely move his shoulders.

Ripp came to the house early, bringing a man named Fleeger. Dickie arrived later.

Ripp was now wearing his blond hair long, and sported a gold chain. Ian did not pay attention to what Ripp and Fleeger said or did. However, sometime during the afternoon, after some provocation, Ripp threw the Fleeger fellow across the room, to show his strength and moral character, and then let Dickie kick him—to show his fury. The man was left bloodied and dazed for no reason—or the reason was that he had said something unkind to Annette and they were protecting her honour. Of course this was not true—that is, it was not true that Fleeger had said anything unkind. But her friends took enormous pride and pleasure in thinking he did, and they had to act. All of this, to Ian, was bogus—but he had been silent in her presence too long to say anything. In fact, he knew many people did not even consider him her husband. Perhaps she no longer did either.

After a short time, many other people left, until by mid-afternoon (and this usually happened when they came over) only Ripp and DD and Tab and Dickie and a few others remained. They apologized to Ian for the fight. It had been inexcusable to act like that, Ripp said, with the kind of mock sincerity violent men have after a violent act.

Ian had hardly spoken all day. He simply stared at Annette until she became uncomfortable. But he was shaking. His hands were trembling.

"What's wrong, Ian?" she asked.

He shrugged.

"You're staring at her beauty, aren't you?" someone else said.

"Yes, I am, in a way." Ian smiled. "And at what beauty does."

He waited for them to go. But for a long while they made no motion to go anywhere. Annette kept looking at him and then walking to the landing on the stairs to watch the storm through the window. Then she would turn and pace across the foyer and look through the living-room curtains.

"Ahhh—it is really coming down," she said.

The phone rang, and Annette went white. She clutched her glass of gin, and looked at Ian. "Ta-da," she said, lifting her glass.

The phone stopped ringing. But then, shortly after, it started to ring again. Annette went into the den and answered it.

"God, she is beautiful," Dickie said.

"Yes," Ian agreed, "she is beautiful."

"She's the most beautiful woman on the river," Dickie said, while Ripp maintained that a McIntyre girl from downriver, the first girl he'd ever kissed, was every bit as beautiful. And then there was Molly Thorn, he said.

"Yes," Ian said, and tears started to his eyes. "Then there was Molly Thorn."

"And Elly Henderson too," someone added.

It was at this moment that Ian remembered what Sydney had said to him all those years ago: "Your wife will be accused of theft."

"By who?" he had asked.

"By you."

————

Evan puffed on a cigarette as he kept his huge hands in his pockets. Like Ian, he too was thinking of his wife. Remembering the note she had left him caused his eyes to swell with tears: *Thank you for taking me to the movie—it was the only movie I ever went to. Remember how the old police car skidded out of control? Ha! I was so proud to go! Thank you for everything, but I want to see Jamie now.*

He walked by the theatre, remembering how she had timidly gone to the theatre door with him as if the manager in his old worn suit was somehow a person of great distinction.

Evan now thought that the condition he most wanted to win back was his luck. It had been a condition of such easy lightness when he'd had it. How had it gone from him? Who had taken it away? And how could one describe it? Perhaps only one word could possibly describe it: faith. When he'd had luck or faith, he hadn't had to think about it because it just was. Once he'd lost it, or it fled from him, in a thousand small and piteous ways he could no longer celebrate it or gain access to what it had been. He couldn't even react to its loss without naming it—something he'd never had to do before. And so with each passing day he decided that this was the day he would get it back. But when he'd had it, he hadn't even been aware of what it was. Now, as a man of luck, he had certainly fallen in all ways. He knew the world as others did, and it no longer sat lightly on his shoulders.

———

At Ian's house the men were still talking about the fight, and how Ripp was right to do what he did, when Ian made his way downstairs to where Ethel had taken Liam.

Ethel had closed the pressed-board door and the two were sitting together, hiding from all the noise and confusion upstairs, with three or four of Liam's toys, a small piece of birthday cake and a candle that he was going to light by himself. Ian came in and sat down on an old wicker rocking chair, holding his cane and trying to think above the commotion, but nonetheless listening to Annette's feet as they moved to and from the back door, and looking up at the cross beams. Now and again he smiled at his son.

Ethel had been telling a story to Liam about a miracle that had happened to her when she was very little, younger than Liam himself. Annette had told her not to tell this story because it was superstitious. Yet the story involved Sara's heroic action, and this is what Annette secretly deplored. And so Ethel had stopped telling it when Ian came into the room.

The only friend Liam had was Ethel. He told her he was going to a party next week, and this party was for Sherry Mittens. No one talked to Ethel more about Sherry Mittens than Liam did. He had saved $7.32 for a present for Sherry Mittens, and wanted Ethel to help him buy it.

The huge basement was unfinished and smelled of oil and pressed wallboard. Ian had had great hopes of finishing it but never had. Other obligations always got in the way. The cottage was being redone, and he had spent close to twenty-five thousand dollars on that although he never went there—and Ripp lived in it half the time, and the bills for the phone and electric heat came to the house for Ian to pay.

He now heard Annette laugh upstairs like a little girl. He said he wanted to hear Ethel's story—although in fact what he wanted was to hear about Sara.

So Ethel continued on: "How did it happen that old Mr. Fitzroy just happened to come around the corner at that time? If he had not, my sister and I would have drowned—and he wasn't supposed to come that way for another week. He told us this later. Yet he had decided to go into the woods at just that time. Out of the blue he got up from his table and started walking—for no apparent reason! And Sara, in spite of her leg being twisted and in pain, kept holding my head above water. If she had let go of me, she could have saved herself—but even though the pain was unbearable, and remains unbearable even now at times, she did not let my head go. She would not. Besides that, neither of us froze when freezing would have been easy. And so even the doctors—and she went to dozens—asked how in the world she managed. And she could not say, except that it was the help of the Virgin." Ethel finished, while loud and long laughter could be heard from the stairs and the snow fell over the green window.

"But what about all of those who aren't saved, and who do die in accidents day in and day out?" Ian asked. "Like Evan's little boy?"

"Well, perhaps those are miracles in another way," Ethel said. "Perhaps there are miracles in tragedy as well."

Ian, who always felt he was far brighter than Ethel, could never seem to win an argument with her. So he said nothing more. Down here in the far corner were his books—he had dozens of novels and histories that he read in his spare time. In fact, each time he heard of a certain book and thought that Sara might like it, he bought it.

A bang came from above, and a thud when something fell. He heard shouting.

He went back upstairs slowly. He looked at Annette, and was about to plead with her not to go—it was on the tip of his tongue—but talk suddenly turned to Evan Young, who someone had seen pass by when Ian was downstairs, and how his child had died on this date. "Didn't he die on this date? He did, didn't he?"

"Yes, he did! But then, sometimes there are miracles where people are saved," Ian said, for some reason, out of the blue.

"What are you talking about—miracles!" Diane asked. "What do you mean by miracles?" And she stirred her drink and looked at the others, wanting them to acknowledge what a provocative question she had asked.

Ian suddenly felt hot and confused, and spoke hurriedly: "Well, think of Ethel being alive today—because of Sara," he said, and he looked here and there.

"Yes." DD laughed. "That's quite a miracle—anything to do with Sara. Right, Annette? Quite a miracle indeed!"

"Shut up, all of you—please, for Christ's sake," Annette said. "Please, let's all just shut up about Sara and about everyone else."

And so no one said anything more for a while.

———

Evan stood at the side of Ian's store in miserable weather, with no one at all around. Far down the street white snow fell over someone's troubled aluminum shovel in a yard. It was Ian, he thought, that he and Harold must seek revenge from. Why should they fight each other? Harold had spoken about this as a way to keep the bond of their own brotherhood together—that is, they must relinquish the one brother and make a new pact. And this had been in the back of Evan's mind all the way to town.

Sooner or later a man must act against he who has cursed him; the pact they had made on the mountaintop all those years ago said as much. What did the pact say? It said they would not be sheep and abide in a Lord who did not believe in them. And yes, Evan had had no money to pay for his child's funeral, and people as poor as he had come with money and food to help. The night before Jamie was buried a man had come up the drive holding an envelope in his large dark hand. Evan had not gone to the door, although Sydney knocked twice. So Sydney just left the envelope on the porch steps. In that envelope—from a man Evan had ridiculed, just because everyone else had—was forty-five dollars. This from a man who had nothing.

What Evan had to do now was put out of his mind the faces of all kind people and the thoughts of any redemption, and he had to say: "It's because of what Ian did to me!" And this was easy to do, except for one thing—it was exactly what Henderson had told them would happen, because a pact between men was a pact with the wind. This angered Evan even more.

He took five steps toward the store, and opened his buck knife to flip the latch at the back door. He knew it was easy, and knew he could carry the safe along the river where the snow scuttling across the ice would blur his tracks—in fact, crossing to the landing the day before was how he had tested this. He would open the safe at the old smelt shed where he kept some tools, take the money, push the safe down under the ice and leave before the store opened after Christmas. He thought of being in the north and living there for good (yes, and how happy he would be), but suddenly he couldn't go any farther. No, he would not do it. It was not in his nature to do it; something prevented him. In fact, he had not thought it through at all. It was the day of his son's death, he told himself—so plan it and do it! But he could not.

Why did you cross the inlet yesterday if not to practise for this danger and prove you could carry the safe on your back! But he could not do what he had come to do; no matter what had happened, he could not lessen himself. So coming to the store at this moment gave his life a sudden and terrible clarity—a clarity that, for the first time, made him hate what he had become.

Clarity was such a big word for a lost man in the snow. But soon something else would happen, something that would turn his life, and all their lives, in another direction.

———

Corky Thorn, Ethel's boyfriend and the half-brother of Evan's wife, Molly, had woken two hours before in Ian Preston's small back shed, where he had gone to get out of the wind and the terrible wet cold.

The shed rested just behind Preston's store. For what strange reason was he there—what had propelled him to enter this old back shed, with the wisps of white snow on the hardwood floor?

He had almost frozen the night before, piling up rags and old newspapers to sleep under in the vacant building. He had been home from up north for almost the same amount of time as Evan Young. And he had made out very poorly.

The truth is, four years ago he had been working on the big staging that Evan had fallen from, but he had climbed down for a break at ten that morning. (He was not supposed to be on break until 10:45 but had gone down earlier than he was supposed to.) And he had left his wrench on the side of the catwalk. He had not even thought of it until he heard, very late in the afternoon when he was back in the trailer, that a man from his own province of New Brunswick had fallen. No one was sure how. But they said management was upset because the man wasn't belted.

He'd heard they had airlifted the man to Edmonton. People waited and listened for news of his death, which they'd heard would come at any time. The man was in a coma and was struggling, and every hour that passed, people said would be his last. So these moments were painfully long. That night, when no one was near the staging, Corky went out and found the big wrench lying in some frozen sand. At first he thought he must turn it in, must let the company know it was his wrench the man had slipped on. Yet he hesitated a second, and then two. No one had seen it, for they went to look up on the staging for any tool that may have caused the man's fall, and of course the wrench had fallen and landed yards away and was hidden. He knew the man had stepped on it and it had slipped out from under him and made him fall the three and a half storeys. But he decided he couldn't admit this to anyone. So he put this large wrench in the canvas sack behind his bed.

The foreman, Arnie Petrie—also from New Brunswick—came to the trailer and asked him if he had taken an early break. Corky swore he had not.

"So you saw Evan fall?"

It was at that moment he realized it was Evan Young, his brother-in-law, who had fallen. Corky knew Evan was working here, but it was a camp with two thousand men and they had only spoken a few times— once when he had asked Evan for some money. But now that he had lied once, he continued to lie.

"See him fall? No, not really—I was at the west section."

"What were you doing there?"

"Bolting down."

"You weren't supposed to be bolting down. What were you doing? You had that sheet metal here to work on."

"I got the worksheet wrong—and when I found out, I come back."

Corky tried to convince himself that it wasn't his wrench that had been left on the staging, and the next day he tried to find his wrench in the tool bay—but in his heart he knew that it was in fact his wrench, and he had found it, and that Evan, his own brother-in-law, had slipped on it. He would be fired if people found out, and disgraced as well. He was an honest man, so why was this happening to him? He'd spoken to Ethel that night by phone, and told her about Evan, and never mentioned the wrench—yet Ethel instinctively felt (and Corky knew this too) something was wrong. And later he lay on his bunk with his face to the wall and wouldn't speak to anyone.

Then Young hovered in and out of consciousness. When he was able to speak, he said that a wrench had been where it was not supposed to be and he had slipped before he had a chance to hook on. The company said that there had been no wrench found. They maintained—especially Petrie, who disliked him—that Evan was rash and too bold, and unmindful of the conditions. Evan was also known to drink late into the night. In fact, Petrie seemed unapologetic about his feelings because he too was a New Brunswicker and had heard about Molly and the boy, and he had the idea that Evan might have poisoned his child and driven his wife to suicide.

This bothered Corky as well, for an animosity had formed against Evan within the company that now protected him. One hundred times or more, he wanted to explain what had happened so that the man could get his compensation. But each day he woke to the idea that it was another day and still no one had blamed him. And no one was treating him kinder now than Petrie himself. Evan had been warned, and now people were pleased by this. That is, like all people, they were always pleased when people not like them were shown up. And Corky listened to the talk now rising against Evan Young. The idea that he had committed a crime and was now being paid back by some higher authority was on many people's minds. So Corky listened and said nothing. And had he planned for this? No, he had not. Worse, the fact that he had not told the truth made each day more a part of the penalty if he did tell. So he would be in far worse trouble now.

Then there was another aspect, one more thing. This, in fact, was the real danger: he was the brother of the wife who had killed herself—wouldn't that in itself come into play and cause people to say all of it was intentional, that he had planned and caused the fall, or maybe even pushed his brother-in-law? As Evan lingered between life and death, all these thoughts plagued Corky Thorn. He had an ugly little face with ears that turned inward, and a blunt nose, puffy cheeks and a mouth with most of his teeth missing. Yet it was, for this very reason, an endearing face to almost everyone. But now he could not look in the mirror when he washed this face, because it accused him.

During inventory late that month, the man in the tool shop, who liked Evan very much, asked Corky where his wrench was.

"I brought it back weeks ago," Corky said.

"Are you sure? I don't have it marked."

"Brought it back!"

The company couldn't prove he hadn't. The man then had the foreman come to the tool bay and look over the inventory in the great big warehouse, where Corky looked like an insect among the tires of giant machines. Petrie looked at Corky with piercing eyes, nodded and told the clerk to forget it. That small moment, that darting look, changed Evan's life as much as anything else that had happened. Corky Thorn knew unless he spoke up now, immediately, Evan, who had cared for him for years, would not get his compensation, for the company had warned him, and had threatened to ticket and suspend him twice before.

How had Corky wanted his life to go? He had wanted to be married to Ethel and work in Ian's store; he'd wanted to help Evan and Molly; he'd wanted to take Jamie fishing. That is all he had wanted when Ian was engaged to Sara. Now he sat out on a pile of sludge and looked down at the great expanse in front of him, the huge, huge trucks, the belted dozers, the great slags of tarp and tar, the miles of grey muddy tracks across the iron ground, and longed for home.

And something else bothered him. Is this part of the main or secondary story? I have not decided. Perhaps it is part of both—but it fits with a logic that is beyond us all, or at least beyond poor Corky Thorn. It was the reason he'd gone out west in the first place: the very fact that Evan's car had needed a new radiator was his fault.

To understand this, we have to go back to that time before Jamie's death.

Angered at Ian's betrayal of Sara, one cloudy Saturday afternoon Corky went to town. He wanted to see Sara to cheer her up. But that was the very day Sara left for university. Despondent at what had happened to the woman, furious that this act of betrayal was taken as a joke by so many, Corky bought forty ounces of wine. Then he went to Bonny Joyce Ridge to see Evan and Molly. Neither was home. But their car was sitting in the yard with the keys in the ignition.

So he had taken Evan's car without permission, ostensibly to go hunting but more just to find a place to drink and worry. He'd thought nothing bad in the world would happen.

He'd tried to drive to the camp at Sevogle, the same hunting camp where Evan and Ian had gone some years before. Halfway along the camp road, the car lurched into a huge rut, and he punctured the radiator. He worked to close the hole, walked down to the brook, got a jug of water, and managed to get the car back out to Evan's by supper.

Evan was waiting for him and was very angry, but decided to let it go. Corky told Evan he would pay him for it, that he was sorry but that what was happening to everyone had confused him. Evan told him not to mind it; he would get it fixed himself.

The next day Corky went to Canadian Tire and bought some new antifreeze, and gave it to Evan to use. "Here," he said. "I can at least give you this!"

So the antifreeze had come into Evan's house because of Corky's good intentions.

Now his nephew was dead, so too was his sister, and he had severely injured Evan—all, Corky felt, because Sara had been abandoned.

Six weeks after the accident on the staging, while Evan was still in hospital, Corky packed his belongings and came home, bringing the wrench with him.

He took the wrench one day and sold it for twenty dollars to Lonnie Sullivan.

And this is when Corky began to obsess about the radiator, and how his act of borrowing the old Chevrolet had caused the leak.

Some months after he came back home, a letter arrived saying that a lawyer had been hired to investigate the accident on the staging. They were asking everyone to write a statement. The lawyer was Jeremy Hogg. Corky tried to write a statement and couldn't. Then he asked Ethel to help him write it, but Ethel did not know how to write letters any more than he did, and simply sat in the corner of her house worried and biting her fingernails.

"Well then," she said, with a big sigh. "What we have to figure out is what happened to that wrench. I know what wrench, Corky—I saw it a dozen times. It was the one you sold to Mr. Sullivan."

"No, it was not," he whispered, and banging his fist on his knee, he protested wildly.

And then Ethel started to cry and wring her hands. "I hate wrenches—I will go to my grave hating wrenches."

Twice during this time Corky went to Ian and spoke to him. He told Ian that he was going to go live in the woods, and snare rabbit and hunt—though Corky wasn't much of a hunter at all. He said he was fed up with people and would live off the land. He saw how Ian walked, how he was in pain, and Corky trembled. If only he'd been at the store like he was supposed to have been, Ian would not have fallen.

He tried to impress on Ian that Ian's sudden and impulsive decision about Sara had caused much unhappiness, and that he was coming to understand how the world was created by such numerous untold events, formed in the vast air about us on a daily basis. "Maybe even in another dimension!" he shouted, to make himself understood.

Ian told him he might need a psychiatrist and not to be ashamed if he did—Ian would help him pay for it.

"I do not need a psychiatrist," Corky said. "I need only to forgive and in turn be forgiven. And if that was the case, none of us would ever need a psychiatrist—would we?"

Corky then went home and asked Ethel to marry him—to marry him right away.

She said she would marry him when, and only when, he stopped drinking. Of course, he said; he would stop immediately. Then he bought a bottle of rum. He was on his way to talk to Ian at the store but saw that Ian was there with his little boy. So he didn't want to bother him. He took the bottle of rum and hid it in Ethel's attic for some future day when he would tell Ian about the wrench and ask him to intercede with Evan on his behalf. Then they could all begin to reconcile, the way they should. This was his plan and he tried to stay sober so that it could work.

Time passed, and Corky received two more letters saying that he still might need to testify in open court. "Open court," he would say to Ethel. "What in hell is open court? I have never been to court and now they want me to go to open court. It's diabolical—that's what it is."

But after a time, Evan gave it up. Jeremy Hogg was no longer retained and went on to other things, for it was no longer to his benefit to seek what he'd said he wanted to seek: the absolute truth and nothing but the absolute truth. In fact, in the end the absolute truth never mattered. And Corky, knowing how it had all transpired, realized there was probably no truth in the world at all.

Corky tried to stay sober, but there was terrible pressure on him to continue drinking. If he did not continue drinking, he would have to change all his habits and everything he had once thought about life. And so in order to cut back on drinking and to please Ethel, he began to buy pills from Rueben Sores. Everyone knew these were supplied through Harold Dew. And soon Corky was not only drinking but using pills to try to stop drinking. So in the end he was using both, and becoming more and more erratic, and saying more and more things he should not say. His body, small to begin with, now looked frail and delicate, especially when he started to shake.

Soon Corky owed Rueben Sores money and Rueben was banging on Ethel's door asking where he was. Then he did something else—he stole one hundred dollars from Ethel's mother's social assistance cheque and went on a three-day bender. This too was not unusual for a person who has told himself that drinking like he did was not unusual and it was people like Ethel who, because of their nagging, were driving him to drink.

"I want you to go to AA, Corky," Ethel pleaded with him after a terrible night at her house where he had nightmares and sweats, began to punch walls and said he would shoot himself.

"Well, Ethel dear, there you go!" was all he could say, hanging his head and mashing his hands together. "I haven't been much of a human being. I am an idiot. There was someone Sara told me about who wrote a book called *The Idiot* and I'd certainly like to read it because it must be all about me."

"But I still love you," Ethel whispered. "I always will love you."

"Even if I die?"

"Even if you did die—which you will not—but even if you did, I will always love you."

"The day you meet someone else I will look over your shoulder and I will sing 'There Goes My Baby'—'cause it's the song that always makes me think of you and cry."

"Ha—that will not happen!" Ethel proclaimed. "I will only love you."

When Corky Thorn received his last unemployment cheque that Christmas, he spent most of the day wandering about the shops, hoping to find a present for Ethel to make everything up to her. He decided he would not drink. But decisions like this are often fleeting.

Finally he walked up the cold highway toward Frenchies second-hand store. There on the back shelf, among some other garments, some silk scarves and woollen mitts, he spied a little fur hat he thought his girlfriend would like. He would never know it was from the marten pelts that had been the start of so much trouble.

The hat cost Corky almost every penny he had, everything except five dollars.

On the way to Ethel's he decided to go to the tavern. He decided he would have his last beer. He carried the hat in a big coloured bag, and sat down near Rueben Sores. Rueben trained his dark unhappy eyes on the little man and asked where his money was. And suddenly Corky began to tell him about the wrench and what he had done to Evan, and asked him to intercede.

"You have to help me," he said. "I didn't mean anything by it, but you have to help me—please! I know I owe you some money—I will get it to you."

One must remember that in the world Corky lived in, owing money was a very desperate thing—even two hundred dollars, which is what he owed, meant he had a grave problem and could get himself killed if Rueben felt he was being disrespected or cheated. So Corky said he had the money, but he'd had to buy Ethel a present, and this was not his fault—it was her fault.

"She's always after me for presents and things for Christmas," he said, forgetting his love for her. He had never in his life felt so badly saying anything, but there you have it: to save himself, this is what he said about the hat he had just bought for the woman he loved.

He went to the urinal, and when he came veering back, his hat was gone. He went out into the street, running from one spot to the other, and after another hour stood dejectedly under the clock in the square. Rueben Sores had taken his hat as payment—and that was that.

A freezing rain pelted down out of the black sky. He hobbled to Ethel's home along a back street, smelling woodsmoke in the air, but the doors to the house were locked. The family was out at midnight mass. He tried the bottom windows, but Ethel's mother had hammered them shut with nails. He now wanted to get the rum that he had hidden in the attic—the rum he was to drink when he spoke to Ian about Sara—but he couldn't get in to reach it. So he staggered off, went into the back of the old derelict shed that belonged to Ian Preston, just behind and attached to the store—and stayed there the night.

When he woke, he realized that Ian Preston was having a great party at his house and Ethel would be working at it. He knew Ethel's mother was out today too. No one would be at Ethel's home. So instead of leaving the old shed, he waited out the storm, smoking cigarettes. Then he put his Bic lighter down on the plywood and forgot it. He stayed in the shed until he could hear the plows on the streets above, over the sound of the snow swishing against the thin tin roof.

He thought about what he had said at the tavern. He had spoken about the wrench! He'd even blamed Ethel for wanting a present at Christmas. He was now wretchedly sick. And he realized, as most of us do sooner or later, that the inner man was where the real struggle was, and in everyone's life there is at least one wrench. Finally Corky walked out of the little shed, and decided to make it to the AA hall. Perhaps someone there could help him stop drinking, stop him from lessening himself as a human being.

But when he got to the sidewalk, Evan Young was standing directly across the street, with snow on his shoulders and an open buck knife in his hand, the blade visible.

Evan must have heard about the wrench and was coming to take his revenge.

"I didn't do anything," Corky said, backing away.

"Pardon?"

"Evan, I didn't!"

Corky kept backing up, even when Evan was yelling at him to get out of the way of the large yellow snowplow, the very plow Evan had once applied to the town to operate. If Lucky had been in the plow instead of running toward him, yelling, Corky would not have been backing into a twelve-tonne machine.

But Lucky was not driving the plow—and in some strange, turbulent way, this was because of a wrench.

———

Corky's old friend Ian—a boy he had grown up with far away, on Bonny Joyce Ridge, and now a man standing in a huge house, a man still worth, after all his hard luck, thousands upon thousands of dollars—heard that someone had been killed downtown on the main street by a snowplow in the blinding storm.

It was twelve minutes later that Ian heard it was Corky—that is, Mr. Charles Thorn, age thirty-three. The plow had hit him as he was backing across the street. A policeman came to Ian's door to find Ethel Robb and tell her.

"Oh my" was all she was able to say. "Oh my. Could someone look after Liam for a bit?"

Ian went and sat with his son. He sat with the boy on his knee and looked out over the snowy street.

Ethel had fled with the policeman and the party had broken up—even though many of the guests didn't know the man killed. He was a friend, Ian told them. Annette had left with the others. He'd seen her putting on her coat and boots, as if she herself was a guest, while Ripp looked back over his shoulder to see where Ian was. Ian could have stopped them. He maybe could have demanded that he go along. But he would not.

He heard the door shut and waited for the outside door to open. She won't do it, he thought and prayed. It will mean the end of everything if she does.

The outside door opened and then closed, and he was alone with his son.

"Are you happy that all the people came?" Liam asked.

"Oh for sure," he said. "For sure!"

"They don't seem like your friends. They seem like Mom's," Liam said. Then he said, "Maybe Ethel and you will someday have the same house."

"What do you mean?"

But Liam said nothing more. He only smiled shyly and said that he wanted to buy a birthday present for a girl in his grade one class.

"And what's her name?" Ian said.

"Sherry Mittens."

———

There was another house that night where people were having a party. They were all sitting in the grand living room. The house was modern, with furniture that often looked austere and artificial. There were many books, and many discussions about life, and many practical solutions to the world's problems. The father was a professor at the university. His name was Jonathan Mittens and someday I would be a colleague of his. I would work in the same department, and we would learn, over time, to dislike each other intensely.

Jonathan Mittens was clean-shaven except for a practised goatee, and had many good qualities. He had a daughter named Sherry Mittens. She had very good qualities too. In fact, the whole family had good qualities. This was the little girl Liam liked—loved—and thought about at night as the trees waved and made shadows in his room. She was so clean and precious and sweet-looking. And Liam thought of saving her from forest fires, or maybe a drowning or two. Still, Liam did not know this: the topic of conversation that day at the Mittens house was how wild and noisy those parties were two blocks over, and how you could hear the partygoers up and down the street, and how those people were devoid of any culture at all. And how Jonathan's wife, Patsy Mittens, had been invited to the party and tore up the invitation and placed it on a log in the fire.

"Christ almighty!" she said.

"There is no one so crass as him," Sherry's father said. He said he had twice thought of phoning the police that very day because it sounded like they were having a fight.

"They're not worth it," Patsy Mittens said. "She's an idiot. We already sent her packing from our book club—she wanted us to read Jacqueline Susann. And that little boy of hers—God knows whose boy he really is."

Sherry Mittens listened to this too, a tiny, very polite, very cautious smile at the corners of her mouth when Liam's name was mentioned because she'd decided that he was the one boy she wouldn't invite to her birthday party. And the invitation to him would *not* be sent.

———

Lonnie had kept track of every penny Ian and Annette had, and now her friends were all planning this robbery together. There were forty-nine thousand dollars in the store's safe. Out of that, Annette would give Lonnie his fifteen thousand. And afterwards—Lonnie will leave me be! she thought.

In fact, if she had just once gone to Ian and said, "I am in trouble, I am in desperate trouble"; if she had admitted everything—everything—Ian still would have done anything for her. Deep in her heart she felt she would have been assured of his forgiveness. But she did not do that.

Two weeks ago she had taken Lonnie's plan to Ripp and Dickie. The day of the party was the one they picked—she would slip out and back in before Ian was the wiser. Then she would be with him all that night, and when the call came from the police, she would have an airtight alibi.

The only problem on the day was that people left the party early because Ripp postured and was drunk, so for her to leave would be far too conspicuous. Then Ian went downstairs and they had a chance—but they hesitated and he came back up.

Corky's death allowed them to go, and her to go with them, all of a sudden. That is, she took a gamble and left. Lonnie had thought of everything down to the last detail—what money to take, what money to leave, the amount to pay Ripp and Dickie.

"They're the real thieves," he said. "Those unscrupulous bastards!"

She felt as if she was in a dream and that it would not happen. But then everything had transpired. Now, sitting in her black fur coat, viewing through the window her white hand waving a cigarette as the car rushed along, she caught her reflection and suddenly hated herself. She thought of the crib notes up her sleeve, and what might have happened that long-ago day if she had not hitchhiked home.

They all three of them were drunk. Ripp, the drunkest of the lot, should not have been driving. They hit a snowbank right beside Victory Warehouse and had to get out of the car and journey on foot. In a few metres the snow had blotted the view of where the car was, and a grey horn sounded, alone and desperate. First they had to drag Annette from the car. Then they dragged her over one snowbank, then another.

Looking up as they dragged her along, with her hat lopsided over one ear and one hand waving to a passerby, she found herself in front of Sara's house. She gave a small cry of alarm, twisted loose and began to run in front of the others, stepping into Evan Young's half-covered boot prints and falling sideways.

Ripp and Dickie hauled her to her feet, and both of them began to brush her off.

Her face was damp with water and snow. She thought of her son and went to turn back, but they held her and pushed her forward.

Of course, Ripp too was frightened of Lonnie, and of the many things Lonnie knew about him. And Dickie was frightened of Ripp. So all of them felt an obligation. They continued holding Annette up and dragging her over the snow. She lost a boot and yelled at them to stop— she had to go back and get it. "Where's my boot?" she asked.

The boot itself was filled with snow, and her white sock was covered too. She took her sock off to clean the snow from it and they noticed her toes were painted red and green. The men began to laugh hilariously at this. Finally she got her sock and the boot back on. They picked her up and began dragging her again, as if off to her own execution.

"No," she said. "Let's phone Lonnie."

But the men did not hear her.

When they came to the store, there was a large crowd in front, and the three of them stopped, making mollifying gestures of confusion and blame. There were town trucks and police cars right outside the store itself, and a photographer taking pictures. It was gloomy and dark, and the snow fell in slashes of grey against Annette's face. This was something none of them had foreseen—that the accident had happened right on this very spot. All of them had assumed it had happened up on the highway.

Ripp and Dickie turned and quickly walked away, leaving her staggering in the snow until she fell on her back. A police office, Constable Fulton, came over to her and helped her up, and she suddenly pretended to want to talk to the police about the accident.

"It's my store," she kept saying. "What happened? Ripp, come back here!"

Ripp came back and stood beside her, looking contrite and smiling at some unknown joke. The constable told them Corky Thorn had been hit by a snowplow. Ripp suddenly smiled again, in spite of himself. He had never managed to stop smiling at other people's pain. Annette noticed this. She noticed everything in the grey dirty afternoon.

The plow had clipped a pole in trying to avoid Corky and was up against the rear of the shed itself. The driver was speaking with a New Brunswick Power employee about avoiding the wires when he backed it out. The storm whistled about her face, as if she was some type of captive bird in a maelstrom. And in fact, she had been now for years. The tears that had run down her face when she'd been thinking of her child had now frozen against her cheeks. Everything confused her. She did not even know if she was or wasn't supposed to go through with the plan, and hesitated, wondering whether to continue to the store or not.

Evan, who was standing there, suddenly turned and looked at her. She started to cry and nodded at him, gave a timid smile and looked quickly away.

There, in front of her, lying across the road, was Corky Thorn, his head twisted back as if it was ready to come off, his ugly little face looking more determined than ever, his stark eyes opened unblinking, catching the snow and boldly staring right at her. It was as if he was guarding in death what he had lost in life.

She became scared and ran home. "Ian," she called when she got there, "is that you? Ian, let me tell you, I went by the store to see what happened—and let me tell you—"

A door closed upstairs and the house became quiet once more. And she understood: he had known her intention for weeks.

She began to shake; her whole body felt broken. At some point she began to pray: "'Hail Mary, full of grace—the Lord is with thee'!"

Some years later I interviewed Constable Fulton. He remembered that day, the wildness of the snow and how Annette was so drunk she was almost incapable of talking.

"So I put her in the back of the police car and drove her home, up streets that were almost impassable. I didn't like her friends," he admitted. "I often wondered later what in heck she was doing with them. Still, to me Ian Preston was in many ways an honourable and decent human being, and was never really given credit for it."

The next morning, early, when the snow was sparkling and the sky was painfully blue, that honourable and decent human being Ian Preston drove down to see the man he believed was his one remaining friend: Lonnie Sullivan. He was shaking and upset—as upset as he had been when he was a young boy and people teased him. He had not known he could return to such uncertainty. He asked Lonnie if he thought Annette could be forced by her friends to do something as reckless as rob her own husband, break into their own store. And he had brought Lonnie a Christmas present from Lonnie's godson, Liam.

"It's her friends," Ian said. "They have much too much influence over her—something is going on."

Lonnie was silent for some time. He looked up finally from under his eyebrows and said in an astonished voice, "Yes, her friends are deep-fried scum. I keep telling her to stay away from the likes of them. But it's nonsense about robbing stores—my God almighty, Ian, have some sense. If you were told that, you were told by riff-raff." And when he said "riff-raff," he looked away in complete disgust.

"No, you are right," Ian said. "You must be right."

"I am always right—always. I think of that little Corky Thorn, and you know I begin to weep. How old was he, anyway? You know he had no one when he was a kid—I was the one to take Corky Thorn fishing in Arron Brook."

And of course, this was true.

It was also true that of the two-hundred-and-eighty thousand dollars Ian had at the time of his wedding, only forty thousand was left.

PART SIX

AT CORKY'S WAKE IN THE SMALL HOUSE, THE OTHER TOWN, the town within a town that did not belong to those Ian had come to be associated with, became apparent. So Ian Preston saw that town again—that is, the town that had existed for him when he was the son of a pulp truck driver. All those boys he had grown up with and those girls, now men and women, came in and out, paying their respects with the air of obligation and duty that was at once mimicking and in a strange way singular and special. Here were toughened men who wouldn't blink if you hauled out a crowbar and threatened to hit them. Here were men who would give you the shirt off their back, or save you in a storm—or hand you their last dollar. To them, Ian had changed, become a part of the town that was elusive and unknown. They simply did not trust him as much anymore. And he knew it, and felt the sting of it, and could do nothing about it.

Sara sat on the couch unable to say much about anything. She had just returned from university and looked like a woman now—that is, a woman who did not rely on beauty tips from Cut and Curl. A woman who had been on her own and did not need to remember him. She had no real need of the town. She was aloof without being condescending, which made him feel his betrayal even more.

That is, somehow he was ashamed of the very things that had once made him seem so special to her. While at the same time, Sara, with her plainness and her lack of makeup and her poor left leg, seemed more than special, almost beatific.

Ethel looked exactly the same. Her big ears poked through her blond hair, and her sad eyes looked up at him. Her sticklike little legs and knobby knees, now not in pink stockings but in black ones, made her scarecrow figure even more endearing.

He tried not to look at Sara, because every time he did the same feeling of betraying her overcame him, and a horrible sensation of waste and loss plagued him. He did not know why, but for a second he believed that everything had happened because of him.

She came up, took his hand and thanked him for coming. Annette had not come with him. It was not a cruel or malicious decision. Annette had always been a coward when it came to death, and she could not accompany her husband now. So they did not speak about her.

Ian went home, and worried a great deal about his wife and his marriage. Yet he could not leave Annette. Why was that? Simply this: with Sara back in town now, he felt he had to stay. He could not prove others right. That is, both he and Annette knew they had made a disastrous decision and were unhappy. And life, such as it was, would have to go on.

"You should leave him," DD started to say at certain times. And Annette would stare through her, as only Annette could do.

"No, that is not possible," Annette would say. "For better or for worse!" Because she knew Sara was back in town as well.

———

Evan Young started back to his house after the accident, after the police had spoken to him, and after the reporter's interview. He only told them what had happened: The more he had yelled for Corky to stop, the more frightened Corky had become, and the more he had backed away, and Young did not know why. But he couldn't have seen the plow, and the wind was blowing ferociously. They questioned him about this, of course, perplexed, for Evan Young, once so lucky, now had a bad reputation. Everyone remembered things about him, and recalled who had said what about his wife and child. So now perhaps he had got Corky too! Perhaps in some diabolical way he wanted the whole family; who would not think that? The cops actually did think this—and in all the fantastic coincidences of life, this one seemed particularly interesting to them. Though they could not prove it, they believed he had done something with this Thorn family, and noted to each other that although they had no proof now, someday he would do something to implicate himself forever. Evan, however, did not know they were thinking this. Or more to the point, he believed that even if they thought this, they would realize soon enough that he himself could not harm anyone.

"I tried to get him to stop" was all he said, and he seemed dazed.

They had no reason to hold him longer than they did and let him go.

For two days Lucky sat in silence, staring at the snow and his cannibalized automobiles. He kept thinking of what he might sell to get himself out of this financial mess. But he didn't know.

He phoned about, asking who wanted a radiator for a Chevy, or a water pump. But no one did. He kept looking into the old chest where the child's belongings were kept, remembering Jamie in the ambulance, his wife sitting beside him. That, he decided, was when his wife died—when she fell to her knees and prayed to God. He thought long enough about the brash and ignorant statement he had made to Sydney Henderson, about taking care of one's family—and how he would never let his family down.

He lay down on the cot and tried to sleep, and wind battered the house.

On the second night he went to the wake and saw Ethel, and her older sister, Sara. Yes, he said, he remembered them. And he said he was sorry he had not been able to stop Corky from walking backward across the street.

Then he hiked back home. It was minus twenty-seven, and he got a drive with an old man from Bonny Joyce, who told him that Ian was in for it: no one trusted him, he'd lost much of his money and he had hurt his back. And the old man said only what Evan himself had heard: that Ian had overextended himself investing in some real estate and even the business he'd bought had liens on it. That he was, in fact, a very good electrician and a very poor businessman who others took advantage of.

And one of the people who had taken advantage of him was his own lawyer, J. P. Hogg, who did not inform him that the warehouse he was buying had a lien of eighteen thousand dollars on it.

"It was done just for spite—I heard the mayor wanted to get back at him—or something—what I heard!" the old fellow bragged.

"I am sorry about that," Evan said.

"That's what comes from stealing—that's what God does to ya if ya steals!" the old man said. There was a sudden hope in his eyes that he was right. He talked too about Harold. The old man had owned a snow blower and had come home to find it gone. He said Harold had stolen it.

"I can't see Harold doing that," Evan said. But of course he knew Harold had.

"Did you know he hurt his back in a fight, and now and again wears a brace himself?"

"I heard as much."

"What do you think of that?" the old man asked. "Both he and Ian? It's like they have to carry their crosses from now on."

"Ah yes," Evan said, "and me too. But you know what?"

"What?"

"The brace—it doesn't do much good."

Evan was let out at the road to Bonny Joyce, and walked the last three miles in the cold.

Back home he burned some boards and wood in the stove, and got the old oil K-Mack going again. He made Kraft macaroni and cheese for the sixth straight day. He was in a bad way, unrecognized by millions of citizens in Canada and just as recognized by millions of others. He was in the throes of poverty. And he was paralyzed with a feeling of unseen forces allied against him. And this was not a phenomenon that was unusual, for in many ways he was correct. Once this luck of his had failed, once he was perceived to be in trouble, gossip and rumour and hearsay had abounded, and in their abounding had separated him from others and accorded him a difference that heightened the initial difference of his luck, and caused hilarity and scorn that he could not extricate himself from and made him subject to the curse of this scandal and the contagion it afforded, until he was as bereft of friends as he was of family. So friends fleeing, he was alone and desperate for recompense. And people knew he was desperate for recompense and did not help.

Because they thought gleefully: Well, look at where his luck got him.

The problem was, he owed nine hundred dollars to his lawyer, J. P. Hogg, and there was no way Hogg would let it go. And Evan knew that anything he did, any problem he had, would be exacerbated by this debt. The office had sent him two reminders. Jeremy Hogg was Jeremy Hogg, and he would go after a penny.

Evan sat in the gloom, stuffing old plank boards into the stove far after it got dark, and now and again lifting the lid to spit, just as men had done for generations. Nor did he want to hurt anyone; nor did he want to take from people. Had he willed Ian to be cheated too—had he willed him to have a bad back? He only knew that Fitzroy's money had been something all of them, at one time, had had a chance at—and look what it had done.

He tried to think of what to do. He realized that Corky had owed him money from the time they were both up north, some four hundred dollars. Perhaps he could go to Ethel or Sara to collect it.

After Molly died, a neighbour had come over and said Molly hadn't paid for embroidering the blue-green sash on the child's crib.

"When did she get it done?" Evan, who was still in a daze, asked.

"After the boy died."

"How much?"

"Forty-four dollars and ninety-eight cents," the woman said, and then looked out into the muddy dooryard, with the long May evening, the smell of lilac condemning him.

So he had sat at the table shaking, and counted out his pennies.

He could not do the same to that family—just as he refused on his honour to take welfare, even if he starved.

———

The day of Corky's funeral, Evan Young picked up the beautiful teak-wood chest and took it to Mr. Hogg. The chest had belonged to Joyce Fitzroy but had been given to Evan's family after his grandmother's funeral some years ago. (This was, ironically enough, the same chest Ian had wanted to buy from Fitzroy as a present for Evan and Molly years before. That is, what had set everything in motion had been in Evan's possession all along.)

Evan was certain it was worth some money, but he was uncertain of how much. He only knew that Hogg collected these things. Last year, when Hogg was at the house, he'd spied the chest and asked if Evan would like to sell it.

"So, do you want to sell that? I'll give you six hundred dollars!"

"No, that was our boy's chest," Lucky had said then. "It's what I remember him by."

Hogg looked disappointed and said nothing else.

Today Evan was hoping on that look of disappointment, and he carried the chest on his back through town. Up along Castle Street at that same time, the hearse with its own chest moved, and people, a few cars at most, followed Corky's coffin toward the great dark Catholic church on the hill, with red sunlight fiery in the new stained-glass windows, which seemed to bleed on the edifices there. Behind the church the gravestones white with snow, and the light lilted on their blessings and names. The light was desolate—that is, the idea of Christ's cry at being forsaken seemed to emanate from those granite surfaces of black and grey.

At that very moment, Evan was at the door of HOGG & HOGG, ATTORNEYS AT LAW.

He set the chest on its side and rested it on his right boot, and waited for his back to stop hurting and knocked on the glass door. He waited, and the wind blew against him, and the snow glided down off the roof in slow motion and surrounded him in light, almost ethereal ways. He knocked again, and then, getting no answer, he opened the door and carried the trunk inside.

There was a reception desk beside a potted plant—a brittle

tubular-leafed plant that hung toward the floor in almost penitentiary sadness. There was a strange darkness in the room as well. A silver Christmas tree was strung with lights that didn't glow. The lawyers were all rich, and some had ruined lives. He'd heard this about Hogg himself.

Seeing the bell on the reception desk, he punched it.

Hogg appeared. "Yes?"

"You asked about this trunk—said you would like it."

Hogg looked confused. "What?"

"The 1840 chest. You asked about it. If you want it, I am willing to sell it—or more to the point, to make clear my debt to you with it."

He waited for Hogg to recognize who he was. A few seconds went by.

"Oh—yes. But that was so long ago—do you have a debt? With us?"

Evan said nothing.

"Well, what are you selling it for?"

"Nine hundred dollars."

"I did not mean the amount—I meant, why are you selling it?"

But when he'd said nine hundred, Mr. Hogg didn't flinch. "Nine hundred?" Hogg asked.

"Yes, sir."

"But you said you put your child's things in it. It was what you remembered him by."

"Child's dead."

There was a pause. Hogg rubbed his fingers together and said nothing for a moment.

"I can't take less than nine hundred—people told me it was worth twenty-five hundred." This was not true, but it is what Evan said.

Hogg asked his secretary to see how much Evan owed. And waited. When he found out it was nine hundred dollars, he agreed. "Leave it, and we will be even."

Hogg looked pleasant in his white shirt and knitted sweater, with its happy childlike design of a Christmas sleigh.

———

For months and months after the attempted robbery, Ian was trying to decide something—trying to understand why things happened, why Annette had been at Sara Robb's house so long ago, having her tea leaves read. And why, just when he'd no longer had a thought of her, did he return to his obsession so fully.

Then one night he simply looked at her putting on her earrings in the hallway and decided that if he remained married to her, he would probably kill her.

So the idea that he would kill for her seemed, in a strange way, to be true. He abused his pills and began to see two doctors at once. And what they said was in fact true: pill addiction was far worse than alcohol. Five times he tried to stop and five times he could neither eat nor sleep—and the nausea and the pain in his back was even more intense. So he would go back to the pills, shaking and angry, only to find that he always took more than before. He also did something else: he began to go out at night, alone, to find cocaine. Then, for a while, he would feel free: free of pain, of his marriage—of his guilt.

Once he was found in an alley, curled up as the rain fell over him, by his little son.

But the pain in his back was worse whenever he came to.

And he was plagued by one idea. "Give me one clue as to what Annette is really doing"—did he ask this of God? I am not sure; but he was plagued by the idea of falsehood acting as truth. And the truth was, the store was suffering and he was down to his last few thousand.

Then one afternoon, coming out of the store and locking it with his large key, he was thinking these morbid things and saw something glinting in the window box below him. He turned and picked it up. It was the buck knife Evan had tossed away in the storm the day Corky had been hit. The knife they had used to draw blood when they were boys. He picked it up and absentmindedly put it into his right jacket pocket.

He spent the next two days scrubbing it and cleaning it, using oil to make it shine. In fact, he became obsessed with having it pristine, as it once was—and although he did not know how it came to be where it was, he was certain it had been sent to him for a reason. But who would send it to him and for what reason?

He was afraid, in fact, that he would use it on his greatest tormentor—Ripp VanderTipp, who still slept at his cottage. He remembered Ripp in a bar, making fun of a woman one night—some poor soul whose welfare payment he took, who waited for him to phone. But worse was that others laughed as well.

Ian became morbid—thinking of betrayal and thinking he should leave before he did something desperate. Thinking he would kill. Then one afternoon, late on a February day, he saw Lonnie Sullivan coming out of Nick's barbershop, pausing to put some bills in his pocket while the wind scowled about his feet. It was at that moment something became very clear: that nothing in his or Annette's life had yet happened that Lonnie Sullivan did not know about. So then, Lonnie Sullivan knew—must have known—everything. And Ian became wide-eyed with shame. For who had been with Annette when he'd met her at Sara's? Who had informed him of Annette's pregnancy? Who visited her when she was ill, and who told Ian that he was delusional to think she would rob his store?

This, then, was the clue he had asked for.

A month after he found the knife, Ian went to his store in the early morning and phoned Sullivan. He was startled when Lonnie answered. But he was able to say, "She told me everything, confessed, and I am coming to see you about it tomorrow night." His eyes were watery and his hand holding the phone was trembling. There was a long pause.

"See me about what?"

He said nothing, because he did not know exactly what it was. And worse, what Sullivan next said made him think he was wrong: "See me about what—what in hell are you talking about!"

Again Ian said nothing. His eyes continued to water. He could hear Lonnie breathing. He could hear him reaching for something and unwrapping it. It must be a cigar. A match was then struck.

"The pregnancy test?" Lonnie asked.

Ian tried to breathe. He felt himself break into a sweat.

"Yes—I am coming to get it," Ian said.

"Get it why?" asked Lonnie.

"Buy it, then!" And Ian hung up.

So after all this time—after seven years—Ian knew. He was sure he would kill Annette if he got to the house before she got home that day, so he left the store and went for a walk along the cold streets.

The only thing he must not do, he told himself, is harm the child. Yet he had already harmed his child—he had become a laughingstock while his fights had caused his business to deteriorate so that almost no one entered the store now. Also, he believed no one knew about his cocaine use. But he was wrong. People knew and talked about it all the time.

So he went back to the house, and sat in the back room.

That night, as they ate supper, Annette spoke about DD and her new boyfriend, who she hoped would work out—and how she might get a job again at Cut and Curl if one of the girls went on maternity. He stared at her a moment, went to speak, and then became silent. He remembered her saying, "You didn't know I had that ace up my sleeve, did you—now you all have jam on your faces!"

"Don't worry," she said suddenly, "things will work out."

"I'm sure of it," he said.

After dinner he went to his store, took his money out and put it into an envelope. He sat in the office and shined his shoes, then put on his freshly pressed suit.

He sealed the envelope and held it in his hand. Then he took the knife out and looked at it.

Finally, he turned off the store lights and headed into the dark.

It was March of 1992.

———

By March of 1992, Evan Young was broke again.

And now people were saying he had forced Corky to his death, that he wasn't satisfied with killing just Molly or the boy. But the police, though they did not relent in their treatment of him, finally said it was hearsay. Hearsay in whispers for three years or more.

The previous week Lonnie had said he had only one job for him.

"What job?" he'd asked.

"I am tearing down the old Jameson sawmill for scrap to be sold over at Jemseg. You can do that and we'll give you six hundred—you owe me two hundred dollars already—so that's eight hundred and you don't have to thank me. It is for you I'm doing it. I don't want Ian Preston to get his greedy little mittens on it! He's angry as a bear because he was outmanoeuvred on the siding, and he is hanging around me again. He has nothing and wants what you wanted. He'll destroy it even more—so I have an offer to sell the land to Helinkiscor when they come. You know I wanted to sell it to you—I waited for two years for you, but it just didn't happen. It was you I was hoping for all along!"

Lonnie wanted him to start work March 6—that is, tear down his dream and be paid at the rate of a hundred dollars a week.

During the first days of March a change came over Evan. He had always believed that the greatest thing in the world was to seek honour and be honourable (this is why he refused welfare, though many thought him crazy)—but it may be just as honourable to seek an end to it. Soldiers did this—they honourably rushed a defensive position they could not in any way surmount; perhaps that was how he should end. And he kept thinking this as the days passed along.

Evan looked up at the stars on the night of March 5, but after a while they disappeared and a mist blew in from the salt bay, still frozen. He thought for a long while about what he must do and what had happened from that moment on Good Friday Mountain with Ian and Harold when they had become blood brothers.

He went outside, and the mist had stopped, the clouds were low, and he could feel spring in the wet snowstorm that would come. In the back of the shed, locked away, was what the police had returned long ago—the container of antifreeze. Why had he not destroyed it? In some strange pathetic way it may have been kept as a memory. Whatever reason, it was still there.

He wondered if he should drink it outside. Then he decided he would drink it exactly where the child had drunk it. For it was the child's birthday this very day.

But first he had to find the container, and he went into the small shed, with its four shelves, and looked for fifteen minutes. He finally saw it, behind the paint cans, hidden away, its form attesting to the very suffering and misery it had caused them all—and yet without conscience or consideration itself. The price tag was still on it, halfway up the container side, just as Corky had spied it and elected to buy it for Evan all those years ago. SALE, it had read on a separate red sticker.

He picked up this container and went out, calmly closing the shed door carefully and thinking even now how he must re-shingle the shed roof. The mist had turned to spitting rain, and soon a snow would come down.

He took off the cap to drink. He had it to his lips. If he had found it the moment he began to search, he would have already ingested its contents. But at the moment—that very moment—a car pulled into his yard. Yes, he thought, the cops have come to question me about Corky. Just as I knew they would, just as people said.

The car made it up the hill, skidding sideways twice. The lights seemed to toss against the harsh dark sky; the fellow rolled down the passenger window and said, "How are you, now, at fixing roofs?"

For more than a few moments Evan was silent. "I'm okay at doing it," he finally answered.

"Then will you be so kind as to look at mine," the man said, "or will I go along downriver to Doan's Roofing and Construction? I can give you a job maybe, but it's up to you."

"It depends," Evan said, "on how big a job you need."

"It's a big job—but you will be paid for every hour."

By now Evan had stopped walking and was standing beside the car.

He stared at the container of green antifreeze and set it in the snow. He shrugged and got into the car. He had no love of priests; in fact, he hated them—more now than when his wife was alive—but this man had been kind to him during Jamie's and Molly's deaths. So he was beholden, and he knew Molly would request that he at least be polite. But why were such men priests? He did not know. He once, in his hopelessness, went to Sydney Henderson to ask him about it all. Sydney said, "It is not the priest but the faith—the faith is miraculous, the priests are only men."

And now the priest was to tell him something that as a man he did not understand. It seemed the priest had started down to Doan's to see about the work, but a sleet started to fall, and he thought of Molly's husband—might he possibly be able to do this work? So he turned and came back to Bonny Joyce Ridge. This is what he told Evan as he drove, and Evan was silent, staring straight ahead.

Then Evan said, "How long did it take you to get here from the time you turned around?"

"Fifteen minutes," the priest said.

The church was in almost complete darkness.

Inside the foyer, which smelled of stale holy water and oak and some requisite half-dead flowers, the priest paced back and forth with his hands behind his back. Suddenly it was as if he was not asking a favour but conducting an interview. And this is why Evan hated priests: they suddenly, at the most advantageous time to themselves, became something else. He thought of how often Molly had entered these doors— walked by this font and placed her hand in to bless herself, took the sacraments, distilled her whole life in this world, only to sit by the window at the end and refuse to go to mass. He stared at the holy water, bleak and stale, and trembled.

"Yer dad fixed steeples," the priest said.

"By times," Evan said, holding back near the door.

"Come in, come in. Could you do the same kind of work?"

"I don't know."

"Come, take a look—what do you think?" And he waited for Young to follow him and they went up the stairs together, then beyond the balcony into the old bell tower, cramped together on the ladder.

"It's in terrible shape. You can see the last work on it was done in 1937," the priest said.

Evan looked at it, lit a match, held it to the structure a moment and then blew it out.

"You need new supports. I would have to put some staging up outside. I would put some steel braces along here . . . put steel rods through here—that would help it. But there is a lot of rot—I could replace it here with maple. It is off a degree or two already. You're losing a lot of heat—I would insulate it again. I do not know if I can straighten it and by the look of outside you need a new roof. I can do that too—tear off the shingles you have, put down some new flash and make it leak-proof, anyway. It's leaking now right down the necks of your holy people, I bet!" he said.

They came down the ladder and stood in the attic.

Evan looked at the dapper little priest with sharp eyes. The sharpness of the eyes came because of worrying over money and his church day to day, because of him and Father MacIlvoy being the only two priests in this whole section of the river and having between them six parishes. The sharp eyes glittered and the wind blew. It was as if the priest had divined what Evan was intending to do just a half hour before, and they both of them were caught up in this mysterious intercession.

"If Lonnie Sullivan won't let me out of my contract, I will have to work for him until mid-July. If he lets me go, I will start on it later this month or when the weather gets a bit better—there is no use doing it in snow. But the staging I rent has to be good and I have to oversee it being setup. I will need three tiers for the roof and four tiers for the steeple. It rents at about thirty-five a tier per week. I set my own hours. I come and I go, but I get it done!"

"That will be fine," the priest said. "But you have to start before July—and the pay here will be better—that is, you won't have to worry about having to pay money back."

"Well, I am honour-bound," Evan said. "I will have to see Lonnie tonight or tomorrow and ask him to let me out of it."

"So if Sullivan allows it, you could do it?"

"Yes, I could do it," Evan said. "I could do the exact same kind of work. But I tell you this, I've had my full of falling and do not wish to again!"

"Then pray," the priest said, "that you do not."

Evan shrugged. Praying was for women and children and he told the priest this. So the priest said, "Well, maybe—but then again you could light one candle for Molly and Jamie."

"I don't know about that," Evan said.

"Well, they were the reason I thought of you on the way to Doan's— because tonight there was a mass said in their honour."

"In their honour—who requested that?" Evan asked.

The priest looked at him, and mentioned the man, Leonard, whom Molly had played horseshoes with all those years ago—the man Molly had seen at the church picnics Evan did not go to; the man who had liked her, and who she too had liked, and who'd brought her home to Evan when she was not in her right mind.

"He often requests a mass for Molly and your son. Leonard Savoy— do you know him? He did so tonight on the anniversary of your child's birthday. He will do one on Molly's birthday as well."

Evan said nothing. He went down the aisle and did not look at the saints assembled, or the quiet face of the Virgin, as he put a coin in the box and lit a wick.

He left in the dark and began to walk toward Lonnie Sullivan's. He travelled toward the highway, wearing his old torn parka. He himself had ridiculed church every chance he got before. He did so until after the child died.

Now it was snowing, and as he thought about the steeple and how to right it, and what he might use to support it, he forgot completely about the antifreeze and about how he'd believed he wanted to die.

———

Harold Dew was at Clare's Longing, some seven miles to the south, looking at the same stars before the mist drowned them and the sleet started. He had stayed out of Evan's way for years. But that did not relieve him from pain. Nor did it stop him from inflicting pain on himself. Why was this? For if he took revenge on Evan's family—though he said he did not take revenge intentionally—why then did he cringe each time he thought of little James and Molly and the death of the two? Why did he get drunk when he was forced to think of it coming unto Christmas, and get into a fight where he fought, and couldn't win against, both Mat Pit and the Sheppard boys? And why had he done so—because they had made light of Sydney Henderson? He did not know Sydney that well, and so it was not rational—and though he had called on Ripp VanderTipp, who he had been drinking with, to help him, Ripp left by the back door, for he was terrified of Mat Pit, and so Harold fought the three men by himself. And why was that?

Now he too had to experience the bane of men who worked with their strength: an injured back that bothered him when the damp weather came. Like Ian and Evan, he believed Lonnie Sullivan was the cause of his trouble. But if truth be known, Lonnie had really done nothing to them; for each of them in their own way had had many opportunities to escape, to say no. And yet, now each of them was plagued by this man—and each of them, while disbelieving in the Divine, had in fact attributed much divinity to this man who they all secretly feared.

In fact, Harold was planning to rob Lonnie Sullivan that night. He had worked on the idea for ten months. To get the pregnancy test—and get his child back. Why this particular night he did not know, but it suddenly came to him, when he woke that day, that this must be the night.

If it was true, the pregnancy test must be hidden there somewhere. For every paper Lonnie had, he kept. And Harold believed he knew where it was: in the workbench drawer, which had a hidden back and where Lonnie kept the notes in which he skewered people's lives. Lonnie had something on everyone—on widows he impregnated thirty years before. So the pregnancy test would be there too. At some points in his reveries Harold thought he would take it—and he would demand thirty thousand from Annette. At times he believed he would demand a blood test and take the boy from them, and rename the child Glen!

But at other times he believed in his heart he would take the pregnancy test and hand it to her and say: "Burn this and be done with it. I knows how yer friends have used you—and they aren't your friends." And he would turn and walk away, and start a new life in the north— the same dream Evan had had, and one that Ian too had entertained.

The same night, and at about the same time Young met the priest, Harold left his house and walked over old Ski-Doo trails that he had helped open, and through the dark of Arron Brook, where the wind always whistled like a mournful cow in heat, toward where the old Jameson mill still half stood, a conglomeration of rusted half walls and withered sluices jammed and bolted and empty.

On the way he passed Lonnie's house, and it was dark, the old truck in the yard—a small yard with a fence. So Lonnie was asleep.

He would confront Annette—in fact, he could not help thinking that this would make him even. Only then would he be happy.

But would he be? That is, happy? For even if he did this, he would still in some way love her—and need her to love him.

Still, robbing the shed would be easy. First, because no one would suspect he'd walked nine miles to do it; and second, even if the back was locked he knew how to get in, since he had been there a thousand times since he was a child. Third, he felt this was his due for how Lonnie had treated him. After Lonnie bragged to him about the test and how he had used the woman, he'd recanted and said that what he told him wasn't really true. That there was no pregnancy test at all.

Harold remembered he'd kept staring at Lonnie as he ate a poached egg—and Lonnie wouldn't look his way, but mumbled something, and sighed as he looked at his egg.

Therefore he decided Liam was his child.

He finally came to Glidden's Hill and moved along the alder bushes at the side of the field, with the hail and snow falling down upon him, and saw one light on at the shed's back entrance. He opened the back door and went inside. When he went inside, the room was dark. There was no sound and so he snapped on the light.

He began to open small drawers, not caring much about the noise, for Lonnie's house was far on the other side of the road, well over a mile away. He knew there were two false compartments at the rear of the drawers and he was trying to find them. But as he took out the drawers, nothing was there except an old pay sheet from 1982 and a bulletin from the Catholic Church, which said: "At this time of Lent please fast, give up worldly desires in order to come closer to God."

Ten minutes passed.

Then twelve minutes.

It was snowing; the little light was still on. Harold left very much the same way, but very quickly.

Then there was silence.

The door was left opened—a light shone on the snow.

Lonnie Sullivan lay on the floor of the shed with his skull bashed in.

Harold was holding the large industrial wrench in his right hand. He had returned everything to its place, and carried well over fifteen thousand dollars in his pocket.

Dawn came slowly over the black trees. The snowstorm stopped. All was quiet in Clare's Longing.

Harold hid the wrench under a plank in his attic, where it would remain for some time. He had found fifteen thousand dollars in a manila envelope stuffed at the back of that drawer, along with fifty-three hundred more dollars tucked under it in loose twenties, fifties and tens. It all seemed surreal.

Still, the money was real, and since no one knew it was there, or that it was gone, Sullivan's death was initially considered an accident: the man, a vicious alcoholic, had slipped while drunk and cracked his skull on the large workbench.

It would be some months—yes, even years—before the investigation would open once again because of all the treacherous finagling Lonnie

Sullivan was known for. The corrupt documents he kept on people in order to blackmail them would someday come to light. By that time, Harold's whole life would have changed for the better, while Ian's life would be a disaster.

Luck, luck, and nothing but.

———

Ian believed in gentlemanliness—or at least, some good part of him did—and above all, a sense of duty. He had married Annette for better or worse. So he must continue on. He went and bought the pregnancy test from Lonnie. And he carried a buck knife in his pocket because he did not trust Lonnie—and he held it in his hand, in case. Yes, he had been parsimonious and thrifty—and he could not understand why he shouldn't be, for a man who grew up with nothing and made his own way should not be laughed at for saving a quarter. Yet now, this was for his son. But it was also to save his own reputation, and out of the fear of being called a joke by Sara (even though she never would). He did not want Sara to know. He knew this was part of his reasoning as well.

There was just one thing: if Ian had not gone down to visit him, Lonnie would have locked up long before and gone home; Harold would have come to an empty shed. But Lonnie was imbibing after Ian left, for the money he'd wanted to get to pay the back taxes on properties he had researched he now had—and this would make him wealthy if he played his cards right. Part of the property he wanted to claim belonged to Ian Preston himself, and was situated on the lowest end of Bonny Joyce, at the Swill Road turnoff. Ian had completely forgotten about this property—but it alone would command thirty-five thousand dollars in a sale to Helinkiscor, Sullivan thought. Ian had no knowledge that Lonnie was about to get it all—that is, five properties, including Evan Young's, for twenty-three thousand dollars in back taxes. He felt he could make thirty-five thousand on Ian's property alone. On the rest he might make forty or fifty thousand more.

So Lonnie thought he would go to town in the morning, pay the property tax with the money Ian had given him, wait until Evan helped him tear the mill down, then put Evan and old Mrs. Thorn out of their places, buy Ian's place, and turn about and sell their properties to the pulp and paper mill that wanted to clear a road right through Bonny Joyce. His profit would be more than eighty-thousand dollars in all. He could make a great deal of money out of this—and the money to pay everyone's back taxes had just come into his possession as if by complete chance that very night. (He had fifty-three hundred more in his drawer that Annette had given him over the last few years.)

He was, for those few minutes before his death, delighted by everything he had done in his life.

So then Ian had arrived first.

Lonnie took out a cigar and lit it, looking at him as the smoke billowed. Then he shook the match out and placed it on the table.

"I've come to give you money," Ian said. "But I want the test."

"What test?" Lonnie said, his eyes streaked with yellow. His mouth was round and playful on the cigar, his eyes suspicious.

"Annette's pregnancy test. I have money for you, but I want it back—and I will destroy it." He clutched the knife in his pocket and stood before the man who had betrayed his wife and his child. But then he let go of it and felt for the envelope. And he took the manila envelope out from under his coat.

"How much is in the envelope?"

"I am not saying," Ian answered.

"Is there anything in it?"

"Yes, but I am not saying how much. I think you should do the honourable thing and give it back, never mention Annette to anyone again, and I will hand you this envelope."

"You want it just to hold over her head?" Lonnie smiled slyly, thinking of Ian as being a man like himself.

"I intend to destroy it."

Lonnie took the cigar out of his mouth and looked at it, paused, then opined on all the things wrong with the world. Look at Africa—big mess; Asia—there was another one. Besides, what about him? Trouble had followed him all the days of his life, and what did he do but try to help people?

Ian held the envelope in his gloved hand—he was a citizen of the town now, dressed in a long tweed winter coat and silk scarf, and he wore a silk yellow tie. At one time, though not in a long while, he'd had meetings with premiers and with deputy ministers over town rezoning and a more efficient snow removal system, but in spite of it all, this was by far the most important meeting in his life. There was something magnificent in this meeting—something that stretched the boundaries of what was just and fair. Because this was the moment his empire, such as it was, was falling away, and all he had built up was going to be lost. The premier, who had once mentioned his name in the legislature, would no longer do so. The town council, which had once taken his opinions seriously, now scoffed. And he knew this, just as a man who gambled everything on a long shot knows this. So in this moment, in asking for this test, he was transcendent, trying to protect his namesake and give him what he could.

But he did not want to be caught here—by someone entering and seeing him. He had no idea that both his childhood friends were already on their way.

"Destroying it seems such a waste," Sullivan said. "I mean, look how she planned it. You know how conniving she was—how she planned it. Now I may as well tell you. 'You know who would be able to get close to him?' she asked me. 'And we wouldn't have to pay them much? His uncles—yes, have his uncles follow him, those town drunks. They would do it just to do it, find out where he goes, when he closes early.' I said, 'Pawnmesoultagod, that it didn't seem fair,' and she said, 'All is fair in love and war!' I said, 'What about Sara?' and she said, 'Sara who?' and laughed as if that poor little girl was nothing."

"That is not important." Ian touched the buck knife with his other hand, once more, and fleetingly thought of his son and Sara—and let go of the knife as if it burned him.

Lonnie looked hurt at this reprimand, and astonished that Annette was so beguiling, as if he too had been caught up in her web. Then he quietly lit his cigar again and looked at the *Auto Trader*, humming and hawing over pictures of snowmobiles. When he looked up, Ian had put the money away and was turning to leave.

"I didn't say no," Lonnie said. He stood and went into the dry room, near an old workbench and industrial wrench that Corky Thorn had sold to him some time before. He came back with an envelope and a slip of paper that he had kept for years. As he rummaged around, he spoke from the other room in carefree disregard of Ian's feelings or honour. He spoke about the trouble he'd been in with Sylvia's Mom years ago. Ian realized after some moments that he was talking about a trotter out of Truro, "owned by a man not like you or me," Lonnie said, but a man who didn't "have no feelings for people."

Sylvia's Mom was a good mare but got caught between a paddock fence and Lonnie's trailer in a snowstorm and had to be put down. So the man—an awful man, religious too, so you know what that's about—wanted six thousand. Lonnie said no way—but said he was frightened of losing his own horses. The man had seen Annette with him—more than a few times—and "That's where it all started," Lonnie said, matter of fact. Annette owed him "big-time" for a lot of things, and this would get her out from under. He insisted that she wanted to go; it was not his idea—he'd begged her "like my own daughter" not to. Now she wanted to go and meet a rich man. He had told her he didn't know any. But she'd insisted. She'd insisted on going with him to Truro. She was thinking she could do something special with her life. He'd tried to talk her out of it, said, "Think about your honour, and what about your future? But she said, 'Never mind that.' Do you understand? I had no choice in the matter," Lonnie said.

"I cried a thousand nights thinking about it," he said.

"I took her to him that spring. Don't think I wanted to! Don't think that!" Lonnie said without a change in his voice, adding, "Now, where is that goddamn paper—awful if I lost it! Anyway, she is with him—in the mortuary, and she frightened to death of funerals. It was an awful painful time. Poor little thing. I wanted to stop it. But what can a man do? Then afterwards she thought he loved her, because he told her how pretty she was—told her that he owned a house in Florida. 'Does he really have money?' she asks me. She goes to town and looks for a present for him, goes to the post office almost daily thinking he will write her. Ha!"

There was a pause for a moment before he continued talking. Not only as if Ian had no humanity, but as if Annette did not either.

"Before then, she wanted to get out of Bonny Joyce real bad, get away from Harold, take some course in Moncton, become a hairdresser. Trying to prove she was worth something—you know. So I pay for that and think my obligation is finished. But she had to meet that man, 'cause she had to be rich. Then what happens? She came to me two months later with the pregnancy test and was too scared to look at it. So I did. Was she really pregnant before she met you? Well, you can find out, once and for all," Lonnie said. "Then we will put all this terrible sordid affair behind us." And he came out smiling and looking somewhat defensive.

His arms were still large and strong, his eyes were somewhat watery at the moment, and Ian thought of killing him.

He handed over the envelope with the pregnancy test, and then went to take it back as a joke. Then he stuffed the *Auto Trader* in his pocket and took the envelope with the money. Eagerly he opened it, counted the money, suddenly breaking out into a sweat.

"Oh, I coulda got more than this," he said, but he looked pleased. His breath was short and his eyes glowed. "More than this. So open up the envelope and see what you think about her now," he said. "Yes or no—was she pregnant or not? It's like a big prize you might win." He nodded and pointed in expectation. "Go on. See if Liam is actually yours. He might be, after all."

Then he looked up, startled. Ian had taken the matches on the desk and lit the envelope with the pregnancy test inside.

"Aren't you even going to look?" Lonnie asked, incredulous.

Ian watched with inquisitive pensiveness as the small envelope burned and the fire grew hot. Some ash scattered, the small slip of paper inside burned too, and Ian held it in his hand until there was nothing to hold, and it fell and scattered—as if it was nothing at all.

He turned and left.

"Do you want to know? I been nice to you—I coulda got a lot more. Ha! I coulda got more—I'm being nice!"

Lonnie turned and shrugged and put the envelope with all that money in the back drawer and went inside the shed, opened the desk drawer, took out a bottle and poured a drink. He had another young girl coming in to clean the place for him. Someday he would tell her about Annette and how she broke his heart. How she robbed him. And he would warn that young girl not to be like Annette.

Now he thought that with this money all the property on both sides of Bonny would be his, and the houses he bought would be sold for a hundred thousand and bulldozed into a road for the mill, and he would get the biggest lump sum he had ever had—after sixty-eight years of life. He stretched suddenly and smiled at the thought of Ian trying to protect that woman.

Must be a point of honour or pride—something like that, he decided, spitting sideways onto the office floor and clearing his throat. God, he himself didn't remember if she was really pregnant or not. Yes, he had her believe she was something special to that man in Truro. Was that right—or what? He wasn't sure. But he'd never done anything to harm anyone. Really, he couldn't think of one instance when he had.

At that moment Lonnie Sullivan had twenty-four minutes to live.

———

A disaster was about to befall Ian Preston. He did not know this, nor could he have foreseen it in any way—nor contemplate the fight that he was about to be immersed in. He had no idea that the next day when he woke and went to his store and locked himself inside, that when he came out, he would become embroiled in the fight of his life.

By this time it was certain that Bonny Joyce was to be given up to a Helinkiscor cut that would include all the tracts of land everyone was concerned about—and more besides. By 1992, people were being offered money for their old properties at five times their price because a large new road had to be made—so many people were simply selling out and moving away. They understood they could not fight both the company and the government. Most were looking into what Helinkiscor would offer them—and these were the same properties Lonnie had been determined to pull out from under the feet of the rightful owners. But he had died in a queer accident at his office. So as I say, people were selling off and moving away, and the world had once again caught up with those on the fringe of it.

To most, Ian appeared to have forgotten all about it.

The little group he had organized in the late 1970s to protect the Bonny Joyce had long since disbanded. Now he never seemed to have a word to say on anything in the world. He wandered out at night alone, preoccupied and friendless. Men shouted insults at him because of the dealings they had had with him. Many things said about him were untrue, yet he had no one on his side. He was able to quell the pain in his back with pills and cocaine, and he was for the most part left alone. He did not drink himself into a stupor as Evan and Harold had—but the pills and cocaine offered the same stupor at a different rate of exchange.

Sometimes wags would come and ask him for money, or his uncles would phone him about a bill, and he would fuss and worry over this. And everyone knew it. Yes, he had been too stingy, even with Annette and his child. Then suddenly his uncles died, within two months of each other, and he was preoccupied with paying for their funerals, and trying to find enough people to act as pallbearers.

His wife no longer had anything to do with him. She went out at night alone. So no one paid the least bit of attention to him. That is, how could a man like this—dispossessed, attacked and ridiculed mount a campaign to save anything?

Yet just when everything seemed to be settled, a month or two before the mill started operation, Ian spoke up. No one had expected this from him at all—least of all Annette. Now and again Annette woke with a terrible hangover, and she would wander downstairs to look for him. He would have left a note with some money—informing her that he was going to see Liam after school, and he was working at the store and might stay there over supper. And she would not see him again that day. DD, in fact, began to plant the idea that Annette had more to live for and should seek a divorce.

Yet in spite of it all Ian looked almost venerable, as if his temperament and pain had changed his very nature. As he walked along the street, his face was strengthened by resolution. He used a cane because of his back, and waited at stoplights even when no traffic was coming.

He appeared at the town council one cold February night the next year. He was august, as if knowing supreme knowledge was bestowed from within. Suddenly the old suit and tie, the derelict face, revealed the contours of fascination and brilliance, a moment on the world stage with his hands shaking slightly as if palsied. His rubbers were covered in salt. His face was strained with worry. He had not spoken to Annette in a week—he had not been home once in that time. He had been making a plan, slowly but surely, to fight for Bonny Joyce.

"The woods won't last five years," he said at this meeting. He held a black briefcase filled with documents. He passed them around, and each councillor looked at them in turn and then passed them to the next councillor and then back to him.

"What is it?" one of the young men asked. A new, brash, understanding, liberal-thinking man—liberal in the sense that as a Maritimer the main concern must be money.

"Well," Ian said, "this is what Helinkiscor has done in Quebec. This is the track on the west side of the Gaspé—it is unrecognizable from this picture taken three years before! They have cut north of that too, and into the river. They have cut right up to the Caribou herd. That is why they have come here—and they have come for Bonny Joyce, which was considered by the Heritage Foundation to be untouchable and sacrosanct just ten years ago."

Ian, coming home from the town council through a dreary drizzle, realized he would be alone. Annette had told him that it was a losing cause, and was waiting for him to agree and to go back to being him. People had long talked about him as being what she'd thought he was when she was a girl—a complete fool. The one thing that stung her was this: many people spoke to her about him as if she should be as amused by him as they were.

"What's that husband of yours up to this time?" the ignorant man who ran the big clothing store in the mall asked her so loudly one day everyone turned to listen. "You'd better smarten him up. I hear he now wants to stop a hundred million dollars from coming to the river."

She turned and rushed away from the store, dropping the new boots she was going to buy, with DD running after her.

But when she told Ian what the man—someone so respectable—at the mall had said, he said it did not matter.

The same reaction manifested itself the next day and the day after. And no matter what she said in protest, Ian said it did not matter.

"I am saying this for your own good," she would tell him.

"But it does not matter at all!" he would say.

And this is what else he told her: Together they had betrayed Sara, and because of that he had tried to change, for Annette's sake—and now he would do so no longer. He had worn what she asked him to wear, made the friends she wanted, and now he would no longer do so.

"Betrayed Sara?" she said, deeply confused. "But don't you remember Sara betrayed me? It was the other way around—you know that, Ian, it was the other way around!"

She looked startled, then bit her bottom lip and tried to think. Tears came to her eyes.

She became worried. But for a few weeks nothing happened at all. And Ian did not go back to the town council—he waited at home. But he refused to take the pain pills for his back. He no longer took the cocaine that would free him from pain. No, he would not do it. He needed to think. And at times he lay on his back in the hallway, trying to sleep. He told her the concessions the government was willing to give Helinkiscor were abysmal and would ruin them all.

"Don't people see it?" he asked. He had lost weight, and his clothes seemed to hang off him. Sometimes he would try to speak and the words would not come.

"You are in despair," Annette said. "Yes, I have heard of men falling into that—despair."

Annette was taking yoga and had her own mat, and was doing jigsaw puzzles like she had done when she was a child. She had Liam help her. For the first time in years she seemed herself again.

Still to Ian, who had long wanted her to be this way, it no longer mattered. The days to him were meaningless and dark. He was focused only on one thing.

So one night after supper when they were all alone, he simply said, "I am about to take on Helinkiscor, and perhaps lose everything doing so."

"What do you mean?" Annette asked, putting down her romance novel, *Love's Desperate Flight*.

He answered her quite quietly and sincerely: "It means the destruction of a hundred thousand acres of land, and maybe all of the great Arron timber track—all the way to Clare's Longing," he said, trying to impress her, as a downriver girl. "There will be nothing left," he said, after a moment, "and if there is, it will never belong to us. It will belong to some Dutchman or Finlander. Everyone sees it, but no one seems to be strong enough to stand up to it—it is our entire downriver heritage."

She looked stunned, and rustled the page of the book as she turned it.

"Well, what does that have to do with you?" she asked sharply. "DD says so what about the stupid old wood! You live in town."

———

By now Helinkiscor knew who Ian was and what he was trying to accomplish—and had consulted the highest levels of the provincial government because, as they said, they wanted no worrisome spectacle. They didn't want trucks or dozers sabotaged. And the source they had consulted told them that Ian was a drug addict.

The deputy minister of forestry, who had actually grown up in the very area they were going to clear-cut, and was Helinkiscor's most enthusiastic champion, said, "He's a total disgrace—no one pays any attention to him. He cheated a dozen people around here."

But there was one thing Ian was waiting for.

The Helinkiscor road would cut along his property line on the Swill, and finally they had to approach him about it. The best way to approach anyone for something like this is to make little of it—that is, to make it seem very standard, and as if they could appropriate his land at any time. Two men came to the house one afternoon unexpectedly, when Ian was down at the store, and offered Annette fifteen thousand for the right of way. She was beside herself—fifteen thousand for a bit of dirt on the Swill way out at Bonny Joyce! She telephoned Ian and asked him to come home. He came to the house, and saw the two foreign men in business suits sitting in the living room, both wearing overshoes with snaps. They smiled at him when he entered and warmly stood and shook his hand, as if they had come to a great meeting of minds already.

When he said no to the fifteen thousand, they offered him twenty thousand.

One was a small fellow with a limp, and the other had a bald head, the surface of which looked like a walnut. Both of them were from the Quebec office. What was it about, money? Well then, they were prepared to offer twenty-five thousand, but no more.

"Twenty-five thousand!" Annette said.

Ian again said no.

They picked up their briefcases—each had one, beautiful briefcases with nice brass snaps—and left.

"Are you nuts!" Annette said. "We can't possibly get more!"

"I don't want more."

"Then why don't you take what they offered?"

"My place downriver is not for sale."

In fact he had been told three days before that an offer would come. His land was ten acres—simply ten acres that had rarely been walked on and had a small brook called Preston Creek that ran into the south branch of Little Hackett, which in turn ran into Arron Brook at Glidden's Pool. Yes, it was up there she had sent him running one time to seek her out—and he did—run.

Ian had not been down to see it himself in three years. It had been his old homestead (which in the papers drawn up in the offer was called a shack), the place where he had made all his plans to be a businessman. The place where he'd sat on the porch waiting for Annette to come up through Bonny Joyce Road, to watch her just as she walked by him. (He and a dozen other young men.)

Still, the idea of taking on the whole province—holding up everyone over a sliver of land, which Annette couldn't even remember—enthralled her. Suddenly it comforted her to think he was like the great Lonnie Sullivan himself. Even though Lonnie had tormented her, she still missed him. So she began to talk not like her innocent self but like her ruthless self, the self that Lonnie himself had helped create; a side of her nature that for Ian was unnatural, and that Liam noticed and seemed ashamed of.

"Everyone said you were cagey!" Annette proclaimed the next day, her beautiful and dreamy eyes suddenly more cunning than before. "Now I know it!" she said with deep enthusiasm. "Now I see it. Ripp? Ha! You have it all over Ripp. Wait until I tell him. He'll change his tune."

"Oh," Ian said. "So Ripp has a tune."

"Well, you know Ripp," she said clumsily. "Wait until I tell DD," she said.

He had never seen her so happy with him. It was the first time he remembered her being pleased she was his wife. He smiled at her tenderly, and touched her cheek. He never answered.

The next day a man came to the store. He walked in and came over to Ian, who was waiting on a customer, and held out his hand.

"Ian," he said. "God it's been a while, lad. How are you?"

For a moment Ian tried to decide who this fellow was, this fellow who was so friendly. And then he realized: oh yes, older, more obsequious, more wrinkled, but with the same pleasant smile, the same admirable way in which to bring men to his side—yes, the man who had interviewed Ian for a job at the mill years before. Now not so proud to come into the store—a place he had not been in before—and now not so proud to take Ian's hand in friendship. Yes, a former mayor, with his dark ring on his little finger and the strap of a gold watch just visible.

"Go away," Ian said.

Then Ian simply turned and continued to work.

There was someone else with him at that moment as well—a small rotund man, waiting and carefully watching. His name was Wally Bickle. Ian knew him from long ago. Bickle was the man who had been called to work at the mill, and had just sized up the person he had come with to Ian's store. Yes, Bickle decided, the man, a former personal manager, was a lightweight—incapable of anything. Ian wouldn't even speak to him. So Wally would distance himself from this fellow in the next week, and begin to assassinate Ian's character wherever he was, tell people about Ian's youth, something so well known in Bicklesfield and Bonny Joyce.

Ian worked until dark, then locked the store and went home. It was bitter and cold and yet some light flared way out in the sky, and he heard the thud of a snow shovel in someone's yard.

A sudden thought came to him: I will lose Annette. And part of him realized he did not want to—that he was desperate not to. I am deceiving her by not telling her what is going to happen—when she realizes it, it will be too late—too late! Poor Annette, she does not know.

And suddenly he felt that everything in his life was over.

At ten that very night a call came—it wasn't either of those two men with the briefcases or the former personal manager but another man, named Mr. Ilwal Fension. He was prepared to offer 27,500 for Ian's land and the right to tear down the old shack that was on it.

"We are putting a road through, you see—we plan to start hauling out of there sometime in the next few months. We will put your whole town to work! It is a very depressed area, and we could have gone to many other places—but we want to put people to work, we want people to be self-sufficient."

Fension told Ian to call him Ilwal.

"No," Ian said.

"No? You won't call me Ilwal?"

"No, I won't take the twenty-seven five," Ian answered.

"You are just trying for more, aren't you?" Annette said, asking a question, yet her voice pleading. "I told DD you would soon settle. So—I want to know when you will, so I can tell my friends, okay?"

He looked at her for a long moment. She was scared now, and frightened of him.

"I will allow them the land if they promise not to cut Bonny."

He knew that all these discussions about what they would offer him were done in consultation with the province, and that he was ostracized for holding them to ransom. But Ian, as much of a failure as he was, would still always be the brightest one in the room.

That night, shadows played off the wall as traffic went by, and the blinds were drawn, and the magazine with the Arborite display was open on the carpet. And the air was still. And the rooms were quiet in a clinging pedestrian way, and the mahogany banister shone with new polish. Annette was smoking and the smoke lingered in the shadows as well. She didn't speak to him; she watched him. She was like a brilliant beautiful cat. And she too had nine lives. She watched him, and butted her cigarette. There was something terrible about him, officious and unlikeable—and she was worried. Couldn't they have some kind of a life together with that money—and a life for Liam as well? She felt he was doing this to spite her, because she had hurt him by some of the frivolous things she had done. She knew now how others disrespected him because of her. Well then, if she'd hurt him she was sorry—but she did not know how to say it.

If she had known, it might have changed everything for the better.

"What will I tell DD about what our plans are, and when we will get the money?" she asked, hopefully, like one asking a favour. "They all want to know—you should see how jealous they are of us now. All of them are jealous of you—and I just say, 'That's my man.'"

He looked at her a long moment.

"Tell DD . . . well, tell DD to go to hell."

She stood and went to bed.

The next afternoon a man, Whitaker, from town council came to see him.

"What they are offering you is pretty good. Mr. Conner and I were saying this last night—that they should offer you something comparable to what others in Quebec got—and I said, 'Ian deserves more than the froggies.' So I'm telling you they went way over that—and that's what we wanted them to do!" He smiled as if this was a secret and Ian should be overjoyed. But Ian seemed unmoved. He asked why they needed his land—there must be another way in to the cut.

"Yes, of course there is," Whitaker said.

"Then they should plow that."

Whitaker said he did not know why they did not do so. Maybe they felt they should give the people of Bonny something.

"Nonsense—there is another reason. They would offer me nothing if they could get around dealing with me. No, the government is hiding how weak they are in dealing with this company."

"The government will just confiscate the land."

"I will make sure the legal ramifications will hold it up for two years," Ian said calmly. "By that time we will know what is going on."

For a few days they were silent. Then the man with a fez on his walnut-shaped head came to see him. He tried to look dignified but was obsequious and startled whenever Ian said anything kind or sensible: "Yes, yes, yes," he would say.

They offered Ian a hundred thousand dollars. Annette sat open-mouthed—one hundred thousand! No one would laugh at them now, she said. Lonnie never did a deal so good, she said. She laughed so hard she had to lean against the counter—just as she had done when she was sick all those years ago. She began to dance in her slippers all around the room, telling him what they could buy—and where they could go for vacation.

"I am not taking it," he told her.

But Mr. Fension came with another offer that very night—he said it would be the last offer: $210,000. He was fit and young-looking and had a tailor-made suit and soft leather gloves, and he spoke, as Annette told DD the next day, like such a gentleman. And she had flirted with him to make him like Ian.

But Ian did not take that offer either.

Lawyers then called Ian, asking if he needed their help. There were two messages left on the phone by J. P. Hogg himself. One said: "If you want to look at the legal aspect of this—I am always here for you."

Then, for four or five days, no one said a thing about the money or the company or the wood. And in the midst of all his Ian started to go to the rec centre and play badminton like he had many years ago, after he and Annette were first married. He was silent to her and refused to speak to the mayor when he phoned.

"I have a badminton match," he said. And lo and behold, the mayor turned up at the recreation centre that night with a badminton racket and squeaky new sneakers.

Annette felt what everyone else did: that Ian was trying to make a name for himself and get on the news, and bring shame to the town. This is what people hinted at, and they said they were not going to stand for it! This, in fact, is what Annette now decided to think as well. Because in order to protect herself, she too had to agree and belong. If she did not, she would be accused of being like Ian. So she was desperate, and Ian knew this is how it would happen. And he felt deeply sorry for her and his child.

But you see, now even if Ian had wanted to take the money—even if he could see what it might do to have this money for his son (and he was only human—he did think of this, and he did think of taking the offer), he could not take it, for he had placed his reputation on the line, had said that the Bonny should not be cut by foreigners who wanted to destroy Arron Brook. If he did take it, everyone would simply look at him as dishonest—an accusation he had been fighting all of his life.

DD told Annette people were saying she was orchestrating it all because she wanted money—that is why she had married Ian in the first place.

"You know that's not true, DD—we loved each other. You said— remember you said!"

Annette could not look at him; she was now like a little ghost—she sat by the wood fireplace and trembled. Her face more than ever reminded him of a porcelain doll's—a woman whose youth was fading. You may have seen her in any court in Europe in the last four hundred years, sitting off to the side in a room of splendid strangers. And she was an innocent too in all this—that is, in her heart of hearts she could never understand why they shouldn't take the money for Liam.

But Ian could not explain it. He could only say he had gone too far to back down now. So this new offer compelled him to be more reckless and more driven, and less conscious about the enemies he now made. The town itself wanted an explanation, wanted him to answer to them. He was invited to the town council to explain his reasoning. He told the town in an interview to "go to hell." They had never cared for him; why then should he care for them? And in fact, he hadn't seen many of them visit him on the Swill Road when he was a boy. So why should they take such an interest in the Swill Road now?

"You have called me stingy and miserly. That is not at all true," he told the paper, and added rashly, "in a week the town will see who I am."

Annette broke down and cried, and begged Ian to realize what he was doing to them. How they would be ruined.

She was right—he knew it. All of his life he'd wanted her to be right, and now she was, for she was trying to save them.

He wrote her a note, which she held in her hand for an hour: *You wanted me to destroy myself—from the time I was a boy. Well, you've got your wish, love.*

On a Saturday during a thaw, just when the cold case involving Lonnie Sullivan was about to reopen, Ian Preston began to hand out pamphlets about Bonny Joyce, and show a painting done by a local woman of the devastation done in the 1970s. He also printed assurances from the same government two years ago that said the Bonny Joyce tract would never be negotiated because of the damage it might cause to two river systems. He stood in the cold for three hours, with Liam by his side. Most people were polite but uncaring, for too many jobs were at stake. Some young boys mocked him, and men came from the tavern and laughed.

One yelled, "You'd better watch your store, Mr. Preston!"

"Never mind them, Liam," he said. "There are enough men like that—and no one like you."

On that same evening, Annette was introduced to Wally Bickle at the curling club. He wore a new curling sweater with one pin. He shook her hand briefly; said, "Oh, the wife of Mr. Preston, the man who is holding us all hostage!" Then he turned his back, and left her embarrassed, the smile still on her face.

As an outsider in town this seemed just the right thing for him to do.

Bickle no longer worked for the finance company and was no longer with the compensation board but was now working with Mr. Ticks, the new senior manager; some said he might be a supervisor himself some-day. All his life, Bickle had been able to size up who might be able to help him. The old personnel manager had got him in the door, but now it was Mr. Ticks who was his mentor—someone who knew the ropes. People said Wally Bickle was religious (so you had to be careful how you spoke) and went to the Baptist church.

The next afternoon, when Ian came home, she looked like a different woman. His intransigence had changed her. Her eyes were red and raw, her hair dishevelled, and she was trembling.

She pleaded, but he did not answer. He simply stared out the window at the dusk coming across the street and night falling. When he looked back, she had fallen to her knees. Shaken, he turned away.

She threw some of his pamphlets at him and screamed, "Everyone knows you're insane—as soon as you got at me, you started to show your other side—that's what DD says! All my friends say it too—even though I don't want to admit it! That's my money as much as it is yours—and I want my money!"

"I am not at all insane," he said, "so there is no use in hysterics. You never even stepped on Swill Road when I was a boy—and I remember—"

"What—what do you remember?"

"I remember how you tormented me because I came from there," he said.

A few days later he heard that his store was to be boycotted until such time as he allowed the road to open.

When he told Annette, she said, "So, what do you think they should do? I have to live in this town, you know—and everyone at Cut and Curl just calls you a big jerk! Everyone wants the mill, and you are calling everyone down. I thought we were going to have a good life. If you sell the land and then write a letter to the paper—that's what my friends say—and admit you were wrong, there won't be any boycott. So do that, if you care about me!"

"I do care about you very much—because both of us were young and foolish. You no more no less than I."

"Well then, please write them." She bit her bottom lip and waited for his reply.

He looked at her seriously for a moment. "No—I won't do that," he said calmly.

"Then I will move out and I will take Liam."

"Then move out—but you will not take Liam! I will kill you first."

And after that, he moved into the basement apartment and lived there.

———

Ian now more than ever before began to see the ramifications of being alone. He began to see what it was like, and realized the one thing the world wanted him to feel was shame.

He would wait for his son after school. He relied upon the boy to help him, spacing the old and new product in the showroom, moving the hundreds of sheets of gyprock into the shelves on the lower floor. But the boy was just a child, and was being bullied and tormented about his father at school. His father was being called a traitor.

The girl Sherry Mittens didn't look at Liam—but later had some other boys and girls catcall behind him as he walked home.

Then the boycott of Ian's store started in earnest.

"It does not matter," Ian told Annette.

"You are crazy—everyone says you are crazy. Ripp says so too."

"I do not know or care. I can only tell you he is a coward!"

The next morning she came to the basement, opened the door carefully, woke him, sat beside him and held his hand: "Okay, I know we haven't been getting along and I will be better, but—well, come on—you know you have to give it up. Sell the land. I was thinking—they are offering two hundred—well, what if you went and asked for three hundred thousand or even four hundred thousand? Well, we can be a family again, and you will be respected."

"How can I respect myself if I change now? I may as well be dead."

"But I—I will respect you. I promise."

He got up, walked her to the door and closed it on her.

Conner, the MLA, retired a week later. He said he supported the government's decision concerning Helinkiscor, but many knew he'd retired because he did not—because of what was given up and because of the government's broken promise about Bonny Joyce, which he himself had stood for in the previous two elections.

"Yes, it's bad what they did to us!" people would say, reading about his retirement in the paper, and then shrug as if they suspected and even approved of what the government was doing—so that Ian informing them of the truth was an unnecessary burden, and his holding up the work was still unconscionable. This, then, became the idea about Ian: that he was waiting for an offer of one million dollars—and the newspaper phoned him and asked him if this was true.

"Is it a million—is it?" they asked, the way newspapers so often do, in the gleeful suspicious manner they wish to inform the public.

Finally Helinkiscor began to make arrangements to cut on the far side of Bonny Joyce, which meant they would have to make the road into Quebec from a far more difficult place (it would cost them many more millions, which is why they were willing to offer Ian so much). Yet the reason for all of this—the reason being that they wanted to use the Quebec mill and not the New Brunswick one to process the New Brunswick wood, and put New Brunswick men and women out of work not for a year or two but for good—would only come out in five years.

Once Conner resigned, however, there was to be a by-election, and Ian Preston decided to run for MLA.

Hearing from others what he was about to do, Annette told him she worried about the money he would have to spend.

"Ripp makes fun of you," she said, staring at him with a look of lonely caution, the sad face of a confused girl, "and we don't want that!"

"We don't want Ripp making fun of me? Why not? When didn't he? When didn't he, with your tacit approval? It doesn't matter! I told you that Ripp and DD and Dickie are cowards!"

"I don't know what that means—'tacit'! How much will you spend?"

"It doesn't matter."

"But maybe we will end up with nothing."

"I had nothing to begin with. It doesn't matter. I already spent my last dime." And he looked at her strangely.

"When?"

"When I bought you an ice cream at Bobbi's Dairy Bar that day—remember? It was my last dime—you didn't mind me spending it then."

"You want to kill me." She smiled. "Is that right? You want to kill me, or have me kill myself. That's what this is about—to drive me to kill myself. I should have known."

The only way Annette could cope now was to drink, and he knew this. But he couldn't help her anymore. When drinking and slurring her words, she began to berate him: Why did he come home to meet the men from the company when she called him that day if he did not want the money?

Why was he so greedy that he wanted a million, as everyone said?

Why did he think people hadn't caught on to him?

Why did he think he could fool people?

He did not answer—he was plagued by other concerns.

Why the company wanted a road into Quebec he wasn't sure—but he knew that was why Conner had resigned, he told her calmly. That was the day she threw a glass of gin at him.

So he began to campaign, and he got the reputation of being an environmentalist who was trying to ruin their livelihood.

He was also leaving himself universally vulnerable to those men who always looked self-congratulatory when they capitulated to the will and ideas of the mob. And that was almost everyone who had ever worked for the mill.

And he did not know this: the real reason Conner resigned—that is file 0991563. It was in Fension's office and drawn up with the approval of the minister of forestry. So furious were they with Ian Preston they decided that at a certain opportune time they would offer his troubled and innocent wife, Annette Brideau, a very good job. That is, they would bide their time, but someday they would pay him back.

———

One night a week or so after he announced he was running and that his platform was to stop the mill, a rock came through his store window. A week after this, Ian applied for an injunction to hold up the mill in court.

Ian went to Mr. Conner's house, pleading with him to reveal what concessions the government was actually making.

"What do you mean?" said Conner.

Ian left without obtaining anything. It was the longest walk, from Conner's steps to the car.

The phone would ring at the house and at the store at all hours, with requests for pipes and insulation and siding and tubing from everywhere and everyone—so Ian did not know who the real customers were. And then came the warning: "Get out of your store."

"His wife hates him," the mayor said to Mr. Fension, who was meeting him in his office that afternoon, Fension trying to force an ultimatum within the town power structure itself and hoping they could bring pressure to bear against the recalcitrant citizen. Fension made a comment about the fact that such a beautiful woman was living with such an ingrate, and the mayor smiled at the universality of some blasphemies.

"Everyone hates him. We accepted him with open arms, and look what happens."

"But his wife doesn't own the land?"

"No, she doesn't!"

"So there is nothing to be done. We will have to go through the other side," Fension said. And he sighed. That meant they would stop trying to convince him to sell, and simply cut road out on the far side of Bonny—though they knew this would cost them much more than they wanted. And they had a proposal in to the government to seek even more financial help. Or to force Ian's hand—but that would mean litigation, and they could not afford the time.

"We will give him one more week," Fension said, "but he is one bastard!"

Sometimes the most fortuitous things one says are said without knowing. For in four days everything would turn in the company's favour.

There was one man who had discovered a flaw in Ian Preston's claim. The night Harold stole the money—not the fifteen thousand in the envelope, a payment for Liam's security, but the fifty-three hundred that was also there, which Lonnie had initially salted away from Annette herself and others who owed him—there was a sketch of all the Swill Road properties. For months Harold had no idea why this was in the envelope along with the fifty-three hundred. So he went to the courthouse on his own, and there he discovered Ian had not paid his back taxes.

Now, in three days, the mill was preparing to start the road on the other side of Bonny and had already begun moving equipment. Harold waited until the last moment because he himself was hesitant and unsure. That is, it was a terrible act of betrayal on his part. But when he decided, he decided once and for all. Yet a secretary at city hall had the audacity to put him on hold, and when the call was taken, he had to argue that he was the one who actually owned the property. Finally, when he was on the verge of hanging up, they realized what he might be saying. So they were very polite and apologized profusely. "Well then, can we see you?"

"Yes—but it better be today, or I will go to Ian himself!"

In fact, Harold still loved Annette and thought seriously of going to her. She could pay the back taxes, get the property and sell it—for Harold and her, and Liam. But on further thought he decided to teach them the lesson they deserved. So he paid the back taxes that had not been paid in years and no one in town had thought to inquire about, and now owned the property outright. And he thought: She would take off Ian's diamond, and someday he would have it!

Later that same day the man with the walnut-shaped head went downriver, and a whoop of approval came from him—a strange little foreign man in high knee socks and flannel trousers, who nonetheless could whoop in delight. Some snowy rain began to fall and a trace of fog lay over the tops of all the great trees in the distance, which were to be cut.

Then, exactly a month after Annette had met Wally Bickle, construction on the road started and Ian Preston's old house on Swill Road, with its windows busted and its steps sunken, was simply bulldozed under.

Ian got into his truck and drove down, passed eight graders and dozers and twelve dump trucks, sluicing all along the dirt road right up the side lane until he crashed into a backhoe. "This is my land—get off my land!"

He had cut his head on the steering wheel and looked dazed. He began to stumble forward, and picked up a marker and tossed it aside. But everyone there ignored him, as if he had become a painful joke. Fension was on-site that moment and passed him a surveyor's clip and a certificate of ownership.

"You should have taken the money," Fension said, his high green boots tied up tight and his heavy pants bulging at both pockets, and the air so fresh it was like an insult in his nose. "All that money could have been yours." He said this very sorrowfully, as if he was on Ian's side.

Not knowing what Ian had been offered, Harold had sold the land to Helinkiscor for a quick twenty-five thousand dollars. Putting the road on this side of Good Friday Mountain would save the company some fourteen million dollars.

Annette was throwing up in the bathroom when Ian entered the house. Harold Dew had phoned her and told her what he had done.

The land had been taken away from Ian and he got nothing at all. He went into the small den and sat down, surrounded by magazines.

She came to see him, opened her mouth to speak, but no words came.

He looked up to see her standing in the door. She had not dressed all day, and her robe was open—she had nothing on underneath, and her naked body was still too beautiful for him to gaze at long because he had never deserved it, and he now knew this.

"Oh God, Ian," she said, "what have you done? Dear Ian, what have you done to us all!"

She stood in her nakedness before him, in her beautiful nakedness, her face flushed, her eyes closed, tears running down her cheeks.

In fact, Annette Brideau's tragedy would begin now.

———

A month or more passed.

In Clare's Longing, Harold Dew sat up late. Yes, he had been forgotten by Ian and Annette. They had thought he was far in their past—a shadow, a ghost no longer noticeable in their lives. But now they were beginning to wake up. Now they were beginning to see things for the way they were!

Now, though he in his lucid moments knew he wasn't Liam's father, in some way known only to himself he *was* the father, and Annette had cheated him out of a son. Long ago he had secretly plotted to take Evan's traps, and look what had happened; now he had Ian's land—so he should let it go.

But he thought: One more thing and I'll be done with them for good. One more thing—and then Liam will come to live with me.

So that night, cold with shadows on the ground from the glimmering roadway light, a man walked toward the old grey farmhouse with its tattered shed and barn, those frameworks bent and twisted down, gone hollow even before the Korean War.

The young man was dressed in a sheepskin coat with a woollen collar pulled up, and his blond hair wavy and combed back. His eyes were dark and his face chiselled in a kind of youthful toughness. He had dark workboots on his feet, the heels of which heightened him by almost two inches to just under six feet four. He was Rueben Sores, Evan Young's half-brother. He believed in nothing and therefore he was free.

He had been called to come to this house by Harold Dew.

He walked onto the soft and dark veranda, where a thought of riches once had been, and even here it drifted in the stifled cold and boredom of a place lonely and faraway. He knocked on the heavy door. A muffled voice was heard inside. He entered to the tinkle of a doorbell.

There in the kitchen, abiding the time by an out-of-date calendar, Harold sat, with his feet in a pail of hot grey water and a woollen blanket draped over his shoulders.

He waved Rueben forward and shifted the table light to look at him. He spoke to Rueben Sores about a clandestine campaign against the one who had taken his money and his fiancée.

"He lost the land—the road has started—all as he has left is his quest to be MLA. So tear down his posters, kill his campaign!" he said in a hoarse whisper, the way he had spoken now for a number of months.

"I don't know if I want to do that. Besides, his campaign is done for anyhow," Rueben said, for Rueben had in some respects always clung to a sense of honour.

Harold took out some money—two hundred dollars.

"Why not? It has to be done when he is down—that's when to kick his nuts off."

Rueben looked at the money, hesitated, and picked it up. Harold licked his large White Owl cigar and lit it.

"If you disrupt him enough, I will get you a truck to haul wood from the Bonny Joyce."

Then Harold went to the door, his wet feet marking a trail, as Rueben was walking away; and holding the door open, so the kitchen light shone on both his bare wet feet and a patch of snow, whispered thus: "Light a fire—we'll see what happens to him without his store."

Rueben nodded, and said nothing. He set out to meet two young friends, Spenser and Kyle, both reliant upon him for drugs (for that is the bond that glued so many). They went to the tavern across the river in Chatham and planned what they might do to disrupt the campaign.

"The campaign is wrong for the whole river," Rueben said. "It's a shame. Is your brother trying to get work up there?"

"Yes," Spenser said.

"Well then, it's awful. So is mine. You see, he stole his money to buy the store from Harold."

"He did?"

Rueben nodded.

It became a solemn and moral moment occasioned by the town's revulsion of Ian Preston.

"Get his boy," Kyle said, as if this was a brave thing. "Give him a whack or two."

Spenser nodded at this: "Yes, get the boy."

Rueben was silent.

They wore their woods vests, their eyes glassy. Each of them had steel-toed boots and a good luck charm in his pocket.

"Tomorrow, then!"

———

Liam continued to protect his father's posters: VOTE FOR IAN PRESTON. STOP THE THEFT OF BONNY JOYCE—FOR OUR FUTURE.

After school on March 26, Liam had climbed a snowbank and on to the pole nearest the lane that led to his house, to try to protect one of them. And he had other posters in his hand, which had been torn down by other schoolchildren.

"What future?" Kyle asked, walking toward him.

"Ya, what future if there is no work now?" Spenser said. "How much yer daddy pay you?"

He did not know who they were.

Rueben needed to say nothing, and stood behind a shed smoking, with the light of afternoon still strong on the sidewalks and the snow. He only needed to feel justified. And since he believed Ian Preston had cheated both Harold and his own half-brother, Evan, he did.

"The mill will ruin the river. It's what my dad said . . ." Liam answered.

"Yer dad—yer dad is a criminal," Spenser scoffed, and not a tooth showed in his head while his stringy hair fell in front of his eyes.

"He's a gutless puke, yer daddy. He run from my dad down at the piles."

Liam was asked three times to give up his signs. But he refused and turned to go home. The street was darkening. And the houses were silent. And then, so sudden it took the wind from him, he was thrown to the road by Kyle and slapped by young Spenser Rogue. They kicked him twice in the side, but he still hung on to his posters. Then they grabbed him by the hood and hauled him backward across the street, as the day orbed toward darkness. Still he would not let go.

"Get some matches and burn them out of his hands," Kyle said. He lit the last three matches he had, and held them until the glassy posters caught afire. It smelled of evening now, of some vague kindle and spark, the sky solemn and whitening to dark.

"Singe his hair!" And Kyle lit the boy's hair until it crinkled and a patch of it whispered and blackened.

With the posters burning, Liam held on to them, until his hands started to burn.

"Kick his face."

So Spenser kicked his face. Finally Rueben came over and threw them off—anxious about what they had done to the child.

"Come on," he said, "that's enough—we don't do that to a boy— leave him alone."

It wasn't until much later that night Ian discovered something wrong. Seeing the boy's hands, he asked calmly who had done this. But Liam, fearing his father might get into trouble, would not say.

"Tell me!" Ian smashed a mirror and cut his own hand.

He rushed his child to the hospital, his own hands covered in blood because of the mirror.

It was when there, having his hand bandaged, he got a call about what was happening at his store.

———

An hour or so after dark, the boys who had torn the posters down went along the sidewalks. Rueben Sores told his two accomplices what he would do. Hatred was exactly that—an exquisite feeling. So it did not matter at this moment who he hated. In fact, with memories of his tormented youth plaguing his budding manhood, he hated the world.

Harold wanted him to burn the store of Harold's old enemy. But Rueben would not be able to get inside easily, so he went around to the back where the old shed was, saw the little election headquarters of Ian Preston closed up and a picture of Ian in the door window.

"Come on," he said to his friends. "Come on."

In this shed there was only a dusty desk with some staple guns and posters, a telephone and an unwrapped computer. Rueben busted the window.

"Who has matches?" he asked.

But strangely, none of them did. They had wasted the last of them on burning Liam's posters.

"Christ, no matches!" he said. Then suddenly he laughed. "Look."

He picked up the small Bic lighter that had been left there by Corky Thorn the morning he died. Rueben stood a moment watching the flame, amazed that he had fire in his hand.

"The gods," he said, and he sniffed. "Hand me some posters," he said to the boys.

He lit the posters they handed to him, and tossed them here and there. Soon the shed was ablaze, and so was the back wall of the store. Everything was going to burn.

Then Rueben, Spenser and Kyle ran. Ran away.

Ian, at the moment his store was afire, was driving Liam to emergency. Liam, whose hair was singed and whose hands were burned. This was to cause the greatest calamity in Ian's life.

He lost somewhere close to $185,000. He was also sued for smoke damage to three other stores and paid restitution of thirty-four thousand. Ian's insurance company contested the claim, and only made partial payment. So angered were people that Ian received many death threats.

Annette kept looking out the window, terrified of a mob. "If the mob comes, I am sure it will be a big mob—for it is a big mob that probably hates you," she said, lighting one cigarette off another and peeking from behind the curtains.

A Social Services lady, Melissa Sapp, visited the house on four occasions and took statements from Liam, which she recorded. People recoiled when they saw Ian. The one young girl who was walking with Liam—Sherry Mittens—said she had not seen any boys doing things, for she had gone home, and she thought Liam had gone home too. Sherry said this very politely, always thankful at being able to help.

Liam remembered there was someone else walking past the armoury. The police made some effort to locate this man but could not. So most people assumed the story was a fabrication concocted to protect his father.

They were suddenly, Ian and Annette, poor. In fact, very poor.

He lost the election by four thousand votes.

Six hundred men and women went to work because of the mill. Six hundred families had a new lease on life. Ten thousand people ignored him and never darkened the door of his shattered business again.

PART SEVEN

ANNETTE KEPT THINKING OF THE MONEY IAN HAD LOST BY not doing what she said—by not listening to her. She spent days staring at her photo albums—the pictures she had taken when she was going to be a model—she had photos of herself in various poses and dress. She had taken a modelling course two years after she'd had the child. The whole atmosphere of this modelling course held on Wednesday nights in the back room on the bottom floor of Saint Michael's was so much fun. So many people picked her out as being someone to watch.

"You will go places," Madam Leslie said.

And everyone seemed to agree. She got a gold star on her certificate.

The certificate read Qualified With Distinction

And it was signed by Madam Viola Leslie.

Annette had paid $457 for the course and to get the photos done—and she'd had an offer to model clothes for a store in Moncton one afternoon, but it had snowed and she did not go down.

Where were those days now? she thought. Where had they gone? She was so sad now. Why did life seem to matter? Nothing mattered anymore.

"He is poor now!" she said to DD. "He is really poor!"

"Oh my God, I know," DD would say, trying to comfort while hiding a slight beguiling smile. So then after the thousands he'd given her from his store; after the parties he tried to throw for her; after the cottage, the house, the car—now was the time. To leave.

In some way, she still did not want to leave him. In some way, she wanted to remain married—whether because of Sara or because of him she did not really know. This gave her tremendous beauty a vulnerability. And people advised her. She found she had many advisers now.

They told her she had done her level best to be faithful, but now he had hurt her desperately. Burned his own store and injured his child.

"You can't be a doormat for him," someone she hardly knew told her one day. And others told her that too. She was frightened all the time.

Another woman took Annette's hands in her own, and blinking back tears nodded, as if recognizing a compatriot.

"I know how it is!" she said.

Annette had always disliked this woman, but suddenly she too had tears in her own eyes.

Belief is emphatic. That is, did Annette believe what they said about him? If she did not believe, she could not leave, so her willingness to believe, even if it was false—that is, her willingness to believe in falseness— promoted the illusion of freedom. And all those around her promoted this at will. When she brought up his name at a card game at the curling club one night (because someone was talking about their uncle having an operation on his back), no one responded. And she kept her eyes hidden behind her cards. So little by little she became convinced that her friends were right.

It is dangerous not to think of your friends as your greatest enemies. It is dangerous not to think that those who have conformed in their views all their lives will not conform when thinking of you, and not want you to enliven their boredom or affirm their belief in how they were told the world works by revelling in your destruction.

Annette did not know that what her friends most wanted from her was not her inclusion but her performance.

A month or so after the store burned down, Fension danced with her and flirted with her, putting his hand down the small of her back when they waltzed. He knew she was married to a hopeless idiot, and he had the grace to exploit it at a dance. He told her stories and pretended he didn't even know Ian. One whole evening they sat side by side, while the snow shone under the lights outside and the avenues were deep and dark and mysterious in the vales of snow. He suddenly felt her eyes were as secretive as dark melting ice that he'd seen as a boy in Norway.

She smoked cigarettes in the quiet maze of romance, and spoke to Fension about her terrible childhood—how she'd had very little, how she'd been used. He took her hand the moment she caught her breath before tears came. Then she smiled when he told a joke in his thick accent, and he kissed her cheek.

But the next afternoon, a Sunday, Mr. Fension arrived at the club with his utterly beautiful wife, who had come from Oslo to surprise him. So Fension walked by her tersely and nodded. She sat alone that day at the back near the kitchen, with its pale smell of soup and crackers, and looked longingly out at the stale air enveloping the icy parking lot. A look of seductive tragedy that she herself did not understand. But it seemed now that everyone else did.

On the way home, she fell and cut her hand. She lay in bed for days. She dialed Fension's phone number and hung up. She thought once or twice of killing herself.

She thought of her cousin Doris Branch, who almost ate herself to death after her husband began to run around on her.

I don't want to eat myself to death, she thought one night as she lay in bed, but I could go for a pizza.

The house was quiet. DD told Annette that she must go to see her the very next day—and decide everything. So anxiousness kept her awake tossing and turning; going over again and again the idea of lost money, and the idea—deep within her—that she had helped destroy Ian's life.

But amid all of these fantastic and fleeting thoughts a sudden strange presence seemed to invade her consciousness. This presence became pronounced for the most fleeting of seconds. Was it even there—could she ever believe in it? It aggravated her that she had even thought of Molly Thorn—beautiful, wise little Molly Thorn. And what did this "idea" of Molly Thorn say in the middle of the night, so softly and lovingly: something that had nothing to do with money or divorce or being important. The voice said:

"Annette—please—stop—love and you will be loved."

But the secret was: if she did so, it meant giving up her new position, a position where everyone was waiting to see what she, Annette Brideau would do. And she realized she valued this new position too much to let it go.

The next day DD told her she must get a divorce. There was no way to live with a man like that, and DD said she would not allow it. "For God's sake, have some self-respect!" she said.

Annette told DD she was not even sure what lawyer to see, for she had nobody to help her. But DD was willing to help and to supply her with the name of a lawyer. That proved she was serious. In fact, she would recommend no other but him, the one Diane herself had when divorcing Clive: J. P. Hogg.

Annette went home determined to phone him. She picked up the receiver half a dozen times, stared at it in a daze, and placed it back.

Then one day, about two weeks after she had talked so privately to Mr. Fension, young Wally Bickle, the man from Bicklesfield, met her on the street and suddenly took her hand.

He looked with his new moustache, like most of the junior managers at the mill. He had a great ability to be arrogant to those who were lower than he was, and obsequious to those above him.

"I don't know if you remember me," he said. "We were introduced at the curling club."

"My God," she said, trembling slightly, "remember you! Of course."

He moved closer and said, with great emotion, "But never mind him—how are you?"

His boyish face suddenly amazed her with its appearance of trained diligence and corporate virtue.

"Oh, I'm okay," she said, smiling, and tears started in her eyes.

"Don't worry," he said, and he squeezed the hand he held. His puffy white coat rustled. "He must have gone through a breakdown—handing out pamphlets and all that. But you must have never seen it coming."

"A breakdown, yes, that's what it was," Annette said, wholly convinced of it. "A complete one too!"

To have Wally Bickle's approval meant that she was included in town society, for Wally wouldn't approve of anyone until they were. Yes, he was unaffiliated except toward those who could help him out. This was her assurance.

———

Some years before, our young Wally Bickle was in the student police, where he wore a flashlight and had an armband. But after high school he didn't get into the RCMP, which he so wanted. He then tried to enlist in the Bicklefield town police but failed an aptitude test.

Still dedicated to public responsibility, he worked as a collection officer, and Molly Thorn was in his register. Then he was hired at the Workers' Compensation Board, where he had to deal harshly with Evan Young (he liked to mention how harsh he had to be). Then, when the Workers' Compensation Board relocated, he was suddenly adrift, looking for another job, and was almost ready to leave the province, when he got a call from the mill. He got this call because of his mother, who knew Mr. Conner.

Wally Bickle went to the interview full of grave determination and was somber when they told him he might be needed in a truly professional capacity. After the interview he turned at the door. The mill whistle sounded, and there was a soft stench of sulphur and copper in the cold night air as shadows crossed the desks and sheets of stencil.

"What will my title be?" he asked Mr. Ticks's secretary.

"What?"

"What will my title be?" he said abruptly.

"Oh! Wally Bickle, Assistant Office Manager in Standard Pulp Products and Supplies," she told him.

"I see," he commented most solemnly. He left and wandered back toward the dark metal stairway.

The next day, he had cards printed that said just that.

———

At first, and for some time after Annette had decided on a divorce, her husband knew nothing and she told him nothing. She listened to his plans to redo the store. She nodded when he told her things, and said he might be right, that his life could get back on track. But she said nothing.

Ian had an idea for a small filter that could be used to monitor the levels of toxins in the water from the mill. He worked on this in his spare time, hoping to make up for things. He would explain it all to Liam, and say he was hoping to make a critical contribution to the river.

He worked tirelessly at his partially destroyed store where no one shopped anymore. And secretly he spent hours at the courthouse archives and in the capital city of Fredericton, and twice he phoned his MP in Ottawa. He collected 170 pounds of documents that came in three taped-up boxes, and were left outside his door in the rain.

"Why did they want my property so desperately, Liam?" he asked, over and over. "Why did they want it so badly?"

What he did not know was in fact obvious: The road into Quebec, which our own government would pay for, would allow Helinkiscor to transport the wood from our own province to a mill in another province with better access to world markets, and force our own mill to shut down in less than five years. A road from his property across the west side of Good Friday Mountain was by far the best access into Quebec. That is why they had wanted it so desperately. And that is what Ian would not discover until others did. Because no one could have ever believed that the company did not even want the mill, just the thousands and thousands of tons of wood they would harvest. Nor did they ever expect to keep the people here working for long.

Ian tried to speak to Annette now and then, but Annette said nothing to him. However, she on occasion thought of Wally—she could not help it. She too had felt the trauma of being ostracized. And she never wanted to feel it again.

Some days she would drive passed the mill to see all the cars in the lot and try to figure out which one was his.

But DD knew what she was doing, and she knew the game being played. And despite all the concern for her friend, the idea of that game is what enthralled Diane.

So Annette went to her fortune teller, had the tarot cards read, played the Ouija board, and discovered that her life was now pointed irrevocably in one direction. That is, in the stern silence of nine at night, in the living room of the fortune teller, with its embroidered oversized cushions on the sofa, the Death card appeared. Annette shrank back in her chair.

The tarot reader assured her that this card only meant change. "Things will change," she said. "It means change, not death!"

Later, when Annette asked the Ouija board if she would find unconditional love, it compelled her to spell yes. "Then it must be with Wally," Diane said, looking over her shoulder and stroking Annette's beautiful hair. "I am more sure now than ever."

That night, as Annette left the fortune teller and ran back along the street, she bumped into someone—much as Ian had all those years ago. It was Sara Robb, who was now a medical doctor here. Annette started to fall, but Sara managed to grab her.

"Annette," she said. "My soul, how are you?"

Annette wanted to speak—she really did. But she turned instead, and left Sara alone on the street.

The next day she went and had her hair done and a manicure at Cut and Curl. She did not understand she was upset because she had not spoken to Sara; she only knew she needed to look special and beautiful again. Her son came with her.

"This is exclusive," DD said, putting Annette's head back gently. "Watch, Liam, how I treat your darling mother."

———

During those trips to Cut and Curl Liam would sit quietly, listening in the boredom of a mid-afternoon winter's day. He was twelve years of age, and old enough to pick out the degree to which things were said and left unsaid. The room would smell of hair rinse and snow, of smoke and boredom, and was filled with the talk of aging middle-class women who were ultimately impersonators of those whose world they aspired to live in. Once, Annette inadvertently made fun of his crooked teeth. Later she looked at him and smiled, as if apologizing, and offered to buy him a pop. He smiled clumsily back, and covered his mouth.

Later that night Liam decided he would get his own teeth fixed, and he applied for a paper route.

Now Liam went to bed worried about debt. Now Liam left for school in the morning plagued by the thought of debt. Now in his scribbler he wrote a household budget, and left it on the fridge for his mom and dad.

———

A week after Annette had seen Sara Robb, Ian left for Halifax to try to get money to help him develop the filter he had invented in his spare time. He was sure that with fifty thousand dollars he could manufacture these filters, distribute them to every mill in the country—and that they would be wanted.

He put the cylinder-shaped object in a box, smiled at his son and said, "Wish me luck!"

He took the train, and spoke to people he met naïvely and hopefully, as if he'd already been awarded the grant. They saw a young enough man still, sitting with his cane, staring out the window.

When he got to Halifax, to the Council of Atlantic Business and Industrial Entrepreneurs, his meeting had been postponed. No one was in the office on Barrington Street apart from a secretary, who had no information except that all meetings had been put back forty-eight hours. He waited two days, and his meeting lasted thirty-eight minutes.

He was asked if he had anyone who knew how to help him.

"My son," he said.

He was asked him how old his son was.

"He is twelve," Ian said.

His was a good idea—peculiar too, because all mills did already regulate their effluence and there were standards and practices already in place. In fact, any other effluent regulator would have to pass the standards and practices, which might take years, before it was authorized. They even made a joke about how this was a Catch-22: they could not give the money unless it passed the standards test, and how could they know it would pass the standards if they did not give the money? But there you go—there it was.

It was a good idea, and the council was most impressed that he was concerned about pollution and river systems. More people needed to be inventive and proactive. "Proactive" was becoming *the* new word.

Ian was ashamed—ashamed of his suit, which was now ten years out of date, and his hopeful pleading face.

The truth was, it was a face these people knew. And Ian they had heard of—he was known as a crackpot. The mill managers had been long aware of his application and they'd informed the person at the council that Ian was the troublemaker from the Miramichi. He came back without the contract.

When Ian arrived home, it was five in the afternoon. The streetlights were already on, and Ian sat in the corner of the living room, looking through his ragged black wallet because he had spent more than he thought he would.

That was the night Liam decided to do his trick.

In his childlike mind, Liam was doing this trick to keep them together, because he believed everything was now his fault. If he had not been so cranky, his parents would not have fought. If he had protected his father's signs, the store would not have burned. Everything that had happened over the last two to four years had forced Liam into a world of model train sets and magic—a place of solitude children are sometimes forced into.

He had practised this particular magic trick in secret upstairs in his room before the mirror. After all this time his hands were healed, with little white scars on the tips of his fingers. He walked downstairs in a black cape Ethel had made for him, and wearing a top hat. Suddenly he appeared like a little Dracula, which startled both his parents. He smiled. He shyly asked if they would like to see a magnificent trick, then told them not to come into the den for forty-five minutes.

Just before he left them he said, "If I do something to surprise you, will you stop fighting?"

"Oh, we don't fight," Annette said.

And so Ian and Annette waited outside the den in silence, both of them as if being rebuked by an authority, both sitting on chairs, awaiting a summons. And when it got dark, long after supper, Liam said softly, "Okay, come in now."

They entered the room as if entering some place of grave mystery. They saw his magic hat and gloves lying across the coffee table, but his cape was draped around him. And there, in front of them, Liam rose a foot or more off the floor, floating as if buoyed by some strange force.

Ian smiled, and delighted said, "How did you do that, Son?"

But Liam only said, "See? It's easy to do things that seem impossible— so please stay together and don't be scared, and I will get a job too and we will have everything we want! Mom, you don't have to ever go away."

Behind him a single light bulb shone, making a halo of his hair.

———

The very next day Annette went to visit her friend Diane. DD was waiting for her.

Annette for some reason wanted to prove herself—not to just anyone but to DD. Why this was, she could not say. She could not say that she was in some way seduced by the very act she was being encouraged to perform. And the more seductive it was, the more its seduction rested upon the fact that she could pretend she was trying to resist.

She had cried the whole morning. The reason for this was twofold. The divorce must come—but she had waited until Ian had lost out on the contract he'd wanted, which he'd said would make a million. She was, in fact, crying because he had lost the contract, and she felt sorry for him. But she also knew her friends—those who protected her— hated him and blamed him alone for all her unhappiness, and she must decide between him or them—and must decide now.

So although Annette had waited to see if the contract would come, it had not. And now that the store was old and spooky and decrepit; now that her husband was disgraced in the eyes of his friends and neighbours, who all were waiting for the marriage to fail—now was the time to leave. To be married to someone so hated, so laughed at and scorned by everyone, was too much. She couldn't cope with it anymore. And that, in fact, was her flaw.

In fact, the final contest would, in some important way, be fought between DD and Ian. And DD was always prepared for a fight.

So Annette went to Diane's house for advice. She sat in silence as sunlight came with high winds against the window and the troubled little yard outside, as DD spoke about her own divorce, and how Clive had wanted to kill her—twice—and how she'd just got away from him in time, and how she worried about Annette and had dreams about her.

"I thought he was so much better than that," DD told her friend. "Talking like a maniac about people and criticizing everything so no one likes him. Is he the only one who has a sore back?"

"Where would I go?" Annette asked.

"You can live here," Diane said. Quickly. "Don't even let on where you are—just leave. That is what you have to do." Her eyes showed her delight.

Diane wanted to help because she would be the confidante. But most of all—knowing Ian did not like her—she wanted to inflict pain.

"I couldn't believe it—I just couldn't believe he would be so mean," DD said.

"I can't get a cent out of him," Annette said. "My account at the bank is almost empty."

"He's a cunt," DD said.

But Diane had only a small prefab house on Becker's Lane, right beside a fire hydrant and a scraggly bush, and it wasn't a place Annette could ever envision moving to. Especially with that drab floating stuff in a bowl that gurgled when it came to the top of the water and that Diane thought of as a decoration, and the smell of the old dog that Diane's husband had left when he moved out with his seven boxes of hairspray.

"No," Annette said, a kind of restive sadness clinging to her voice. Then she added, "I have my son. As I have my son, I have my hope!"

These were women unlike those who talked in theory about equality and subversive tendencies. In fact, most women who spoke about independence for women would have been scared to death of them. These were women who could smile as they cut you to ribbons and skewered you around a barbecue. Lies? Fuck, what else was there?

———

On those long-ago days, Ethel took Liam down to her house and spoke of applying for a job at a restaurant near a bar called the Warehouse. The restaurant was called the Pudding Lounge. Then she and Liam would have "heaps of fun," she said.

Ethel was the one who took him to church, and had been the one to prepare him for first communion, and had talked to him about saints and popes and God. She gave him a small daily-mass book and signed it in her crooked handwriting: "With love, Aunt Ethel." She talked about Saint Faustina, who said the only measure of love is to be measureless. And it seemed that if anyone had this capability, little Ethel Robb did.

Liam would lie about his mom and dad, and not tell on them, and not say that they were in the throes of a special kind of tragedy. He bragged about them always, and made up stories to tell his teachers about them. He said that his father might work for NASA. Often he was unable to stop telling fibs. He tried, but he couldn't stop.

He would say that his father was inventing a machine that would help the province and his mother was going into business with her friends, and they would soon move to Toronto or somewhere very special. He said that the prime minister had visited the house and that they flew on a private jet. He invited children to his birthday party when there was no birthday party to be had. They came with gifts while he was in the kitchen trying to make them peanut butter sandwiches.

Liam climbed on the roofs of houses when other boys chased him home, and walked with dexterity far above the earth, and had a fort he called the Shelter under the big backyard trees. There he kept certain things: magnets and Spider-Man toys, and small parts of computers that he collected and wanted to build.

He was spied on, and reported to police, and gossiped about to others, by the neighbours like Ms. Spalding, who lived in the broad white house next door.

Ethel, however, did not lie and dislike, but showered him with affection, and told him that he must believe in God.

"Why should I believe in God?"

"I don't know—maybe because God believes in you!"

The days were long and drawn out in school, and he was alone. He would fall asleep with his head on the desk. A teacher would yell at him, "Do you know the answer, Liam, to the seventh equation?"

"Z to the fifth," Liam would answer without moving his head, not counting on the teacher's displeasure that the answer was correct.

Sometimes when Liam would see a man waiting after school for his child, he would close his eyes and whisper, "Make it be Dad, make it be Dad—make it be Dad!"

———

Back on a day after the last blizzard in late February some years ago, two or three years after Lonnie Sullivan was found lying in his blood, Harold came into town to look at empty shops. It was the right time to get his pawnshop going, he decided, because so many buildings were closing up. He wanted one right in the centre of town.

Before he went to check out the best building available—an empty square block of a place, with the plaster already turning yellow and a grey water stain running the length of the ceiling—he saw Ethel Robb walk across the park to the restaurant where she worked, holding Liam by the hand. Harold was doing much better because of his uncle's death—ruled an accident. He had been left two old trucks and three thousand dollars—and of course no one knew that he had found much more. He had sold Ian's property to Helinkiscor. He smoked cigars now himself, and had gained weight—so he looked very much like his uncle once did. He always had a cigar or two in his pocket, his shirt opened, showing his medallion and chest hair. He talked so loud at times that people in the mall would turn to look at him.

He went across the street to see the boy, who he now believed was his son.

He ordered three cheeseburgers, and watched as Ethel carried them to him. She was scared to death she would slip and spill them, for it was her very first day on the job.

"You got a big appetite," she said.

"I do. Yes, dear, I have a big appetite—I'm big in every way." He smiled. He tweaked the little boy's ear and made him smile and said kind things about him, and asked if he would like some french fries.

"Share my plate," he said.

He was the only customer, and the windows were covered in snow. He moved his seat closer to where Liam sat, and they talked about hockey. He talked about school and said Liam had better study and get an education so as not to end up sorrowful. He said he knew many people who were sorrowful, and didn't want another person in town to be so.

The way the boy looked at him Harold was moved. He hugged him and asked him how he was.

Ethel wore multicoloured stockings and had two blue ribbons in her hair, and her big short-sighted eyes blinked rapidly and hopefully under her pink glasses so he felt a sudden compassion for her. Yes, he said, he remembered her as a girl at Bonny Joyce, and hadn't time changed them all.

Ethel asked him if he knew what had happened to his uncle Lonnie Sullivan.

"Oh, that was years ago now—slipped, I guess," he said. And he patted Liam's head as he said it. He was attracted to Liam because Liam looked so much like his own dead brother, Glen. He kept glancing at the boy and smiling.

"Oh," she said. "My Corky slipped too."

Suddenly, as if to change the topic, Harold pulled something from his pocket: the fur hat he had got from Rueben Sores, who had stolen it from someone at the tavern a few years ago. He was taking it to Frenchies, the used-clothing store, to see if they wanted it. But he changed his mind now.

It was a woman's fur hat, in fine condition, but he had no use for it. Rueben had given it to him because Harold had been so angry they had burned a small boy's hands.

"Take this, for Christ sake, and shut up about it," Rueben had said.

Now Harold told Ethel he had just bought it, and there was only one person he would ever think of giving it to. And he handed it to her.

"A present for you, dear!" he said.

She herself had nothing—just like Harold, and two generations of people from Bonny Joyce Ridge. She tried it on and smiled. She wouldn't think of keeping it. The radio played some bebop-alula song from long, long ago that Corky had said was his very favourite song. It was called "There Goes My Baby," and when she heard it, she should think of him. The snow hit the green window and melted, and she looked like a little doll in her big fur hat. She tried to hand it back, but Harold wouldn't take it.

"My God," she said, "that's so expensive!"

"What do I care?" Harold Dew said, taking her hand and holding it gently. "It looks like it was meant for you."

Then he did something so spectacular: he gave Liam a ten-dollar bill.

"Someday when she doesn't know it, I'm going to send Mom a note that says I love her—and a chocolate doughnut," Liam said, mostly to himself. "And make her guess who it's from!"

"That's a good idea—your mother is the most important thing," Harold said, and he smiled gently, and kissed the boy's cheek, and took his hands quickly in his to see if they were scarred.

———

In late April, Annette Brideau got a phone call from Wally Bickle himself and was offered a job at the mill. This came so suddenly and unexpectedly that she went into a state of euphoria, and went shopping, ordering almost an entire new wardrobe—skirts and slacks and blouses. She did not know about odious file 0991563; but neither did Wally Bickle.

It was over a week later when Ian heard of this job. Someone came into his store and told him. At first, Ian did not catch on. But once he did, he saw the disaster of it, felt it through to the pit of his stomach.

He sent Liam away later that afternoon, telling him he did not want to see him anymore. Then he went out later to bring him in, but Liam had gone.

So, like the remark he'd once made against Corky, Ian could not believe he had said anything so unkind.

He planned never to go back to the house. He would live on his own and move into an apartment on Charles Street that he knew was available. He would continue to fight the mill—no matter what! He would be able to walk to work, although he also thought of simply selling what was left of the sorry old store and going back to fixing radios. In fact, this was the only thing that might be available to him. Yet when he received the bill for the wardrobe, and realized the amount she had spent—twenty-three hundred dollars—he went back to the house in a rage, staggering along the street.

When he got home, he saw that his clothes had been moved and packed in boxes, and those boxes placed near the basement stairs. But at this moment, Annette attempted to be reasonable and sanguine. She shook as she lit a cigarette. She stood and then sat, and then walked away from him and back toward him. Then she sat again. She told him that she had tried desperately to save the marriage even when people had told her it was hopeless—and that she had lived in a state of denial about what he really thought of her, and now she had to finally begin to live for herself. She said that he had never thought she was good enough for the likes of him. But now people were look-ing out for her, because they knew what she had had to endure. That she had endured too much—and everyone said to her, "How can you endure so much?"

He slumped down on the very chair he had slumped into the night he had come back from Halifax. And suddenly she began to lecture him.

She had a job now—so there was no use in him crawling back to her—he should just crawl somewhere else—maybe under a big rock. He glanced at her a moment and said nothing.

She continued speaking. Look at all the money he had spent frivo-lously on elections and posters.

"Big election boy!" she said. "And where did that get us?"

They could have had money; they could have been set—but he was too pigheaded. When she mentioned how her good friends, like Ripp, had warned her, her eyes brightened like a sudden flame.

"Leave me alone," he kept saying, "leave me alone!" Then he said it once more: "Shut the hell up and leave me alone!"

"But I am just saying," she continued, "I told you not to do what you did—I told you. Now you are broke and everyone says you are so fuckin' stupid, and that's not my fault. And you used Liam to burn the store."

"Why would you ever talk like that—why?"

"Ha! Everyone says you're not right in the head—that you might need a lobotomy of some kind."

Then she suddenly began to count on her fingers. "Here is what DD herself said just last week: that of all the women, you had the most beau-tiful one—and look what you end up doing like a total nut job. So anyway, DD is right. And Ripp says, 'Let me at him if he comes near you.' That is what Ripp said, so you should be careful, my boy. Me talking? You should hear what they say about you. In fact, they said to me—and I mean a whole whack of people—that you should have stuck to a person more your speed is what they say: Sara Robb!"

And she began to laugh at the unintended joke and put her hand over her mouth, giggling.

He didn't remember doing this: he grabbed her hair, threw her down and slapped her so hard it bloodied her lip. She was suddenly, and for the first time, terrified of him. He straddled her on the stairs, looking down at her manically.

"I'll kill you. I swear I will kill you," he said—and it was said so calmly that she had no trouble believing him. Then he hauled her to her feet. Later he was so ashamed because he remembered he could feel her shaking in his arms.

Liam ran from the den and tried to get between them. But Ian, seeing only a form coming toward him, thought it was Ripp VanderTipp. He hauled out his knife and swung it backward, and in a second he cut the boy on the arm. Not a bad cut—but some blood did fall on Ian's shirt.

"Dad, stop!" Liam said. "I want to show you my new Pokémon cards. Dad—that's why I came to the store, okay—when you sent me away—I was just wanting to show you my cards. I'm sorry."

Ian looked at his child, gave a shout of agony and left the house.

Liam picked the knife up, and after taking it upstairs hid it.

And with this, a new age was dawning on the river, one where, as DD said, all her real friends would be finally and truly free.

————

Sara Robb had been called to the death scene of Lonnie Sullivan a few years back. He had been found by one of the young Wizard boys who had come to collect the garbage. He called the town police, for the old shed was just on the expanded town line, and Dr. Sara Robb was then called by the coroner, Jarvis, to accompany him.

They met at Lonnie's place. Wind had blown the snow deep inside the shed. Sara asked that nothing be moved, but the young Wizard boy had already turned the body over to see if it was Lonnie—and then he'd turned it back once more. Jarvis instructed Wilson, the photographer, to take a number of pictures—three of the roadway, five of the outside of the shed, et cetera—until they managed to get inside the shed itself. There they took pictures of everything—of the tool box from four different angles, and the bench, and the way Lonnie lay. The coroner walked about the shed itself, measuring footprints.

The body was already stiffened and the right arm extended out. There was a broken rum bottle, the glass scattered over most of the floor. There was an *Auto Trader* lying open between the bench and the body.

The first thing Sara noticed, besides the body of Lonnie, was the blood on the corner of this metal bench, as if he may have fallen and hit his head. It had solidified on the bench and had seeped along the bench leg. So she took a scrape and sample of that blood.

She also looked at the wound on Sullivan's head and collected some of his blood. She took the samples of blood back to her office; but then things happened, and the death was ruled an accident, and she went on to other things.

Over time, Sara went back to Africa, twice almost fell in love—thought of moving to Belgium with a divorced co-worker—was recruited by the UN to act as a liaison officer in Rwanda for the World Health Organization. She decided against this, for she wanted to have her own practice in the little place where she was born. The modern world was closing in on her, just as it was on those in Africa who she doctored and tried to care for.

When she came home, the death of Lonnie Sullivan was forgotten.

Over time, no other theories were presented. Sara discovered that the test on the blood had come back when she was away, and a few weeks after she came home she looked at it, and was surprised that the blood on the corner of the bench was not the same type as that of Lonnie Sullivan. She handed her results over to the coroner but heard nothing back.

So Sara Robb kept what was left of the sample of blood from the corner of the bench in a refrigerator in her office, as simple prudence, and life went on. She was smart to be prudent, because when the coroner himself retired, he discarded all the blood evidence in his possession.

———

Annette went to Jeremy Hogg and asked him what she should do.

"You really need to divorce him," Hogg said. "Everyone knows he's crazy as a bag of hammers—he trashed his house, his store, you have already had to call the police. Your friend Ripp tells me how he has to stand guard for you. So then, no one will blame you."

"Oh, I don't know—I wish he was back to himself," she said, wringing a Kleenex nervously and sitting in Hogg's dark office near the old travelling chest, looking about uncomfortably—for now she was here, and now she was doing it.

She was propelled to divorce because people expected her to, and she could do so and be certain that she would be applauded for taking this step. This was, in fact, not only part of it but its greatest part—the tremendous tearing away of all that once was had now started. That is, divorce was an institution as much as marriage and she was now a part of it as an institution, so she must follow the rules of this institution. If that sounded cold, it would only be if she was the one who was totally vulnerable and alone—and though this was the state she and her new lawyer projected, she was neither of these things.

Now Hogg stood and closed the office door so they could have privacy. This in itself made her feel not only special but somehow selected.

As he walked back to his desk he said, "I usually tell people to reconsider—for the children." He always said he usually told people to reconsider, and he always followed this with "But in this case—if your mind is set. He has probably hurt the boy—has he?"

"Yes, yes, yes, yes, yes, many times, all of that," she said. "Stabbed him!" Annette looked at him.

She was still beautiful; there was no doubt. However, her face was starting to turn puffy like that of her mother. She was not the youthful and irrational woman he had heard so much about—but she was still striking—and in a certain way he was overcome by her, which allowed him to dislike her husband even more.

Ian was hated on the river. He was hated at the mill where she worked. Both Hogg and Annette knew this. They also knew how people (Hogg's wife being one) cynically spread rumours that the boy was not his son.

"A young woman like you should make something more of your life. He already hurt one woman, I hear—Sara Robb," he said, not knowing the implications of this remark. Not knowing that Annette's fury was, in great part, fury that Sara had succeeded in a way she never would, in spite of capturing him. In fact, the real lesson being that Annette capturing him allowed this transformation of Sara. Annette looked at Hogg with a transfixed look and said nothing.

Hogg caught this delicately and showered her with praise for standing up to him on her own to protect the boy. "You got a black eye protecting your son," he said. "He probably would have killed the boy! A knife he had on him to do his dirty work, if it came to that."

"Yes," she said, "yes, I had to fight him off!"

"Yes, I have heard as much," Hogg said, suddenly yawning.

Hogg, however, had the vulgar male trait of immediately and bellicosely taking the side of women's independence, as long as it wasn't his own wife. It was politically expedient to do so, and Hogg was nothing if not expedient.

But to say that Annette did not know this was to say she did not know how the game between men and women was played. She knew it ruthlessly and predatorily from the time she was fourteen.

So they played, miming both the importance of her hard fight for independence and the child—whose name Hogg kept forgetting (some goddamn Irish wannabe name, he thought), and the sudden ruthless attitude of her husband, who, "in this day and age," would act the way he did, insanely jealous because she had to take a job and had danced with someone at a dance.

Then, finally, the money was mentioned. She looked about and said secretively that Ian kept his money in a safe. That she had money in her account, but she knew he had lots in the safe. That she was worried because the store had suffered a fire.

"A safe in his office is the worst place for it," Hogg said. "He might decide to blow it. You should have some investments—do you have any? Do you know what he does with his earnings?"

She was shocked as this sudden realization took hold. She shook her head and tears came flooding to her eyes.

"I don't know anything about it," she said truthfully.

"What? No investments—in this day and age! Well, I'll help you with that! I can increase your money tenfold—but he should not control it. And he will fight this, I know. So we have to get a court order to get it out of the safe and into a bank, where it belongs. Put it in trust for the boy until all of this is settled."

He told her to make sure she had a friend stay with her, change the locks on the doors, and he would see that the money was removed and put into a bank on a court order.

"Yes, yes, yes," she kept saying, adding that it would be the hardest thing she'd ever had to do. Her newly bought wristwatch with its juvenile black leather strap seemed to accentuate her defencelessness.

Her father worked daily in the Department of Motor Vehicles; every once in a while he came out with a prurient off-colour joke to show how lively he could be. He had a stuffy chair he sat in, and an enclosed living room that always smelled of damp and cigars. Her mother was a little shrewish woman who disliked her and was envious of her beauty, always saying, "Oh yes, it's all Annette, all the time!"

But Annette had made her own way. She had used her magnetism all her life. She knew it and Hogg knew it. But now that was nothing compared with how she'd been traumatized.

"What would your dad say about all of this—a fine man like him?" Hogg reminded her now. And when she began to cry, he too seemed choked up. So he said what he felt he must: "Maybe someday you will find another man to heal your wounded heart."

And she smiled through her tears.

Sorrowful, yes—and the first hour of many innumerable hours of consultation was charged: three hundred dollars.

Diane stayed with Annette throughout her ordeal. She wouldn't leave her side. Annette didn't have to answer the door and Diane took her calls. Everyone wanted to know things. (Ripp did not come over to the house at this time, fearing Ian's insanity and the look in his eyes. No— Ripp didn't want to get involved in that—that is, with anyone willing to fight back in spite of the consequences.) They said Annette was suffering severe mental anguish at this time and was constantly at the doctor's.

She started going to the therapist at this time too, and for many months was seen entering the building and coming out after dark, even into the fall after it began to snow.

Liam continually asked why. In fact, that is all he seemed to ask.

He was told his mom had to leave his father.

"He just can't accept your mom for the way she is," DD said. "All of us are only human—isn't that right?"

"Yes," Liam said, and suddenly he smiled his still-joyous smile. "And my dad is only human too—and people should be kinder to him because he is! He is a greater man than Wally Bickle. Or any of the other men Mommy knows!"

But no matter what Liam hoped and prayed for, the divorce became final—and Liam was left alone. He was left alone almost entirely, day and night for weeks on end, while Ian paid his own lawyer and had his own fight trying to obtain visiting rights.

But it was during this time his cocaine use became known. So visiting rights were denied.

"That is why he was up to all his dirty tricks—to get insurance money for cocaine," DD said.

Annette was a secretary in the mill's main office. Her boss was Wally Bickle. Ian had, Wally said, stolen a fortune from her—and many other things. Wally had come to her aid, he told people, and was taking care of the boy.

"Really?" one of the men said.

Wally shrugged.

"I don't mind that at all. All that boy needs is discipline, a man willing to be a man."

Except, of course, Wally had spent no time with the boy.

And Annette was famous at the mill—someone desired, beautiful and on her own.

One day she got an anonymous note with a chocolate doughnut from a secret admirer. *I love you with all my heart*, it said.

Who could it be? she thought, looking about. It made her smile.

"It's a sad thing," Harold would tell Ethel. "I never thought I would live to see the day—but the world catches up with people, it always does!"

However, there was one thing Harold had not foreseen: Evan Young's luck seemed to have come back by this same circuitous route. Evan had joined a construction company, Doan's Roofing and Construction, and had recently paid off all his debt and built a new house miles away. He had begun to read again, voraciously—books of all kinds, like he had in his youth—and play the bagpipes so well he was invited to join the Scottish Society. One night he spoke about the Battle of Culloden, and Sara Robb was there. Though they did not speak that night, she was suddenly taken by his intelligence and kindness.

Harold, sitting in his big happy pawnshop on the far side of the square, guessed how it must have happened. If he had not gone to find the pregnancy test, he wouldn't have encountered Lonnie. He wouldn't have been attacked from behind nor would he have got into that terrible fight in the centre of the room. He wouldn't have used the wrench as a last resort to defend himself.

The demise of Sullivan had allowed Evan to escape his obligation, just at the time the priest wanted him, and Doan saw him work and needed a good man in Halifax.

Doan said, as he hired him, "You go to AA—quit drinking and fighting—Molly would not want that!"

This tore at Evan's heart. And he had been sober well over two years. And the man he met there—the man who helped him stay sober those first few awful months, when all he wanted to do was to drag himself back to the bottle—was Leonard Savoy, the man who had been kind to Molly at the church picnic so long ago.

Now, after all this time, he could not imagine ever drinking again.

———

The two policemen who'd worked on Lonnie Sullivan's death were not the officers who had decided it was an accident: Constables Jarvis and Roy, who had driven the photographer there the next day and stumbled upon the scene in the bright morning air after the storm had blown itself out. No, the files were transferred, and the death was now being reinvestigated by the RCMP.

It was some years later, of course, but there were still a few unanswered questions. This is what the two policemen, both RCMP officers, now spoke about.

"It is a burning question," Markus Paul said to his mentor and friend, John Delano, in the snowy cold winter of 1995. "And the burning question is this: how does a man slip and hit his head on a dry floor when his body is found two body lengths away from the narrow bench he supposedly hit? What I am saying is, he couldn't have fallen like that. If anything, the body should be facing the other way—if he hit the bench like the report says."

"Well then, maybe someone killed him, someone who had a loan," John said. "Someone who didn't want to work it off. Someone who'd had a car or a motor confiscated from him—something that he did if people couldn't pay."

They were talking by phone, one in Neguac and the other in Newcastle, thirty-three miles away.

"Maybe, yes . . . Do you know what I am looking at?"

"The pictures of the scene?" John said.

"Yes. So he comes in and finds someone stealing something—or whatever—and pushes this fellow, so that the fellow he pushes hits the end of the bench . . ."

"And then this fellow turns and hits him—"

"In fact, if you wanted to be smart about it—looking at the picture of Lonnie now, I could say two blows did land on his head. And I don't think anyone picked up a bench to hit him."

"No—so what was lying on the bench?"

It would take an inestimable time to narrow it down.

———

Two more years passed. Wally and Annette organized staff parties, and even went on a company retreat to the spa resort at Bald Mountain. Wally tried to fish. Wally tried to paddle a canoe. Wally tried to horseshoe-toss. Wally was gruff with one of the waiters because his shoes got wet. Wally wanted things just so.

And if you saw Wally at work, you saw Annette. He drove her home almost every second day, Wally did.

Years ago, after he was in Ian's store that day, Wally had shifted loyalties slightly, from the man who was in the main office to Mr. Ticks himself. For many a week and month he was seen wherever Ticks was; and then, realizing Ticks was beginning to be disliked, he shifted again and was suddenly seen at Mr. Fension's table when they were at the golf or curling club. In fact, sometimes he would not even speak to Ticks anymore. Ticks no longer got along with the upper management at the mill. Wally did not know why, but the trouble Ticks found himself in was advantageous for Wally, who never missed an opportunity when someone was down.

Wally was a company man because it was most advantageous to be one.

Wally handed out his cards, and left them in places to impress others, places like the office of J. P. Hogg.

Why was Ticks no longer a force at Helinkiscor?

Mr. Ticks was from Maine. He was a woodsman, like many here. And he was a good woodsman—and he walked the cut in his heavy boots, and with a knapsack to have lunch—and soon he realized what Helinkiscor was planning for the wood—and within eleven months he was disturbed by what was happening. And he called a meeting first with his own bosses and then with the new MLA—the one who had defeated Ian Preston—the young man who looked terribly concerned and forward-thinking, and who was initially fired up to do something but who, suddenly, did not get back to Mr. Ticks at all. Because if he did, he would have to admit—and his government would have to admit as well—that Ian Preston was exactly right.

And on occasion Wally himself was summoned to a meeting, and the only thing Annette could tell DD was, "He is at a meeting, so something important is going on."

"Does he run the mill?" DD would ask dreamily.

"He will," Annette would answer, "he will." And she added, "I've heard the rumours, DD—about Wally—that he has someone in Bicklesfield. Let me tell you—that is not true!"

"Oh, I know," DD would say, looking at her and smiling. "But won't you have to become Baptist for him?"

Each day the huge mill rumbled, the smoke belched out into the huge sky, the great river boiled darkly. Yet each day the price of paper and wood product plummeted, while the price of electricity, which the mill was so concerned about, went up—because the price of oil went up, and therefore the price of energy.

Then layoffs came, because there was no sense keeping men at work when no profit was made. This is what was said in the offices where Wally worked. This is why Wally was asked to call men into the office and give them the pink slip.

But if one looked closely, one would see: The layoffs were necessitated by a lie—and the lie was predicated on a truth, and the truth was this: the mill would have been in difficulty if it was selling its product only to the US market, where an ongoing dispute was entering its fourth year, but in reality this mill was sending 80 per cent of its finished product to Japan. Yet the province simply assumed it was a depressed market because the mill kept telling our government their product was coming under unfair regulation and tariffs in the United States.

By this time, a quarter of the mill workers had been told they were going to be laid off, and the government was in meetings to try to bail Helinkiscor out a third time. What was more subtle was that both Helinkiscor and the government were using these talks to assuage the public. All of this is what troubled Mr. Ticks—for Ticks knew, after one year, that Helinkiscor had a timetable to close the mill.

And this was for one reason: the deal to bring Helinkiscor here had guaranteed the company a free hand to cut wood and to own whatever they cut, whether the mill stayed or not. Now, the people who had negotiated this deal with Helinkiscor had no idea that the mill would have thousands of tonnes of wood on the ground that the company did not intend to ever process here. They simply assumed this was impossible.

Yet this was why the Swill Road property had been bought, and it was why there was now a road into Quebec. From the first, Helinkiscor was thinking two or three steps ahead, and knowing two years before the government did that such talks would begin, such talks would fail, and that once the company culled the thousands of yards of timber, they would leave the province for good. They would leave as soon as they got the amount of wood on the ground that served their stockholders best. They would process this wood not at this little mill in New Brunswick but at their larger mill in Quebec, with its more acceptable access to markets through the Chaleur Bay and St. Lawrence Seaway. And how would Helinkiscor pay for the transfer of wood? It would get our province to help subsidize it and to build the road into Quebec itself.

Then, after a few more years, they would leave that mill in Quebec as well for one in Russia. Helinkiscor was using the real difficulty in the softwood dispute with the US as a bogus infliction upon itself, and getting guarantees of more money from a province already broke and desperate to keep its own people in jobs.

Helinkiscor leaving is what Ticks was trying to stop. This is why upper management was silent and antagonistic toward him. Therefore he was alone, and therefore Wally Bickle, without the wherewithal to know why Raymond Ticks was now on the outside, took advantage of his being alone and no longer sat with him.

Wally saw this—as he told his mom in his twice-weekly phone calls to Bicklesfield—only as a potential bonus for himself. "If Ticks goes, I'll get a raise," Wally told her. Wally, as people knew, loved his mom.

So a third time Helinkiscor was bailed out, and a third time people came away from the meeting ecstatic that this company was going to stay. And a third time people like Mr. Ticks and Mr. Fension, the mill's senior management, were given dinners and talked about as businessmen of the year. Ticks sat in his old wrinkled suit, wearing a pair of winter boots and eating his salad without a word as the speeches railed on. Only once did he look up, blinking his strained eyes. That was when the premier, looking like a little boy, saluted them and gloated that Helinkiscor's commitment to the river was unequivocal. And got a prolonged standing ovation for his remark.

When Wally went home to see his mom, he would often talk to his friends there—who believed what he said to be true, for they had no reason not to. He told them he took care of a child of a violent man, and protected him, and helped the child's mother. He spoke of it so often that he believed it all.

One day at the old Copps service station in Bicklesfield, Wally was saying how much he did for Liam, and a man was there waiting for a ride north, to work the power lines. It was Sydney Henderson. He listened to this young man quietly and was about to leave, when Wally Bickle said, "So, where did I go wrong, Sydney—trying to help out a youngster? Isn't it what you are all about?" And this got some of the wags laughing.

"Nowhere," Sydney said.

"Well then, thank me, Syd, for doing all this good work—you're the boy for good works." And the men there laughed again. And Wally winked and grinned. He was wearing new pants, and a new shirt and a new buckled belt, and at that moment he took from his pocket and opened a brand new pack of gum.

He smiled as he put a stick in his mouth and winked at Sydney.

Sydney nodded. He went to the door, but suddenly he turned and said, "Excuse me, Mr. Bickle—except—"

"Except what?"

"You have made everything up. You do not care for Liam. His father does. At times in his life they could not afford milk for him—not once did you experience that, nor have you spent time with him. And not only have you not adopted him, as you pretend—you will soon allow a son of yours to be destroyed in the womb rather than to be adopted. So I think, well—you have made it all up, and used this family's story and their child to your own benefit. So you mustn't talk about ANYONE betraying another, for no one has betrayed that child and that family more than you. It was the same with Molly Thorn and her two hundred dollars, though you do not remember her."

"Yes, blame me—for other people's violence. That's irony for you," Wally scoffed.

"No," Sydney answered, "I could never use irony against you. On the other hand I could never take credit for one bit of pain I never myself had to endure from anyone else's life. And," he added, "I have had to endure much pain—and so does little Liam Preston."

Then he stopped, for his drive north had come, and he looked ashamed at what he had just said. The men were now silent in their coats and hats, and immobile.

"I remember Ian Preston. He is the one who actually loves his child and he, not you, should be given credit for it—and about the mill, he was exactly right," Sydney mumbled. Then he added, "Forgive me. That's all I was going to say."

Sydney Henderson, as you might remember, was never seen alive on the river again. He died on his way home to his family almost three years later.

———

This "Mr. Ian" now lived in a tiny room, surrounded by thousands of pages of documents; had a little computer he worked on at a small desk. And he was almost there—that is, he had discovered very much in the last three years. It came to him slowly but surely, when reading the stock market reports daily: he realized the stockholders and the price of Helinkiscor shares were all very solvent in a market where Helinkiscor continued to say they must cut back or leave. So he realized, this small wan man, that the wood was not going to be processed in New Brunswick. He asked for a meeting with the premier and did not get it.

He was not allowed on Helinkiscor property and the union hated him. He began to send his letters to the editor of the newspaper, begging people to realize that their jobs were in jeopardy and the terrible destruction on the Bonny would not even benefit them. Four letters were published and then the fifth was rejected.

———

Harold Dew married Ethel.

He had opened a pawnshop in one of the closed-up buildings (where Annette once upon a time wanted to open up her tanning salon) along a street of endlessly closing buildings, of taxi stands and trinket shops and faceless half-empty stores. It was not only Ian Preston's store that had closed; everyone had moved to the malls on the outskirts of town.

But Big Harold had no worries. He was finally well off. He had a bass drum and some small pieces of furniture from Millerton, and some nice silver trays. He made a little money, and endlessly thought of ways to make more. He went into Ian's old appliance building and brought back ovens and fridges, brazenly carrying them right across the street with the help of Spenser and Kyle, and sold them on the black market, moving them off within a week.

FIRE DAMAGED GOODS the sign proclaimed.

He had asked Sara and Ethel's mother if he could take things from her upstairs attic to put as teasers in his shop. He would be over at Sara's office every other day so she could look at his tonsils or his abdomen. He was a constant sufferer, pains and whatnot. That is, like more than enough large tough men, he was a hypochondriac. While there, he would talk and gossip with his sister-in-law. He was a perennial gossip, which as much as he would deny it, showed his puritanical side. He was a big man with floppy boots, his shirttail out and a wide grin.

"Where did you get that odd-looking gash on the back of your head?" Sara asked one afternoon.

"God knows. Drunk, I guess."

"How long ago?"

Harold shrugged.

"It's quite a peculiar mark—did you hit the corner of the table, fall backward?"

Harold yawned.

"Did you ever get it taken care of, get stitches?"

"Nah—don't even remember!"

Sara placed the wrap to take his blood pressure.

"What about that loser, Preston," he said. "Are you glad you never got hooked up with the likes of him? He got on the coke 'cause of his back. They now tell me he weighs about 102 pounds—that was what Annette did to him!"

Although it was through Harold's protégés, Kyle and Spenser, that Ian was able to buy cocaine, Harold looked quite sanctimonious when he said this.

People came to his shop with all kinds of things—Harold never asked the youngsters if these things were stolen. "Times are tough," said a slogan at the entrance. "Get more," he simply told them, paying them twenty bucks if he felt he could get sixty.

The pawnshop, which had not existed when the town was whole, existed now when the town was fractured and the downtown had become more broken and closed, when the sanded winter streets looked empty under the glare of the sun. And it existed to entice people to use it. So, in fact, it existed to entice people to bring items to pawn, and those items did not necessarily have to belong to those who pawned them. The store also held wedding rings, and mementoes of dreams now dashed, of men starting to realize that the great broad mill did not hold any future for them. For so many men could not get hired on and others were already being laid off. The West beckoned them, and they left their dreams behind to go to work the sludge piles north of Edmonton, Alberta. There they made money to send home, to keep dreams alive.

Harold stood in the pawnshop's perennial gloom, near the metal lamp and an old bass drum, and watched as the men became more and more scarce as if they were in some black-and-white movie from the 1950s where people were targeted by some alien gamma ray, and suddenly and simply disappeared. He watched, in this sad black-and-white movie, that ghost of a man Ian Preston move along a sidewalk with his head down, his arms filled with documents, his legs thin and unsteady. Sometimes children teased him, and he would look at them in splendid confusion, almost as if they had entered from another dimension and he did not understand why they were tormenting him.

Once, all his documents dropped and he knelt and tried to pick them up when some of the boys kicked them away as a joke. Harold went out and spoke one word and they all scattered.

"Go!" he yelled.

He helped Ian pick the documents up and gently handed them to him. He had no idea what they were about.

———

One spring day, the boy Liam ran past Harold's pawnshop, legs flying, on his way to see his dad. Still running back and forth from one place to another—from his father's tiny room in a motel to his mom's house, trying always to keep both parents in mind.

Liam waited for his dad all that day in this room, sitting in a chair that faced the old door. He wanted to show his father his braces. But his dad did not come home. This little room, with its hot plate and dated microwave oven, its forlorn chair and black-and-white television, was the loneliest room in a series of rooms on Ian's downward spiral. The door had been broken, and the field outside was covered in hard drifts of unmelted half-white snow. Yet Liam waited for his dad as long as he could. He had been working on his father's cylinder invention and trying to fix it for him, thinking still that if they could sell it, his mom and dad would get together again—and so he had fussed with it now for eight months—and maybe someday he would fix it, and maybe someday—all would be well.

Ian's room was in the Blue Heron motel. The motel was once owned by Lonnie Sullivan, and had been repossessed and put on the market and bought by J. P. Hogg, who had given it to his son to run.

Ian didn't have a lock on his door—room 17—because it had been kicked open too many times. He was fixing radios for extra money, and still wrote letters about the contamination of the water system by Helinkiscor.

But Ian did not come back to his room that day.

So eventually Liam walked home to show his mom his braces. He was going to smile as soon as she came home. He had paid for them mostly by himself, though she had helped with two hundred dollars. He had delivered papers for two years now, because the divorce was financially crippling both his mom and dad. Neither of them knew where the money went; they knew only that the great savageness of divorce had swept them up in its claws and ravaged them. The boy was left solitary during much of this time.

Annette wanted to have her divorce be as public as Princess Diana's. So she was a star for a while in town. And being a star, and having friends, soon compelled her to spend whatever money she had. She threw a huge party the day it became final. She blew money everywhere. There seemed to be no end to what she would do. She even had loaned Wally Bickle eight thousand dollars. But after all was said and done, she realized quite tragically that the divorce had cost her thousands, and Hogg had not, in a long time, returned her calls.

That day—years ago now—Liam waited in the chair in the foyer to smile when his mom came in. Yet his braces keep hurting, even though the orthodontist had said the hurting would go away. When he telephoned, the orthodontist had already left for the long weekend. So he took an aspirin and pretended the pain would go away. He had paid for these braces almost fully by himself—and they had made quite a joke of it at the office, which was across the street from Hogg's law office. The orthodontist had taken his money in dribs and drabs, and he worried about all of this endlessly.

Today as he had walked back to the house, the picture window in Mr. Hogg's large law office was busted, a piece of plywood and plastic covered it, and he'd wondered what had happened.

"Yer dad's gone to jail," said Sherry Mittens, coming over to him and smiling. "My daddy says no one can help him now, and no one wants to anymore. Not any of the good people, anyway—not any of the people like us!" She had three or four friends with her, and she looked at them out of the corner of her eye as she spoke, delighted that they were delighted too. Liam watched them very carefully, saying nothing. Then they turned in front of him and he walked behind. And they spoke as he walked behind them, and Sherry Mittens spoke most of all.

He learned that his daddy had been taken to jail in a dispute with Mr. Hogg. This is what Sherry Mittens said as he walked by Harold Dew's pawnshop on his way back home. Sherry said his father had been taken to jail in handcuffs with his forehead cut open.

"He is not Liam's father anyway," one of the youngsters said.

"My mom says it wasn't Mr. Preston who was a father to him, ever."

"Be kind—be kind," Sherry Mittens said.

At home Liam waited for his mother, who did not come home.

Finally, he lay on the leather couch in the back room, tears coming down his cheeks because of the pain in his mouth. It had been his father's favourite couch. But all of that was over now.

———

The last four years had cost Ian everything. The store was gone. His wife had spent even more than he had trying to keep the house and the furniture, but in the end the house would have to be sold. That is what her lawyer told her. After a while—after all things were settled—Hogg sent his last bill, for $13,782.75.

Many days fixing his radios, Ian would think over his life. Ten dollars a week he tried to put aside for Liam, but sometimes he could not manage to do it. He tried as best he could to keep in contact with his son as well, but at times it was difficult—and he knew he was losing him without wanting to. Long after Liam had stopped hoping he would, Ian would walk to the school to meet him—but as so often happens, it was too late, and Liam seemed more and more solitary and alone. And Ian would return to his room and his own solitude.

At times he would reflect on Sydney Henderson, the boy he and his friends were supposed to be different from—the man who was so poor he could never put money aside for his children either. In so many ways, Ian thought now, he was the same.

Ian never drank. Syd Henderson did not drink. Ian was not violent. Syd was not either. Ian loved his child, although it was said he didn't— just like Sydney, and too, just like Evan. In fact, Wally Bickle constantly told people that he loved Ian's child more than Ian did himself.

Both Evan and he were, in fact, now accused of some of the same things Sydney had been accused of long ago. In fact, so little seemed to be different in their lives that they must in some way have devoted themselves to the same causes. Yet, Ian knew, their causes were entirely different. It was the world that sought to destroy them all. Sydney's wife, Elly, had been accused of theft, and this was completely false. Sydney told Ian that someday someone would accuse his own wife of the same crime, and he had.

The night before Liam went to visit his dad in the motel room, Ian had gone for a walk, his mind plagued with thoughts of Sydney

Henderson and with the idea of getting his luck back by finding out in his heart what had caused him to lose it. To lose everything.

It was almost Easter, and he thought of the blood of the saints for the first time in a long time. That is, he thought about what his forefathers had believed. Yes, and they died for their belief, many of them—and he had died for his belief as well; or one could say with a good deal of truth that he was prepared to die for it. And his belief was looked upon as insane—so he was now, in many ways, more than a little like Sydney Henderson, that man they had grown up with and mocked. Ian in fact had, like Job, called out to God many times to stop his pain. He just did not admit that he had.

He looked up through the leafless trees toward the moon and found himself on a side street, walking down toward the town square.

The trees themselves seemed pitiless, and his shadow showed how he walked stiffly because he was unable to bend his back. Annette's friends had accused him of spending money on quacks to find a cure, but he had not seen anyone about his back in years. He no longer cared. That is, though he fought the pain, he no longer cared to be cured.

He thought of it this way: Corky should have been in the store helping him move the fridge—why wasn't he? And was that the start of his business's decline? Once the decline had started, so his marriage had started failing too—and because Annette was so impressed by all those men at Helinkiscor, he had decided to fight the mill. Now he could see clearly how every moment had led only to his destruction. Then, as he got to the bottom of the street, he thought of the trunk—the thing he had wanted to buy. Why wasn't it there at Joyce Fitzroy's—that in itself would have changed every other event in his life.

And as he walked by the law office of Hogg and Hogg, he glanced in—just a glance, nothing more, and at nothing in particular.

And there it was—the travelling trunk that had belonged to his family that his mother wanted, that he had tried to buy seventeen years before as a wedding present for Evan and Molly.

He stopped and looked closely. No, there was no mistaking it at all.

The night air had that glaze of spring, when there is still ice in the ditches but the snow is gone.

He looked around for five minutes or more, trying to find a suitable weapon. Finally he loosened a frozen rock from the soil and threw it through the plate glass. Then, with another rock, he broke the rest away. He entered the office and began to overturn everything, even as the alarm was sounding. He picked up a fire extinguisher and crouched down behind the trunk. When the police came in—one of them was Constable Fulton, who had always been very kind to him—he stood and sprayed them. Fulton told me that Ian held off the police with a fire extinguisher for five minutes, and then with his boots for as long as he could, until they threw him down.

"We threw him down very hard, and I was worried we had hurt him," Fulton told me in that interview.

Reports circulated that he had died, but that was not the case at all. He only wished he had.

———

Sara went down in the afternoon to see how her sister, Ethel, was, because it was close to Easter and the earth was warming, and they sat together on the porch in the glare of sun and the fading scent of winter. And Sara spoke with the soft certainty that had directed her life now for the past fifteen years, and her breath made a faint outline and was gone, and she whispered, "Something happened, Ethel, long ago, and now everything is wrong—I do not understand it at all, but something, some small trick of fate, caused all of this to be, don't you think? Ian was so gentle, and still is, but he has been betrayed—and lashes out at shadows."

Ethel nodded and said simply, "People get married to the wrong people—and things get mixed up when they do. I was supposed to marry Corky, and you were supposed to marry Ian, and Annette should have married Harold, then Molly would still be alive. But here we are, mixed all up. Still, things always turn out, in some way."

"Do you hate Annette?" Sara asked her.

"No, no, no, I love Annette. At times, in the house when I worked there, I know she loved me too."

Sara smiled and nodded.

Ethel took the fur hat Harold had given her and started to fluff it with her fingers. Her little house shook as the great trucks filled with Bonny Joyce timber went by, still smelling of dying sap. Everything along this road was heaved and pulled away, as desolate as a marsh in late fall. The smell of machinery entered the rooms, diesel on the air mingling with the shouts of men, harsh yet loving at the exact same time.

"Can you stand those trucks every day—and all that noise?"

"Maybe I am thinking someday they too will be gone!"

Sara kissed her, put forty dollars on the windowsill and left.

Ethel had the mind of a little girl, as Sara said. Ethel would try not to—that is, she would try to be bright. She would sit at the kitchen table and try to remember things, like how to make pancakes.

She would forget she had a mom who loved her and a dad who used to tickle her and say, "My little angel who will go straight to heaven— not a moment in purgatory—right up to the clouds—and all nice clouds too, because you are the kindest child in the world!"

Even when she failed grade two, and then grade three, and had to go into something called "remedial" in grade four, and walked home alone all those winter days ago. Once last autumn she had tried to carry a huge pumpkin into the house, thinking she could make Harold a pumpkin pie. It had rolled on top of her at the bottom of the steps, and it had taken her almost twenty minutes before she could get it off.

Sometimes Harold didn't even have to speak and she would say, "I'm sorry," because she did not know what it was she had done wrong.

She sat in the room with her long hair in pigtails, her eyes staring into the dark and her tights wrinkled at the knees, and her legs so thin they looked like sticks. And there wasn't a person you could mention that she didn't love. And if you thought that wasn't important, she would say, "Just go and ask God."

Today when Sara left, she picked up the rosary blessed and given to her by Father MacIlvoy, and put it in her big dress pocket. She thought long and hard. So hard she squeezed her eyes shut. Yes, it was up to her. She was the woman who had managed to get Liam his first communion. Annette had in the end relented on that. Now she decided he needed to be confirmed. If he was not, he might get in trouble. For who knew what might happen if a person was not confirmed?

She told Harold this when he came home from the pawnshop. He said, "Sure, confirm whoever you want."

———

Harold had asked Ethel's mother to allow him to go to the old house and take some things from it for his pawnshop. The first time he went he took a little windup monkey that had once belonged to Sara, which her mother had bought her long ago for being brave that day they'd almost drowned.

He went there once more, to get the wicker chairs he believed he could sell for seventy dollars. He looked into the dark back closet at the end of the attic to see if he could find anything else. He suddenly noticed the bottle of rum Corky had bought when he was worried about the wrench. Harold picked up the bottle and put it in his jacket pocket, and carried it with him into the future. Then he went back to the pawnshop and brought the newspaper with him.

LOCAL BUSINESSMAN INVOLVED IN LATE-NIGHT BREAK AND ENTER, it said.

———

Sherry Mittens told her friend Liam about his father being in jail. That is, Sherry was Liam's great friend, always telling him things to try, in her little heart, to inform him, and say it was for the best that he heard all these terrible things from her. She was filled with sarcastic irony, always willing to undercut his dreams. She would wake in the morning and prepare herself in front of the mirror, thinking of what she would say and how she would say it, and her little mouth would turn up in a slight smile. Then she would time walking to school so that Liam, pants rumpled and hair uncombed, came out of his front door, and she would catch up to him. Her whole body would smell of nice pink soap, and a scent of cleanliness would pervade his senses. He would wait for her, and she would entertain herself by speaking of non-specific things—how her cat, Muffy, was—how she herself would never have children, and how she would like to live in a city like Toronto. How her father was from Toronto—did you know? How the university here was not for her father, who was so much more devoted and brighter than others in his sociology department, don't you know.

Then, when others joined them, she would drift ahead of him and walk a few paces beyond him with her other friends.

She was devoted to this, and she would sometimes whisper to people that Liam had done something with little boys, for that's what her auntie, Ms. Spalding, had told her. She maintained she said this for his own good as well, dressed in her sweet flouncy dress, her fine white coat and her decorative yellow mittens. Yes, yes, it was better she say it. No one could ignore her pretty smile, or how her eyes flashed when Liam's name was mentioned. Or when she thought of him during the day, and remembered something more to say.

Because she knew so much about him and could tell; and could help him. Yes, she was the only one who could. For her father was a professor of sociology.

The only trouble in all of this was Liam himself—Liam thought Sherry was his one and only friend.

And then one day, one grey afternoon, he walked behind her after she said his father was in jail; she shook her pretty head and said such horrible things about this boy Liam that for a little while he did not know that sweet middle-class Sherry Mittens, who loved kindness to animals and wrote an essay on equality for everyone in the whole world, was speaking—speaking, speaking—about him.

That night she waited to walk home with him, tremendously anxious to tell him something she had heard, but he turned down the back stairs and sat in the gloom by the garbage bin until the school was empty and everyone had gone away.

———

Sara was taking care of Spenser Rogue's grandfather Mange as he lay dying. She was pleased to do so; she even talked to him about the old days when the pulp was piled up behind the house and the chips looked like pieces of gold in the sun. And that seemed to help him get by. Then one evening as she walked into the room—D48—where he lay, his body so shrunken that his large hands looked like paddles, his face white and severe, she suddenly—as if it had all been recorded someplace and she was seeing it for the first time—realized that he was the man who long ago had given her and Ethel the hermit wine when her parents were away. She remembered him in the back porch by the box of old bottles, with the flour sacks nailed up over the window. She had been reading to Ethel about a prince in a castle, and he said—yes, he could show them a prince, and give them a special honey, and if they drank it, they would see the prince. It was suddenly his Humphrey pants and the gold clasp on his suspenders that came to her—almost like a violent intrusion—when he turned his head toward her as he lay there now, and raised his hand—

She suddenly remembered the smell of pulpwood, and her standing in between him and Ethel and saying, "No, don't hurt Ethel. She's my sister." She remembered, even worse, Ethel standing watching, not knowing what to do.

And how much he had hurt her, hurt her and hurt her, when she was a little girl, when her mother had cut her bangs so short she didn't like them at all and she hid a little bottle of perfume in her room. She had nothing more than one dress, and they had run down to the pulp yard because she and Ethel were going to see a prince.

He looked over at her now, a sack of urine at the side of the bed and the veins in his arms punctured. He did not know her, did not even know that she was his doctor.

"I'm in pain, Nurse," he whispered. "I'm in pain."

She felt his pulse, ordered as much morphine as he could handle and made sure he drank the orange juice. For the next few weeks she did what she could to allow him peace at the end.

———

The notes we have about Sara from the time she and Ian broke up are both scattered and somewhat elliptical: Sara, whose average grade in high school was ninety-seven, left for the university on the hill. She lived in an apartment with three other girls, just off Head Hall, and then moved to Dalhousie University, where she rented a small room with the toilet two floors above.

"Medicine," Ethel said, when Sara came home. "I bet that has an ingredient or two."

She fell in love with another young woman when in university, and they were constantly together. Had a serious affair. It was something she had tried not to have, so it was said, and couldn't help herself, so it was said.

That was the rumour, nor did she once deny it. She would stay in touch with this woman most of her life.

Still, nothing is certain in life. Sara came home, and people threw parties for her and had many kind things to say about her in the paper. People could not help liking her and wanting to be seen with her—for she had met Desmond Tutu, she had met Nelson Mandela. So then, in this dreary little backwater, she was a blessing. People could not help but ask her to join with them. Her paper on medical and military inadequacy during the genocide in Rwanda had been read at a UN subcommittee and its findings were endorsed by the Secretary-General and mentioned on CNN.

So at first, everyone paled compared with her.

The initial idea—that Sara was a modern woman and a renegade—certainly helped her; all the book clubs wanted her to join theirs—and there were four serious ones on the river that studied all the favourite Canadian authors (but not the author from their own town, who, they decided, wrote such troublesome things and did not really truly understand or represent their values, which were progressive and modern ones best explained by fashionable women or by books from Oprah's Book Club). So everyone thought Sara was heroic and wanted her on their side.

Yet little by little by little, this attitude changed and then dissipated. Sara over the last year or so had damaged this early beneficence and managed to become embroiled in a terrible controversy herself, because after coming home from working with Doctors Without Borders, from working with the poor in many places in Africa, from being a witness to the inexcusable lapses by the United Nations in Rwanda—in short, from being considered a hero—some part of her, wherever it was, had declined to do abortions. So after a time, this cancelled out many progressive people's ideas of who she was.

"What a cripple," some sniffed.

She was no longer invited to the book clubs to read books written by substantial and progressive ladies.

It had started simply enough—people had asked her to support a petition that would help Dr. Morgentaler set up an abortion clinic in the province, saying his human rights were being violated. She not only said she couldn't—she tried to dissuade these people from their idea, and said she believed human rights started before one was born. So a group of women who played bridge and did yoga, and had once been ecstatic that she had returned, were now trying to sue her. It was a frivolous lawsuit started by Patsy Mittens, but nonetheless it deeply hurt her.

Yet, with all of these having deserted her and questioned her competence, she found solace in duty and obligation. So that is why she was in the ICU and happened to be Mange Rogue's doctor.

"Some terrible thing has happened," she told her mother, "to all of us, something that even you did not foresee!"

She wanted to tell her mother of the thing the man had done to her when she was young, and that she was now barren because of it. But she could not. And if it ever got out now, she thought, many from those progressive groups would think she was making it up.

They kept at her—her enemies. So Sara, after many months of stoic silence, finally answered letters in the paper and said yes, she had given it much thought, debated it with herself and had been under much pressure, but she had decided she could not personally perform this procedure, that there were others who would. So she worked with infants, both those who were premature and those with fetal alcohol syndrome, and to her these lives were sacred.

She became known as Sacred Sara, the Immaculate Conception. And people said, "She doesn't have children, does she? Well, what would she do if she was raped and got pregnant? People like this never think of abuse happening to them!"

"No."

"You see."

So she looked, with her limp and her short hair and her small dark eyes, bundled up in winter in her jacket and boots, to some of the women she looked to be an enemy of the people. This in fact is how she was thought of by everyone in Annette's crew. And they did lessen her worth whenever they could. Yet it seemed none of them had written about the genocide in Rwanda, had spoken to Nelson Mandela or had hidden men women and children under her medical hut in the mountainous gorilla region of the north, when men with machetes roamed the area and at certain intervals in the nighttime one could hear them as they wandered about with steel blades and clubs, singing in French as a Beatles song played on a boom box in the dark. DD told Annette that some people said Sara was medieval and should join a convent.

"You see what an outcast she is—ha!" Annette said to Liam with grave triumph, leaning against the counter. She was drinking and slurring her words. "You see! I knew it, I knew it—I knew what she was like—you see! She'll have no friends now. No one invites her out—she is all alone, you see! I knew she was all alone. I knew she would have no friends, and look at the friends I have—see!"

PART EIGHT

THERE ARE VIGNETTES WE HAVE ABOUT LIAM—MY students have found them over the course of years, here and there, by interviewing those who knew him, or now say they did. There are, I suppose, a thousand moments in childhood that might register if looked at in photos as being moments both elliptical and profound— and Liam had those moments too—and now after it is all over they are thrust upon us, deliberate, ordinary and accusatorial, in complete and utter silence, from small memories of his life.

There is a scene when Liam is ten years of age. It is late at night, and he is trying to get his father to stand up. His father has cut his face. How, we never found out. Liam was looking for him. He must have woken, found his father gone and searched the snowed-over streets. His father had tried to get some documents that would save the Bonny and had been attacked by members of Union 187.

There is one day when Liam is performing a magic trick at school. The girl Sherry Mittens remembered it distinctly. It is before he has his braces. Suddenly the auditorium goes silent. The young boy everyone tormented is now rising behind a desk, into the air. And they begin to clap and shout and holler and even say, "Bravo."

There is a moment when he and Sherry Mittens are together on a bus and it is late. He is staring down at her and she is speaking. Her eyes are downcast—and at this point he is thinking how wonderful it was to confide in her. The next day was the day she nodded spitefully when she spoke, the small crinkles of hair sticking up, like bent pins, from her little oval head, and amid all the hope and dreams he had for friendship—the one she was speaking so cruelly about was him.

There is a moment when he and Ethel are walking home after going to a movie. Liam had phoned her and asked to take her on a date—for he wanted to see the movie and had no one else to go with.

He is running downstairs. It is noon hour. He is waiting for the mail. He is trading Pokémon cards with someone somewhere in Alberta.

He is sitting on the steps outside, wearing his hockey helmet and knee pads, asking people if they know who killed his pet pigeon. Of everyone who comes and goes he asks, "Do you know who would do such a thing? Who could? Does anyone know who could—it was Joey, my pet."

He wears his helmet and knee pads to tackle anyone who would—to tackle the evildoers.

His mother begs him to come inside. It is almost one in the morning. But she sees how stubborn he can be—stubbornness burned into him by ridicule. So that even those youths who took his pigeon—Kyle and Spenser, who broke its neck as a joke—even they do not go by his house, worried that he will know it was them.

He is all alone. It is night and he is coming home. He has no one anymore in the world. The memory of his father shutting the door on him at the store that long-ago day has shaken his heart.

Trees wave in the warm July breeze over his head, and he whispers into the soft trees, "Someday I am going to go away."

He buries the pigeon near the back fence, in the shade.

———

Sara once told Ethel that people are fascinated with what is bad because they believe bad can actually hide the good that is underneath. That this is the true reason for the attraction to bad, and that people never really like the bad, but love when bad or feared people act with a degree of kindness and spontaneous generosity. This is a defining idea, and the idea that bad men are misunderstood because of this hidden goodness allows many of them to play the con of being good underneath. They often do this in spite of good intentions, and do this to and with themselves, because the con is in so many ways and for so many reasons self-beguiling.

Sara did not say this about anyone in particular, but she did see how many, many people were attracted to Harold Dew, and how even she was fascinated by him. For he had been a rough and a bad man many times; he had done things most men would not do, and yet people—even some he'd cheated—were fascinated and attracted by him.

There were still some very kind things about him, things that Sara herself saw and liked. He could give you the shirt off his back—many said he had done this, many times. It was true that he had a good deal of charisma, especially with the young, and the young flocked to him and did his bidding, just as in years gone by they had done for Lonnie Sullivan. For instance, he gave a five-tonne truck to Rueben to haul wood—just as he said he would do.

Still, he always wanted and needed something in return. So therefore, like Lonnie Sullivan, he did not know that he had to con himself in order to con others, and to gain the confidence of youngsters he had to believe that he would do them no harm. But in ways he did not know or consider, in ways he did not comprehend, the very conditions of their friendships led to harm.

And this had happened all his life—first with Rueben Sores, who sold drugs for him, and in a way with Corky Thorn, and now with others like Kyle and Spenser, who ran and did his bidding and who both were doing things for him to work off loans, and who, in fact, if they did not watch out, would go to jail for him.

So the courting of Liam Preston was a natural phenomenon. Liam was alone now, and so was Harold, and Liam needed a father figure, and Harold believed—even though, when he thought rationally, he knew it couldn't possibly be—that Liam was his own son. Liam had, in a way, lost both his father and his mother. Harold realized this and tried to be nice to him. When Harold was nice to anyone, he was like his uncle Lonnie—he could be exceedingly nice without even knowing it. And he felt sorry for the little boy too. He told Kyle and Spenser never to bother this boy

again, and he told others as well that if they ever in their lives were anything less than respectful to this boy, he would hear about it.

So, though Liam did not know why, he only knew that it had happened and that no one bothered him anymore. And Liam began dropping into Harold's happy pawnshop after school every day. For there
was no one home, and there were no friends either. One day he came to
pawn his Thomas The Train set. Harold looked at it, realized it was not
much good but offered Liam twenty dollars. He also said that Liam
could have a job at the shop, cleaning up.

Harold was Ethel's husband—and of all the people who had been
kind to him, the one who had been kind to him the most was Ethel.

Liam's teeth hurt and he needed money. He did not talk to Annette
anymore. He had waited for her to come home for supper too many times.
And she had her own life again, and it was a life where she excluded him,
because she was once again youthful and beautiful and single.

So Liam would cook beans and wiener's for them both and sit there
waiting in silence. Sometimes, on occasion, when he saw her walking
along the street and she did not notice him, his heart would go weak
with love. Once he called out "Mom!" but she didn't hear.

Where would Liam go? This was one of the main questions my students
asked.

A few years before he met Harold Dew, Liam had a fort he had built
by himself. He worked on building his own computer and putting his
own bicycle together. He would send away for parts for his bicycle or
seek them at second-hand shops, spending afternoons alone, and he
would find computer parts in the dump, which he would carry home
through the streets on sunny afternoons in summer. And after a while
he had friends—Jack and Dan and Brad and Gordy and Fraser and Pint
McGraw. They were all much younger than he was, for no one Liam's
age bothered with him.

So he told the children stories about how he wanted his computer to
work and how he would take them for a trip to the pond. Someday when

the day was hot, he said, they would all go back across the tracks to the pond. He just had to wait for the right day. And he knew the situations of all those boys; he knew when Gordy's father was out of town or when Pint was teased; and he would say, "In my fort no one is teased, and no one's father is out of town," and he would smile at Pint and sit Fraser on his knee. Pint had weak eyes and wore thick glasses. So he gave Pint twenty of his Pokémon cards. Pint McGraw often came to the fort and sat on the bench in the corner, and folded his hands on his lap and looked up at you and smiled. Sometimes he came there at seven in the morning, just to wait for the others.

Pint was so skinny his socks would fall off his feet, so Liam made small pins to hang from his shorts, and attached thread from these pins to his socks. Pint and Frazer were five, Gordon was six, and Dan and Brad were eight. These were his friends from those summers long, long ago. Brad and Dan were the ones who helped him search the dump for old computers, and Brad was the boy who helped him with his bicycle. He would tear the backs off the computers and look for the right chip and bring it back. Or sometimes he would carry the entire hard drive back to his fort and take it apart. So computer parts lay all over the back lawn, and bicycle parts did as well. Liam's eyes at this time were deep grey and beautiful. He had read books on computers and showed the older boys how to win the computer games everyone was playing. And the one thing about these children from Injun Town and beyond— from near the old sawmill and on those lanes that ran toward the water—was this: all of them were in one way or the other as orphaned or as alone as he was.

It was easy for them to be alone that summer around the back of the house, beyond the garden, near the wall of elm trees where the sun came through. When Brad and Dan wanted to do something without the other kids, who were too young, Liam would say, "In my fort every-one does things together."

And sometimes he would have a pitcher of lemonade and plastic glasses that came from the basement. He also had a marble pot. And once or twice he brought out a bag of chocolate chip cookies, and Spider-Man comic books. They sat about the small benches while Liam worked on the computer or found new shocks to try for his bicycle. He found it was easier to get the power source from the house beyond them. Sometimes they would sit for an hour or two as quiet as could be, watching him.

In a real way, he was their hero those long-ago days, when kids often had no heroes at all, and when Liam never had a friend. He brought out a little TV for them to watch as they ate their cracker snacks.

Sometimes some of the boys wouldn't show up. Sometimes it would be only Pint and Fraser who would come across the back gully, hauling an old wagon. He would hear the wagon arrive at eight in the morning and look out his bedroom window. Sometimes they would come, rain or shine, and sit there on the bench. He showed them the computer motherboard and RAM discs and pointed to them, saying, "They sent a man to the moon with a computer as big as my house. Now there is enough power in what I hold in my hand to send a man to the moon."

The children would look up at the sky, blinking.

"To the moon," Pint McGraw would say, rubbing his thick glasses.

But then Liam did something else. He took his father's cylinder, the one Ian had worked on in better happier times, and examined it. He knew it was just a pastime, but he also knew what his father had been trying to do: he was trying to use filters to take readings of effluents from the mill. Liam took the cylinder apart and redid it. That is, by midsummer of the year he was twelve he had essentially solved his father's problem, for the cylinder worked simply: by the shades the effluents made on the filters, and each filter caught the minerals in the water and made the filters dark blue or pink or red.

Then one day he took his father's invention back to him and placed it in his hand.

"I think I fixed it," he said. But Ian said he was no longer interested in it, and he placed it on his small shelf in the little room he had rented.

So Liam went back home. He sat on the bed, staring at his Game

Boy and his Spider-Man. Far away down the street, there were cat-calls from boys his age who always teased him and sometimes slapped his mouth.

"When I grow up, I will go away," he whispered to himself.

Liam told the children about mathematics, and how he thought his dad's cylinder would work when placed in water or any liquid. That it would do readings of what was in that water—so it would work in wells or houses, in mills too.

"It will make a million for my dad." He smiled. And it might have, if his dad had known it.

He told them that people from all over the world who would never understand a word of each other's language would still understand mathematics. So mathematics was, in fact, the universal language, and even if humans went to the moon or stars, they would have to travel to them on the peculiar principle that two plus two equalled four. And he said, smiling gently, "That's why there is a God. There is a God because two plus two equals four," he said. "There is a God because Sara had to go away." And he told them about Sara and how she had doctored twenty people from the reserve and from Bonny Joyce; and those were the people no one cared about.

"Twenty?" Fraser asked.

"Twenty people." And he said that if she had married his father, she never would have learned to save those people. "So," he said, "that's why there is a God."

They would sit still and listen quietly as he spoke. His voice would trail off into the leaves and branches where small birds flitted in the afternoon or dipped into the bird bath he himself had constructed at the side of the house. At night he would sit in the dark. Sometimes he would say, " 'Our Father who art in heaven, hallowed be Thy name,' " and then he would listen to the sounds of the trees at night—the wind in the willows—and he would sleep.

"I will be a saint," he whispered, "and I will—be a saint."

Liam was always repairing his fort as well, to keep the wind or the rain out. At times he would take the wagon with the kids in it and go down to Randolph's lumberyard to look for scraps of lumber. The manager would see them coming down the streets, against the hard sun of midday, Liam pulling three kids in a wagon, all of them talking and laughing, with the wind from the water blowing their soft brown hair. Their bodies were as thin as twigs in the summer air, and their little wagon was dwarfed by the lumberyard's great mesh fence.

The manager often gave them a piece of lumber to take back with them across the flat empty sidewalks of a town in disrepair. Far off the big pulp mill stack loomed. Far away a whistle sounded at noon hour. Now and again someone would hoot at Liam from the pool hall as they passed back toward his fort.

"Goofball!" they would yell.

But Liam never paid attention to people who yelled at him anymore. Once upon a time he had. But not anymore. Now he simply sat at night and thought of the trains that moved people, and how someday he would go on a train. You see, he had never been on a train, or ever outside of town. As the dispute between his parents grew, and gossip grew about who he was, he found his mom and dad had no plans for trips they once thought they would take. And he never looked their way when those people yelled at him.

The children held fast to the idea that Liam was the bravest and best person in the world, the one who gave them lemonade and was making a fort, and knew—well, let me tell you, he knew why two plus two equalled four. Around by the trampled weeds toward the far end of the house, as the trees swayed in the afternoon breeze, they pulled their little wagon with the lumber.

Then that day came when he promised he would take them to the pond, and out they went, all of them, Pint and Fraser and Gord, in the wagon, holding the pitcher of lemonade and the loaf of bread and some peanut butter, and the older boys wheeling the bicycle that they had just finished making, and Brad holding the towels, with Liam leading them all over the tracks to the old pond in the stillness of August when all those other children, those children with mothers and fathers, were at the cottage.

They went to the pond the front way, between the two new subdivisions that were spreading mercilessly toward the future. It was cool and the mud was worn, and there were broken beer bottles on one side, and the ruins of a fire. So they stayed on the side where they were, in the sunlight of afternoon.

Liam acted as a lifeguard, and watched them swim. They had towels and blankets and peanut butter sandwiches, and Liam made them a lunch and laid it on the blanket. They watched the sky. Fraser and Pint and Gord lay naked because they didn't have underwear and didn't want to get their shorts wet, and Dan and Brad lay in their underwear, which was almost black from dirt, and they all looked up at the trees, and spoke of going to school. Then they started talking about going to heaven. And it didn't matter what religion they were; they all wanted to go to heaven the same way. And in case they didn't know where it was, Liam told them that it was beyond the clouds, and a place where the fort was too. And as Ethel had told him, in heaven—why, in heaven any wish, as long as it was kind, would come true. He knew he was saying this because he was older, more assured, and most importantly because someone had taken the time to say it to him.

Then he took out some sugar from a small bag and mixed it into the lemonade and they sat around the pitcher. Then he took their photo. Then, as the day passed, they had to look for Pint's glasses and they couldn't find them. He didn't know where he had left them.

They had to go back home without them, with Pint McGraw sitting at the front of the wagon, blinking rapidly, and Fraser holding on to him, and their shirt collars damp. All of them spoke about the movie Liam said he would take them to, and about how they could get money to go. Liam told them he could use his paper delivery money. But he said they would wait until Pint got his glasses. That he and Brad would have to go back tomorrow to look for them. So Liam and Brad divined when they would meet and where.

Then Liam told the joke about the scarecrow who was scared of crows and they all broke out laughing, and it was growing dark and the wagon veered to the right down the path between the trees to the back of his house, so it sounded as if all the houses were suddenly laughing and talking about scarecrows.

Then, when they got home, the police were there. Liam's neighbour Ms. Spalding had counted six times Liam had used her outlet to get electricity. So the police had confiscated his computer parts and taken his bicycle. All the children stood around him, with their collars still wet and the day growing darker and a robin twittering as it hopped in the backyard grass. But there was something even worse: The police man had also heard from Georgie at the tracks that Liam had had the children's clothes all off at the pond. And what was he doing taking photos of the children? And no, he couldn't have the computer back or the bicycle. The police officer, Constable Jarvis, took him into the house and told him he was never to go near children or he'd be run in. The boys stood outside listening to this, and heard Liam's mother yell at him, "What kind of person did I bring up? Going around and having little boys naked!"

And she hit him hard on the back with a belt.

They all stood in the silent evening, and it was growing dark. Then the boys were taken home.

The next day it rained; the wagon, overturned, had been left in the dirt at the side of the house; black squall blew the trees, and the back of the fort fell. Liam sat in it alone. He looked around his small fort in a daze. And he was shivering, but it wasn't from the cold.

After that, he was alone again. And he would often go to the park and sit.

One day he went back to the pond and looked for three hours and finally saw Pint's old glasses under a small piece of driftwood. So he ran downtown, smiling. And he saw little Pint walking down the street. He yelled and waved, saying he had gone back to the pond and found them, but Pint was with his foster mom, who'd told him never to speak to Liam again, and so passed him by.

"You leave him be. You little cocksucker pervert, you is—little faggot is you," the foster mom did say.

But then Pint, when he was way, way down the street, did look back and smile.

Liam sat in the park after school most days. On occasion, people would still holler at him, "Goofball!"

He almost never went home until he needed to go to bed, for there was no reason to anymore. He was called an "odd little goofball," but he still walked the streets to find computer chips and motherboards others had thrown away. And he stayed up long into the night working in his room, listening to music from his headphones.

Once his mother beat him for playing his train at two in the morning. He did not know why she did this, but she was drunk and had fallen into a kind of hell without real borders. That is, a hell so borderless it could be anywhere at all.

So the next day he went into Harold Dew's to sell his train set for twenty dollars. That is, without his parents knowing it, he began to sell or give away everything that had once belonged to his childhood: his Toronto Maple Leafs cap, and his Spider-Man collection that his dad had bought. His beautiful marbles and plumpers. Even the pictures in the scrapbook of him in the wheelhouse getting his picture taken with Captain John. One day, walking alone, he simply tore it in two. That is, he was going away already; already he was leaving them forever, though they did not know.

When he went inside Harold Dew's pawnshop that late-April day, his teeth were aching and his gums were bleeding because his mom had slapped his face without realizing she would hurt him because of his new braces. She had cut his mouth deeply and it was sore, and he had spit blood most of the way there.

Harold's heart went out to him, and he gave him a drink from the bottle of rum he got from the attic. He saw the pain in Liam, just as he had once seen the pain in himself. His own teeth had been destroyed when he was a boy, by a kick in the mouth. His life had been ruined because his mother had told him he was in a will, his friends too had gone away—and he had been on his own from the time he was fifteen. So he knew what it was like to be Liam. And Liam looked so much like his brother, Glen, he couldn't stop staring at him, and then smile vaguely, as if in some kind of apology. And he began to think of him more and more as his own child.

"Here, let me pour you a glass—poor little fella, poor little lad," Harold said, with utmost compassion, and he poured out a double shot with a little Coke.

And Liam drank from that glass, and suddenly he felt very giddy and happy. He had never known he could be so happy.

On Good Friday, he went to Harold's again, just to talk to someone.

The shop was open—the place was dusty and filled with clutter. Harold Dew sat behind the counter doing a crossword puzzle.

"How is yer teeth?"

"They still hurt," Liam said. The idea that his teeth would be fixed, and that everyone would love him if they were, had been his constant hope. Sometimes children pour their hope out like gold and it falls clinking to the ground, and is lost.

Liam had thought that his mom would love him once he had them fixed. And perhaps his dad had slammed the door on him only because of his teeth.

Now all they did was give him pain.

Harold asked him if he would like another little drink.

"Yes—good, please!"

Harold took the bottle of rum that he had got from Ethel's mom's attic and poured out a double shot, and set it on the counter near the boy.

"It's good—it always takes the pain away is what I found!" Harold said. "But you have to moderate. You can't drink all the time."

Liam took a drink, and then again and again, while Harold talked about how he had been kicked in the mouth at school.

Liam put the cup down on the cluttered countertop and Harold winked at him, and he smiled. It was the first time he had smiled with his braces on. He had been waiting to show either his mom or dad.

Now it didn't matter at all. Now the boys he had made picnics for didn't matter either.

"Name a seven-letter word for scandal—it begins with an *o*," Harold said.

"*Outrage*," Liam said, picking up the bottle and taking another drink straight. "That always works."

———

It was when Mr. Ian was in jail that Liam was most on his own. This was also when Wally started to distance himself from Annette. When he veered away from her, when he began to ignore her drunken phone calls late at night.

And this is when Annette declared she was going to write a book. She would phone Wally and tell him a book was coming.

The woman who read her fortune told her that someday she would write a book, and she knew now was the time. Her therapist told her she might try to heal by writing of her terrible abuse. So she would have to write it soon. Why? She did not know. Except to those who still listened to her, and they were becoming fewer and fewer, it seemed to have something to do with an insult once from Patsy Mittens's book club. She blushed when she remembered it, and wanted more than ever to prove something.

Yes, there was a man in town who she heard wrote—but what would he know? Her character would be a character women could relate to—at one point this character would save a woman from abuse, or live in solitude on an island because men had treated her wrong. And as for religion, she said, "Don't get me started on the priests."

This is what Liam listened to as Annette and Diane spoke about perverts. Liam did not know what a pervert was, but he knew he had been called one by Ms. Spalding with her big straw hat and her dark glasses and her homey, civilized, no-nonsense life in her garden with her new soil.

Annette talked about how she would spare no one; her heroine would be the one to destroy bishops and prime ministers. At one point she said she would destroy all the men at the mill—show them for who they were and how they cheated on their women. Wally, too, if he didn't watch it.

DD would say, "Oh, I know—wow! What will you call it?"

"*Love's Journey*—or *A Woman's Heartbreak*. Or *Love Island*, or *Love's Elusive Flight*."

Then Annette would tip her drink back, and bringing the glass down and pushing it away with her beautiful hand say, "DD, you will be my agent. I will have an agent and it will be DD. We will probably have to go to Los Angeles. Would you mind going there, DD?"

"If I have to. I won't mind," DD said, adding dreamily, "I am so glad you are doing it. For what man could ever write about women who live like you or me?"

Annette said it would be almost imperative that they go to Los Angeles, for that's where the movie would be made. Then, one night, she said that Liam wouldn't be able to come.

"Why?" Liam asked, heartbroken.

"I don't know why."

"Why do you have to go?"

"Because of the movie, dear," Annette said.

In their folly, she and DD would often laugh at all the men who were now out of work, and speak about how Wally had to order them out of the mill yard, and how she—that is, Annette—had a hand in firing people. "You did—you fired them?" DD asked.

"Yes," Annette said, affirming this with a quick nod of her pretty head. "Wally said to me, 'Annette, you know more about the damn men here than I do—should Greg Milton go?' and I said, 'Yes,' and Wally simply crossed his name out."

DD laughed and said, "Oh wow."

And Liam would know that Greg Milton's little girl was ill, and they had no money, and he would be ashamed of what they said. And one night he saw Annette in a state of complete hysteria, unable to contain herself, tears of laughter in her eyes, and he became terrified that something terrible would happen—and it would—soon.

Then after they spoke and drank, DD and Annette would leave him. They would take their coats and purses and the door would close, the smell of alcohol evaporating in the evening air.

Liam would sit at home. Sometimes he would sit in the den for an hour or two, and then he would get up and sit in the basement near the old pool table. Or he would go upstairs, far up to the attic, and look down toward the great bridge far, far away.

Once she came home from the bar at ten o'clock. He was so happy she had come home early. He heard them and ran downstairs. That was the night she had promised them all a surprise. She wanted him to float for Ripp and Tab and DD.

He wouldn't do it.

She said she would get a belt.

Tab said, "No, you leave him alone if he don't want to float."

Ripp said Liam couldn't do it.

"You couldn't float," Ripp said, "even if you wanted to."

Tab said, "Leave him alone—he is just a kid. He doesn't have to float."

Annette said, "You little bastard—you know how I bragged that you did, you little son of a bitch—so go and float!"

But he did not.

And perhaps it was in the way Ripp grinned when he heard that someone was beaten up at a tavern; or perhaps it was in the way DD could turn on anyone—suddenly, as soon as they were down and alone, with a fleeting look of brutal pleasure in her eyes. Perhaps it was in the way he remembered his father, who had spent money taking them out to dinner on Liam's eighth birthday, being rebuked in the restaurant by his mother, who drunkenly said, "If you were half the man Ripp is. God, there are times . . . yes, there are times—!"

Liam at that moment was smiling and waiting for his cake, and then he looked down, ashamed. Perhaps that was when Liam's heart was broken.

Some nights long, long after Annette went out, he would sit in the den in the dark, listening to the wind, his bare feet on the white carpet. He would think of the cylinder and how he and his father almost made a million—but what was worse, he'd read in *Scientific American* about something just like it, already in use. And thinking of how his father had almost, almost, almost won, tears would flow from his eyes, not out of shame or frustration but out of longing and pride. It would have only taken fifty thousand dollars from the Atlantic Canadian Opportunity Agency—and yet, frightened, they did not award his father the money and had left him alone and broken.

Liam had run to the school the day he had corrected how the cylinder worked, his hair sticking up because it was so dirty, and his sneakers rundown at the heels, and his nose running. "I know how it works," he told the high school physics teacher. "It is a stabilizer—it works on the premise that every rinse at the mill or any other industrial site can be washed, and effluents can be kept at a minimum. We can test the leaks in any pipe for chemical spill, the leaks into the river can also be monitored—so we will know exactly how much pollution we are causing. All we do is get a male and female coupling and attach it at any given point along a line that is flushing, and we will record by these filters what is in the water and how to devalue its impact!"

The physics teacher had told him this might be good in theory, but was it practical to think a mill would even care?

"Those who are left to clean up the mess might," Liam said.

But he was given no indication that this was a very significant invention, and the teacher talked about it as just one of the many toys men brought forward when they were whiling away the time.

The teacher held it up to the light and smiled, saying, "I see your father is quite the little gadget maker," with the scent of chalk dust in the afternoon air.

Now Liam did not know where that cylinder was, and now it did not matter anymore, and the secret, secret bond it had made between him and his dad had gone away.

Liam would walk at night, alone. Sometimes until almost morning. His hands were scarred from trying to protect his father's signs, and he often had to keep them warm against his body, and at times, because the skin was thin, they did not warm and tears would bright his eyes. Yet he would take the streets or climb trees or run along the walls near the convent—no one knew where, in fact, he would be.

Once, some boys saw him in the park at the top limb of an oak tree, eighty feet in the air. They called Sara Robb to please come and tell him to get down.

He would climb the storm drain and slip into his window at the top of his house.

Annette planned her book. She went to the bookstore and asked if they would buy copies from her, and they asked her who her publisher was.

"Oh, they are all after it right now," she said nervously. "But I haven't chosen one yet."

She bought herself champagne to celebrate this book, and even bought a computer and set it up in the den.

————

Now the weather was changing and the smell of spring was in the winter soil. Easter had come.

At three in the afternoon, Liam walked through the desolate town. He may or may not have remembered his father had predicted this and had fought against the company coming in, and had destroyed what was left of his life doing so. But it was not the company, it was his father who was heroic.

So Liam had taken three drinks of rum from Harold.

"You're a smart little fellow," Harold said, "but do you still love your dad—Ian? Do you still love him after all he did to ruin your life? You should hear what people say about him now. Can you love a man like that, that he beat you and your mom? Do you love him?"

"Heart and soul," Liam said, tears flooding his eyes. "Heart and soul."

They had tried to take him away—Ms. Spalding and the social worker, Melissa Sapp—when his mom and dad were being pulled apart; but he would not go—he hid, sometimes in the big garbage bin on the second floor at the back of the school. What was wrong with those nice people like Ms. Spalding and Melissa Sapp, Harold asked him now; what was wrong with their concern?

"They have the concern any vulture has over an animal it is waiting on to die! They are ironic and sarcastic to all, and both of those things lessen their souls," Liam said, looking up from under his eyebrows because he was giving away his brilliance and did not wish to have it exposed.

Harold only shrugged. "You are a strange boy—I'm sure if they went and got degrees from university, they want to help people!"

"Well, I'm sure they say they do!" Liam said.

———

This was the time of the great foreclosures on houses and businesses and certain other places that dotted the river. Old families like the Conners had been debilitated, and their huge nineteenth-century houses sat bleak and uncared for. This was happening more as more people fled the area, and as sons and daughters no longer came home but travelled west or south to the cities of Fredericton or Moncton. The streets had been patched and paved twenty times, and the docks lay bare and empty.

Harold would go with Kyle and Spenser in the back of the truck to those houses—they would start as early as seven in the morning, rifling through things that old men and women wanted to sell.

"Inspect that. No, that has an added arm—you see, it'd fetch almost nothing. Here is what we want—I'll offer thirty for this and won't go higher than forty-five." And he would send the boys to do the deal with the elderly couple peering at them with dull eyes from the door. But he kept Liam with him when they went through the real stuff—the libraries of certain places, for example. The libraries might be those set up by a daughter or son, and forgotten sometimes for forty years. Harold would go through these happily and meticulously, because many times he would find money, or even the number and contents of a safety deposit box— and once he found a will. Liam would bring him the books.

"No, God—throw that one out—this book and this book, not that—no, this—yes, that one too—we can sell those."

At first Liam believed that the books Harold kept were the ones people would pay to read.

"Read? Who in fuck says anything about reading? No one reads— look!" He would show that each book he had chosen had old prints or maps inside them or were collectible because of when they were printed—that is all he was after—that is what the owners of those books never knew to value. Harold Dew, in fact, was very bright—he might never have read D. H. Lawrence, but when he found an original first edition of *Lady Chatterley's Lover*, he guarded it, knowing it would bring him money. In fact, it brought him four thousand dollars at auction. He gave Liam three hundred dollars from this windfall.

Sometimes he could get two hundred or three for a print, or even four hundred for a map. The prints and maps were always worth money to collectors in Fredericton or Saint John, who would buy such artifacts.

From this Liam came to collect his own books and brought many home—that is when he brought the books of that other writer, books others in the town refused to read. He had heard so much of how terrible this writer was, how violent, that at first he himself wanted to throw them away. Yet he began to read this writer who people said they hated, and he lay in the upstairs room with the light shining on the obscure pages and the world of his river opening up like a terrible beautiful blossom that in its countless tragedy had hope of another bloom—and in this world of despair and darkness he saw much beauty, and many times his own mother and DD too, and the writer's love for them in spite of endless frivolity—and once or twice he wanted to tell his mother he had spied her in the very books she and her book club friends hated yet had never taken the time to read. Of course, he saw his father too, and he saw someone else smiling at him in the pages of those tattered books published back in the seventies and eighties: he saw the face of Harold Dew.

There were other books he kept from the old libraries—in particular, *The Diary of Anne Frank*. It too was a first edition—but he did not let on to Harold that he had it.

For a while he went along with Harold to find books. But even then he seemed always alone. Sometimes he told the darkness, the sky, the great beyond, that he loved them. He still had an open face, a worldwide grin—and a sheepish hope that the world would love him too.

————

When Wally moved to the alcove on the other side of the office, with his own window (which is what all enterprising office boys and girls long for) and his direct line to upper management, things started to change for Annette. She did not know why—but now, suddenly, she was no longer in Wally's inner circle.

Wally was aloof, preoccupied, although as always, his face was still bright and juvenile. He was a man who had no point of view but all of his life greedily held the views of others.

"Try every trick," DD said, "and you will have him. A perfect date and a perfect supper—and a perfect bed."

For two years she had given him information, become his spy. She stayed late; she worked behind the scenes for him. Not that she got him very much information—but once he'd told her she'd hit the mother lode. That is, that Mr. Ticks had sent off a letter to the premier about how the mill was working, and he'd sent the forestry minister a private management memo also. Wally instantly reported it to head office. He saw the suspicious and dumbfounded look on Fension's face, but Wally himself was really unaware of what was going on. Within two weeks,

Ticks was gone—gone for good. And Wally was certain he had done something beneficial in his capacity as a company man.

And that is why he now had his own window.

But Annette was saying she was thinking of writing a book. So Wally moving to the alcove was a sign that he had got whatever it was he wanted—and wanted no part of her anymore. Once again he was unaffiliated.

Yet he didn't speak to her now. Not like before, when he had been a mentor, when he had spoken to her each noonhour about her son, who he pretended (and actually believed) he cared for. This preposterous arrogance had lasted for some time, this pretense that he cared for Annette and her son because they were vulnerable. He did not seem to see how Liam looked through him at times with bright, so bright eyes.

But now things had changed. She was no longer the Annette who he was concerned about and helped, but an office girl he had no use for, and who the company no longer needed; and of course her son, that boy, was not his concern. In fact, he disliked that boy intensely.

Three weeks passed. The supper Annette had planned did not turn out, and she was never at her desk at work. Her chair was empty.

How did I ever get mixed up with that thing! he thought. He'd tried to help her—but help could only go so far.

Then she told him what was going on. And over the following week he acted as if it was all up to her, and said it was bad timing—and that she must know it too.

"We could keep it," he said one night as they talked in his car, "but if we did, Ian might abuse it if he found out. In fact, he is not like me or you. He has no use for children. He would really injure it, like he did Liam. We are well aware of how Liam suffered at his hands! Everyone in town was concerned about Ian hurting the boy. So this would just be another case in point. It's best for the child to get rid of it now. That's all I am concerned about." He stopped speaking, abruptly.

Annette, in fact, had wanted to keep the child. But now she looked at him, and saw behind his boyish round cheeks a very different Wally: cunning, arrogant, and, in some very important ways, stupid.

Until this very moment she had actually thought they would be married. The child would be their bond of love. This is what she had imagined—and imagined a new life. It had been, in some way, her last hope.

"No—we are too mature for that!" She smiled. She then thought of adoption, quickly and hopefully. This too seemed to debilitate Wally.

"Adoption—no. That's even worse, isn't it? It might go to a bad family—God knows what might happen! A lot of people want to adopt just to hurt children—I know that for a fact! And besides, the new couples live for their careers. This is the best thing." The best thing was to rid himself of it as soon as possible.

But Annette too knew that adoption was not a possibility. Why was that? Because her arch-enemy, Sara, had started a group counselling young women to give up unwanted children for adoption. The group met in Sara's office once a month. So even if she wanted to allow a child to be put up for adoption, the idea that she would ever do Sara's bidding was anathema to her.

"I'll pay for everything," Wally said, and he smiled. "Everything. You could even make a day of it—take DD—is that her name? Yes, and it'll be my treat!"

She looked at him, her face a study in brilliant curiosity. She touched his limp arm. He was sweaty and uneasy.

"Well—I know, silly. But what about you and me?" She kept rubbing his sleeve with her hand.

"You and me—"

"Well, yes."

"Well," Wally said, staring straight ahead, "what I like about you is that we didn't have to get too involved. You're so independent—you've suffered enough in a bad relationship. And I have a fiancée in Bicklesfield," he said. He moved suddenly, started the car.

"Who?" she asked. And she smiled, as if he must be joking.

"Well, her name is Missy—but I don't want her involved in this," he said, still looking out the window. And a very corporate sternness came over his face and features, accentuated by his heavy coat and scarf.

The next day he passed Annette's chair at work, saw a used Kleenex on the desk, and the picture of Liam, and the little toy monkey that you wound up to play the cymbals, which Liam had bought her for her birthday from the pawnshop downtown.

———

Annette and Diane went out of town that day. They called it a "working holiday," and they were going to have lunch in the Miramichi Room at the large hotel. That would be nice and comfortable.

It came to pass that they were the only ones in the room. Their seats were austere and the waitress was stern. And the lunch menu was beef bisque, veal or Fundy clam chowder.

Then they went to the clinic, and sat in the doctor's office on a back street, holding hands. But Annette was not comfortable holding hands. So she stood and went to the small window overlooking the dowdy street. She knew Diane was there because of the excitement associated with what they were doing, that Wally had phoned her and asked her to be a companion. But Annette had telephoned him twice before they left, hoping against hope that he would tell her not to, that it would be all right—that they must reconsider. But he said nothing like that. In fact, he didn't even want to speak. So it would be done.

"Sara would never be brave enough to do this," Diane whispered to her.

For years Diane had dressed and acted like Annette did, until she had become a mimic. And now, in this situation, Annette was a mimic too. She had become, like so many others, a social mimic. But Annette did not know what mimics were really, or why society dismissed those who were not mimics. Annette did not know this, but she did know the mimicry she had displayed in the last few years had turned her relationships to ash, had made her husband homeless and destitute.

She also knew that Diane was a gossip, and she had begged her on her honour not to speak about this to Ripp or Tab or Dickie. Not only for her relatives' sakes but for the sake of her little son.

"For Liam's sake," she pleaded. "Please, if not for me, for his sake!"

Diane said, "Omigod on my life! Not a word—I mean, if people find out!"

"What would Ian say?" she added with a small beguiling smile. This was the same smile Annette had seen whenever Diane was ready to betray. And Annette had to look away.

Annette wanted most of all to know if it would have been a boy or girl, but they looked upon it differently. Annette had no sophistication in this regard. That is, she still thought of it as a child.

"Boy," she whispered finally to herself, taking in the peculiar smell of blood and antiseptic. "I know it would have been Liam's brother."

But what was most peculiar is she did not know what to do afterwards. She lay on the table in the separate room in a white johnny shirt. She even asked DD if she had all the information.

"What information, dear?" DD said.

"I don't know," she said, stupefied and alone, "information about it—just—" But she stopped. Then added, "So what is done is . . . done!" Still she refused to leave. DD asked her twice more what it was she wanted. Twice more she seemed to be confused.

Then, after a while, the doctor came out and walked toward her, holding Annette's coat.

———

"Why is it," Annette said on the way home that late afternoon, when it became cloudy and snow scattered along the scarred road, and they had to pull over for a pulp truck that had lost its load, as two young men tried to get it upright and stabilized, "always the women who suffer." She lit a cigarette. She looked into the dark.

DD said, "Omigod, I know, sweetheart, I know—it is because we are progressive, and continually save the world."

"Oh," Annette said. "How?"

DD shrugged and smiled, DD did. Because that philosophical question had no answer.

———

The truck, the one Harold Dew had inherited from Lonnie Sullivan's estate and had given to Rueben Sores, now sank in the snowy mire and the bog. The wood had to be unloaded in the freezing cold. Rueben threw the eight-foot pulp to the side and it sank in the ditch scum and ice. The other boy, Rueben's young brother, was under the tilted machine, hoping to right it before the great squall came from the north. Their family had worked this way for generations. Yet they had only managed twenty loads in the last month, for the old truck was always breaking down. Both boys, tough and anger prone, were fed up with their quota. They saw how the wood was being harvested and how tonnes and tonnes and tonnes of it were being taken to the yard. Rueben watched the cutting at Bonny Joyce, saw the ugliness of it all, and realized that there was far more wood being cut than they were processing.

"They must be going to take it somewhere else," he'd told his friends the previous month.

His brother and he were fed up and disliked the mill now, and all it stood for. For they had helped build the road that not only took our wood but hacked an opening from Good Friday Mountain into Quebec. So Rueben knew where the wood was to go. That is, he and the other workers were not so stupid. They knew the Quebec mill that Helinkiscor owned was now closer to the great trucks' farther hauls than the mill here. So what would happen to the mill here? And what would happen to them, who would not be allowed to haul wood into Quebec? By now they had taken all of the wood in Bonny Joyce, and left a thrashed heap, snow blown, desolate and barren.

DD drove around them in the darkness. Rueben looked at them both, his stare filled with a passionate indifference. It was now six years since he had burned Mr. Ian out, over Ian's concern for the mill.

"Cunt," he said to his brother, because he had just cut his hand wide open once again.

Darkness, night coming, end of the world.

———

Annette went home. She sat in the kitchen with her high boots leaving slush on the tile, and stared out the back window at the night.

That night she saw a book by that writer from town, the one who was so despised. Annette remembered how they'd all cornered him one night at a bar—Ripp and Dickie and her and a few others—to tell him his books were terrible, and that all of them could write something better if they wanted.

He had simply drunk his dark rum and ignored them. And now he was dead, and some said he was famous.

Liam had brought home one of his novels and had read it. Some weeks ago Liam had asked Annette if she'd ever met this writer. And Annette had postulated a good deal about why this writer had been rejected by his people. That he was morose and drunk and violent.

"Perhaps he was all of that—I am sure he was. I do not know. I only know he actually wrote—wonderful things," Liam said.

She picked the book up and then set it down quickly, as if it would burn her, and walked to the fridge. Yes, she rarely spoke about her own book now. But oh, what she could tell if she ever really wanted to.

———

She still had her own problems, Annette Brideau. And soon after she came home she began to realize it. From that moment forward, Wally did not speak to her or look her way. Now when she smiled his way, she looked like a frightened girl.

He would spend time staring out the window, tapping his pencil and listening to phone messages. Sometimes when she went in to see him, knocking on the side of his little office cubicle, her lunch in a paper bag, he wouldn't even turn around. He would stare, his hands cupped behind his back, at the parking lot.

She asked him what the matter was.

"Oh, I'm just busy."

Then she heard that Diane had mentioned something at Cut and Curl about their trip. Once again, she begged Diane not to tell.

"Of course not—you have my word!"

And so it spread all over town, what Annette had done, to the mill where Annette still worked. And when it spread there, Wally was furious and cut her cold. They had better not blame him. He was willing, as he often said, to go to the ends of the earth for women, but not for that! He left by the back door, ran past the back window, and soon began to tattle about her too.

So Annette was now alone. Suddenly, irrevocably alone.

Cosmo was the magazine she relied on. She kept two copies at her desk. But to say this is foolish is to say that *Cosmo* did not entertain women, and men as well, with an idea of moral superiority. These magazines she and DD read, published in faraway New York or Los Angeles, did not know of the little house with pitch-black eaves where she had grown up. And now that she felt abused, she had no one to turn to. Nor could she say she felt abused by this treatment—because supposedly this treatment wasn't abusive. Yet Sara—alone and berated, and in fact betrayed—had said that it was.

One night Annette called out to Wally at the end of the chip yard.

"Wait," she said, "please, Wally, wait. You have to know—I am—in pain. It's like it was when I was a girl—remember I spoke to you about it?"

He did not see her at all.

Now, after work, she was on her way—with the streets sanded and the night air growing softer and glazed with ice—toward a bar called the Warehouse.

Later, sitting in a booth at the gaudy Warehouse, with its fake salute to marine life most of the people never experienced, she found herself nervous and in pain. The crew were gone, many already laid off. She did not know that soon the office would be split up and many more would go. That her "crew," who told jokes and snapped gum, had recently switched places to drink. They were going down to the Zanzibar—a place they said they wouldn't go last year because it was where Annette's store once was.

But Annette was suddenly no longer part of their equation; now they felt free to go to the Zanzibar, which Jeremy Hogg's oldest daughter ran.

So Annette sat all alone and stared about her, looking up in expectation, ready to smile.

But tonight she began to feel something wrong.

The pain started in her groin, and was at times a ferocious pain inside her. But she dismissed the idea that she should go to the hospital to see if anything was amiss. For she was confronted now not by a congratulatory nod of the head, like the one from DD when Annette left the clinic, but by a more rueful salutation, one that came from an unshakable sense of loss. Something that she was not supposed to feel, and had been told as much.

Now too she was suddenly worried she had AIDS. She had heard of a woman who contracted that just by being out once. And then she knew something else. A woman who worked at the mill—Mr. Ticks's secretary, Ines, furious that her husband was divorcing her and leaving town, had told Annette she'd hired a woman with herpes to sleep with him. And she had met the woman, a person named Kitty, who had arrived at the bar like an assassin, whose eyes burned into Annette when she looked her way, and reminded Annette of the stories she had heard when a little girl of hell. But hell was something they all laughed at, because hell was not believed in anymore by anyone. Even though they walked through it during their waking hours.

Annette had entered a different world, a world of the fallen, of angels beating their wings against a smoky bowl, and she no longer wanted this world, this world of the fallen. She wanted to hold someone in her arms, a child perhaps. Even the money Jeremy Hogg had placed for her had been lost in the savings and loans failure out west—and she had lost all she had hoped to gain. But worse, there seemed to be no recourse to get any of this money back.

Annette was not brave. She was not noble. She was simply alone and sick and hurting, and did not know what to do. She had done what people advised her to do, and now she was alone—like 95 per cent of humanity at any given time. But now that she'd had the procedure, surely she and Wally would be happy? That was it: he did not want the child, and she had been promised happiness if she did what she wanted, for herself. Wally should know that their happiness was now guaranteed. This is what her notes had said to him—the ones she'd tried to leave on his desk.

The night was cold when she left the bar. Long ago she had been sworn to the calendar of what she was told were the superstitious events of the Catholic Church. She followed them darkly. But now that was only a dim memory. When she got home, she went in through the side door, crossed to the stairway and climbed up in the dark.

She called, "Liam!"

But the house was still, and empty as a cloister, and she was alone.

She was alone because others, many others, those people who'd watched with relish as she destroyed her marriage and hurt her child in ways that cannot be mentioned, had now drifted away, and said the same cruel things about her that she had said about others all her life. And she, she, Annette Brideau, was finally aware of this. But now the show was over. Her freedom such as it was, was complete. And the articles in *Cosmo* moved on to other things.

———

That night, Wally went to see Diane. They went to the Zanzibar. The music played languid and indolent at the booth where they sat. He kept twisting the swizzle stick from his drink and tapping it on the table. He asked her what had happened to Annette. Why had she changed so drastically? Why wasn't she fun anymore? He asked if he could confide in Diane.

"What are friends for?" Diane said.

"Do you know what happened?" he asked.

"Yes." For Diane always knew what had happened.

"I don't even think it was mine," he said. "It was probably someone else's. She was mixed up! I mean, I tried my best to help her. For her husband was vicious—sadistic, really. You know that. It was Ian's fault, so I tried to help her out. I don't know what she is telling people, do you? About me, I mean—what she might be saying about me?"

"Oh God, no—I don't know what she says, ever!"

"What should I do?" Wally said in a kind of panic. He knew his mom, whom he loved, might visit soon. "I think I got mixed up with a liar," he added, almost hopefully.

"Yup," Diane said, greedily confirming his assertion.

He begged Diane not to tell.

"Omigod, I won't ever," she said.

He asked her what she would like to do. She wanted to save the forest by starting an eco-project of her own, and use environmentally friendly hairspray.

"That's commendable stuff," he said.

———

Ian sat in jail. All through Easter of 1998, he sat in jail. The cool air was white and soft as the world drifted toward spring.

Ian had kept all the monies, and figures of monies, in his head now for fourteen or fifteen years. He tabulated and calculated in his head the amount of money spent and given away and lost. Yes, even worrying over every penny had not saved him in the end.

His store had been sold off—at one-fifth the price of what it should have been—last March to pay both his and Annette's legal fees. That is, it was sold at forty-one thousand dollars.

The amount of money paid to Mr. Hogg by Annette was in the thousands. The money Ian had paid to his own lawyer was in the thousands. There had been liens on properties he had bought in good faith—the ones he'd had to declare insolvent after two years and sell at an enormous loss. (These were the properties the old man who had given Evan a drive in his truck had spoken about.)

Now there was nothing.

Nothing at all.

And yet, he had captured Annette—the young girl he had loved and longed for. He could never have imagined hurting her. And look at what had happened!

He knew how much he'd loved Annette in high school, how he had planned to love her, how he'd longed for her when he met her again and how he desired her even now. But had she tricked him? He did not know. He only knew that he had done what was honourable; he'd had to do it. When he'd heard the child wasn't his, he'd said nothing. But he had bought Lonnie Sullivan's silence for the sake of the child. He had gone down in the night to protect his family. And Harold had left at the same time to find the pregnancy test and declare a family. And Evan had left the churchyard illuminated by the lit candle to honour his family.

Ian also knew that some people felt divorce was nothing much, that men were often at fault in divorce. He could not deny either premise.

But what bothered him was something more than this. He had been culpable from the first moment he pretended that the only reason he was walking with Annette was that they were both concerned about Sara Robb. And if he thought of it—if men and women were culpable in these increments every day, and they understood that they were, why did they not take measures to improve? And if these small manipulations caused wrong, how could they be thwarted?

Or if doing these things—as he and Annette had done—was not wrong, then why did such terrible things swell from them? And this is actually what the trunk was telling him. That is, the trunk was telling him, as much as Evan's antifreeze and Corky's wrench—that as a matter of fact, there was a God.

The trunk from 1840, which had been loaded on a ship out of Liverpool and brought across the high sea by an eighteen-year-old woman named Ruth MacDonnell in a blue-and-white dress, was his boondoggle, and each rise and fall of the waves upon which that ship had sailed 150 years before bore witness. Poor Ruth had not figured long in the New World. She'd died in childbirth at twenty-two and was buried in the small church in Bartibog, the gravestone crumbling and covered in embedded moss. Yet the trunk remained pristine.

Why did he go to buy that trunk from his uncle? It was on a sudden whim, just a thought—when he felt kindhearted and filled with the lightness of being. If he had not thought of that trunk—if he had simply gone to Evan without seeking the trunk—he would surely have helped Evan get the money. Perhaps he would have worked for Evan—then things would have been like they should have been. Yet, getting the money—was that the transgression? Not if the money had not changed him. But the money did—and the final proof of that change, that transgression came in the form of Annette. Yet he did not blame her. He blamed himself. They had started out, after the honeymoon, to destroy each other—they had to, in order to be free of guilt. If Annette did not see this, he now did. But for the first time, perhaps, he was seeing that they did not want to destroy each other; each in their own way was determined to destroy and ruin only themselves. And now he knew—both had.

The amount he now tabulated, quick as a wizard, that he and she had lost over the last fourteen years, their dreams for Liam washed away like gutter rain: $2,231,651.43.

Ian was given two years in jail for break and enter. It seemed to the spectators who came to gawk and say "I told you so" that Ian didn't care what happened to him.

As he prepared to go down to the medium security facility, a few people did drop by to see him, out of kindness. He was ashamed that Sara was one of them. The first thing he asked was for her to forgive him.

"Ahhh, but that was so long ago," she said.

"No—it was just yesterday afternoon," he replied.

He told her that one day years ago, he had snuck one of the books she was reading, a book of short stories, and had read a story by someone who had an old river man saying that the best a person could hope for was to want nothing. How foolish he once thought that was, in his youthful anger, ambition and pride. Who could ever want so little? Now he would, if he could live his life over, live it for one dream only: to want and need nothing.

"It is a story by Anton Chekhov," Sara said. How terrible Ian looked, his mouth split open, his eyes haggard, his skin grey, his voice a whisper.

"Well, whoever it was—he knew me." Ian smiled.

She reached out and touched his cheek.

And looking down at her leg and seeing the brace she sometimes wore, he asked for forgiveness once more.

———

Annette Brideau entered her Golgotha. Not because she was destitute and not because she had done something she felt in her heart she should not have done. It was because of something else entirely. She felt she must do something to help her son. All of a sudden, she realized this. She was ashamed of how she had treated him, because she had not been able to show the love he deserved.

That is, like many mothers and fathers, there were years of lost time and wasted moments that plagued her. Was this because she was infinitely bad? No—she was at moments in her life infinitely good. She simply needed to concentrate on winning Liam back.

She asked DD what Liam might like.

"I don't know—maybe a bicycle?" DD said. Annette could tell DD was bored with her now—and had once told her she had better stop drinking. But Annette did not seem to be able to.

I will buy him a new bike, she thought. Yes—he would like that!

She pawned her diamond—the one she and DD had picked out. Harold told her he didn't want to take it. But she begged him to.

Then she picked out the bike she thought Liam would like, and people soon realized she herself had never ridden one. She was seen walking it along the street toward the house, as proud as any child, with a red bow on it. She was even singing.

"But you can't afford it, Mom," Liam said.

"Ha—what do you mean, can't afford? And I don't want you down working for Harold Dew anymore. That won't happen with my son." And she kissed him. After she kissed him, she said, "See!"—as if she was trying to make up for something now gone away. Years that had drifted out into the street and had disappeared.

"You and I will live together. We will buy a smaller place—and you know what? Well, anyway—wait and see. Now . . . " She tried to think. "It is your father's birthday—I want you to write him a letter."

"You really want me to?"

"It is not hard—once you forgive him" she said. That is, she was trying to forgive Ian because she had to forgive herself. She tried not to think of the money they might have had, or the store she had tried to destroy.

"I promise I will never see Wally Bickle again," she said. "And you are not to roam around the town anymore," she told him. "I will be the mother I was supposed to be!"

She sat upstairs, refusing to allow Liam to go out at night. "You have to stay away from Harold," she pleaded. "And I will change—I promise."

But Liam still tried to get back to Harold to work his shift. One evening, knowing she was in the hallway, he opened the bedroom window and got out on the drain far above the ground. From there he tried to jump to the maple tree nine feet away. And he fell, knocking himself out cold, his wrist broken. Annette was terrified he had died.

But he simply sat up in the driveway with a smile. "Ouch," he said.

He got a cast, and Harold wrote on it: "Big Harold Dew—like a father to you."

Liam came home that day hoping his mother would sign it too, but like the child she always was, her old self had come back. She had gone to Halifax for a facelift.

I love you, she wrote. *Please don't be angry, Liam. I want to look pretty again, so just you wait and see!*

PART NINE

THE CASE OF LONNIE SULLIVAN HAD FIRST BEEN TERMED an accident, then "undetermined," and finally it had been declared a homicide.

In the weeks after Easter in 1998, Markus Paul and John Delano compiled lists of names of those who may have had something to do with the case, and sent them to me, a social psychologist and profiler who had worked on these things before, both in Boston and here on the river. I had never thought that these kids, who were in a photo I had of them from grade two, would now become my focus.

The police officers as well were known to me.

John Delano was a boy I had taught in summer school, years and years gone by, when I was still working on my degree. The thing I most remembered about him was his forceful personality—and yet this forcefulness is what it would take to see the case through. Markus Paul was a young tough First Nations constable, and in his own way as clever as John. They sent me names and asked for my opinion.

So after three weeks, I came up with three names out of the twenty or so on the list. And of those three—and I believed the guilty person was one of them—one name stuck out. I said nothing was written in stone, but I was almost certain it must be one of these men. I met John Delano and Markus Paul in Markus Paul's office on a day of wind and rain, and placed these names down:

Harold Dew.

Ian Preston.

Evan Young.

We talked it over for more than an hour.

Harold Dew?

Yes, it may have been, but we did not think so—for of them all, Harold had the best relationship with Lonnie and was a relative in the traditional sense; he was the one that was treated the most fairly, we felt. That is, we missed what was most obvious—that crimes are not always overt or recognized.

Ian Preston?

We thought it might be Ian because of something Lonnie had on his wife—some secret. Some said it was a pregnancy test. But nothing like that was found and no one could be sure what Lonnie had on her.

Then there was Evan Young, the man who had left the church to visit Sullivan that night in order to get some kind of dispensation for what he owed.

"That would be about the right time," Markus said.

So we concentrated on Evan Young. For Evan had changed from being a champion of skeptics, went to church, fasted, took the Eucharist. Neither Harold nor Ian had changed in this radical way. That is, neither had made such a substantive change in their very persons. Only Evan had done so.

John Delano and Markus Paul began to collaborate fully in June of 1998. They already had solved many cases, but this one, which they worked on only in their spare time, puzzled them.

"He may have gone in to ask for some kind of leniency—and Sullivan wouldn't give it to him," John said finally.

"That would be enough to enrage anyone," Markus noted. "So he finally snapped, after losing his wife and boy. After having his compensation taken from him, after being almost killed himself, only to be back where he started when he was a child."

"But he could have told Sullivan that he would earn what he needed to pay him back—or more for that matter, and in half the time," I ventured.

"Sullivan would have still refused—for he had Evan at his beck and call. And he loved that idea," John said.

The photos were obscure and we could not be certain if there had been one or two sets of footprints because of the snowfall that had started later that night and turned into a blizzard. But worse was how little evidence had been collected at the scene, for it was presumed to be an accident.

"If Evan had got the money from Joyce Fitzroy—would his life have been different?" Delano asked.

"I am sure of it," Markus said, "but in what way, I do not know."

"If he had got the money—Molly and he—well, what would have happened?"

"Who did get the money?" Markus asked.

"Ian Preston," I said.

———

Wally Bickle had suddenly been given a good deal of authority at about this same time. It was a promotion that he did not expect and was not prepared for. He was by June no longer a junior manager but on-site manager of the mill itself. And his was therefore the main management signature on the closing of the Kraft mill and the firing of Mr. Ticks, his onetime boss.

He had been called to the main office on a bright cold day in late May. He walked in certain he was being fired. Then suddenly someone handed him a telephone, and from the main office in Finland, he was told that he would oversee the function of the entire mill for the best part of the next six months.

There were two main reasons for this.

By June of 1998 the company had almost filled their contractual obligation. All the wood was cut, much of it yarded and ready to be transported to the great lots near the mill ground. But suddenly there was talk that the mill would close.

Helinkiscor's obligation, firmly stated in the last bailout, had been fulfilled. That is, they had paid the power rates, and paid the men, and brought in the wood from the woodlots in three counties. But staying to process the wood at this mill would cost them too much money. And there was no stipulation that they must process the wood here. Their contract said the wood belonged to the company, but nothing in the contract ever said they had to process the wood at the New Brunswick mill.

No, they did not want to betray the fine people of New Brunswick. The company too was part of the family. They did not want to seem ruthless. But if being ruthless was in their best interest, then they would be.

Since there was no actual stipulation that they must process the tons of wood cut, either in the woodlots or onsite, they were in a fundamentally untouchable position. Now, anyone in an untouchable position has a moral dilemma. A company in an untouchable position can easily sidestep ethics. This was the catch that the government itself had allowed by its own negotiator's incompetence.

"Oh," that negotiator kept saying as he lapsed into subservience, "yes, that can be done—of course. Well, let me say this, we treat our companies well here—always have!"

Helinkiscor knew by 1997 that they could cut their costs dramatically if they processed this wood at their other Canadian mill in Quebec, on the far side of Bay Chaleur. It was just a hundred miles away, and they had a ready-made road—plowed out of the wilderness by New Brunswick men cutting the New Brunswick wood for them over the last five years.

But in order to facilitate their next move, the company needed a Canadian in place to take over Ticks's job. And Ticks, a man from Maine who wore his hair like men did in the fifties, and his tweed suit jacket and heavy boots, was simply lied to and replaced. Then the company started full-scale layoffs of men both in the yards and in the mill.

"Coming into fall we will feel the pinch," they told Wally, not only as if it was natural but as if it was the workers' fault. They told him he was their last hope. He was the one they had chosen to get them out of a financial mess. If he couldn't, in October he was to oversee the closure of the mill, and destroy all the machines the province had bought. That is, get the very men they had hired to work the mill to rip out and destroy it, so no other company from Europe or North America could ever take over and be in competition with them, Helinkiscor.

They told him they didn't want to do this.

"Yes, sir. I know—I see—it's a large responsibility. I will try my very best!" Wally looked at them with stupefaction and a childlike hope for approval, and nodded around the room.

The government could easily have stopped this by moving in, confiscating the wood and demanding repayment of the bailouts. By the time Wally got his promotion they knew what was going to happen. But, you see, "principle" was involved. They had given their word, and in the way of unworldly people they believed others would take note of this, even as their land was being plundered and raped, their people ridiculed and falsely accused of poor workmanship (for this is what Helinkiscor was telling stakeholders, that the New Brunswick worker was incompetent), and laid off.

————

Sometime after her facelift, hearing of Wally's promotion, which appeared in the second section of the provincial paper, Annette dropped by his place with a bottle of champagne.

No matter how much she had told herself she would not speak to him again, she could not help herself. This became her last desperate gambit. Just as Sara had once walked to the store in the rain to see Ian, now Annette came in the rain to see Wally.

But she did not look at all like Sara.

"We finally got rid of him," she said as she knocked quickly and opened the door. She was speaking of Mr. Ticks.

Wally stood up in a flash, looked at her, mortified that she had come to his house.

In fact, Wally's mom was there. And Mrs. Bickle was shocked to see this woman, much older than her boy and divorced. His mom could feel the tension and knew in a second what was what between Wally and the woman.

Wally's mother, Verna, was a stern, big-bosomed Baptist woman from Bicklesfield. Everyone knew Verna and her raspberry pies. Everyone knew how she could make jokes about men, and laugh so loud she shook the cutlery at the church suppers. Everyone up and down Bicklesfield knew her boy had a big promotion, a white hat at the mill. Everyone believed in Bicklesfield what people wanted to believe here: that he had been promoted because he alone could save the mill.

After Annette arrived smelling of alcohol with a bottle of champagne in her hand, Verna, dead against alcohol (but not raspberry pies), sat in the chair in the parlour and would not come in to meet her; she sat with her big hands flat on her big knees and said, "I am fine, Wally. You and your friend have your little talk, and I will wait here."

Now and again Verna peered into the room. She could see the makeup and the new facelift. Worse, of course—Annette was Catholic and French.

Finally, Annette walked into the parlour, and standing over the big-bosomed woman reached out her hand.

"You must be so proud of your son," she said, lisping slightly, the top of her mauve sweater unbuttoned to show the edges of a black brassiere.

"Everyone is proud of my Wally," Verna said, taking the hand so lightly so as almost not to touch it before she let it go. "All the girls he graduated with just a few years ago love my Wally!"

Then Verna gave one of her looks that would freeze you in your tracks, a look at the unbuttoned see-through sweater only a mother could give, a look that had death and utter Baptist hatred of Catholic mass deeply embedded in it. And Annette turned her face away quickly and buttoned her top button. When she looked back, Verna was smiling kindly, with her eyes fixed on some distant point.

Verna said nothing more for the longest time. Until Annette left the house. The champagne was left unopened on the table in the far corner of the room; perfume still lingered in the lonely affixed places.

"You're not mixed up with her!" she asked, still sitting by herself. "Missy would be devastated—little Missy would!"

Missy, Wally's girl from Bicklesfield, had gone to community college. Missy liked things just so, was a church girl, and had bought a thigh reducer advertised on television but had not used it yet.

"No!" Wally said, almost hysterically, and walking first in one direction and then turning and walking in the other. "No—no, no, she's had a painful marriage. It is terrible—her husband beat her black and blue and is now in jail for breaking into her lawyer's office," he said. "I tried my best with her is all—but what can you do, what can you do!"

"Well—she's trash pure and simple," Verna sniffed, "showing off her tits—trash to be beat black and blue, trash not to be, as far as I'm concerned. A woman like that needs a good whack in the ass!"

"Oh, don't you worry, I know what she is," Wally said suddenly. "I know all about her!" he said in the voice of a child. He stopped pacing and looked shamefully up from under his eyes.

———

That very same night, Liam left his house at ten thirty and walked the streets looking for his friend. When he found Harold smoking outside the tavern, he said, "I need some pills—you must know where to get some."

"For who?"

"For my mom."

"Pills for your mom—what does she need pills for?"

"She has a sore stomach or something and she won't go to the hospital—she refuses to go, so she needs pills. She is crying and everything."

"Do you want me to go with you?"

"No, Harold, she won't see no one—just pills for my mom!"

Liam waited twenty minutes and Harold came back with the pills in a small box. "Here, Boss," he said. "You take good care not to lose these."

Then Liam turned and ran back down the lane toward his large house in the dark with pills for his mom.

She was sitting on the bed in her nightgown. There was some blood on a Kleenex. She smiled at him.

She had been drinking to ease the pain in her stomach. He came upstairs and into the room slowly, and smiled tenderly. But he could smell her body as soon as he came into her great carpeted room, with its large floral bedspread on the bed.

"Mom," he said, "you have to take a bath—you peed yourself again."

He ran her bath and made her a drink, and came back and gave it to her.

She looked at him as if he was a stranger. He told her she looked pretty and kissed her forehead. He didn't know what else to say. After all this time, being pretty was the thing she wanted to be.

He gave her one pill and then one more. Then he helped her take a bath. She told him that they would be happy—she would see to it. She asked him if he wrote Ian the letter.

Later, sometime later, she simply fell into a sound sleep.

When she woke at six in the morning, she was dizzy. Her child was standing over her, with his face pale, his lips protruding just a little because of his braces.

"What did you give me?" she asked.

"A pill."

"What kind of a pill?"

"I am not so sure—but I wanted to help you. I think it is something like Dad takes for his back sometimes."

"Did anyone phone?"

"No."

"No . . . Wally?"

"No."

She lit a cigarette.

"Do you think my face looks some good?"

He smiled at her in a certain way, a way that was knowing. It was awful now, her face. It was pinched forward as if suddenly she was in a casket.

She shrugged.

"Of course, Mommy," he said, "you are beautiful. Daddy knew that too," he added.

She asked him if she should wear the blue skirt with the jumper top. She asked him to find her shoes.

Liam ran about to find these things for her. To find the pieces of jewellery she hadn't lost.

That is why his mom had the facelift. Her resurrection, as she called it. So many jokes now were at the expense of a religion she had once believed in as a girl. But she had needed her facelift. To look beautiful once again.

"Here, Mommy," he said, trying to clip her necklace on, tears in his eyes.

———

The night Annette visited Wally's, he and his mom went to the Kingsway and had the big fish-and-chip special. Verna looked at the menu for a long time, contemplating every dish, it seemed. He waited anxiously, wondering what she would say. She sniffed and said her nose was itchy. She said she liked Bicklesfield.

Wally felt the screws of convention plague him. He thought of the bottle of champagne. Yes, there was no foolishness with his mommy. No champagne for his mom. He came back from the Kingsway in the dark, and sat in his house smoking his little cigarillos. Two girls had to be let go in the main office.

He took his pen out of his pocket pen holder. He sat forward as he had done as a boy when reading over a test, as if in an impertinent way he was judging what was about to judge him. His stomach protruded over his pants buckle as he went through the names.

He picked Ines Drillion to go. He looked over the list again. He lit a cigarillo.

He picked Annette Brideau.

———

That very morning Annette decided not to go to work, but took a drive along the coast all the way to Bicklesfield.

She waited by the community college. Then, at three in the afternoon, she saw her, the girl she had hunted down just to find out who she was. Missy Melonson, in her purple leotards and her woollen skirt, walked by the car.

Missy had '99 on her jacket. So, Annette thought, she would graduate next year—and then she and Wally would be married.

Annette watched the somewhat homely pouting child plod along, all the way to the river.

She suddenly shivered, and rubbed her nose like a little girl.

Then, shrugging at the immense folly of her own life, its bewildered journey toward the dark, took a last brazen drag on her cigarette, looked at the red polish on her manicured nails, and started the car.

———

Ian was called on by Markus Paul, and for a few hours spoke to him. But Ian, being a gentleman, never once tried to sway the opinion of the officer.

"Did I kill Mr. Sullivan?" he said. "No, I did not. I did not know he was dead until after he was buried—it was the strangest thing. I was speaking to him, yes, about a private matter—and then four days later someone tells me they had just been at his funeral. So I must have been on a hunt for information about what Helinkiscor was doing—or I might have just not opened the door to my store for those days."

"What were you and Sullivan speaking about?"

"A private matter—nothing important."

"There was a rumour you took money to him, but no money was found—did you take money?"

Ian did not answer. He did not answer because he felt Evan had killed Lonnie in a fit of rage and had taken the money—and he wanted to say nothing about it. The money had destroyed them all, become hubris unleashed. It had destroyed his wife, who in some way he still loved.

And he had harmed her enough. He remembered her terrified childlike eyes when he'd raised his fist to strike her. That was not what a man should ever do.

Markus closed his notebook and asked Ian if he thought the mill would remain solvent. All the pain he had gone through, was it worth it?

"I thought Helinkiscor would be gone by now" was all Ian said.

Markus Paul left. The day was bright, and Ian thought of Evan—and thought about how he had caused it all, all of it. He finished his cigarette and lay in his bunk.

Ian had predicted the mill would close in 1996. He was dead wrong. It closed in 1998. But that was because our little provincial government reinvested another twelve and a half million in the mill. This was called "Wally's reprieve"—though Wally had nothing to do with it, and the money was already spent by the time he was made boss. But suddenly, because he was made boss, this was his reprieve, one he had organized— he had, rumour had it, walked into the office, cleared those people out who did not want to co-operate, and took things over.

So Wally was called a "take charge kind of guy!" People wanted him in politics; they wanted him to settle things.

At this time Helinkiscor was loading their yard with timber. It was piled so high some people thought the mill would last another fifteen years.

———

J. P. Hogg himself was unmoved by the town's plight. He knew the mill would go in a matter of months. He had no intention of staying either; he had no interest in staying someplace so removed from what he felt he was. He was in the process of selling the Zanzibar, his percentage of the prefab-home business and three other ventures. In fact, he was moving to a law firm in Fredericton. He'd been offered a partnership and couldn't say no. The firm had bought him a house and he was trucking his sailboat down. There was a going-away ceremony for him at the town hall, a dinner and dance at our curling club, and the unveiling of the street sign in his name.

Annette herself attended this. She thought Wally would have to be present and perhaps, just perhaps, she could corner him.

Hogg Street would intersect the main highway just before the mall. Everyone clapped. But Wally was not there.

Certain things Hogg decided to sell. Sara Robb had half a day free and took a walk over. She spoke to him as if he was an old friend, because she spoke to everyone like that. Besides, Hogg was only a year or so older than them all.

Hogg told her he didn't want the teakwood chest anymore, because of what had happened. "Ian," he said. "Yes, a hard case you know. It breaks my heart."

So she bought the chest for a thousand dollars and decided someday she would give it to Liam. She did not understand why it was so significant in Ian's life.

The good news, she told JP, was that she was engaged again, this time to Evan Young. JP put his great arms about her, hugging her and brushing his lips to her hair.

"You can't imagine how happy that makes me," JP said. And he told her he agreed with all she said about, you know, the rights of the unborn and stuff like that—"But please don't tell anyone I said that." And he added, "Tell me, do you think I look better with or without the beard?"

———

Evan had left the priest that night years ago and walked up the lane, across to the old back lots of the pulp yard, and then along the road for four miles. He cut through the woods. He stopped walking at Grey's Turn, for he heard someone—or something—moving toward him.

He breathed silently in the cold air and waited. He listened for a while and whoever or whatever it was trailed off toward the Ski-Doo trails near Arron Brook. He thought it might have been a young moose walking the cold off, though it sounded more like a man. He continued on his journey, hoping to meet Sullivan at the shed. He planned to tell Sullivan he would pay him twofold to let him out of his commitment. He blamed much on Sullivan. Even the death of Molly and his son. This was the state of mind he was in.

But when he got to the shed, the door was open and Sullivan was lying face down in his blood. There was a strange silence about the place, with snow beginning to wisp about the open doorway. There was an extraordinary feeling of being watched, and for a split second Evan did not know whether or not he was witnessing a glimpse into what he himself had done. The sudden sight made him think that he had in fact committed the very crime he had often thought about, and was standing at the door afterwards. Perhaps now he was just coming to from committing it. He began to get dizzy, and he fell sideways and bruised his eye. He stumbled away in the night.

He made his way back home, feeling his body shake violently. He was to have flashbacks for years.

The next weekend, Evan reported for work at the church. He was sure the priest suspected him. He began to go to mass. The reason he went to mass again was fairly complicated. But he saw a death that night—Lonnie Sullivan's—and realized that something somehow had protected him from being found the same way. After a time when he began to go to AA, he met a man who was to become his best friend, Leonard Savoy.

Now, after some years, he was in fact wealthy. He had built a new house. His income was established and he gave five to eight thousand a year to charity and helped people who needed to go to Moncton or Halifax for cancer treatment. Doan and he had branched out, and operated in three cities. He was going to marry Sara. They had come together at a small group of singles who went to the same church. He felt silly going there to find a date. His life had brought him back to faith; the church had not. Those who did not see the difference could never know Evan. But finally he was cajoled into going, and there was Sara Robb, the woman Ian had once been engaged to. He hadn't at all followed what she had done.

He didn't even know that she was a doctor. He found that out because he helped transport three prostate-cancer patients to Moncton one afternoon, and this little woman stepped from the shadows and got into an ambulance with a patient. Then she simply disappeared again.

She had been working for months in East Africa with Doctors Without Borders. She had come back just that week—had decided to come here to the church social because Ethel had kept telling her to. That was some months ago. They sat together at picnics and went for walks along the lane down to the bay, and sometimes sat for hours far off near Arron Brook. And one day when all the others were going to wade over to the island and she said she would stay where she was, he picked her up and carried her across the inlet. Far away stood Annette's dilapidated worn little cottage—the place where Ian had lifted Annette on his shoulders to help her through the window so long ago. Now little remained—a broken window, a pane of shattered glass, and a feeling of dreary sadness and isolation.

It was that night when he waded to the island with little Sara Robb on his shoulders that Evan knew he would ask her to marry him.

So, everything would work out.

He did not know, and nor did she, that he was soon to be arrested for the murder of Lonnie Sullivan. And it was the mistaken profile I had given the police that might have led to this.

———

Ripp at first thought he would show the boy. He stood up and took his stance. But in four punches he found out.

He fell back out the door, and ran from the tavern as fast as his muscle-bound legs could carry him. He ran across the street and tried to get away. Rueben grabbed him, hit him again on the back of the head, and he fell across the hood of the car. Rueben beat him until he was barely conscious, and said, "That'll teach ya, ya big-feeling son of a whore, ta make fun of no one like Diane."

———

Liam travelled back and forth to Harold, and did odd jobs for his friend to get money. Even though Harold offered him money, he didn't take it without working. He cleaned and swept and made Harold lunches, and now and again shined his cowboy boots. Then he would get a pill or two and take it home to Annette.

Harold was his only friend, and told him jokes as Liam worked in the solitary way he always had now. Harold was mad at Quebec because of the mill. "So, Liam, what do you call a bra in Quebec?" Harold would ask.

"I don't know."

"Sepper tits," and Harold would laugh.

Then he would set one boot up on a stool for Liam to polish.

"What is the difference between a Presbyterian bra and a Baptist one?"

"How should I know?"

"A Presbyterian bra keeps them stiff and upright and a Baptist one makes mountains out of molehills."

Then he would smack his gum, and grin, and put the other boot up. There was one moment when Harold fell in love with Liam—when he thought of him as his own son. He did not know exactly when it was. Perhaps it was because Liam reminded him so, so much of his younger brother, Glen. Perhaps he began to realize that everything in the world sooner or later comes back.

The lost life in Harold's small dark room held diamonds and pins and necklaces, and half of Ian's wardrobe, and small mementoes, and children's boots and hats. Annette's diamond was there, and so too were many others.

Liam was working to get the diamond back. Every day he wondered what he could do to earn the money. Then one day Hanna Stone's son—the one she breastfed in front of Molly Young—came in with a shotgun. It was the shotgun with the beautiful silver barrel and hand-carved stock that Harold had lost years before playing horseshoes. He would do anything to get it back. And he traded the shotgun for the diamond, which Stone planned to give to his girl-friend, Ines Drillion's daughter Penny.

———

Liam stood by the town clock. People walked by in the dark. and they didn't know what he was going through. Not at all. He looked into the faint store windows, and threw his Pokémon cards into the fountain. He watched them disappear like his youth. He remembered his mom taking him to Steadman's store in the early afternoon long ago. They went and had pie and ice cream at the counter. Afterwards they sat in the park, and for a while she even held his hand a little. Would she remember?

He left the park now and walked blindly toward the pond, where he and the boys once had a picnic. He remembered Pint McGraw and Fraser. He smiled, remembering how they were all going to go to the moon.

But there was no picnic anymore. Maybe there was no more moon. He had come here to throw himself into the pond and go to the bottom and take all the pain away. He sat for a long while, thinking. But he could not do it. For if he did, who would be there to help his mom? He took the buck knife his father had used to cut for blood and tossed it into the air. It fell into Liam's secret pond, and he watched it disappear.

He went home with the morphine pills in his pocket. Now his mom waited for them, expectantly like a child.

"Do you have any pills?"

"Yes."

"Where did you get them?"

"I can't say."

"Well, when I get better, I want to know everything—but now, well, I don't feel good. It's just if I can get over this little rough spot, I will be fine. I don't know why Wally hasn't phoned. I put a phone call into him about my job—he is supposed to phone back. I went to Mr. Hogg's party—you know JP. Has a street named after him—anyway, I was there."

"I will take you to the hospital."

"No! I have to wait for Wally to phone now—I just told you that! He has a job and can hire me again . . ."

"Mom—please, you have to go to Sara. She's nice. She likes us and she will help."

"Please, dear, you have to help me get my nightgown on."

Annette couldn't go to Sara. She had perverted their friendship, and that now prevented her. Sara and she had gone in different directions, in different worlds. Also, she was afraid. Sometimes she would remember looking at the statue of the Virgin in her little room when she was deciding what to do the day Lonnie had called her. And she remembered the voice came, saying: Go to Sara, for she loves you more than anyone. If she had only done so, how different and better all their lives might have been. And again, what if she had said: No, Wally, I must not do this, for I do not really want to—Sara will know what I must do.

But no—always she had been too afraid. And yet now she realized something more deeply than ever: Sara, lame and left all alone, had never been afraid of anything.

"I wish I was more like your friend Ethel was to you," she said to Liam one night. "She was so good to you. I would give anything to go back and change things. Do you know—shhh—I tried to rob your dad's store—shhhhh." Here she sat up and looked at him with such terror he almost looked away. "It was the worst thing I did. And then I went with Wally—oh God, why did I? Liam, I got mixed up—with bad people. It started when I was so little—Ripp and all those people Lonnie introduced me to. Who can love me now?"

"I do!"

"Shhh—I do not deserve love."

"Maybe none of us do—and that is why love is so . . . blessed."

"I am still loved," she whispered, looking around again in terror.

"Forever—" He smiled.

"By who?"

"By me. And by Dad."

"But I beat you with a belt," she said. "Shhh—I hit you with a belt!" She reached up and touched his face.

"Yes—and it hurt," Liam said. Then he laughed. In his laugh was the sound of more pain than she'd ever imagined.

And then she said, reaching out to hold his hand, "I wish Ian and I were still together. Do you think we could be a family once more—do you think he would want me?"

And then she whispered, as if to some dark certainty in the corner of the room, "No—not anymore. It's too late now, I think, for that!"

Then she smiled bravely and said, "Oh well."

The morphine pill would soon put her to sleep. But in her daze, complete with a pleasant irrepressible numbness and gentle fatigue that would increase moment by moment, she would realize how little she had shown her son love, and how much she should have. Staring at the door of his bedroom, she would become frozen in a kind of melancholy she could not control. Once or twice she would cry, thinking of him as a little boy standing in the backyard all alone.

Diane had been so important to her. They had held hands and promised never would they divulge each other's secrets. Never! Diane had been more than a sister to her. So what had happened? Time and disillusion, and Diane's sudden realization that Annette wasn't part of the group, and to be a part of the group DD would have to forgo the friendship.

She often tried to find Diane, to ask her what was wrong. To ask her what she had done.

"Remember," she said, suddenly trying to sit up, "when I took you for ice cream and pie at Steadman's?"

"Yes, Mom." He smiled. "Yes, I do and—"

"Boy," Annette said, "did I ever look fuckin' good that day!"

————

Harold had everything he wanted—almost. He had made a little fortune—little to be sure, but his cigars and pawnshop and gold rings and pompous stare and affected concern were the same as Lonnie's had been, and Lonnie had ruled a backwater for thirty-three years. The one thing Harold did not have was Liam. Not officially. And more than anything else, this is what he longed for.

He did not tell Liam anything about this, but he made two phone calls to Annette.

Then he went to see her. He went on a rainy afternoon, and held the same envelope Ian had taken to Lonnie years before, with the exact same money in it—the very same bills.

She let him in the back way, thinking he was bringing her diamond back—that he wouldn't be so cruel as to keep it. They sat in the kitchen at the granite counter—the last new thing she had bought—glinting under the stove light. She seemed at times to be hardly awake, drifting in and out of time and space, and looking at him startled when he spoke. She sat in a kitchen chair with her arms at her sides, her legs straight out and her body limp.

And once he snapped his fingers in front of her. "I want to offer you something," he said. He whispered it kindly, and he took the envelope out and pushed it across to her with a clandestine gesture.

"I want Liam to take my name—Dew—and I will offer this for it."

She looked at him, now like a porcelain doll upon whose surface years have left bruises and darkness, and she tried to speak but couldn't. Her mouth opened and closed and her lips trembled. She looked to the right and left as if to find a friend. And as she turned her head to the left, she smiled at nothing.

"Ian," she whispered, "shhh—I loved him. You did not know—that Lonnie made a mistake—shhhh. He thought I wouldn't lov-love Ian—but I did. He made a mistake."

Harold snapped his fingers in front of her face again, and lifted her chin.

"No, he didn't make no mistake. Listen! What would it matter to you," he said. "You want to pay Ian back for all the bad things he did. We will do this—take this money, have a good time. I will adopt the boy and give him my name!"

Here he took out seven more pills and placed them in her hand—enough to kill her if she took them all at once. "You can have these pills if you say yes."

She began to shiver and look behind her.

"No," she whispered, "no, I won't. Well, you know—remember—Liam—you see it's—a bicycle—once as a young girl I tried to ride one—I was just a little girl."

Tears flooded her eyes, and her porcelain face and dyed blond hair seemed to quiver slightly at the insult.

"Who does a bitch like you love?" he shouted, grabbing her face for a second and glaring at her. "I loved you all my life—but then, who does a cunt like you love!"

"Everyone." She trembled, smoothed her hair, and tried, in the end, to sound dignified, like those people like Patsy Mittens she once wanted to be might have sounded. But yes, at this moment she loved them too.

"Everyone—I love everyone. And I am . . ."

He snapped his fingers once again in front of her face to wake her. "What—what are you? What are you?"

"Don't you understand?" she whispered. "Shhhh—please, please forgive me—I am sorry."

Love in fact was the only secret irony could not understand. The one condition of irony those I knew who mocked and used irony never really understood. And Harold took the money and went away, confused, and breaking down on the street, sorry he had called her those names. And wanted to ask forgiveness too.

———

Helinkiscor's idea after they fired Mr. Ticks was this: you could do a rip-out job—hire Doan or some other company to come in and take the paper machines out. But then everyone would find out what your intention was to begin with. It would also make the provincial government look corruptly inept. It would also show that Ian Preston was actually right and justified in saying what he had said. Why? Because weak, soft men in provincial power had given their word. And they had—and this went to the highest provincial office—poured money into Helinkiscor and worked very hard—and this too went to the highest government seats—to destroy Ian Preston's reputation. They had leaked one-sided and bogus information about his dealings to the press and had—this also came from the cabinet—made a point out of offering his wife, Annette, a job to show him up. The resulting disaster in her life, as well as his, however much appreciated, had not been foreseen.

This government had ignored all the warnings about the mill from both Ian Preston and Mr. Ticks, and in fact had helped Helinkiscor draft a statement against their own government bailout when Ticks went to the press, in order to allow another, huger, bailout to happen. So if a rip-out was to come, which it was, how could Helinkiscor do it to make themselves and the government look good? In fact, this was the only thing the government wanted: an assurance that they wouldn't be seen as complicit. Because if they were too complicit, Ian Preston might, after all this time, have a legitimate case for legal action—and especially so if certain documents were published.

Helinkiscor knew this, and so gave their word. That is, they knew very well Ian Preston and his wife had been manipulated and used by the very company that had called him mad; and the government was so hoping it would not come out that they had asked Helinkiscor if Mr. Ticks had any information about a file numbered 0991563.

In May of that year, Helinkiscor claimed that they would not do a rip-out job as long as the men did not strike. But from the moment they said this, they also indicated the world of softwood and pulp products was such that men could not be kept working.

And Helinkiscor was actually hoping the men themselves would destroy the machines. The mill would be useless and Helinkiscor would say it had been betrayed by the men, and leave. The government, of course, had paid for these machines in the first place. But, you see, the government needed the men to destroy these machines as well because they did not want to be accused of putting their faith in a company that would take their millions and then destroy the very mill they had spent millions in good faith upgrading.

So both the government and Helinkiscor pressed Wally to lay off more and more men, and he did so with the certainty that he was a company man and had his duty to perform. And both the government and Helinkiscor knew the layoffs that Wally Bickle was hired to make would sooner or later force a strike. It would only take a few more weeks; the discontent was so great that Helinkiscor would refuse to negotiate, and lock the men out. Sooner or later these men would break down the gates and come in and destroy the paper machines themselves. Then Helinkiscor would say they were forced to go, even though they'd had a new two-year contract drawn up, ready to be signed, between them and the union. They had no intention, of course, of showing this contract to anyone until the machines the province had paid for were destroyed. Then they would say, "Look at the contract drawn up in good faith!" The mill would be useless, and Helinkiscor would have no competition when they moved into Quebec—and all the wood on the ground would still be theirs, ready to truck away.

And this is exactly how it happened.

In July, the men walked out because of layoffs in June. Annette was simply one of almost two hundred workers who were let go. It all happened within a week. And Wally simply put a large padlock on the steel mesh gate to keep them out. Because he was ordered to do so.

"You men are doing it to yourselves!" Wally warned, his round soft face fraught with duty.

But the strike needed a leader—so Mr. Fension inquired about Rueben Sores early one morning.

"He's in jail for assault," someone in the office who knew him said.

"Ah," Fension said. And he went into his own office and closed the door—and the door remained closed for most of the afternoon. You see, the company did not need the president of the local, or the secretary treasurer, to do this; they didn't need the political hacks who ran the union and spoke of brotherhood and honour. They needed a man who could take over a huge crowd and decide for that crowd what must be done. They needed an actual leader—a tough charismatic man, who as Fension said, in his thick accent, "Don't give a hell's bells."

———

When Rueben Sores got out of jail late that day, the streets were empty. Even the tracks leading out of town were bare. The church bells weren't ringing and the schoolchildren weren't on the playground. The great mill was shut down, so there was no smoke. There were no cars, and most of the stores were closed. Downtown he went to buy a paper, but the papers were sold out. He went to a tavern and sat in the same chair where he had sat the night he stole Corky's hat. Today he was the only one there.

Sometimes he wondered about that fur hat, and what had happened to it, and whose life it influenced. But then he forgot about it once again.

"Yer mill has betrayed you!" young Spenser Rogue said when he came into the tavern later, after his grandfather's funeral.

"We'll see about that," Rueben answered.

In the next five to ten days, as more layoffs came, strikers arrived and milled about in increasing numbers and frustration. The men called for support from other mills across the province, then set up a barricade and started a protest.

And as Fension would tell his wife, Linky, who was packing to go back to her summer villa in Norway, Rueben Sores did not "give a hell's bells" and "all those idiots will follow him."

———

Harold Dew made sure the boy Liam made his confirmation—and his good qualities in fact supported his claim that he was concerned for the child and his welfare. That is, he wanted to do better and so he did. And "the poor little fella" whose mom was sick and whose dad had abandoned him was the object of his greatest concern. And it was a great concern—more than just what I might call a pawnshop concern. For Harold still believed the child was his son.

So on one certain evening when Liam went to Harold to get pills for his mom, Harold reminded him about his confirmation.

"Aw, come on—I don't want to do that," Liam said. He was trying to act like the man who was now influencing him, Harold Dew, just as Harold himself had been influenced by Lonnie Sullivan thirty years before.

But Harold said this wouldn't do. He was astonished that Liam did not understand how important this was. "Your mom is sick and you are going to be confirmed if I have to take you by the scruff of the neck and haul you up there myself."

"But you don't believe in that superstitious stuff!"

"Believe in it? Why, I stake my life on it—on Jesus Christ—so don't you think for one minute you are getting out of this."

So Liam had to attend confirmation classes and write a letter to the priest explaining why he wished to confirm his faith within the church. Harold helped him draft a letter to the very angels who would protect him. Read the final draft, hummed and hawed over it a bit—said it needed some punctuation or the archangel Michael might have a bone to pick—and finally said it was ready.

"Is your mom coming to the confirmation?"

"I don't know," Liam answered.

"Well, poor thing—that is really too bad." And Harold for those next few days spoke very highly of the church, of confirmation and of going to mass, and of all the saints who had lived a life of denial and trust in God. He began to take stock of himself and the world around him. He wondered if all things, down to the minutest detail, were happening in some ethereal transmutation of human consciousness. Well, you might think he did not think this way, but Harold did, in this one question: why—and with why he asked, why was there water, why was there earth—why day and night and why the sun, why stars, galaxies, and why beyond that the void? Why did the void exist—and what was beyond the void? What measure defined the millions and billions? He, like Ian and Evan, who since their moment of blood brotherhood had all asked the same questions, came to no conclusion, but then Harold became fascinated about this transformation in the other direction— that is, why plants and photosynthesis and then animals and bone, and blood and molecules and atoms crashing crazily inside the wicker chairs that he wanted to sell, in a way in a universe of their own that was perhaps exactly like the universe we ourselves lived in? Yet still he could come to no conclusion. So taking the Host, saying the Our Father, was a way to structure this dynamic, and to see the dynamic in terms of spiritual nobility that overcame all powers and portents.

But more foreboding was this: he had just found out that Evan was the main suspect in the death of Lonnie Sullivan.

Now Harold could tell himself he did not want this—but how in the world could he stop it, for just as Annette and Ian had progressed from innocence to destruction, so he himself had done the same. And he could not go back now to say he had done what he had done, for he would lose Liam and Ethel if he confessed. Nor did he mean harm to Sullivan—he was only protecting himself. But no one would believe this if he told them, so he must be silent about it. Also, the reason he had been at Sullivan's was to steal a pregnancy test in order to blackmail Liam's mother about Liam himself.

So then he too, Harold, had begun to pray—like millions and billions of others who say they do not believe.

"Perhaps Evan will not do any time and the case will be forgotten," he decided. "Or perhaps this has come to pass because he allowed Glen to climb with him that day! I did not ask anyone to be arrested. So it's not my fault."

This is what he told both Ethel and Liam one night while staring at them both mysteriously so they did not know exactly what it was he was saying.

"I did not mean to do the crimes I did—like most people," That is, like everyone else he was not a moralist; he was a humanist. He did not crave or hypocritically assume his moral stance until he saw the disaster of his actions. Then he tried to cling to something else in his soul.

But Harold had made one mistake.

Amazingly, after all this time, the wrench was still in his possession. And up until this time he had thought no one would ever know it existed. He had at first taken the wrench and hidden it upstairs in the attic. Now and again he would even use it out on his tractor or to tighten or loosen the big bolts on the high end of the shed. But then he hid it again. Forgot about it really.

One day just recently, Ethel went into the attic to find some clothes. So he took it again into the shed, and near where the old muskrat pelt hung like a ghost on a nail, he buried it in the dirt under a board.

He had never known what to do with it. That is, Harold, like all of us, simply wanted the past to go away.

———

The priest had come forward after the rekindled investigation into Lonnie Sullivan's death to speak of his concerns and his guilt that he may have spurred Evan on to committing the crime.

So the police could do nothing less than take Evan in.

The problem was this: Evan had no memory of that night—except seeing the body.

He had a black bruise on his head close to that time. This was remembered by five or six people. So this too seemed to indicate that he had been in a struggle. That is, out of all the snow and sleet and darkness of that long-ago night the bruise was remembered by people who saw him walking along the road toward home. In fact, two youngsters had asked him if he had been in a fight.

How would any jury in the world believe he had gone to Lonnie

Sullivan's without intending to do what had actually happened? Like a man dropping back to walk with his fiancée's best friend.

"Is that when you became religious?" John Delano asked.

"It is," Evan said bluntly. "Yes, it is, was, or whatever. I go to communion now four or five times a month. Maybe I am trying to atone for everything, for wanting that money so bad—that Joyce Fitzroy gave to Ian Preston—that I couldn't handle life."

But then he told the police how he had been seconds away from taking his own life. Could he then have taken someone else's?

"Is that what happened?"

It became common knowledge all over town that the murder of Lonnie Sullivan so long, long ago had been solved. Reporters took pictures of him in his cell, and because of the case, the idea that it had not been resolved before, he was refused bail.

Sara had come back from Rwanda and had found love—or so she thought. Worse, Evan did not deny the charge against him. He could not because he did not know. And this is what he continued to tell her: "I cannot deny it because I do not know."

"A human tragedy," Harold would say to Ethel, and Ethel would start to cry. Harold would weep as well—that is, have tears rushing down his cheeks.

For Sara, it meant ruin. Harold knew this as well.

"Yes," he said. "That poor little woman—that bodice of human dearity, who tried to be nice to an old curmudgeon like me."

More peculiar is what was now being discussed. Lonnie had told the Wizard boy, the night before the boy found him dead, that he was keeping something grand and that Ian was going to pay him a large amount of money to get it back.

"Tonight I will get my UI" is how he had said it.

The Wizard boy had, in fact, told this to the town police five years before. The Wizard boy, now in his late thirties, became very well known for a little while. People reflected that he had no reason to lie, and he was a Wizard boy, and he was going bald.

Annette Brideau was called into police headquarters and asked about her past. Not only was this terrifying to her—not only did she not know Ian had done this magnanimous act on her behalf—but she herself swore it was not the reason she had married Ian.

The hilarity over all of this, and about all of them, was unending that summer. All of it seemed frozen in time, and their faces became the faces of those intertwined in disgrace.

———

Here was Sara Robb's choice: to hand the blood sample she had kept for years preserved in her fridge to the detectives, or to throw it away. For if it was Evan's blood, she was in fact condemning her own fiancé. Perhaps she could convince herself it was too corrupted to be of use. Perhaps she could convince herself that it had nothing to do with anything. But worse, if it was the blood of someone else—say, one of her patients—then she would be laughed at, called a conniver who was trying to frame someone else for the murder her fiancé had committed. And she had every man from Bonny Joyce as her patient—she had her hand on every man's chest and every man's penis, had taken every man's blood. Who would now believe anything she had to say about a blood sample that might exonerate her fiancé that came from her own office, or condemn the one who had betrayed her? That is, if it was not Evan who had murdered Sullivan, then it must be Ian.

If Evan had nothing to do with Lonnie Sullivan's death, this blood sample would exonerate him. And she held this little sample in her hand many nights thinking this. But if it was him—if it was—then she would have been twice fooled by two former friends. Worse was her plight—that is, her moral plight. It could not be Ian's blood—it could not be!—but what if it was? How she would be looked upon!

Sara Robb was silent. In this silence her whole life seemed a great trick played out against her.

For many days she did not know what to do at all.

Then one night, just after the report came out that Evan was to be charged, she sat straight up in bed, long after midnight, listening to the tick of the clock down the hall. In a half-slumbering state she was thinking of three years before, parting Harold Dew's hair.

So there was one other scenario now, one that was equally bad. That is, what if it was the blood of Harold Dew? She had in fact drawn his blood four times in the last two years.

Sara went to work, depressed and gloomy. She stared at the vial and began to write a note to the chief provincial coroner.

But then she tossed her pen down and sat staring into nothing.

To send the vial away was to condemn either Evan or Harold, or implicate Ian. But if it was Harold's blood, people would say she had taken this blood just to condemn him and ruin her sister's life. It would be every bit as bad as condemning Ian, who, they would say, she had a clear motive to seek revenge against.

Rumour would destroy them all.

What would spur this hatred against her was her own editorial in the newspaper during the time certain women were accusing her of being old-fashioned and insensitive. She had written that God calls on people not to do what is easy but what is right. She also quoted scripture, which is always a dangerous thing to do: "I knew you before you were in the womb. You were consecrated before you were born."

How could that insignificant amount of matter—that bright blush of someone's fine makeup—hold such power?

So even she, who was innocent, who tried her best to be fair, was paying the price of living.

I will allow your fiancé to be free, the universe said, but you must condemn your sister's husband—a sister whose life you saved and who you swore to protect. And if you do save your fiancé, no one will believe you. In fact, they will accuse you of being untruthful . But if you do not do this, the one who you love will go to jail, and may in fact die there. Then there is Ian, a man who betrayed you—you were the doctor on duty and made sure he was treated the night he came to the hospital A vial of blood—what is that to seep out of him? And if it is his, no one will believe you either.

Or you can take the seed of blood you have collected and you can throw it away—into the dark bay below Bonny Joyce, and in tossing this seed you can live assured of the uncertainty that anyone around you, or you yourself, will ever do the right thing again. Because no one can do the right thing if you do not.

Sara lived with these thoughts, lost weight, but she found no resolution. One afternoon she told Ethel a story. She asked Ethel to come and sit with her and said, "I want to tell you a story."

"Oh great," Ethel said. "I love stories."

"Well," Sara said, "there were two men, and one committed a crime. But both men had turned their lives around—and both men no longer were the men who at one time were guilty of thinking of this crime, because both men had at one time thought of this crime as being just. Yet one, out of misfortune or a moment's indiscretion, committed it. Perhaps even by accident. But by his very act of committing it he set many free—even the other man who might have done it. Now both these men were better men now than they had been in years. Both simply wanted to be kind. But if someone turned evidence into the police, that someone would condemn one of these men to a place where being kind would cost him his life. So whoever gave evidence was condemning one of these two men to a life where his direction, his hope for goodness, would become a casualty of what he in rashness had done years before. And is this fair? So if you, Ethel, had the means to find out which of the two men it was—what would you do?"

And Ethel simply said, "Harold is very good to me. He is not a bully anymore—like he was at first. Liam has changed us both. Liam is like our son. Much like our son should be. I can't have babies you already told me—so Liam is my child now. I want you to know I love Harold, and I want you to know he loves me—and I want you to know we both love Liam, okay?"

Sara kissed her, like she always did.

And now a rumour was spreading across the town that the spinster who doctored children but did not have one of her own was in fact the kiss of death. She left the hospital at night under this suspicion, and was left alone again.

This was exquisite torture—which man might she save by advancing a cut of blood that she could have collected at any time?

————

Annette by this time in her life looked fifty. It was two months after she'd been laid off. She had put her big house up for sale in a bid to save something. She'd received notices of foreclosure and requests that she call the bank.

She wanted to buy herself and Liam a little trailer on Becker's Lane. She asked Diane to help her with a loan, but Diane couldn't afford it. The little trailer was nice, she thought now—though a year ago she would have laughed about being seen in it. It had a small porch and two bedrooms, a little kitchen and a small living room. Yes, yes, yes, that is all one ever needed!

On the night Liam was confirmed, he came home to find Annette in agony. Earlier he had knelt as his sponsors, Harold and Ethel, placed their hands on his head. He had whispered fidelity to the church and to God. Harold had hugged him and there were tears in the man's eyes as he held Liam out at arm's length.

"I'll take care of you. Don't you worry about a thing," Ethel said.

But Liam left the reception because his mother wasn't there. He left the old church basement and came home. His blue suit was too small and his ankles showed above his socks.

He had now, after all this time, the gentlest smile his mother had ever seen.

She was slumped near the window in her bedroom. She had been looking out the window for him to come home. He told her he was going to take her to the hospital. She was too weak to say no.

He sat her up in bed, and took the golden necklace that Wally had given her for Christmas two years ago and tossed it onto the floor. Then he took the beads that Ethel had received from Father MacIlvoy and had given to him that very night, and started to place them around her neck.

"They will probably burn my skin." She smiled.

"No, Mom, they won't," he said. His white lips trembled. He tried to remember prayers as he held her. But he could not remember any prayers at all.

"Father, Son and Holy Ghost," he said, his lips trembling.

She looked at his face and touched it gently.

He helped her dress—he was used to it now. There were red blotches on her face, and her breasts were scarred where she had had her implants. He got her best shoes and helped her put them on.

"I am so sorry I hit you," she whispered, touching his hair, which was damp with sweat.

"All of us are sorry, the whole world, and those who aren't don't know. Little Wally Bickle is not sorry—but he does not know," Liam said, not looking up while he tied her shoe.

"You have to take me," she said. "I don't want no ambulance. Busybodies."

"I'm going to take you to Dr. Sara," he said. "She is only four blocks away—she is still in her office tonight."

"Dr. Sara—she hates me," Annette whispered, almost spiteful with terror.

He laughed, then wiped tears from his face. "Oh Mommy," he said, "don't you know! She is one of the few who doesn't."

They went out into the hot night, the trees gloomy and damp. They passed the FOR SALE sign. Yes, he remembered her pounding that into the soil just last week, as if she wanted to prove to the world she was going to make a change. And sadly, as if the world would care if she did.

Sara Robb was at the office late for one reason: she had the vial of blood in her pocket, ready to either throw into the water or take to the police, when the boy appeared with his mother. She put the vial away, for suddenly she had to try to save Annette Brideau's life.

Annette said, "Oh my dear, dear Sara," and clutched her hand, the prayer beads resting under her white chin and softly against her cold breasts. "Pray for me now. I am too young to die."

Sara discovered that Annette had a massive blood clot. She phoned an ambulance immediately. But the clot moved suddenly, stopping Annette's heart at 10:15 p.m.

Sara continued her heroic measures in the hospital for almost two more hours.

Annette was forty years old, but almost no one heard that she had died that night, an old woman forgotten by everyone.

Liam sat in the waiting room staring at an orchid in a large pot. He remembered going to first communion. The sky had been threatening that day, the wind blowing the big trees; Ethel had him by the hand. A little shaft of light was falling from the cloud. "Angels," Ethel had told him, as she combed his hair by the church's big archway. "They are everywhere. Do not believe those who tell you they are not!"

He was sixteen now. So where in the world would he go?

Ethel and Harold told him their house was open to him as long as he wanted.

"I am your father if you want," Harold said gently. "You come live with us and I will be the best father I can be. It is not too late for that to happen!" And he added, "Liam, if there were more people like you in the world, there would be fewer people like me," and he'd kissed his forehead.

Sara made out the report on Annette's death. She thought of how little Annette had been left with, how much she had lost, the prayer beads against her skin as a last resort, the sadness and confusion in her eyes, and her last words: "God forgive me." She thought of everyone suffering the same way in this world, in one fashion or another, and made her decision: she would turn the vial in.

———

Markus Paul interviewed Evan.

"The problem is, I was once unconcerned about anything. Then I went into the woods hunting with Ian Preston, thinking only of money, and did not have a peaceful moment until I was standing over Sullivan's body. Except what did I kill him with?"

"Oh, we know what you killed him with," Markus said.

"What?"

He showed Evan photos from the top and side of the red tool box, evidence taken by the photographer Wilson all those years gone by.

"There was a wrench sitting there. Sullivan did not slip and fall—he was hit hard with a big wrench."

"A wrench?"

"Look, you can make out its outline. Do you remember it—a wrench?"

"No, I do not remember a wrench."

———

There were seventeen people at Annette's funeral besides the pallbearers. The priest was young—in his twenties still. He had never heard of Annette. He spoke of the treasure of Catholicism, and the need for people like Annette in the Catholic Church. Strangely, it all seemed true. The day was warm, and the bright spaces between the many, many empty pews looked hopeful in the sunlight. The choir sang "Ave Maria," and the coffin made of dark oak sat before the altar just as Corky's had a very few years before.

The death of Annette, although hardly noticed in the town at first, had over the course of that summer a profound effect on many. Some people who knew her became very depressed, and then quite suddenly became angry at themselves and others because they saw her youngster in the town park or going alone to the enclosure to swim, and became aware of the tragedy they had all been party to. They had participated in creating the very plight she'd found herself in that last night of her life, when little Liam was trying to find her best shoes.

Wally began to be shunned everywhere he went. He came back from bible camp and tried to be humble. But humble did not sit well with him.

Now he too was alone.

He went to Diane to ask her if she was telling secrets about what had happened.

"Omigod, no," Diane said. "What do you take me for?" And she gave him not a smile this time but an astonished and spiteful look reserved for people she'd been told to dislike.

But then she went on to Cut and Curl. She was going out with a younger man now, a bold and indifferent kind of fellow, sixteen years younger than she was, who seemed to care for nothing.

His name was Rueben Sores.

The dour great mill seemed to swallow Wally whole, the caking machines laying in wait for him to enter through the small back door, the ghost of forgotten office laughter echoing.

Now he opened the locked personnel office where half the chairs had been stacked. He saw under Annette's old desk the little monkey Liam had bought for her. It was lying on its side, as if ready to bang its cymbals in defiance. And there was a note on a yellow sticky from one secretary to another, written more than six years before: "Meet you in five minutes."

———

Liam was alone again.

Once, Pint McGraw saw him and tried to catch up to him. He said, "Liam, wait! I have to tell you something very important—they are going to take me . . ."

But Liam kept walking. In the far corner of a downtown building in the middle of the afternoon, he hid, and watched Pint as he looked for him, up and down the deserted street, trying to catch his breath.

"I am sorry, Pint," he whispered. "I am sorry."

Pint never had his own room. He never had a birthday party—the closest he ever came to a celebration was when Liam took him to his fort. He had a few Pokémon cards that Liam had given him long ago and a small case to put his glasses in. But sometimes he was so exhausted he would fall asleep with his glasses on. When they took him to the hospital, to the children's ward, to the room with one window, it was already late in July. He had no visitors. They promised him his own harmonica. He asked them if Liam could visit.

"Of course," they said.

He didn't want to be there. Scared of being alone, he told them that he was feeling much better, so maybe he could go home.

After a while—and a short while too—his hair fell out. He never saw Liam again.

Liam lived alone. And his house was big, so he could hide there. He never spoke to people, so he didn't know about Pint at the hospital, who was asking him to visit.

He began to go back and forth to the beach at the enclosure. He began to notice that outside the huge mill, men had gathered in protest. Leading them was Rueben Sores. Rueben offered him smokes and told him stories—once placed a ten-dollar bill in his hand.

Liam would remember that his mother had driven these roads for four years, working, believing she would have a good life. She in a way was a star—as close to a celebrity as we had here—and that is why they needed her to destroy herself.

Once, he snuck under the gate by the lower entrance and placed the necklace Wally had given her on Wally's car's inside mirror. Then he turned and walked away.

I don't think he liked Mom at all, he thought.

He would go visit his mother's grave and sit beside it in the day.

He didn't think of things she had said to him about his teeth and how they were crooked. He knew that she was in many ways like a spoiled child. Even when she saw disaster all about her, she couldn't stop pretending to be loved. He sat at the fresh grave, not able to bring himself to leave. His mouth would open in agony, and he would shiver the same way he had when they took the boys away and said he couldn't build them forts.

No one bothered with him anymore if he walked by his old school or toward the playground in the long dreary afternoons, or when he went out looking for beer bottles to drag up to the bottle exchange so he could go to a movie. So he could see Spider-Man like other kids. Or go swimming for fifty cents at the Kinsmen Pool, and sit in isolation near the rusted mesh fence.

He could tell the town had come to its end.

Sometimes he walked by his mother's grave and did not go and visit it anymore. And once or twice someone asked him, "What are you going to do, Liam?"

And he said, "I am going to go away."

Once Liam went away no one would bother him, no one would care. This is what he thought. He often thought of his mom, and tears would start. The treatment she had was, he believed, a crime against his brother. But she had been forgiven—if only she had known.

He never answered those who called out to him. He never spoke to classmates at the beach. He never listened to his messages on the telephone.

Then Harold and Ethel asked Liam to come and stay with them.

Some days it got cold, and you could see fall would come. Harold said he cared for poor little fellas and he wanted Liam to work for him—he had started getting contracts that Lonnie Sullivan once had to move garbage. They would go and clean out sewers, sewer lines and septic tanks. It was a good job, and was how he himself had started out thirty years before.

"How are things at the pawnshop?" Liam asked.

"I had to close it up—too many people selling and no one buying. Couldn't afford the rent—the downtown, boy, is dead!"

"In some ways I expected that," Liam said.

"We will go and bring the stuff back here," Harold said. "You can help me."

So they went and loaded what was left of the world. There were two table lamps, a wicker chair—the shotgun that Evan had once won on the horseshoe toss, that Ian had used, and was traded to the pawnshop by Hanna Stone's son, along with two slugs, for the diamond of Annette Brideau.

They put it all in the back of Harold's half-tonne truck.

Harold said that he had waited years to get that shotgun back. He told Liam how he had lost it and said, "You can have it."

"I can have it?"

"Sure, it's yours!"

Harold bought Liam a Coke on the way downriver, and tousled his head.

"How much did you love your mom?" Harold asked.

But Liam couldn't answer. His eyes filled with tears.

"I'll be the best father you ever had," Harold said. There was a long pause as he shifted gears.

Harold and Liam went fishing, and out on the bay one day they spied an old drifter, half covered in sand, lying on the beach in Neguac.

"Do you want that?" Harold asked Liam and Ethel.

"What could we do with it?"

"What could we do with it? Well, we could put a new wheelhouse on it and redo the Cuddy—repair the keel, keep it for ourselves. I can drop an engine into it."

They hauled it home by truck. It was called *Isa's Morning Star*. Harold said, "We will change the name to *Ethel's Hope*."

At night they sat on the porch and drank beer.

Harold had contracts for fourteen houses. It could have, might have, should have been a very good life.

But was it fair, now that Harold had turned his life around—because of Liam and Ethel—was it fair that he would have to pay? And pay with twenty years? In doing so, in paying this way, would this redemption and change that he was experiencing for the first time in his life continue, or would he fall into bitterness and hatred again? And those other two—Evan and Ian, now both in jail—was it fair in any way that they were paying for things unseen? For Molly's and Sara's pain?

This is what we spoke about in my class just a few years ago, before I retired to my house in Burnt Church. If Harold paid, what would that do to Ethel and Liam, who'd had no one in their lives until Harold? If Evan remained certain he had killed, what would that do to Sara?

A fair country—that is what they often said on CBC Radio.

Did my students, living in such a fair country, have any answer for such things?

Harold and Liam worked on the old drifter together in August and gave it the new name *Ethel's Hope*. And Harold and Ethel took the boy to mass on Sunday, and they all played horseshoes, and Harold taught Liam firearm safety and showed him how to work the shotgun.

Then one morning Harold and Liam got up and went fishing together. It was a beautiful day and the sun was on the water by ten o'clock. Harold showed Liam how to cast behind the half-covered rock on Arron Brook, where the famous Lyle Henderson used to fish. He taught him how to follow his fly, and how to cast up against the current with a White Wulff dry fly or a big bug—and that day they came home with seven trout, all over two pounds and two over five pounds.

"I have never caught a fish before," Liam said.

"Well, with me, Glen, you will catch many."

"Who is Glen?" Liam asked, smiling.

"Oh well," Harold said, hugging him gently. "Oh well, my boy, oh well!"

Yet there remained the matter of Lonnie Sullivan's inventory.

What inventory? Even my students laughed. Who would think a hardscrabble shop at the end of the world could have something called inventory? A shop that had sat through thirty-seven years of summer and winter, spring and fall where Lonnie Sullivan plotted his empire out of scrap metal and copper wire; his empire of leftover bits of the past, built using boys who had nothing, to work for next to nothing for him. A place such as this, a shed torn down a year after the funeral, to have anything called inventory?

And yet, of course, it did. And one piece of this inventory was something both John and Markus were certain existed, from magnifying the pictures of the crime scene on a wall at the back of the RCMP office in July of 1998. It was not there, but its outline was obscure yet visible, and so they published this photo in the local paper in August. It was a long shot, certainly silly and perhaps meaningless in the ragtag drift of years, this partial outline of a huge industrial wrench.

It appeared in the paper, with a small caption: "Outline of industrial wrench quite possibly used as weapon in the murder of Lonnie Fitzgerald Sullivan, March 5, 1992. Persons with any information contact the RCMP or Sergeant John Delano, cell: 506-476-4746."

There were no callers, of course, but people spoke about it. "Look," they said, "it's perfectly visible—so clear!"

"No, it's not," others said, "what a joke." And the local paper drifted here and there with this outline on the front page some few weeks.

For Harold, when everything else in his life was going well, it seemed like a trick played upon him by the heavens.

It was worse for Sara. She became the target of a personal scrutiny. Engaged for the second time—the first man deserted her, the second accused of murder that even he says he may have committed.

Both these men sitting side by side in jail.

Cruelty, hilarity, laughter, kick in the cunt—nothing but.

————

Once in a while, far up in the office on the sixth floor of the main building, a light would burn. Sometimes Wally would open the doors and go into rooms where the laughter of years gone by still lingered, the sexual tensions between men and women in offices near the edge of the world. Sometimes he found things that spoke to him only in sadness for a past that was wasted. He was trying to do his job, and waited for obscure orders at obscure times. Sometimes the phone would ring, and a voice with a French accent would tell him that only two trucks had made it through the new Good Friday Road that afternoon, and what was he doing about it? And Wally, his hair receding, his moustache bushy and his eyes bewildered, would try to look up work orders and invoices and general directives, only to be hung up on. Sometimes he would look out of the window and see men milling about in front of the barred gates. He was alone and scared—Fension and the rest had left him and gone back to their own country. One night, someone threw a rock at his car.

All the great wood was being sent to Quebec—and Wally, without fully knowing he had done so, had seen to it. Now that he realized this, he too was to be laid off in two or three weeks. This came suddenly to him, in a thunderbolt—that is, he too had been left behind. Then about a week after the calls from the Quebec mill stopped, he began getting other phone calls.

"Leave the building for your own good." Then the caller would hang up.

The corridors were empty, like spokes running into a hub—the plaster cracked and the calendars two years behind. Some afternoons when he was checking the rooms, his keys on his belt, the phone would ring somewhere—and keep ringing, and he would rush from one corridor to another, trying to find which phone it was.

"Get out now!"

Late one afternoon the sun disappeared beyond the clouds and rain started. He heard men at the gate yelling. Terrified, he thought he should find a place to hide.

He took his briefcase and his jacket, and walked along the long second corridor that led down the metal stairs, toward the small side door. He thought he'd be safe going out the back way.

It happened that this was the day Rueben and his brother had planned to enter that very door. So a crowd of men, led now by Rueben Sores, who had busted the gate down with his old truck, which had once belonged to Lonnie Sullivan, stood before him.

Wally smiled at them timidly, took out a handkerchief and wiped his mouth. He stood there, with his heavy gut, in a cheap ochre suit. All the pain he had been ordered to cause over the last three years was now on the faces before him.

"It's not my fault," he said. But Rueben Sores simply picked him up, and tossed him aside.

They ran over him, breaking his jaw as they came inside.

They jammed the paper machines with plywood and straw until they smouldered. They laughed and roared and used the forklifts to damage the walls, used the fire extinguishers with glee. They shit on the floor and wiped their arses on the executive towels.

Then they all of a sudden realized what they had done and ran—ran away.

Rueben had a gold necklace he had stolen from Wally's car. He carried it in his pocket, then gave it as a present to his girl, Diane. She wore it to Cut and Curl.

Later he was arrested for sabotage, and the workers turned on him. He was not true union, they said, not a brother. So it was Rueben who did the eighteen months' jail time for that.

"Animals!" Fension said to his demure beautiful wife. "Canadians are animals. My father knew that much fighting the fuckers in the war."

———

Liam sat in the home he had come to, after running errands and helping out at the woodlot—helping Harold as they trucked away the remains of the pawnshop and put them in the shed that lay sunken and deformed at the back of the house.

Harold was waiting for the bay to freeze so he could walk straight out toward the icebreaker's path and toss the wrench away, under the ice in the middle of the bay—never to be found, for this was to be the last year the icebreaker came into our bay.

But the days passed. And November came and went, and the month of Advent, when Ethel was busying for Christmas and waiting for the third Sunday so she could light the pink candle—to her, the most joyful and solemn candle. The bay had not yet frozen enough for Harold to walk on the ice, and Ethel and Liam had gone to the woodlot and got a lovely fir tree, and put it up near the mantel with the manger.

It had started to snow the day they got the tree, and they had hauled the boat up on logs, near the back shed, and made a cover of tarp and wood for it.

Sara too lit the third Advent candle on Sunday, December 16. Then she went to the jail and asked Evan what she should do. "Is it your blood?" she asked.

"To tell the truth, I don't know."

On December 17, Sara gave the vial to the RCMP, and they sent it to Moncton for testing. It would take two to three weeks before an answer came back. Still, it might never be used, John Delano told her, for as much as he personally believed her story about collecting the blood, it hadn't been secured at the time of the murder.

———

On December 17, Liam woke to an argument in the house. He lay listening to it, thinking it might be about the Christmas tree. Wind rattled his window and a pale crust of snow lay on the tin porch roof. He sat up finally and said, "What is it?"

But no one answered him, so after a time he came downstairs in his underwear, shivering.

Ethel was sitting in her old knitting chair. She had been knitting Liam and Harold socks for winter, and the night before had both of them try them on so she could finish the toes, and her pile of yarn was piled around her feet.

The phone was upset in the middle of the room and there was a bruise on her eye. There was a patch of mean snow outside. One window was frosted and an icicle hung against the window.

The night before, Harold had taken the wrench down to the shore and started out on the thin ice, but the ice had cracked.

Tomorrow I will get rid of it for sure, he thought.

He put the wrench back under the same small board in the shed—the old board with the nail that had once, years gone by, held the two marten pelts he had taken from Evan's traps.

Ethel had got up the next morning when Harold had yelled at her to go across to the old shed and get his jigsaw. He wanted to finish the cover for the boat, and he was in the midst of putting on the name: *Ethel's Hope*.

So she went. She hated this dark spooky shed. She stood by the door for five minutes, and Harold yelled, "Come on now, Ethel—I has to get this here done. Then I'll take you and Liam to the Pudding Lounge for dinner—how about that!"

She took a deep breath, opened the shed, picked up the saw and started to leave, when her face brushed the old muskrat pelt that had been brought there by Evan years ago, and hung from a beam over the stall. In the darkness it frightened her. She tumbled backward and fell on a board, and a nail punctured her leg. She dug at the board to get the nail away and picked up a handful of dirt as she did.

She wouldn't have looked at the wrench if she hadn't touched it, buried as it was under the plywood board she'd fallen on. Late last night, coming back from the shore, Harold hadn't buried it properly at all.

Ethel sat down on a little wobbly sawhorse and looked at it as if inspecting a new piece of equipment.

There was the smell of straw. She could smell snow too, and remembered how she had once said she hated wrenches. She kept staring at the wrench and then her eyes widened, and she began praying to herself in a whisper, as if she was trying to answer all the questions she was asking herself. She hid the wrench in the same place, put the dirt over it again and put the plywood back. But she could not stop looking at where she hid it. So she dug it up again.

She walked toward the house, stopping every few feet to try to think why this was important. When she got to the boat, Harold was waiting for her. She hadn't even put on a coat and only wore her blue jeans, a sweater and short winter boots.

"Come here and see your name on this here boat, love," Harold said.

But she simply turned and started walking up toward the road that led away from Clare's Longing, with the wrench in one hand and the jigsaw in the other.

"What are you doing—bag o' bones!" Harold said.

"I'll be back in a while," she said. "I think I will go to church."

"Church—are you nuts? You'll freeze yer arse off!"

Then suddenly he could make out what she carried. "Hey!" he shouted.

He ran across the snowy yard and grabbed her.

Now, as Liam appeared, she was sitting in the room and was asking Harold about the wrench.

"Where did you get it?"

"I got it a long time ago—I won it at bingo."

"No, this big wrench has caused so many problems," Ethel said, tears in her eyes.

"Give me the wrench and I will toss it in the sea, and it won't be seen no more," Harold said.

"No. It was Lonnie Sullivan's—Corky sold it to him, and you know how it got here. So—well, so it was Lonnie's."

"It weren't ever, but so what if it were?"

"I don't know, but it might get Evan off—it just might be a valuable piece of evidence, about how Lonnie died. And I think you hit your head that same night—because of the mark on your head—and this is what I think about this valuable piece of evidence."

"A valuable piece of evidence—you brain-dead idiot!"

They argued for five or ten more minutes. Liam said nothing; he just listened to it all.

Harold then told her the truth. But, he said, he had changed completely—his life was new. He would not do anything to put the new life in peril. To turn him in now, when he had a new life, was not fair.

"I know, love, I know" was all she said, and she sounded far wiser than he or Ian or Evan. "But I will be here for you, and they will say it was self-defence!"

"But if they don't?" he said, his voice almost hysterical. "It's no longer fair for me to go to jail."

"But you might only do three years," Liam said, for some reason, and he touched Harold's shoulder and smiled.

"No—they will turn on me and I'll do twenty-five!" Harold roared.

Harold tried to take the wrench away from her. Liam told him to leave her alone. Ethel broke free and Harold began to chase her, first around the living room then across the hall, then into the kitchen and then outside. The day was snowy but still. There wasn't a sound, not even that of a bird, now that the wind had stopped.

Ethel would not give the wrench back. She made marks in the snow as she tried to crawl to the culvert to hide.

"No, Harold—I have to show them! It might be important for Evan."

Every time he picked the wrench up, her whole body came with it, and he would toss her down on her back.

"Don't!" Liam yelled. "You are going to kill her!"

Liam ran into the house and found the shotgun in the spare bedroom near an old box mattress. The shells were on the dresser, covered in dust. He snapped the gun together and came into the yard. Harold, in a blind rage, had the wrench in his hand.

When he lifted the wrench, Liam yelled for Harold to stop. Then he simply closed his eyes and pulled the trigger.

The blast blew Harold forward into the ditch and peeled away the back of his head. He lived close to four more minutes.

John and Markus were called a little later. When they drove up to the house, Harold was lying in the ditch, face down, with his feet sticking up over the culvert. Ethel was sitting on the culvert, holding the wrench. Many other people were standing around.

Liam sat alone in the house.

————

When John Delano called Liam into the RCMP office, he offered him a pop and chips. He asked him how he was feeling. He asked him if he'd heard from his dad.

"What do you plan to do?" he asked.

"I am going away," Liam said.

"Did your mother suffer a lot?"

"Yes."

"I am sorry that your mother suffered. I don't want you to suffer anymore. Is that why you went to get the pills for your mother?"

"Yes."

"Well, we don't want you doing things like that anymore."

"No, I won't."

"Was Harold good to you?"

"Yes—he was very kind."

John didn't tell him about Pint McGraw. Liam was to find out the next day; Pint left him his harmonica.

He visited his mom's grave no more. On the day he heard his dad was getting out of jail, he boarded the train. He did not wait to say goodbye.

In the last letter he ever wrote to us, he left instructions about how he'd done his magic trick and risen above the ground.

————

Wally gave testimony against the men who had destroyed the mill, and Rueben was sentenced to two years in jail, which meant eighteen months with time served. Then our Wally went back to the collection agency in Bicklesfield to work and phoned people about arrears.

Missy worked for the same agency and called people on another phone down the hall.

She had a nice picture of Wally and a few hand puppets she liked to play with. But she did not have her own office window. Missy wore purple and had a wide face. In five years, she and Wally looked exactly alike: rotund and self-righteous and, like Verna, a party to gossip.

Missy and Wally weren't planning on having children. They were too noble for children—you know, in this day and age. No, they wouldn't think of adoption. It wasn't really for them. They would sacrifice the need for children and be forward-thinking instead. Wally Bickle would never would have to suffer the torment, worry and love of bringing up a child. And that was nice for him.

However, they both snapped to it whenever Verna was around. She was terrible with Missy, some did say, and gave the girl a nervous breakdown in 2003, which was hushed up—you know, the time Missy heard all about Wally at the bible camp with that young seventeen-year-old girl named Ju Jube Malone, and tried to swallow pills and take her life.

"I'm not on no diet," she would say later, you know, at the church suppers—until she got so large you could hardly recognize her anymore. Both, it was said, were interested in politics, and once had dinner with a Member of Parliment.

———

On September 11, 2001, Evan and Sara were married at the church in Clare's Longing by the priest who had hired him to fix the steeple. It was a clear and beautiful day all down the eastern seaboard. Leonard Savoy was Evan's best man.

Ethel and Ian were married in 2004, after Ian sold his little invention to Doan. It was used on industrial sites to test effluents all over the Maritimes until better inventions came along. It wasn't the best invention, but it wasn't bad. He must have made a profit of about ninety-five thousand dollars on it. And with that, he and Evan bought and refitted Jameson's sawmill, and used the wood stands far up beyond Little Hackett Brook, and began to sell the best lumber in the province. They also began to replant Bonny Joyce—and after a few years they put up a headstone for Harold Dew, with the inscription

OUR BROTHER, GONE HOME TO GLEN

Sara gave Ian and Ethel the house on Pleasant Street as a wedding present, along with the travelling trunk she had bought at auction. Ian and Ethel kept mementoes of Liam in it. It became sacred after a while. They put in it all the things they remembered he once had loved.

Every vacation, Ian, who I got to know fairly well after I retired and who was Evan's partner in the mill, would get in his truck, and he and Ethel, who now worked in the office of Dr. Sara Robb, would spend three or four weeks trying to find his son. But as time passed, the chances became more and more remote that Liam would be found.

Someone said he'd seen him on a street in Toronto on a July day under a great building that offered little shade. But that lead went nowhere.

They came close a few years later, after a sighting in Windsor. Someone said he'd worked with Liam at a video store. Liam would tell the kids stories about how he built forts, and he'd talk about his friend Pint McGraw. In fact, he seemed comfortable only with children. But then, after a few months, he went far, far away. He had his passport and a work berth on a ship to Australia. "There is nothing for me here," he'd said.

The person who had invited Liam to come to Australia was in fact a forgotten neighbour, Sydney Henderson's son, Lyle. He had sent Liam four emails asking him to come down and work with him like a brother at the other end of the world.

Before Liam left, he told someone he had no family.

With the reverence certain young men have for the new age, this man spoke of Liam, how he could go to the highest levels on the most difficult video games in the world and was a master at fixing computers. Everyone wanted to retain him because of how well he could solve cyber problems. He played the harmonica, had grown tall and strong, and had the most beautiful white teeth and smile.

He was a whiz at mathematical problems too, and had read *The Diary of Anne Frank* and talked about it always, and carried it in his duffel bag when he went west to board the *Southern Star* one grey evening in autumn.

"What did he say?" Ian asked, his face filled with tears and premature wrinkles, while Ethel stood beside him holding his hand.

And the man recounted what Liam had told them before he went into the dark.

"Men!" Liam had said. "Those lads, let me tell you, they drink nothing at all—but blood."

ACKNOWLEDGEMENTS

I would like to thank my agent, Anne McDermid; my editor, Lynn Henry; my dear friends Liz Lemon Mitchell, Jeff Carleton and Philip Lee; and my family: Peggy, John and Anton, and sisters Susan and Mary Jane.

I remember my parents and many others who are gone, such as Peter Kelly, whose lives touched me deeply; two noble unsung writers: Rick Trethewey and Wayne Curtis; those at McCord Hall, such as Bob Gibbs, the quiet genius; and Michael Pacey and Brian Bartlett, who knew me way back when.